THINNER THAN BLOOD

Edward K. Ryan

THINNER THAN BLOOD

Cover Design : Ashley Fetterman
Published by Slate Run Publishing LLC.
www.slaterunpub.com

Ed Ryan can be contacted at www.edwardkryan.com.
Sign up for my mailing list and receive a free short story!

Other Titles by Edward K Ryan

THE MARK OF THE DEAD

Thinner Than Blood

With Their Bones

Anthologies

The Black River Chronicles (Fall 2020)

Slate Run Annual – Vol 1. (Contributor)

Slate Run Annual – Vol 2. (Contributor)

Short Stories Available Now

The Reckoning

Mercenary Law

Ugly Whores

Ghosts of Kiranon

Confrontation

Ed Ryan can be contacted at www.edwardkryan.com.
Sign up for my mailing list and receive a free short story

FOR DANIEL AND CHRISTOPHER.

MY OWN LITTLE BITS OF MAGIC.

ACKNOWLEDGMENTS

This book would not have been possible without J_m Slattery, Steve Slattery, Steve Kuehn and, of course, Dan, Chris and Tracy. Thank you all.

Chapter One

Hello, mother.

She looked no different today – the last day he would ever see her – than she had any other day.

She was so beautiful. A pixie face framed by hair red as the summer sunset. Eyes as green as freshly cut spring grass. Her smile dazzled like the moonlight on soft winter snow. The touch of her fingers was as cool as the autumn breeze on his face. Her voice was sweet music in his ears. He understood nothing that she said, but it made no difference to him. She was there. Like a hand that reached down into the cold, black water he drowned in all day long, she was there to pull him up and let him breathe if only for a few breaths.

He was sitting in the front room of his parents' home, the early morning sun cutting a sliver of gold through the shadows as it slipped through the long windows. Without, the red and gold leaves swayed in the autumn wind and his father's hounds raced through the yard, nipping and barking at each other. His father was out there, axe in hand as he split logs for their fire and arranged them in a neat stack on his wheelbarrow.

Strange that I hear the barking and the fall of the axe. Strange that I hear nothing else.

He focused on his mother as she lifted a cup from the small table beside him and put it to his lips. He looked down as her little hand clasped his big one where it rested against the arm of the old chair. It had been a while since he had last seen his move. It no longer worked. Nothing did but his eyes and his ears and those none too well. Whatever it was he was drinking was neither hot nor cold, sweet nor bitter. It was wet, he supposed, but nothing else could be said for it. She was still talking, but it was like the buzz of a hummingbird's wings in his ear. Gentle, soothing, but nonsense nonetheless.

She spoon-fed him something out of a bowl, thin, gray, and tasteless. He ate it because she seemed to want him to. There was sadness about her, a pained look that creased her face with long lines and dimmed the light in her eyes. It was for him, he supposed, but he was not sure why. This was the best part of the day, after all. A moment was all it ever was, but it was an escape, a brief respite from the eternity of darkness he endured between her times with him. Deep in the sea of nothingness that surrounded him most of his hours he always held tight to the thought that he would wake and she would be there.

He dreamed sometimes. When there was neither the impenetrable darkness nor the wakefulness that mother brought, he would dream of another life. It was the past, he thought, but he was never sure. He was a child in some of those dreams, living in the same house, playing in the yard his father worked in. There were other children, faces without names. The dreams never included sound, and he could not even put voices to them. Other times, he was grown as he was now, but his arms worked. So did his mouth and his legs and he walked and talked and lived among others. He saw more faces in those dreams, some he recognized as the grown children from the first. Others were new and he could not identify them. Always things were confused and disjointed, fragments that did not fit together and formed nothing but nonsense when taken as a whole.

He thought about them sometimes while he was awake, frozen in his chair with his mother doting over him. While she washed him and changed his clothing and fed him, he made a game of the fragments of the dreams, trying to fit them together like some puzzle. It never worked. It always left him tired, anxious, and frustrated. His mother would sense those times. She would rub his hand or speak to him. She was singing sometimes, he supposed, but he was never sure. When she was done, she would sit, her hands on his, and cry. Those were the worst moments of the best part of his days.

He looked up as his father entered. He was a tall, strong man, with a face lined by age and hard work. Father dropped his armload of firewood in the box by the hearth and wiped his hands on his leather apron. He came and knelt before his son, one strong hand on his shoulder, and spoke to him as he always did. Father was sad too. He did not cry like mother, but there were the same lines, the same emptiness in his eyes. When he was done, he squeezed his son's shoulder, kissed the top of his head and straightened. Mother gave him food and they sat and ate with their son, talking to him as if he understood, including him as best they could.

Good people, mother and father.

When they finished, father left. Mother cleared away their plates and cups and then returned to sit and wait. She said nothing, her hands holding his again as she stared at the dancing flames in the hearth. Father was back soon, washed and changed. He wore splendid trousers and an embroidered tunic with a long, white cape. He was an important man, father. He kissed mother, spoke to his son, and then left.

It would be soon. He was never awake much after father left. Sometimes the sun would rise high into the sky before he slipped away again, but he was usually falling into the blackness before then. Mother never left him while they waited. She was always holding him, sobbing sometimes, talking others. The talking was not to him, though. She was praying, he guessed, but not to a god he felt. Perhaps if she kept trying, she would find one who listened.

She gave him more to drink a few times while they waited. Mostly, they sat and she prayed to gods who did not care.

She was just adding wood to the fire for the first time since father left when he felt it start to come over him. It was the same every time. It started deep inside. Like a fire a thousand times more intense than the one mother fed, it rose up out of belly and spread through him. It crept. It oozed. It dragged itself through every inch of him with excruciating sloth, burning, searing, making him want nothing more than to die and end it all. He opened his mouth to scream, but nothing came out of it. His hand tightened on the arm of the chair, but it was not his doing. He began to shake first, the legs of the stout chair tapping against the wooden floor. Mother turned at once, reaching out to hold his arms, talking again, tears streaming down her face. He began to convulse, arms flailing despite her efforts, his back arching as the pain tore him from within. His head thrashed from side to side and his legs stiffened, heels pounding on the floorboards.

In an instant, it was over. Mother was gone. The chair was gone. The house was gone. He saw only blackness. Solitude. Emptiness.

I am alone.

Mother? Mother? Where are you?

It was all wrong. He was awake, but it was not morning. It was dusk. He could tell from the shadows that lay across the trees that it was not dawn. Father was not working in the yard. Mother was not beside him to greet him. His eyes flickered from side to side, but found nothing. The fire still burned high in the hearth, but most of the logs in the firebox were gone. The front door stood open, the cold autumn wind blowing into him. His cup and plate were not on the table next to him.

Where are you?

He listened, but his ears were not good. He made out sounds, but from where or what he did not know. Outside? Was that why the door was open? Behind him where everyone went to wash and dress? He had to know. He looked down at his hand where it lay on the arm of the chair.

Move.

It stayed where it was. Of course it did, he realized. After all, it does not work. He tried to get his heels to pound on the floor, but they stayed where they were. His head stayed where it was too no matter how he tried to move to either side. His breathing quickened, harsh and desperate in his ears. He blinked because it was all he could do, faster and faster as he grew more panicked. She had to come back. She could not leave him alone like this.

Where are you!

She was outside, on the porch. She was not looking at him as she backed into view, blocking the door as a tall man in a dark cloak stood over her. They were talking and their voices were loud and harsh. His finger stabbed down as he bent over her and mother raised her chin to shout back.

The man had to stop. He was not to speak to mother that way. Father would not have it. Mother backed away again, into the house with the man still outside. They were still yelling and the man's finger was still stabbing at her. Why did he do that? He had to stop.

Mother tried to close the door, but the man put a foot inside to block it. His face was visible in the fire light now. He was one of the men from the dreams, one of the older people who had not been a child before. He never looked so angry in the dreams. He had been smiling, happy, and friendly with mother and father.

The man tried to step around mother and she blocked him, her hands against his chest, trying to force him back. She was so small and he so big.

His hand closed on her arm and his face turned black. He shoved her with one hand, knocking her over one of the small tables. There were little things on the table, trinkets and baubles, and they bounced on the floor next to her. The man looked down at her. He was surprised. Had he not meant to do that? Then he was moving past her, coming close.

A pinching sensation flared in the pit of his stomach, something like the burning he always felt when he was about to return to the darkness, but quick and more intense. The approaching man felt it as well and turned just as mother regained her feet. Her hands came up and the hearth roared to life. Fire sprang forth, rushed to her and wreathed her hands, burning and spitting, but leaving no mark upon her. She held those fiery hands out toward the man, her eyes burning red with the reflected flame.

Magic.

The man hesitated, but he did not look afraid. He stared at mother with an expression that might have been sorrow. The man raised his hands to her and the fire flared between them in an orange flash and the pain intensified.

He swam in a moment of darkness and when it passed, everything was fire and smoke. His ears buzzed as people shouted. Everything was a haze. His father's face flashed through the smoke for a moment, smeared with dirt and blood. The strange man was there was well, teeth bared, clothing singed and torn, and his dark hair coated in ash and soot. His eyes were solid black, dead and glassy like some sort of doll. Perhaps he was dreaming, but he had never seen these things in his dreams before. He looked down at his hands and feet and begged them to move, but they still did nothing.

Mother, where are you?

The smoke cleared and he saw father and the strange man locked in a fierce struggle. Fire danced along their hands and blood dripped from them. The walls, floor, and ceiling were ablaze and smoke billowed through the shattered front windows. Men moved from without, fighting to get past the flames and enter the house. Magic flared and brought burning pain. His eyes flickered about, searching.

Where are you?

She was near him, slumped on the floor before the hearth. She lay on her side, facing him. Her green eyes were open and staring and dull. Her crimson hair was singed black. Her gentle fingers were twisted and bent at odd angles. Her brilliant smile was frozen and drooling blood. She seemed to be looking at him, one hand stretched out flat as if reaching for him. Her head was bent oddly, her neck turned too far.

He tried to scream but made no sound. He tried to reach for her but could not move. His gaze flickered back to where father struggled with the man in black. He silently urged himself to move, to do something – anything. But the flames flared again, the smoke closed in. The sharp pain of the magic all around him still burned, but he felt the slow, creeping agony join it. His body tensed, his vision began to fade.

He was slipping away again.

Back into the darkness....

Chapter Two

Where am I?

He woke staring at the deep blue of the autumn sky. The sun beat down and the whole world was in motion. His head pounded and his lungs burned with every breath. Blankets surrounded him and his head rested on something soft. He looked about as best he could, but saw only blue sky, gray blanket and some dark bulk to his left that he could not turn his head to see clearly.

He was conscious of the sound of earth crunching beneath him and the squeal of an axle. He was in a wagon or cart, he assumed, but he could not be sure. There was the creak of wood and leather as well. Nearby, birds were singing, a sound he had not heard in some time. His father had moved him close to the front door of the house a few times when the weather was nice and he had heard birds then, but it was still cold and he was not home.

"Awake, boy?"

His breath caught in his throat. A voice. Had he imagined it? Were those words in his ears or in his head? The only voice he remembered was his own. Everything else was a humming. He waited, listening to the turn of the wheels and birds' songs and decided he had imagined it.

Then, a face poked into view, an elderly man with a dark beard shot through with gray and a wizened face. "You are! You are!" A calloused hand reached down to grasp his as he started to panic, his breathing labored. "Rest, lad. Rest. You're safe enough. Just rest. We're almost there..."

He slept. It was the first time he could remember actually sleeping. It was not the strange emptiness of the dark he was so used to, but more like the land of dreams he escaped to almost by accident. He floated through pictures and sounds, smells and touches and tastes that were all new and frightening but bore some odd touch of familiarity. He visited places he could not help but think he had been before and people he did not know but somehow recognized.

At first, he was afraid, so rocked by the strange sensations that he was sure it was some sinister facet of the dark prison he lived in torturing him anew. As he dreamed, he grew more comfortable. He sensed that it was all right and necessary, as if his mind were trying to sort through all the previous dreams and order them that he might finally fit the pieces into a larger picture.

The dreams were endless. He experienced confusion at first as with the others, but this seemed more of an honest mistake than a torturous denial of answers. Slowly the ordering of the dreams began to fall into place and create a narrative. He watched it all unfold as if he were watching actors on a stage playing out someone's life. It occurred to him early on that it was his life he was watching unfold, but something made him resist that thought for a long time.

He had just begun to accept it as such when he woke.

He was lying in a bed, surrounded by stone walls in a circular chamber pierced at regular intervals by shuttered windows. Timbers framed the ceiling high above him. He was wrapped in blankets and soft pillows cushioned his head. A fire blazed in the hearth at the foot of the bed and he shut his eyes against it, remembering.

Mother. Aralyn.

He opened his eyes slowly. Yes, her name was Aralyn. He was not sure how or why he knew that. The name sounded strange, a label. He tried to remember what process had brought him to the realization of what she was called and failed. Everything he dreamed for so long up to that moment scattered upon waking and he found himself holding on to fragments.

A clicking sound from the door to his right as the latch slid back drew his attention, and he turned his eyes toward it. To his surprise, his head followed. It took a titanic effort, but he turned until his right cheek was against the pillow and watched as the door swung inward. A squat candle on a long iron stick came first, throwing a feeble, flickering light. The candlestick was gripped in a small, pale hand that reminded him of his mother's in a way that made a hollow in his stomach ache. The hand belonged to a young woman, a wispy little thing in a white robe that almost swallowed her up. She had a basin of water tucked under her other arm and a towel draped over one shoulder. She did not notice him watching as she turned about and nudged the door closed with her knee. Balancing everything she held, she padded to the bedside and placed the basin and candle on the nearby table.

She started when she saw him staring up at her, her hand coming up to her mouth. He would have done the same if he were able. The face that looked down at him in the soft candle light was thin and delicate, with high cheekbones and a narrow chin. Midnight hair tumbled down about her shoulders and the eyes that widened in surprise were a smoky gray. A smattering of faint freckles sprinkled across her small nose, a faint hint of the mortal beneath the almost magical beauty. Her gentle hand reached out to touch his forehead, cool and soothing.

"Do you know where you are?" she asked, her words soft, almost musical.

He opened his mouth to respond, but no sound came forth. He was aware for the first time of how dry his lips and tongue were. He swallowed as best he could and forced a small shake of his head.

She eased his head back to the center of the pillow and bent close. "You are in Marcester. You are safe here. Can you blink once if you understand me?"

He blinked. He expected everything to vanish at any moment, revealed as a cruel trick or an excruciatingly detailed nightmare. He closed his eyes and opened them again. She was still there. Her hand was still cool against his skin. Her gray eyes still stared down at him with a mix of curiosity and uncertainty. He wondered at his lucidity. He could feel her hand, hear her words. He could even smell something vaguely sweet about her, a perfume perhaps.

He was trying to absorb it all when he realized his blood was stirring as well. It was the same reaction he always experienced before – when he was slipping away or when the strange man had come to his house. It was different now. It persisted, but it was more muted, more subtle.

He tried again to speak, countless questions flooding his fragmented mind, screaming for answers. He managed nothing but a dry, hacking cough. The girl pulled away from him, dipped the towel she held in the basin of water and put it to his mouth. He held it between his lips and sucked the moisture. He blinked rapidly when she removed it and she wet it for him again. When he was finished, she wet the towel once more and wiped his face, neck and arms. He sighed and closed his eyes as she worked. He was tired, but for all the sleep he seemed to have gotten, he could not imagine why.

His head lolled to one side and he felt something heavy settle over him. He forced his eyes open and looked up at the girl. She bent over him and spoke, but he could not hear her. His eyes closed again despite his efforts and he slept.

When he woke, the girl was gone. He did not remember having dreamed while he slept, but he could not recall the oblivion of darkness he had floated in for so long either. The windows were still shuttered and he had no sense of how much time had passed. He was sweating, his blankets soaked through, but shivering as well, his teeth clicking together as his chin trembled. His head pounded and his bones ached. His throat was raw and dry. He shifted his eyes to the small table near his bed, hoping for water, but it was gone.

Was the girl a dream too?

He let the thought play itself out in his mind and decided she was not. That settled, he began to wonder what was a dream and what was true. He asked himself how much of what he remembered might have been a delusion. Were the things he had seen for so long real? Were mother and father but illusions created by his mind? Was he ever in his own home, in his chair looking out his windows?

The girl needed to come back. He needed to know. But how? He could not speak or move. He had questions but no way to ask them.

Someone help me.

His eyes squeezed shut and his mouth opened wide in a long, anguished scream that made no sound.

He floated in and out of consciousness after that. The world was a hazy, drifting collage of sounds and pictures more confusing than the dreams that once baffled him. He saw the girl once, but so briefly that he supposed that was a dream. Mostly, he saw the strange man with the gray streaked beard. The wizened face was friendly as the man cared for him, changing his bedclothes, cleaning him, and giving him water and broth. The girl placed cool towels on his head and the old man kept the fire roaring. For what felt like an eternity he drifted, never sure what was real and what was a dream.

He began to question his sanity until, one day, the haze and confusion vanished. It was a bright, cold afternoon, the windows of the room thrown wide to let in the fresh air. He woke to the sound of the door latch sliding back and watched as it swung inward to admit the old man and the black haired girl. The man went to tend the fire while the girl came to his bedside with her basin and towels. She placed the basin on the table and seated herself on the edge of the bed.

"Awake, I see," she said as she dipped the towel in the water. She looked over her shoulder at the old man. "His fever broke overnight." The old man grunted in response and she turned back to resume her work.

Her hand had not yet touched his face when he reached up to catch her wrist.

"Durn!" she called to the old man, bringing him rushing to the bedside.

She was more surprised than frightened by the movement. As small as she was, the grip was weak enough that she could have broken it with ease. Instead, she took his hand in her free one and squeezed it gently.

"Easy now," she told him. "You are safe. No one will harm you. Blink if you understand me."

"I understand."

A stunned silence hung in the room as they stared at him. The sound of his own voice echoed in his ears. It was a strange sound, almost wrong. They were the first words he could remember ever speaking, but he knew that could not be. He was a grown man and his dreams had shown him a life he had spent walking and talking - living. So much was still in pieces, that he was not sure what to think of it all.

The old man leaned close. "Do you know-?" He paused and drew a breath. "Do you know who you are?"

He thought a moment, replaying bits of the dreams. Nothing substantial formed out of the tendrils of smoke he grasped at. "No."

The old man nodded as if he had expected as much. "Do you know who we are?"

"No." He stopped himself and nodded his head at the old man. "Durn?"

The old man nodded again. "Durn." He pointed to the girl. "My niece, Halonni."

Halonni. A pretty name, he decided. It suited her. "H-Halonni."

She nodded encouragingly. "I'll bring you some water and food."

She started to rise, but he held onto her hand. He did not want her to leave. Something about her presence made it all real. In a way he could not explain, he feared he would slip away when she left. She reached down and gently peeled his fingers open. She flashed Durn a look of concern and then slipped out of the room, closing the door behind her.

He picked his head up from the pillows, staring after her, but Durn pushed him back.

"Not yet, lad. Your fever is broken and you seem to be coming back to yourself, but you need time. Rest. Gain your strength"

He did not have anything resembling enough strength to fight the old man and collapsed back into the bed.

"Good, lad. Good. Get well. Then, we'll see about things."

He stared up at the old man, hard. "Who am I?"

The question hung between them for a long time. The old man seemed to be thinking of the best way to explain things. He sat on the edge of the bed and stared down at the floor while he mulled it over.

"I found you on the road outside of Drappel. Do you know that place?"

"No." The name meant nothing to him.

"It's a town halfway across the valley from here." He paused. "The Censharn Valley. You know it? No, I thought not. This land is Kronos. How about that?"

He shook his head. None of those names meant anything to him.

Durn shrugged it away. "Well, regardless, Drappel is where I found you. I was passing though when I found you and the other man lying in the grass under an old oak tree. You had been there for days, I think."

"My father?"

Durn frowned, the lines on his face deepening, and shook his head. "No. I don't think so anyway. He looked nothing like you. I never did get his name before he died. He spoke only long enough to beg I take you away. Somewhere safe he insisted. Somewhere no one would find you." The old man blew out a long breath. "He called you 'Jantalus'. Do you remember the name?"

Jantalus closed his eyes. In his mind, he gathered what images he could and tried to hold them in place. He managed to stitch a few together and then concentrated, trying to hear voices, to make out words. No matter how he tried, he could not pick anything sensible out of the chorus of gibberish and noise. He shoved the images away in frustration and opened his eyes.

"It means nothing to me. You are sure that is what this man called me?"

Durn did not hesitate. "I am. Jantalus is your name."

Silence settled over them for a time. Jantalus. Drappel. Two names that meant nothing at all were the only links he had to who he was and where he came from. Two answers that satisfied not one of his countless questions.

"Shall I tell you something more?" Durn asked as the quiet of the room grew awkward. "Do you want to talk more?"

He did not. He was tired, beyond tired in fact. How he could be was anyone's guess, but he felt himself drifting again. "Tomorrow."

"You are sure?"

"Yes."

Durn rose from the bed. He stopped halfway to the door and looked back. He paused as if he would say something but thought better of it and let himself out, closing the door behind him.

Alone in the room, staring up at the shadows of the high ceiling, unable to move and barely able to talk, he considered his name and what it meant.

Nothing. It is just a name.

Jantalus.

Chapter Three

He spent several more days in the small bedchamber. He grew stronger with every sunrise, sitting up by the third day and feeding himself by the fifth. He still slept more often than not, and his dreams remained elusive. He was conscious of having them, but they slipped away from him on waking and he remembered little. It was beyond maddening. For so long, the dreams were all he had beyond the stolen moments of wakefulness with his parents. He had cherished them even though he did not understand them. Anything was better than the nothingness that had consumed most of his hours. Now, he was awake and alert and regaining function at a rapid pace and he wanted nothing more than to sleep and dream and hope for answers.

One of the first things he learned was that more time had passed than he could have imagined. His last memory before coming to Durn's home was the day his home burned. The day mother died. It had been early autumn, just cool enough to turn the leaves. The chill wind that rattled the shutters of his windows now carried the first sweet smells of spring. He had missed all of the intervening winter.

Durn came to him every day, bringing food and water and fresh linens, but Jantalus did not speak to him, no matter how many times the old man tried to engage him. He only nodded when Durn asked if he was well and ate his food without a word. He did not want to talk to the old man or anyone else. He needed time, as foolish as that seemed even to himself considering his life to that point. His hope was that he would dream while he slept or remember something in the quiet hours of wakefulness that would bring some meaning to the things he had seen and learned. Despite his silence and isolation, nothing more revealed itself.

He did not see Halonni for those five days. He almost asked Durn why at one point, but decided against it. He resolved to put her from his mind and focus instead on willing himself to remember. He failed on both counts.

It was the afternoon of the sixth day since waking and learning his name that he first swung his legs over the side of the bed and placed his bare feet on the cold stone floor. Walking was something he had spent the last few days wondering if he would ever do. For the last several months, Durn and Halonni had spent their days moving his body through a series of exercises meant to maintain his strength and flexibility. In theory, his body would be strong enough to begin normal movement.

Durn detailed it all to him one day, speaking even though Jantalus would not answer him. The old man spent hours relating different things, hoping for a response of some kind. While he did not answer, Jantalus heard every word of it.

"I'll help you if you want to try."

He had not heard the door, but Halonni was standing with it opened behind her, one shoulder against the wall as she watched him. She looked worn and disheveled; her gray eyes shot through red and ringed in black. She was paler than usual and her midnight hair was tangled and unkempt. He was aware, as he always was when she was near, of the burning sensation in the pit of his stomach.

What is it and why do you cause it?

He almost asked her aloud, but the more he looked at her, considered what she and Durn had done for him, the less sure he was that he wanted to know. One corner of her mouth turned up in a wry smile when she realized he was staring.

"A long night and a longer morning," she said, misreading his hesitation. "Marcester is a small town and we're stretched thin when it comes to work." She cocked her head to one side. "If I can get you up and about, you might be of use."

He steadied himself on the edge of the bed and pushed off a bit with his arms, testing his strength. "All right. I'll try it."

She raised an eyebrow as she pushed herself away from the wall. "You speak after all. I was afraid you'd forgotten how again."

Halonni came forward and ducked under one of his arms, draping it over her slender shoulders. He reached out to steady himself against the headboard with the other. He hesitated, considering the consequences of falling. She was half his size and the chances of her catching him, let alone lifting him off the floor and back into bed, were absolutely nothing.

"I'm stronger than I look," she told him when he looked down at her.

She was overestimating her strength. Fortunately, he was right about his own. He wobbled and clutched at the bed for support as he forced himself up, his legs shaking and threatening to buckle. After a moment, they settled beneath him and he was standing on his own. He no longer supported himself with the bed, but he held on anyway. Her intentions aside, he had no faith in Halonni's ability to help him if his body decided not to cooperate. Not fully trusting his own strength, he staggered a few halting steps, walking from one end of the bed to the other, constantly in contact with one hand. Halonni held on to him as well, firm and close at first and gradually easing away until she stood at arm's length, watching.

"I'd be lying if I said I wasn't impressed," she admitted. "I half expected to see you on your face after the first step."

He did not respond, his attention focused on the shuttered window across the room. It was far enough away that he would not be able to reach it without letting go of the bed. A small goal, perhaps, but one he immediately set for himself. He had been a prisoner long enough.

He shuffled to the end of the bed and inched forward, holding on to it as long as he was able before letting go. Behind him, Halonni began to object, but he ignored her, forcing himself forward with short, unsteady steps. The dozen feet of cold stone floor between the bed and the window took forever to cross. It was six steps that were six victories as he took each, slow and deliberate. His hands were clutching the shutters, drawing them open in a rush of cold air before he realized that sweat beaded his face and his heart was pounding.

Marcester spread out before him as he looked out the open window. He had assumed he was high in a tower judging from the room, but he was at ground level. All around him, the little homes were mud and wattle and the few more permanent structures were clapboard and thatched roofs. He saw no other buildings of stone. A scattering of goats and sheep were clustered amid the dirt paths that spider webbed about the town and pigs and chickens milled about in pens. A few worn and hardened townsfolk tended to the animals or pushed carts along, none paying any attention to him.

Halonni was at his side in an instant, reaching around him to slam shut the shutters. She took his arm, steered him away from the window and back toward the bed.

"You have to be more careful than that," she told him. "You cannot be seen."

He sank down onto the bed, sitting at the edge, his elbows on his knees and his head bent. He was exhausted from that small effort. "Why?"

"You're-." She stopped, looking at him in a way that said she was not sure how to say what she meant. Finally, she crossed the room to the table and picked up the small mirror there. "Look."

She held it up in front of him, and he stared at the distorted image in the polished surface. Her meaning was apparent immediately. His eyes were completely black with no pupils, dull, solid and lifeless.

Like the man who killed mother.

He tore his gaze from the thing he saw in the mirror and looked up at Halonni. "What is that? What am I?"

She lowered the mirror. "Durn should be-."

"Tell me!"

His voice reverberated through the room like a thunderclap. Halonni stared at him.

"Tell me," he repeated, calm now, but insistent.

"That," she pointed two fingers at his eyes, "is the mark of the dead."

The mark of the dead. He had no idea what that meant. Other than the man who had killed his mother and destroyed his home, he could not remember ever seeing it before. To Halonni it was obviously something of importance. More to the point, it was clear this mark was not something he was fortunate to bear.

"What does it mean?" he asked.

She drew a deep breath and seated herself on the bed near him. "To me? To Durn? Nothing. To most, it is the sign of the Necromancers, people who practice spirit magic. They steal the souls of the dead to fuel their power. The contact with the spirit world marks them." She gestured again. "Marks them like that."

"Is that what I am?"

She stared at him for a long time before answering, "I don't know."

He stared back. Strange, he thought, that I am too vile a thing to be seen through the window but she and Durn have no objection to me in their home. They might have been people of uncanny patience and tolerance. More likely, they had seen this mark of the dead before.

"Who are you?" he asked finally. "Not your names. I mean more than that. Why did you take me in? How did you come to even find me? If I am too twisted by this mark to be seen, why am I here with you?"

Halonni glanced to the door as if she were considering leaving but sighed instead. She tucked her legs beneath her and sat back a bit, her hands folded in her lap. "No one. That's who we are. Castoffs better hidden and forgotten about. That's why we're here. Marcester is a nothing town buried in a place no one cares to go to. We don't bother anyone anymore and they don't come looking for us."

He shook his head trying to make sense of what she was saying. "What makes you better off here?"

"Magic." She shrugged when he tried to object to her vague response. "How do you think you are alive? You have been here months unable to drink and eat. You just stood and walked for the first time in what Durn thinks could be years. If not for his magic, how could you even draw breath?"

"His magic heals?"

"Of course it does. It is not strong, but he is skilled with medicines as well. Between the two, he has helped many people."

Jantalus studied her face a moment. "He helped you. You are not his niece, are you?"

She shrugged again. "According to whom? I am if I choose to be. I suppose he is more like a father, but there are fewer questions about an old man and his orphaned niece than a daughter when his wife has been dead thirty years."

That made sense enough, Jantalus decided. "So why you?"

She brushed a few stray black hairs from her face. "Durn was once a wealthy man. He owned land and had a wife and son. He hid his magic as most who do not want the Vicars who control the Alliance after them. I imagine he could have made peace with them, perhaps even served them, but Durn has never been of a mind for the politics of the powerful, I think. Regardless, when his son fell ill, he tried every remedy possible to cure him. When that failed, he used his magic. His wife was horrified. She accused him of practicing dark arts and murdered their son lest he be a tool of the spirits of the dead. After telling everyone in their village about her husband's secret, she joined her son."

"Word of his magic spread, of course, and Sentinels came to arrest him and take him before the Vicar Council in Haven."

She was beginning to lose him, but she seemed to realize it from his expression.

"The Vicars are the priests of Enyara. The oldest of them sit on the Council of Elders that rules over the Free Lords' Alliance. The Vicars wield power over the elements. Gifts from their god they say." Her frown said she doubted that claim. "Use of magic by others is forbidden unless sanctioned by the Council. That usually requires oaths, service, and favors. Those who refuses usually finds themselves hunted by Sentinels and either brought before the Council to face judgment or killed outright."

"And Durn?" he asked.

"Had enough money and land worth confiscating. The council has that power, of course, but Durn was well enough known that they could not simply execute him when he refused to join them. For all their power, the Vicars would lose control of the nobles if they appeared too quick to eliminate anyone they wished. So, the price for his life was forfeiture of his lands and money. He came to Marcester, a forgotten village in a remote region that is only a protectorate of the Alliance. Here, he can hide and they can pretend he no longer exists."

Jantalus digested it all for a time, leaning his back against the headboard. He believed her. He had no reason not to. He would be dead without them. If he could trust them with his life, it was reasonable to trust them with just about anything else. When he was done thinking it over, he looked back to her.

"I have two questions."

She held up a finger. "One."

"How did Durn happen on me if he is hiding out here?"

She flashed him an impish smile. "Durn's considerable talents are a bit wasted in such a small place. He still has a few friends who call on him when family and friends are ill. When they do, he goes to them and they pay well enough to make the risk worth it. Sometimes, people come to us. We think the man you were with was bringing you here."

"But Durn did not know him?"

She shook her head. "No. That was odd."

He drew a deep breath and let it out slowly. Not much of an answer, there, but he imagined it was all she knew. "All right."

She held up a second finger. "And two?"

"Why me?"

She cocked an eyebrow at him. "He saved your life and you question his decision?"

"He owed me nothing. Why make the effort if this mark I bear could invite trouble for him?"

"I don't know." She held up a hand to stop him when he tried to argue the point. "I'd tell you if I did. The truth is, he is taking a fantastic risk by having you here. As much as the people here think of him, they know nothing of his magic. They respect his skills as a healer, but they have no reason to suspect he uses anything else to help people. If they saw the mark of the dead in his home, they would send soldiers to summon Sentinels and Vicars for sure. His reasons are his own."

"And he tells you nothing of them?" Jantalus pressed.

"No, I don't." They turned to see the old man at the door, his face dark with anger. "Obviously, she likes to talk. The more I share with her, the more of my business there would be to spread about."

Halonni came to her feet with a concerned look. "I was only answering questions, Uncle."

He straightened. "You've other matters to attend to. Do so now."

She nodded, cast Jantalus an uncertain glance and crossed the room to leave. She paused when she reached her uncle, looking as though she might say something, but slipped past him and was gone.

"If I have offended you-," Jantalus said.

"You have not," Durn said, cutting him off. Despite his words, his face was still flushed and his voice laced with steel. "Rest. I will return with your supper and we will talk more."

He nodded. "Halonni-."

"Has much to learn. She and I will discuss this. It is not your concern."

"Durn." The old man had his hand on the door when Jantalus called him. He paused. "Perhaps I can join you. Leave this room, I mean."

Durn thought it over a moment. "Very well. You will join us."

"And you will tell me more – answer more questions?"

"As best I can."

"Thank you."

The old man drew a deep breath. "We will talk more at supper."

Without another word, he was gone.

Jantalus watched after him for a moment, staring at the closed door. He sifted through all of what he had been told for several minutes before he realized something. For all of her explanations and recounting of who Durn was, Halonni had managed to say very little about herself.

He pulled his legs up on the bed, leaned back against his pillow and stared up at the ceiling, wondering. Something about the girl made him think she was more than just a wayward soul Durn had adopted along the way. She claimed Durn possessed magic, but it was her presence that always triggered the burning sensation in him, not his. She was deliberate in avoiding his questions and he wondered if the infrequency of her visits was deliberate as well.

Supper, he supposed, might be more about questioning her than Durn. *Who are you, Halonni?*

Chapter Four

He never had the opportunity to ask her that night.

A commotion rose up from outside the house less than an hour later and Jantalus could hear pounding hooves and shouting men. When no one came, he pushed himself up from bed, bracing himself against the wall for support. He pulled the door open and peered down the short hall beyond. It was empty. He stepped into the narrow corridor and shuffled along the wall to the opening that led to the front room of the house. It was a small, cramped space with a stone hearth and a few well-worn chairs gathered about it. At its center was a table consisting of little more than a collection of old boards set across two sawhorses. The room was dark save for the dying sunlight that peeked through the front windows.

The voices were louder and he crept forward to hear them better. His shoulder to the wall, he made his way to one of the windows. He stopped and listened. The voices were gruff and demanding, an air of authority hanging on every word. Durn responded to them with an even, measured tone, neither belligerent nor deferential to their demands. Several men were talking at once and the voices were too jumbled for him to pick out anything.

"Enough!" a gruff voice called finally, dropping the chorus of shouts into silence.

Jantalus turned to glance out the window. Durn stood alone at the edge of the earthen path that led to his front door, a semicircle of eight horsemen arranged before him. At their fore was a broad-shouldered man with a short black beard who scowled down at the old man. He was clad in blued mail with a sword strapped across his back. Jantalus did not know this man. He glanced at the seven arrayed behind him and saw no familiar face there either.

"The question is a simple one, old man," the first stranger said. "Have you seen the man we are looking for?"

Jantalus focused on him again. Something about the man drew him back. After a moment, he saw what it was. The man's blue cloak was emblazoned with the device of an oak tree with a pair of crossed swords before it. Jantalus had seen that symbol before. In fact, he had seen it many times. The symbol was everywhere in the countless dreams he spent his nights trying to piece together. Shields, cloaks, tabards, and pennants bore it in almost every fragment of dream and memory he could recall. Whatever it was, it had been part of his life in the past. It was important, but Jantalus could not remember why.

"I have seen no one," Durn told the strange man. "I have kept to myself as promised. Honor your end of the commitment by leaving me now."

"We will do as we please and in our own time." The man stabbed a finger at him. "You are in no position to make demands."

A hand seized Jantalus's arm from behind before he could hear more and he turned to find Halonni there. She dragged him away from the window, nearly pulling him to the floor before he caught himself on a nearby chair.

"Are you mad?" she whispered through clenched teeth, her pale face dark with anger. "If you are seen, we're all dead!"

"Why?" he asked as she all but dragged him back to the hall that led to his room. "Who are those men?"

"Sentinels." She pushed him back against the wall, listening. "It sounds like they're leaving. Lucky for us."

She put a finger to his lips when he tried to ask more questions, her head cocked to one side as she listened more. Nothing moved for a moment and then the front door opened and closed with a loud thump. Footsteps approached, one set only. Durn appeared in the doorway of the front room and heaved a sigh of relief on seeing them.

"Bastards must have found someone who saw us bring you here in the fall." He shook his head as he joined them. "They'll be watching me now. Zeronis knows I'm lying to him, even if he can't prove it."

"Zeronis?" Halonni asked.

Durn nodded. "Anadom Zeronis, nephew to Telena Thel, the Vicar Elder. He's head of his own cadre of Sentinels. Someone has him after you." He turned his attention to Jantalus. "I don't suppose you remember why?"

He pointed two fingers at his own eyes. "Other than this you mean?"

Durn shook his graying head. "No, no. That's enough to get a Sentinel after you for sure, but not Zeronis. He's Telera's little pet. He does her personal work. Someone important has taken an interest in you, boy."

Jantalus thought on it a moment, but nothing new came to him. "What is that symbol he wore?" he asked instead.

"The oak and swords? That's the symbol of the Free Lords' Alliance. The settlements of the Censharn Valley formed it with the Vicars ruling them as the bulk of the Council. You know it?"

"I've seen it."

"And you'll be seeing it more if we don't get you out of here," the old man said.

"Out of here?" Halonni narrowed her eyes at him. "He can barely walk. How, exactly, is he supposed to travel? If we send him out on his own, he'll be dead by wolves or starvation or exposure even if he does manage to evade those Sentinels." She shook her head. "Not that he will."

"Alone? No, he won't," Durn agreed. "But you can see him through. You'll have to get him beyond Alliance lands. South to one of the frontier towns maybe or deep into the mountains-."

"I can see him through?" Halonni demanded, stepping forward to meet the old man's eyes. Durn tried to look away, but she caught his bearded chin in her hand and turned his face about. "What are you suggesting? That I take him away from here and leave you behind? I'll fight every Sentinel the Alliance has and all of those worthless Vicar shits before I do that."

Every bit of energy drained from the old man, his shoulders slumped and the lines on his face appeared to deepen. In an instant, he looked ten years older. His weathered hands reached out to take her delicate face and he bent to kiss her forehead. "I know you would, my dear. I know." A sad smile cracked the mask of pain and fatigue that had settled over him. "You'd give them hell, too. But that won't help us here. We'll pack some things tonight, all of us. I'll send the two of you ahead and then wait here until Zeronis and his bastards lose interest. When things have calmed, we'll meet somewhere and start over. Kronos is a big place. They can't chase us everywhere."

The tension eased out of her and Halonni reached up to take his hands. The look of concern in her eyes said she was less than confident but, clearly, she liked the idea more than the one she thought he was proposing initially.

"We have work to do," she told them and started away.

"Wait," Jantalus called.

Durn faced him again, one eyebrow cocked. "What is it?"

Jantalus looked him over carefully, measuring every inch of the man. He did the same with Halonni before returning his black stare to Durn. "Why? Why not cast me out? I am no one to you. I am a stranger found on the road who bears a mark that means only trouble for you. Charity for a sick man is one thing. Risking your lives for a freak who is hunted by the people who rule this land is another matter. Why are you doing this for me?"

Durn stared back at him for a long time, his face devoid of all expression. "For you? This has nothing to do with you, boy. Nothing at all."

Without another word, he turned away and disappeared back into the front room.

"Halonni?" Jantalus called as she moved to follow him.

She paused with a sigh and looked back. "Can you just leave it alone? Can you just accept that he's helping you and let it be?"

"Did you when he helped you?"

The girl shook her head. "Why are you so sure that is what happened?"

"Because you didn't deny it the first time." He took a step toward her, drawing close in the narrow hall. "Why is he helping me?"

She looked up at him, her lower lip clenched between her teeth. Her eyes closed and she drew a deep breath. "He isn't, Jantalus. He's helping Evon."

"Evon?"

She nodded. "His son. You remember I told you he healed the boy?"

Jantalus nodded.

"When the boy's fever broke, he was marked." She pointed. "Like you. Exactly like you. That was why his wife murdered the boy. He bore the mark of the dead and she and the people in his village blamed Durn for cursing him with it."

"So I am his penance? He thinks he'll save me to atone for failing his son?"

Halonni shook her head. "No. He just needs to find one of you, one marked person who is not what the rumors claim you all are. He has to find a reason to believe that his son died because his wife was mad with fear and grief, not because the boy was a monster."

Jantalus was quiet for a time, thinking it all over. It explained the risk Durn had taken and continued to take. Even so, Jantalus could not shake the feeling it was too great a risk for a stranger.

"You still don't know anything about me," he said. "Even I know almost nothing. What if I am what the rumors say marked men are? What if I am just a monster?"

She stared at him, hard. "That is why he has me. Pray, Jantalus, that you are not that monster."

Without another word, she turned from him and disappeared after her uncle.

Jantalus spent the remainder of the evening back in his room. Halonni and Durn appeared for but a moment to provide his supper and left without a word. They were making plans and preparations he imagined and he would have had little to add. His fate was theirs to decide, but then, it had been for some time. Whatever his questions about their motives, he held no fear that they would do anything to harm him. They had ample opportunity to abandon or betray him over the last few months and they chose to risk their own safety instead.

So, he had eaten, settled into bed and drifted off to sleep for lack of anything better to do. He dreamed old dreams, images and sounds he had seen many times before, all of places and events from his childhood that offered no further insight into the dark void that was his memory. Even as he slept, he tried to manipulate the images, to will himself to other times and places in his mind to find things of substance, but it was useless. Finally, he accepted what was and let himself watch the stories that unfolded before him with the casual peace of a man who sat beside a river and watched it flow by.

At least until the door came crashing down.

He bolted upright in his bed at the sound, throwing his blankets away.

He was over the side and on his feet with an instinct he had not known he possessed and without the caution he should have remembered. His legs went weak beneath him with the sudden movement and weight, his knees nearly buckling from the effort. He caught himself on the bedpost and straightened, drawing a steadying breath.

He was just reaching for the door when it burst inward and Durn and Halonni scrambled through. Halonni was dressed in a long, dark cloak and boots and held similar clothing under one arm. A worn leather pack hung from one slender shoulder. Durn slammed the door shut behind them and secured the latch.

"They're back," he announced and Jantalus did not need to ask who he was referring to.

Halonni shoved the cloak and boots into his hands. "Quick, now. We left the back door open in the kitchen to draw them, but they'll be here soon enough."

He dropped back down to the bed and started pulling the boots on, rushing so much that he fumbled and struggled like a fool. Finally, she knelt down to help him as she would a child. Durn had moved past him and was feeling along the far wall, his calloused hands digging into the edges of the stone blocks. Finally, he found what he wanted and pressed his fingers into a small hollow. To his left, a section of the floor swung away, revealing a hole just large enough for a man to squeeze through.

Durn beckoned them forward just as someone tested the door from without, the latch jiggling. Jantalus hurried as best he could, Halonni all but pushing him ahead to where Durn waited.

Something heavy hit the door and it shook in response, the wood splintering.

Durn took Halonni by the shoulders and kissed her forehead. Then, he dug something out of his pocket and pressed it into her hands. "Go. Do not wait for me. You know where." He laid a hand on Jantalus's shoulder. "Watch out for each other. I'll come when I can."

Halonni, half his weight and a full head shorter, was pushing him to the opening in the floor. He dropped through, landing awkwardly on the floor of the earthen tunnel below and dropping to his knees. She was next to him a moment later, swinging the trapdoor closed just as the door above finally came apart. A chorus of shouting and cursing erupted and feet hammered on the floor.

Her face barely visible in the thin slivers of light that slipped through the cracks in the floor, Halonni closed her eyes and set her jaw as she drew a deep breath. Her hesitation lasted but a moment. With a look of iron determination, she began crawling forward in the low tunnel, beckoning him to follow.

Through the pitch black they crawled, feeling their way, blind. Halonni moved with a confidence and familiarity that spoke to having been there before. Jantalus stayed close enough that she kicked his hands more than once as she moved, but he was willing to bear it instead of falling behind. She finally stopped ahead and he heard her grunt as she strained against something. He heard nothing more and she did not move from where she was.

"Come here," she said finally.

He groped ahead, catching her leg. She reached down to take his hand and guided him up to a kneeling position beside her. She pushed his hands up to the ceiling and pressed them against what felt like wooden planks.

"Push," she told him, her breath hot against his cheek.

He braced his knees against the ground and pushed up with all of the strength he could muster. Something shifted above and gray light seeped through a square outline that formed above. Halonni's hands joined his as she reached up to push with him, and, finally, a trap door opened away from them. Something heavy fell back as they threw the door wide, crashing to the floor. Jantalus strained to see in the weak light above them, trying to determine where they were.

Halonni did not wait for him. She grasped the edge of the opening and pulled herself up, disappearing into the gloom for a moment. Jantalus remained where he was, still trying to determine something about their surroundings. The structure above looked like a small shed, the gaps in the siding allowing gray moonlight to seep through. A small barrel was overturned nearby that he assumed had been what was atop the trap door. Tools hung from the walls and large bulks of unidentifiable material covered in canvas tarps filled the space. He heard the metallic click of a door latch and then Halonni was back, peering down into the hole where he was kneeling.

"Are you waiting for those Sentinels to come pull you out of there?" she asked.

He drew a deep breath and shook his head. He placed his hands on either side of the opening and pushed with his legs, trying to lift himself out. It was harder than he imagined, his strength sapped by the long crawl and the effort of opening the door. It was all but impossible, his arms and legs rendered almost useless with fatigue. He cursed himself for his weakness and crawled out awkwardly, throwing his leg up as if he were mounting a horse and rolling onto his belly. Halonni grasped his arm with two hands and helped him to his feet.

She led him to the door and pushed him ahead, closing it behind them. They were in a small, empty lot between the shed and another, larger building. The spring air bit into them, turning their breath into icy vapor. Nothing moved in the half-light of the moon. Halonni glanced over one shoulder at a building behind them. Jantalus assumed it was Durn's home, but he had never seen anything but the inside and was not sure. She gave it only a moment, then took his arm and guided him away, heading through the sleepy village toward the dark bulk of a forest that lay a short distance south.

Jantalus hesitated. "Durn-."

"Made his instructions clear should it come to this," she said without looking at him. She pulled at his arm. "Keep moving. If we are spotted, you'll never outrun them."

His legs weak with fatigue, his mind swimming with questions about her, about Durn and about himself, Jantalus let her lead him on without another word.

Chapter Five

They spent the next few hours groping about in the dark, slipping and stumbling as they made their way through the dense trees. Branches slapped at them and thorns tangled in their clothing and cut their faces and hands. Jantalus managed only short bursts of movement, stopping constantly, his body aching and refusing to cooperate. He sagged against the stout trunks of the trees, shaking and panting, each time swearing he was at his limit. Always, Halonni would wait with him, never saying anything, her hands still locked on his arm. She had a sense for when he had regained enough energy to move again and pulled him on. The cycle continued for agonizing hours that he soon lost all track of in his haze of pain.

They finally stopped just as the sun broke over the horizon and lit the forest with streams of hazy gold. Halonni chose a fallen tree at the edge of a small clearing where the light slowly crept across the bare earth, steadily sweeping away the shadows. Jantalus dropped down, missed the log entirely, and landed on his backside. He did not even bother to move, but slumped back against it and closed his eyes. Halonni knelt before him, and placed a hand on his shoulder. He opened his eyes as she put a skin of water to his lips.

"Not too much," she warned, pulling it back as he gulped it down. "The nearest stream is far enough away that we have to be mindful."

"You know where we are?" he asked, his head tilted back against the log. He felt like something huge and heavy was pressing down on him.

She shrugged. "Of course."

"And where we are going?"

"Ulis," she answered. "I don't suppose you know the name." She did not look surprised when he shook his head. "A town south of here. It sits on a trade route. Easy enough to find - which is the point. Most importantly, it is sworn to Duke Armus of Turgin. That means no Alliance soldiers or Sentinels. Of course, the Duke's lands have their own dangers."

None of the names she mentioned meant a thing to him, but he nodded anyway. "I'm sorry. Sorry about Durn."

She tucked the waterskin back into her pack and rose. "Don't be. He knew what he was doing. He'll wait those Sentinels out and join us when they are gone."

"If they ever leave. He might have finally pushed them far enough."

She ignored him. "We'll just wait in Ulis until he comes."

"And if he doesn't?" Jantalus pressed.

She glared down at him, her pale face all hard lines and her eyes narrowed. She opened her mouth and then closed it again. Halonni paced away a short distance and then returned, dropping to one knee before him. She reached into one of her boots and withdrew something. She leaned close, her gray eyes on his, her delicate face all dirt and grime from their crawl through the tunnel and no less appealing for it. The girl opened her hand and held it out to him.

A steel ring with a raven emblem and a pendant bearing the design of a winding river attached to a silver chain rested in her palm. "Do you know either of these symbols?" Doubt filled her eyes as she stared into his black ones.

He took the items from her and held them up to the streams of sunlight, examining them. He recognized neither, a frustratingly predictable experience. "What are they?"

Halonni shook her head. "I have no idea. Neither did Durn. The man we found you with, the one who died, was wearing them. He had nothing else of value on him and no other mark or symbol that could identify him."

"Durn did not want the Sentinels to see them," Jantalus mused. He hunched over, examining the ring and pendant as if doing so would reveal something more. It did not, of course, but Jantalus was thinking about something else.

He looked up at Halonni. "We need to find out what these symbols mean. We need to know who I am and why those Sentinels are after me."

Halonni put a hand to her hip. "You mean 'you' need to know. Meeting Durn in Ulis is my concern, not chasing down who you are and where you came from."

Jantalus held up a hand to calm her. He could not be angry with her words. She was worried about Durn, he imagined, though she did not show it. The old man was foremost of her priorities and she was minding Jantalus because she had been told to do so. It was hard to blame her for that.

"Durn saved my life," he told her. "I still can't imagine why, especially with everything you have told me about this mark and what it means. Perhaps you are right that his dead son haunts him and he helped me in a search for answers. Whatever the reason, I owe him. If I am what he hopes I am, I owe him my best effort to help him in return."

"Help him?" She shook her head and puffed out a breath. "You can barely walk."

"A few weeks ago, I couldn't even do that," he reminded her. "I owe him. If I can find out who I am, who the man was that this ring and pendant belonged to, perhaps it will answer the question of why those Sentinels are so eager to find me."

She looked away a moment. "And if the answer is simply that you are everything Durn hopes you are not?"

He thought on the possibility a moment. "Then there is no reason for you not to run back home and tell them exactly where to find me and put an end to all of this."

"I might do that," she suggested.

"You would have by now if you believed it. If Durn believed it," he added after a short pause.

Halonni rubbed her eyes with her palms. For all of her strength and energy throughout their flight through the forest, she looked exhausted in an instant. "All right. We'll ask around in Ulis and see if anyone knows those symbols."

"Ulis?" he shook his head. "I thought he found me near a place called Drappel?"

"He did," she replied. "But Drappel is a week away from here and straight through the heart of Alliance territory. Ulis lies along the Krilizanian Way. Everyone in the Censharn Valley passes through there at one time or another. By my guess, we have as much chance of finding answers there as Drappel."

Something about the idea told Jantalus he should doubt it, but he had no standing to argue. Drappel and Ulis were names to him and no more. He had to trust the girl's word on this just as he did with nearly everything. If she felt it was best to go to Ulis, he had little choice in the matter. Even if he had had the strength to argue the matter, he was hopelessly lost. He needed Halonni where she had no use at all for him outside of Durn's direction that she look after him.

"I'm tired," he told her, closing his eyes.

"So am I," she admitted. To his surprise, she seated herself next to him, their shoulders touching. "We'll rest while we can."

He looked up at her. "Is it safe here?"

"No. But, for us, it's not safe anywhere. Get some sleep while you can. Ulis may be closer than Drappel, but it's still a long walk."

He heaved a heavy sigh and leaned his head back against the old log. "Thank you."

"Go to sleep."

"I mean it."

"Shut up."

He left the matter alone and drifted off to sleep.

It was noon by his estimation when she shook him awake. He was cramped and sore, unsure how much of it he owed to the flight from Marcester and how much to the way he had been sleeping. He pushed himself to his feet with a groan and stretched his legs while he rubbed his aching neck. Halonni had her pack over one shoulder and was tying back her hair with a leather cord, her attention focused south.

"We should reach Ulis by nightfall if we leave now," she told him.

She waited for him to join her and then started off, setting an easy pace. The trees were as thick here as they had been, but their progress was much better in daylight. Jantalus kept pace with an effort, but surprised himself with his ability to do even that. He was conscious that she was keeping her own progress slow for his benefit, but she made no mention of it as they went. They paused frequently to rest and, after a few hours, happened on a small creek that Halonni admitted to have forgotten about. They refilled their water skin and drank their fill before moving on.

They spoke sparingly. Halonni seemed preoccupied and of little mind to engage in idle chatter. Considering everything that had happened, he was not sure he would have felt differently. She spoke only of their progress or to point out potential dangers like snake holes and brambles to be avoided. For his part, he wrapped his cloak close to ward off the chill in the air and did as he was directed.

They came upon the road she had called the Krilizanian Way an hour before sunset. Ulis, she advised, was a short distance away to the east and they had drifted slightly during their trek south. Halonni shrugged off the misdirection and started down the hard packed earthen road without hesitation, beckoning him after.

They managed only a few dozen yards before Jantalus saw the first Sentinel emerge from the tree line to his left. Halonni saw him too, freezing where she was. Another man appeared beside the first and then two more from the opposite side of the road. Jantalus could see at once that none of them was Anadom Zeronis, the man who had confronted Durn and he was reasonably sure he did not recognize them as being among those who had been in Marcester. What he did recognize was the oak and crossed swords symbol that they wore on their distinctive blue cloaks.

They approached slowly, cudgels gripped tight and swords belted at their hips. They formed a loose half circle across the road ahead.

"Evening," one of them said as he stepped forward. "We'll have a word if the two of you don't object."

Halonni stood her ground. "We do. We have business in Ulis and time is important to us."

"Only a moment," he insisted. He gestured toward Jantalus with his cudgel. "Have him lower his hood for me and then you are free to go."

"I said we were in a hurry," she answered. Jantalus did not move.

The Sentinel cocked his head to one side, flashing a smile that was nothing resembling friendly. "You don't know who we are, do you pretty girl?"

She returned the cold smile. "I know Sentinels are not welcome on the Duke's land. Why don't you boys get back across the border before someone finds you here?"

The smile vanished. The speaker took a step back while the other three men started forward, cudgels ready. They moved slowly, deliberately, taking no chances, but showing no fear. Halonni retreated several steps until she backed into Jantalus.

"The leader is the one with the magic," she advised. "He'll wait for me to use mine to defend us and then try to counter me."

"Can he?" Jantalus asked, squaring himself to meet the closest of the Sentinels. It was almost laughable. Jantalus was bigger than any of them, taller and broader in the shoulders and chest, but likely not a physical match for someone the size of Halonni. He would be good for little more than slowing one of them for a moment.

"It doesn't matter," she answered out of the side of her mouth. "All he needs to do is distract me so these bastards can club the piss out of us."

Jantalus felt fire rise in his belly as she summoned her magic, reminded at once of his mother and father and their battle with the black-eyed man. It reminded him too of the stupors he once fell into and how similar it all felt. Durn, Halonni had told him, possessed magic. The old man had never provoked any reaction from him like this, though. It was always Halonni.

Jantalus had no time to think on it as the closest of the Sentinels made a grab for Halonni's cloak. She ducked away, slipping out of it, leaving him with only the empty garment. Before he could recover, Halonni thrust a hand toward him, and the torch he held in the hand opposite the cudgel flared to three times its normal intensity. The wooden stick was a cinder in an instant, the flesh that held it seared and stinking. The man shrieked and dropped it, clutching at his smoldering hand.

Another of the men had just seized the front of Jantalus's tunic, pushing past his feeble attempt to block him away, when he felt his blood begin to burn anew. It was the leader of the Sentinels summoning magic just as Halonni had promised. Halonni hesitated as the last of the cudgel wielding men approached, struggling as if she could not summon her own magic now. The man latched one hand on her white throat and raised his cudgel. At the same time, the man holding Jantalus jabbed him in the ribs with his own weapon, dropping him to his knees.

He fought for breath, but the pain of the blow was nothing compared the magic rising in him. Like an inferno that had started as a mere candle flame, it was growing at an exponential rate, raging inside of him in a way he had never felt before. The Sentinels stopped where they were, all eyes, even Halonni's, on him. His cowl fell back and he looked up at them with his black, dead eyes, face flushed red and twisted with rage.

"Crush his fucking skull!" the lead Sentinel shouted, desperation and fear cracking his voice.

The man holding Jantalus raised his cudgel to strike. Before the blow could fall, Jantalus surged up, one hand grasping the man's face. Despite his weakness, he took the Sentinel by complete surprise and the man made no attempt to ward him off. Jantalus's thumb and third finger gripped the man's temples. His palm flattened the thin nose against his face. The man screamed in agony as Jantalus's magic exploded forth in a rush, crashing over him and hammering him to his knees.

The world faded to black for an instant and Jantalus found himself for a heartbeat's time in the impenetrable blackness that had been his catatonia for so long. It did not last. As soon as it engulfed him, a light appeared at the center. He rushed toward it in his mind's eye and found it was an image of the man he grappled with in the physical world. He was kneeling in the darkness, shrieking and convulsing, his cries high pitched and terrible. As if he were looking down at it all from above like an eagle soaring overhead, Jantalus watched himself grip the man's head in his hand once more and squeeze. The screaming intensified to a deafening screech.

And the man's head broke apart like ripe fruit dashed against a heavy stone.

The darkness vanished and Jantalus found himself on the road to Ulis once more. Halonni and the men surrounding her stared at him, shock and fear twisting their faces. Even the man whose hand Halonni had burned was staring, horror overpowering pain.

At his feet, the man who had attacked Jantalus lay in a heap, blood seeping from his nose, mouth and ears, empty eyes riveted to the clear spring sky.

Jantalus fixed his horrible black stare on the man holding Halonni by the throat and started toward him, stepping over the dead man.

Without a word, the man released her and, his companions at his side, ran back into the trees. They never looked back.

Gasping for breath, her hands at her throat, Halonni slumped to one knee on the hard earth. "Almost broke my damn neck," she whispered, her voice strained and raspy. She looked up at him. "I had no idea... I mean, we knew you had some magic, but we didn't know what you could do."

He held out a hand to her. She took it and let him help her to her feet.

"Neither did I," he replied. "But now that I do, I am sure it is not the first time I've done it."

Chapter Six

"It doesn't mean anything, you know."

They were the first words either of them had spoken since their encounter with the Sentinels. They were waiting at the main gate of the timber wall that surrounded Ulis as a group of farmers fought to move a pair of oxen that refused to pull their cart. The guards at the gate were shouting and cursing, ordering them to clear the entrance, but the beasts refused to budge and the farmers' prodding, slapping and whipping were having no effect. The sun was nearly set in the west, and the gates were due to be closed and locked for the night. The soldiers were furious at the delay and letting their displeasure be known.

Jantalus looked over at Halonni and found her staring up at him. She was huddled in her cloak against the wind, her face burned crimson by the cold. Bruises had begun to form on her throat, dark and ugly against her fair skin. She might have been waiting for some kind of response, but he was not entirely sure what she was talking about. He simply shrugged instead.

"I mean the magic you used," she explained after a moment of silence. "It doesn't mean you are or aren't anything."

A monster or simply a victim of an undeserved mark was what she meant, he realized. "You've seen magic like that before?"

She looked back at the farmers and soldiers arguing nearby and paced away from them to be sure they could not hear. He followed after a moment. "Like that? No. I've heard Durn tell stories of Vicars who had the power to sense thoughts or even project their own to others. But overwhelming another person's mind to the point of destroying it from the inside out? No. Never."

He thought it over a moment. "Then I suppose I am not a Vicar."

She looked at him as if he were mad and snorted. "A Vicar? No. The Vicars are priests of the goddess Enyara. Their order is selected from those born with the gift for their magic and the recruits trained from childhood. They claim their goddess gives them the power to control the elements around them. A few, as I said, claim to have the power to read minds. The most powerful serve the Alliance in Haven. Those with lesser gifts are trained to be Sentinels. Their power is not like what you did to that man. The Vicars are not marked like you either."

He looked her over for a moment, thinking. "What are you then? A Vicar? A Sentinel that left their ranks?"

She shook her head. "Neither. I'm something of an oddity by Durn's evaluation. My magic is inborn like the Vicars, but different. It... It's complicated."

He wanted to ask more, but the farmers at the gate finally managed to get their beasts and carts moving and Halonni was quick to notice. She was obviously not interested in discussing the matter further and started toward the open gate at once. The soldiers stopped them only long enough to ask their business in Ulis and let them go when Halonni claimed to be visiting relatives. The men did not even bother asking for any kind of verification and waved them through without so much as a second glance. Halonni led Jantalus through the street beyond with a marked familiarity that said she had been to Ulis more than once.

Jantalus followed her, his hood pulled low and his black eyes downcast to hide his mark. Halonni might have been sure that he was not one of the Vicars she had told him about, but she had not offered any alternative explanation either. The idea that she might be hiding something was the first in his mind, but he dismissed it quickly. The weeks he had spent in Marcester with Durn had been ripe with opportunities to reveal anything they knew about him, and yet neither she nor the old man had volunteered a thing. They were as ignorant as he about who and what he was. Beyond his mark and the personal interest Durn had in him because of it, everything about Jantalus was a collection of blank pages in a book without a title. Halonni might be with him because of circumstance and lack of alternatives, but that did not mean she was lying to him or hiding something.

She stopped at the corner of two streets, her attention fixed on a long, single storied building on the opposite corner. The place was alive with all manner of activity. Men filtered in and out of the front door, gathered to drink in the street without and could be heard shouting and brawling within. Musicians played along the street outside, their dulcimers and horns barely audible above the roar of the revelers. A few coins were tossed into their hats as people passed by, but they were largely ignored. The flicker and glow of warm fires chased the growing darkness away from the door and windows of the place and puffs of white smoke rose up from beneath the eaves. A painted placard hung from an iron bracket over the door, but it was so faded and peeling, Jantalus could not make out any words or symbols.

"The Bloody Nail." Halonni gestured toward the place. "The owner, Temicus Vey, is a friend of Durn's. We should find some help here."

She did not sound as confident as he would have hoped and he flashed her a sideways glance from beneath his cowl. She sighed in response and shrugged.

"He doesn't know me," she said. "We'll have to rely on Durn's name and hope it's enough. Vey, I was told, is far from the trusting sort."

"We'll see," he said, starting forward.

"Wait." She caught his arm and he turned to her. "Your magic – don't use it unless you have to. Sentinels can sense it. The leaders, at least. That's how they are used. They can smell magic like a hound after a deer." She paused. "Not that it will take those bastards from the road much effort to figure out where we went anyway."

That was something Jantalus had considered more times than he cared to count in the last few hours. The surviving Sentinels would either begin tracking them again immediately or run for aid. As much as they did not need more people after them than they already had, Jantalus actually hoped for the former. If the Sentinels went for help, it would cost them time and that was time Jantalus and Halonni needed. If the friend of Durn's that they sought would not or could not help them, they would have to flee Ulis. For a busy town, it was not a large one. They would not be able to hide from determined hunters for long.

He adjusted his cowl to be sure his face was well hidden and nodded to Halonni.

She led him across the street to the entrance of the Bloody Nail. Several of the men gathered on the street whistled and made crude remarks as she passed, but none took any action. Jantalus stayed close regardless. He doubted his chances in a brawl with any of them, but his sheer size at least deterred them from any thoughts of misbehavior. They pushed their way inside, squeezing through the crush of patrons that clogged the whole of the taproom.

Drinkers and brawlers, gamblers and musicians and all manner of others packed the room so tightly that Jantalus wondered how they could even breathe. Halonni managed the duck and squeeze her way through, pulling Jantalus along by the sleeve of his cloak as she went. He held his cowl with his free hand as they went, pulled and bumped about so much that he feared it slipping and giving him away. No one paid him much attention beyond a curse or two as he pushed and elbowed his way through the crowd.

When they had finished navigating the sea of bodies, they found themselves at a well-worn counter made of lacquered oak. A short, bald man with hard, dark eyes stood behind it, barking orders at the serving girls, the slop boys and the cooks who worked the ovens in the room past the open doors behind him. Coins were continually slapped down on the counter by the passing staff and he slid them all into an iron box as they arrived. A pair of huge men, broad shouldered and bulging about the middle, flanked him. Halonni flashed Jantalus a concerned glance and then approached.

"We're looking for Temicus Vey," she told the man, her voice barely strong enough to rise over shouting men, clinking glasses and crackling fire.

The little man did not respond as he counted several stacks of coins and deposited them in his strong box as he went. He paused for a moment, screamed something to one of the serving girls and then went back to his counting. Halonni tried again, but the man simply held up one hand, never looking at her. He waited until he finished counting every coin before finally acknowledging her.

"Temicus don't run the Nail anymore," he said, flashing a gap-toothed grin. "Mine now. That sorry son-of-a-bitch is gone."

"Gone?" Halonni asked, her face losing all expression. "How do you mean? Is he-?"

"Dead?" the man anticipated her. "Aw, shit! No, he's not dead. Well, not last I knew. Got himself in some trouble with his gambling debts. Lost the Nail. I bought up the deed."

"Do you know where he is?" she pressed.

"No." He shrugged. "Don't much give a damn either. He's not here. That's all I care about. Now, you're drinking, gambling or whoring or you're out of my face, girl."

She bit her lip and shot Jantalus a desperate look before turning back to the man. "I don't suppose anyone else around here would know?"

The man stopped counting a new handful of coins one of the serving girls had slapped down before him and paused to look up at her. "Deaf, are you? I don't give a shit if the bastard is alive or dead. You can leave before I have a few of my lads finish what someone else started on your neck."

One of the brutes next to him smirked and rubbed his hands together. Two more men that Jantalus had not seen as they entered approached from behind them. One of them laid a huge hand on Jantalus's shoulder and squeezed, hard.

Halonni held up her hands and took a step back. "We're leaving."

The men walked them to the door to be sure they left, clearing away anyone who barred their path. One of them gave Jantalus a rough shove as they reached the street, an unnecessary punctuation to a clear enough message. A few of the revelers in the street snickered, but most ignored them as they continued their drinking and brawling. The sun had set and large iron braziers burned on the street corners to ward off the chill of the night air for the musicians and those who crowded close. The transition from the warmth of the crowded gambling hall to the frigid street made Jantalus want to rush over to join them.

Halonni paced away to the other side of the intersection and set her back against the building there. She reached up and rubbed her temples with her fingers. "I'd be lying if I said I had any idea what to do next," she told him as he joined her. "Temicus Vey was the only person here I knew. Without him, we're not going to avoid the Sentinels for long."

Jantalus swept the nearby streets with his black eyes. He counted a dozen more alehouses, gambling halls and inns in the immediate area. Every one of them was as overrun with patrons as the Bloody Nail, with people crowded in the streets nearby. They were mostly farmers and common laborers by the look of them, all soiled clothes and calloused hands and leathered skin. A few had the pasty complexions that marked them otherwise, but they wore the same patched tunics and their hands were just as calloused. Bakers, scullions, coopers and all manner of other occupations mixed with the rest. Those were not the men Jantalus focused on.

Organized in small islands among the others were small groups of men that kept to themselves. The glow of the fires glinted off mail and shields, helmets and blades. They were a mixed lot, some rough and unkempt while others looked the professional sort with cleaned and polished equipment. None of them bore any mark that matched the crest of the town or the Duke that ruled the area.

Jantalus nodded toward one of the groups. "You see those men?"

Halonni sighed, pushed herself away from the wall and looked. "Probably mercenaries or caravan guards. Now that the roads are clear, merchants will be on the move. That means raiders and slavers will be too. Men always flock to the bigger settlements hoping to be hired on as guards for the caravans."

Jantalus reached into his pocket and produced the ring and pendant Durn had given Halonni when they had fled Marcester. "Well traveled men will probably have a chance of having had seen these."

"I imagine so," she agreed. "But, even if we discover what those mean, we are no safer here."

"I was thinking they might point us in a certain direction." He pointed to the men again. "A direction some of them might already be headed."

Halonni was shaking her head before he finished the thought. "We don't have much money and no caravan master will want us along unless we pay. Besides, Durn will be looking for us here."

Jantalus turned, his black eyes staring down at her from his cowl. "Durn isn't coming. You know that. If Sentinels are willing to risk crossing into this Duke's lands to have us, they'll not be letting Durn go until they do. We are on our own."

She did not speak for a long time, her gray eyes smoldering. He was not sure if it was the fact that he was right that angered her, or the idea that he had questioned her at all. From the moment she and Durn had taken him in, they had made every decision for him. It was the first time he had asserted himself and he wondered if she found she did not like it. He was sure he was right about, but she never challenged him. She held his gaze a moment longer, her delicate face red with the cold, her gray eyes shadowed with fatigue, and then simply nodded.

"Let's just be careful about who we ask and how." She held out her hand. "Give them to me. It's best that I do the talking. The less attention you draw the better."

He nodded and dropped the ring and pendant into her open palm. They spent the next hours walking up and down the nearby streets, approaching everyone that looked the part of a mercenary soldier or a traveling merchant. They showed the marks on the ring and pendant to all, asking for any information that they might be able to share. Most of the men dismissed them without even looking, assuming they were swindlers or selling stolen jewelry. More than a few were more interested in Halonni than discussing anything else and she spent almost as much time rejecting obscene advances as she did asking questions. A few men took the time to listen and look, but none who did had anything to share that helped them. They were told the markings were everything from the crest of a trading company to an ancient family of long dead noblemen. None of the stories ever rang true and few of them came out of a mouth that did not reek of ale.

As the night wore on, they lost their enthusiasm, too tired and frustrated to force the matter. Finally, after assuring what Jantalus guessed was the tenth mercenary in a row that Halonni was not a whore and no amount of money he promised would change that, they decided to give up on the matter. Their attention turned to finding a place to stay. Every inn in the town was long since filled to capacity, and the taverns and gambling halls had already rented out every bare patch of floor to anyone willing to pay to sleep on it. The few citizens willing to speak with them did so only to inform them that they had already rented out space in their lofts, storerooms and sheds to travelers and none could think of anyone with available space. Posing the question of where they might find lodging to a member of the city watch who happened by got them nothing but a stern warning that they would be arrested if they were found sleeping in the street.

They gave up completely and were headed back to the gate to take their chances sleeping in the forest when two massive shadows detached themselves from the alley between two nearby buildings and stepped into the street ahead. The men were the biggest Jantalus had ever seen. Each was a full head taller than he and built like great walls of corded muscle. They were armored in blued mail and wore battered old cloaks and boots. Jantalus had never seen men like them before. Their skin was the color of freshly tilled earth and their eyes small and deeply set beneath their broad brows. Their huge heads were shaved bare and the smaller of the two had a short, well-trimmed beard. He also bore a huge steel hammer strapped across his broad back while his companion carried a massive double bladed axe.

Halonni and Jantalus stopped where they were as the men approached. They were midway between the gate and the collected inns, taverns and gambling halls they had been searching. This area of the town was all but abandoned and poorly lit by the few slivers of moonlight that filtered through the clouds. The patrolling soldiers that had made at least cursory checks of the busier areas of the town were nowhere to be seen now.

"Peace," the smaller of the two giants called, one empty hand raised in their direction. "We will not harm you."

If you could, Jantalus thought as his magic stirred in his blood, his body alive with the fire of it. Beside him, Halonni's magic was rising, adding to the intensity of his own. She did not seem to notice him in turn, her attention focused on the dark skinned men.

"What do you want with us, then?" she asked.

The men stopped a safe distance away, doing their best, Jantalus supposed, to assure their peaceful intentions. "We've heard you need a place to stay," the smaller man said. "We've come to offer you one."

Halonni stared daggers at the man. "In exchange for what?"

"You telling where you got that ring you've been showing around."

Chapter Seven

Jantalus and Halonni allowed the men to lead them back to the stable they were using for shelter. Discussing the matter in any place public, they advised, was unwise. They refused all other questions as they led the way, simply saying that they would answer everything as soon as they were sure that no one was in earshot. Jantalus could not help but feel the whole affair a foolish one. They did not know these men and had no reason to trust them. He was letting the fact that he was cold, exhausted and desperate overrule his common sense, but followed along in spite of it. As desolate as the section of town they found themselves in was, these men could have attacked them at any time. If they had not done so the moment the four of them had entered the first alleyway, Jantalus assumed they were not interested in robbing or killing them after all.

The promised shelter was small, big enough for two horses at best, and situated at the rear of what appeared to be an old smithy. The owner, the men explained, was retired and the shop abandoned. It was a simple storage shed now, as was the attached stable. It provided barely room enough to sleep among the barrels and crates and canvas bags, but it was a protection from the wind at least and kept the rain off of them.

The men ushered them in and led them through the cramped spaces between the dusty old crates and boxes to a small spot of bare floor they had created by restacking and shoving aside everything they could. The larger of the strange men worked for a moment with flint and steel until he had lit the wick on a rusty old oil lamp that barely cast enough light to see by.

"Sit." The smaller man gestured to a pair of small crates in the corner. "I am Stilthius Menion." He pointed. "My brother, Tyris." A hint of an accent tinged his words, but Jantalus could not place it.

Halonni nodded slightly. "All right, Stilthius Menion. What is your interest in us?"

Tyris Menion dragged another small crate over and lowered his massive bulk onto it. "You don't have names then?"

The girl cocked an eyebrow at him. "Halonni Vilcris. He is Jantalus."

Jantalus said nothing as the brothers nodded to him. In all the time he had spent with her in Marcester and on the road, Halonni had never bothered to share her full name with him. He found himself staring at her rather than paying attention to the Menion brothers. She noticed him after a moment and shrugged one shoulder before looking back to their hosts.

"You mentioned the ring," she said. "Do you know something about it?"

Stilthius sat on the floor next to his brother and stretched out his long, thick legs. "Us and half the men you questioned, I'd wager."

Halonni shook her head. "Everyone we talked to said they did not recognize it. The ones that were sober enough not to make up wild stories, at least."

"And rightly so. It's the river design on the pendant that is actually important here. It's the symbol of the Black River mercenaries."

"Men fear them?" Jantalus asked.

"Not anymore." Tyris Menion drew a finger across his throat. "They're all dead. Rumor is the whole lot of them ran afoul some dark power and it did them in. Mercenaries are a close group. You never know who you'll be working for or against day to day, so you keep an ear to the wind and try to learn what you can. With what happened to Black River, word spread fast. Now, no one wants to even admit they knew the poor bastards."

"Not you, though?" Jantalus kept his eyes on the floor. The talk of dark magic made him conscious of his mark and concerned of what they might think if they caught a glimpse of his face.

The brothers looked to one another for a moment before Stilthius answered for them. "We were Black River for a time."

Halonni leaned forward and dug out the ring from her pocket. "Do you know this raven symbol then?"

Stilthius did not hesitate. "Shit, everyone in Black River knew it. That's the mark of Peridor Finn. He was the man who formed the company."

"You knew him?" Jantalus was almost lunging at him, filled with a sudden hope that he might have his first answer as to who and what he might be.

"Knew him?" The big man shook his head. "No, not personally. Black River was eight hundred men at full strength. We were scattered all around the Censharn working all manner of contracts. Finn owned the contracts and did the dealing, but his officers ran the actual meat of it all. Word was Finn was a rich man once, a landowner who pissed someone off and got himself stripped of his titles. Forming Black River was more about a thumb in the eye of the people who fucked with him than anything else. We worked for the Duke of Turgin more often than not. Finn liked sticking it up the ass of the Alliance whenever he could."

He paused and rubbed his hands together. "So." He let the word hang a moment. "Would you like to help us find him?"

Halonni and Jantalus stared at the men in stunned silence. Stilthius looked thoroughly confused as his eyes flickered between them.

"He-." Halonni drew a breath and licked dry lips. "He's dead."

Tyris Menion spat on the dusty floor. "Fuck."

"You're sure?" Stilthius asked, his dark face creased with disbelief.

"My uncle buried him," Halonni answered. "He died last autumn near a town called Drappel on the other side of the Censharn."

Stilthius sat back against the wall of the stable and heaved a heavy sigh. Beside him, Tyris was shaking his head and pounding his massive fist against his knee. Jantalus had the sense that it was anger and disappointment, not grief. They had clearly been hopeful of finding this Peridor Finn and the news of his death ruined their plans. A long, uncomfortable silence hung in the little space for a long time before Stilthius drew his long legs up under him and leaned in toward them again.

"He died in battle?"

All eyes turned to Halonni Vilcris as she shook her head. "Finn was nearly dead when he found him – my uncle, that is. He had been wounded more times than he could count. Finn spoke only for a moment. He asked that someone look after Jantalus and then died. He never had a chance to explain how he got there or why."

Stilthius turned to Jantalus. "What do you know of-?"

"Nothing," he told the big man before the question was even finished. "I remember nothing at all. The name Peridor Finn is meaningless to me and I have never heard of the Black River mercenaries. I am not even sure where Drappel is."

They fell into silence again and Halonni rose to her feet. "I am sorry we were no help to you. We appreciate what you were able to tell us."

"Where are you going?" Tyris asked as Jantalus joined her.

Halonni paused and bit her lower lip. "I assumed you would want us gone since we couldn't help you."

Tyris waved them back down. "We offered a place to stay the night and it stands. As pitiful as this old hole is, there's nothing else in this shit town. Rest while you can. We're broke and only paid through the night. Might as well share what we've got."

Jantalus shrugged when Halonni flashed him a questioning look. They were not likely to get any other offers. With a nod of appreciation, Jantalus retook his seat on the old crate and Halonni settled down next to him once more. Halonni opened her pack and pulled out their blankets, an old bottle and a small bundle wrapped in an old cloth. She pulled the cork out of the bottle with her teeth, took a quick swallow and passed it to Stilthius.

"Not the best," she told him, "but cheap wine is better than no wine."

Stilthius grinned and took a long draught. "You're my new favorite person on Kronos, Halonni Vilcris."

The bottle passed to Tyris and then to Jantalus. Halonni opened the bundle of cloth to reveal a small wedge of dry cheese that she cut into four parts and passed around. The Menion brothers thanked them again.

"What's your interest in this Peridor Finn?" Halonni asked as she chewed her food. "Work?"

Tyris nodded as he accepted the bottle back from Jantalus and washed down his cheese. "We spent the winter in Turgin and pissed away what money we had on whores and cards. We came back here hoping Black River would be recruiting again. Looks like we'll be taking work with someone else this spring."

Halonni flashed him a faint smile. "Seems so." She handed Jantalus his blanket. "We'd best get some sleep. We'll be leaving Ulis in the morning ourselves."

Stilthius held out the half-empty bottle to her. "Sleep well, then."

Halonni held up a hand to the bottle. "Yours. We owe you at least that for letting us stay here."

He shook his head in return and looked around them. "If you say so."

Jantalus slid off his crate, wrapped himself in his blanket and laid his head in the crook of his arm. Halonni settled down beside him, her head at his feet, and rolled herself in her own blanket, using the empty pack for a pillow. She was asleep in a matter of minutes. Jantalus lay awake for a time, his eyes closed as he listened to the two outlanders. Despite the foolishness of it, he was still wary of the big men. He told himself over and again that they would have tried to harm them already if they were of a mind to, but he lay there and listened for a time regardless. They spoke of Peridor Finn and Black River, speculating about what might have befallen both and how they wished otherwise. They discussed the other companies they might find work with and how much they needed the money, but little else.

Finally, more exhausted than convinced he was wrong about them, Jantalus drifted off to sleep.

A searing, breathtaking fire in his blood woke him a few hours later. He bolted upright, kicking Halonni in the back of the head with the heel of his boot as he did. She came awake with a groan of pain, clutching at the spot where he had hit her. He did not even look at her; his attention riveted on the doors at the opposite end of the stable. Something or someone was close. He knew it.

He could feel it.

Halonni sat up to look at him, rubbing the back of her head, her face a vague shadow in the darkness. The oil lamp had gone out, only the dim moonlight that outlined the door and windows was visible. Jantalus threw off his blanket and rose, senses on alert. There was no sound, but the fire in his blood raged.

As Halonni struggled up beside him, the doors on the other side of the building burst open. Half a dozen men rushed in, naked blades gleaming in the light of several torches. To Jantalus's left, a shuttered window crashed open and another man swung through. Half blind in the darkness and still shrouded in a sleepy haze, Jantalus hesitated... paralyzed. He saw dark shapes and torches everywhere, rushing toward him, men shouting and leather creaking. He had nowhere to run and fighting seemed laughably futile.

Still overcome by indecision, he heard a bellow as if from some maddened animal. With speed that should have been impossible for a man his size, Tyris Menion leaped forward, his massive double-bladed axe gleaming in the torch light. Like a great cat ambushing its unsuspecting prey, he launched himself at the knot of men.

"Pig-fucking sons-of-bitches!"

Like a rabid beast, he tore into the stunned men, his axe whirling and cutting, shattering flesh and bone and spattering walls and crates with blood. A moment later, Stilthius was beside him, his hammer raining thunderous blows, leaving men crushed and bleeding. In a moment of total chaos, three of the men who had broken through the door where hacked apart and lying on the floor in pools of blood. Two more were wounded and retreating with the rest as they hurried back to the street. Tyris and Stilthius chased after them screaming obscenities and promising to finish them all.

Instinctively, Jantalus rushed after them, pulling away from Halonni as she tried to stop him.

More men waited in the street and Tyris and Stilthius had their backs to the wall of the stable, weapons ready. The men had formed a semi-circle about them, a dozen strong with the Sentinels who had ambushed Halonni and Jantalus on the road outside of Ulis at their center. They were not pressing the attack, their eyes on the Menion brothers and the axe and hammer that dripped the blood of their fellows. For their part, the brothers did not show the least bit of concern for the numbers they faced, their eyes wild and hungry in the fire light. One of the men spotted Jantalus as he stepped into the street and started forward, but Stilthius feinted toward him and he fell back at once.

Tyris raised his axe toward them. "What are you waiting for? I don't need to rest you filthy bastards."

Jantalus swept the line of men with his black eyes, searching. His blood was still burning. Pain flared through him when he settled his gaze on the lead Sentinel, but that was not the source of the strongest magic. The power causing his blood to stir and burn so violently was nearby, but he sensed that it did not come from any of these men. He concentrated on the raging magic inside of him, trying to focus. In an instant, it was as if an invisible line had been drawn ahead of him, leading him toward the source of the power. The more he focused, the more specific distance and direction became.

Someone was approaching from an alley just behind the clutch of men that surrounded them. The magic he was sensing approached with this person. The men who had ambushed them inside were waiting for this other one to join them. Jantalus turned to warn Halonni, but she was gone.

He risked a glance into the stable, but he found no sign of her in the darkness.

He looked back as the enemy ranks parted and a handful of others joined them. Jantalus recognized the aura of power among them as the one he sensed. All five were wrapped in long, hooded black cloaks, their faces hidden. They paused among the others, making no threatening move. One of them, taller than all but one of the others, came forward a few steps, stopping midway between the opposing groups. One gloved hand came up to pull away the hood, revealing a strong, square face that was only vaguely feminine. The woman's black hair was short and spiked out from her head.

The eyes that fixed on Jantalus were solid black.

She stared at him, sending the fire inside of him raging at a new intensity. She held his gaze a long moment and then turned it on the Menion brothers.

"This is not your affair," she told them. "I give you your lives. Leave us while you can."

Stilthius spat toward her, a stringy glob of phlegm catching the edge of her cloak. "We go where we choose and decide for ourselves what concerns us."

The woman glanced down at her cloak and then back to the outlanders, her face impassive. "Why don't you take a look at what you face and think about what you're doing? Leave or we'll kill you."

Stilthius laughed like a mad man, white teeth showing in the torch light. He raised his huge hammer toward the half-moon overhead. "Hunnaris laughs at the weak fools of this land. You do nothing but talk!" He waved her forward. "Fight us you puny shits!"

Before the woman could respond, one of her black cloaked companions, a small, thin man, lunged forward, his hood falling away from a hideously scarred face. "I'll take them!"

Saliva dripped from his ruined lips as he snarled and raised twin swords. The woman grabbed at him to stop his charge, but he was beyond her grasp and sprinting toward Tyris Menion.

The street exploded in a rush of confused action. Swords and knives flashing, the assembled men joined the rush as Tyris and Stilthius stood against the tide like two great steel walls, axe and hammer scything. The black-eyed woman stood at the center of it all, fighting to restore order to her men. At the same time, a mass of town watch and armed militia arrived from an adjoining street, come to investigate the commotion. There were shouts and threats, demands and refusals and more violence erupted without a clear sign of which side had been first to attack. The majority of the men who had ambushed Jantalus and his companions halted their charge and turned to meet the militia while two of the men in black pressed the attack against the Menion brothers.

The remaining three black-cloaked figures charged through the melee and headed directly toward Jantalus, the woman leading. Jantalus glanced over his shoulder at the alleyway behind him. He would not get far if he ran. He was still weak and he had no idea where he was going.

His attackers closed quickly, rushing up to him, seeking to seize him by the arms. He could see the glassy black eyes under the hoods of the two people who accompanied the woman. The larger of these was a man and the smaller a woman. Each clutched at his arms as he tried to pull away. The woman could not keep her grip, but the man found a hold on his wrist and jerked him about. Jantalus tried to shove him away, but the larger woman with the spiky hair was on him as well, her hands reaching for his face.

Her hand closed on him, her fingers digging into his cheeks and eyes, a white-hot eruption of power exploded between them and the woman gasped, her black eyes going wide. Images flashed through Jantalus's mind, quick and vivid. He saw himself and the people who grappled with him in other times and places, friends then and there. Names spoke in his mind. Shantara. Rossin. Caleb. Faylor. Samarus. He knew them all. He had known them all his life. Tassaren – that was their family name.

Shantara gripped him still, her face stricken, her mouth wide with an anguished scream. The power continued to build between them, rising like a mighty wave. He could feel her magic surging, fighting to counter him, desperate to break free. To either side of him Samarus and Faylor were also summoning magic. Yet another magic flared from behind him, blocking theirs away. It was Halonni. Her power and theirs wrestled for control, the tension in the air building.

For a heartbeat, the world stood suspended in time around him. The fire of his magic struggling against theirs cooled. The sounds of battle fell silent. The pressure of Samarus's hands on his arms and Shantara's jagged nails against his face vanished. For that heartbeat, the world stood still.

And then, his magic exploded in a shockwave of pure force.

The air around him shimmered and then rolled out from him in a ripple. A thunderclap shook the whole street and Shantara, Samarus and Faylor were hurled away from him. With the rush of magic, his strength seemed to flow from him as well and he crumpled to his knees. Samarus hammered into the wall of the stable and broke through completely, disappearing inside. Faylor tumbled away to his right, collapsing to the street behind the clashing townsfolk and the assassins. Shantara was hurled straight back, crashing into a pair of her men, knocking them all sprawling.

Jantalus tried to rise, but his knees buckled and he had to brace himself against the ground to keep from falling on his face. He could see the men fighting Tyris and Stilthius begin to give ground and their fellows fall back as well. Tyris and Stilthius screamed another challenge at them as they gathered up the fallen, Shantara and Faylor, and fled down an adjacent street, vanishing into the darkness.

Jantalus's head swam as he tried to move again, his vision blurring. He could vaguely make out the huge bulks of Tyris and Stilthius as they started toward him. He slumped forward, his forehead against the ground as the world began to spin out of control.

He heard a voice in his ear and a slender arm came around his shoulders. He turned to see Halonni kneeling over him. She cradled his head as he collapsed completely, shouting something he could not understand.

And then, he was falling into darkness.

The darkness that claimed me before.

Chapter Eight

Tassaren.

The name echoed through the impenetrable darkness he found himself swimming in. He was trapped once more in the too familiar nothingness that his mind had retreated to so many times. There was nothing to see, no sense of time or space. He could move, but felt no actual movement across any distance. He could scream, he thought, but he could not hear it himself. What he heard, the voice that spoke to him, came from somewhere else. For a few moments, he tried to answer it. Then, he realized it was his own mind talking to him.

He stopped trying to see and hear and feel and taste. He stopped searching the emptiness for something that he now understood was not really there. That darkness, that emptiness, was an illusion. He could not be sure it always had been or was only now. In the moment the distinction did not matter. What mattered was that it was not real here. It was a trick, a ruse, a bit of fantasy his mind retreated into in order to protect itself when it was overwhelmed. It was still his mind, though. He was still in control. He still had a choice.

And Jantalus chose to wake from the darkness.

It was not a physical awakening. He was still sleeping. What he did was pull his mind from the blank corner it was staring into to shield him from the onslaught of magic that threatened to pull him under. It was something as simple as turning about at a dead end and walking back the way he had come. His conscious mind was still there, still his, and waiting. He had simply to reach back and take hold of who and what he was.

He did so easily and without the pain of his magic. He slipped into a dream state as easily as he might wade into a gently flowing stream. In an instant, the darkness burned away like a morning fog and he was surrounded by a world of sounds and pictures. They rushed by him like leaves in a storm wind, whirling and scattered, uncontrollable and chaotic. In his mind's eye, he saw himself among them, a solitary rock in a raging river of light and sound. He settled himself and concentrated. With a calm, controlled effort, he bent the raging memories to his will, slowed them, ordered them and then selected what he wanted from them.

His success was minor at best. It was still too much to manage and too fragmented to understand as a whole. But he concentrated on the name Tassaren and those who had come for him. He drew the images and sounds of those people to the fore and drank them in. He saw Shantara and Samarus and the others as children and then as adults. He saw himself among them, a companion and a friend. He studied them in detail and memorized everything about how they looked and sounded and acted.

Then, when he could force no more from his tattered memories, he returned to the waking world.

****

He was lying on a thick bed of old blankets that insulated him from the cold, hard earth beneath them, his head propped up on a balled cloak. Two more blankets had been placed over him and he lay only a few feet from a roaring fire. A canopy of stars and moon stretched above him, and spruce and pine trees formed walls around him. He eased himself up, his head pounding and his back and shoulders aching. His face stung where Shantara's nails had dug into his flesh. He turned to find Halonni stretched out an arm's length away, her pale face gone ashen, her eyes lined with dark circles. She was sleeping on a makeshift bed of old blankets similar to his.

He reached out to shake her awake.

"Don't."

He turned to the sound of the voice as Stilthius Menion stepped into the circle of light thrown by their fire. He was stripped to the waist, his dark skin mottled with deep bruises and welts. He was trim and all hard muscle, his massive body a patchwork of dark scars. He was drinking from a wooden cup he held in one hand. His steel hammer hung loosely from the other.

"The girl was all but dead on her feet." He seated himself on a fallen tree trunk that had been dragged close as he spoke. "She's been sitting up with you all day and night. Let her sleep."

Jantalus withdrew his hand and looked about. "Where are we?" A sudden thought sent a cold shudder through him. "Tyris?"

Stilthius waved a dismissive hand. "Standing watch. It takes more than a few lice ridden inbreds to end the Menion brothers, lad. Soft, you

Kronans." He sipped from his cup and gave Jantalus a measuring look. "Well, not all of you. Most, though." He gestured to their surroundings. "We're in the forest outside of Ulis. The town watch didn't give a shit who was who; they just started rounding up everyone. We tried to explain it all, but it ended with Tyris caving some poor bastard's head in and we ran. Wasn't easy either. You're heavier than you look."

"It seems I owe you my life," Jantalus offered.

The outlander shrugged his huge shoulders. "Some answers, at least. If you have them."

Jantalus squared himself before the fire and pulled his blankets around his shoulders. "I can try."

Stilthius leaned forward and handed him the cup he held. "Took it from the dead before we ran out of Ulis. Got a good bit of their gear too." He jerked a thumb in the direction of his missing brother. "He kicked in a door while we were running and we helped ourselves to some poor bastard's blankets and food while we were at it."

A quick sniff of the cup told Jantalus it was some kind of spirits and he drank down a swallow. It burned all the way to his toes and then back up again. He nodded and handed it back.

"The girl says you've been sick and don't remember much. How true is that?"

"Mostly," he replied. "I see things sometimes, flashes of events from my past. It is my childhood one time and later another. I wrestle with it, but I rarely get the answers I need. I am not even sure Jantalus is my real name. It is the name Peridor Finn called me when Halonni's uncle found me."

Stilthius pushed a few stray sticks into the fire with the toe of his boot. "What do you know about those black-eyed shits from Ulis?" He gestured toward Jantalus. "You have the same look, the same eyes."

The same mark of the dead. Halonni's warning that reaction to seeing it would cause trouble appeared to be lost on Stilthius Menion. "We were friends once, I think. I see images of us together, but I don't have any context for it. I don't know why they were after me, but the men they were with were Sentinels."

Stilthius nodded as he spoke. "The girl told us about the Sentinels. She didn't know the others though."

"Tassaren," Jantalus told him. "They are from a family called Tassaren. I know all of their names and faces. I just don't know what they have to do with me." He looked Stilthius Menion over. "Where is all of this going? Why are you even here? This is not your problem."

"It is now," Tyris Menion announced as he came in from the dark to join them. "I finish fights once some son-of-a-bitch starts one with me. Besides, we were dead men back there. If that girl hadn't used her magic to save us, we'd have been overwhelmed. We owe something for that."

Jantalus shook his head. "They are not ordinary men. You'd do best to stay clear of them."

Stilthius snorted. "Halonni tried the same warning. You don't understand. We are the servants of Hunnaris." He lifted his eyes to the moon. "The moon god is the god of death, war and struggle. His great ivory skull looks down on us every night and judges us. We must be brave and strong in this world. We must be fearless and eager to fight against worthy foes or we will spend the next life battling the hordes of hell to prove our worth. Better that we earn our grace here, now, and spend eternity at Hunnaris's side eating and drinking."

"And fucking pretty girls!" Tyris added with a roar.

Stilthius joined his thunderous laugh and raised his cup in salute before draining it in one huge gulp. He wiped his mouth with the back of his hand. "Those men we fought were exceptional swordsmen and ferociously brave. Perhaps it was the magic in their blood like the girl says, but regardless, they are worthy opponents. If we kill them in combat, we'll earn our kullar."

"Kullar?" Jantalus asked.

Stilthius nodded toward his hammer. "There is no word for it in your language. The warriors who serve Hunnaris believe that when they have earned their place at his side though their courage, they will hear a name spoken to them by the god himself. This name will be that of a soul, chosen by Hunnaris to join with his servants in this world. That dead warrior will become one with a favored man's weapon." He held the hammer out for Jantalus to see. "When we are young, we forge them; it is our rite of passage to manhood. It must be a perfect vessel or no great soul will find it suitable. If a warrior's courage is strong and his weapon worthy, it will earn the soul of an ancient warrior and take his name. When our weapons have earned that name, we are worthy and have also earned eternal life with the moon god."

The giant withdrew the weapon and rejoined his brother. They were quiet for a time as Jantalus watched the two men from across the fire. Tyris refilled his brother's cup from a bottle he carried and they drank greedily. The calm easiness about them was almost perverse considering what had happened in the last day. They simply sat on the log before the fire, their eyes lifted to the silver light of the moon and drank as if they knew nothing at all in the world apart from the night, the fire and the spirits.

"Another drink?" Stilthius offered after a long silence.

Jantalus shook his head. "Why did you fight those men for us?" he asked instead. "They were after me, not you."

Tyris tossed his empty bottle aside. "Well, that is something of an interesting turn. Stilthius and I have been on Kronos for a few months now and have managed to gamble, whore and fight in the finest of places in that time. The whoring and fighting haunt us the least. The gambling is the hard bit. More than once we've had men who take exception to being parted with their money come to collect." He shrugged his huge shoulders. "When that mess started back there, we just assumed those bastards had come for us."

"Wouldn't have been the first time," Stilthius put in. He leaned forward a bit, his elbows on his knees. "These men we fought, these Tassaren siblings, will they come for you again?"

Jantalus stared at him, at the eagerness in his dark face. Beside him, Tyris looked just as hopeful. These mad men, he realized, were hoping they would meet the Tassarens again.

He drew a deep breath and nodded. "I believe they will."

Stilthius clapped his huge hands together. "Excellent. We travel with you then."

"I am not even sure where I am going next."

The brothers looked to each other and then back again to him. "Just let us know when you decide," Tyris told him. "If you're going to be up, we'll get some sleep while we can. Fair enough?"

Jantalus nodded, still more than a bit taken aback by everything that had transpired. Without another word to him, they gathered cloaks about themselves, lowered their heads against their packs and drifted off to sleep beside the fire. Jantalus watched them for a time, trying to sort out everything, and then gave up. He was hardly in any position to refuse their help, regardless of what was motivating them. If the Tassarens did return, he would be far better off with the Menion brothers at his side than not.

He pulled the blankets tighter around his shoulders and inched closer to the fire. The question of where he was going next stuck in his mind. The Menion brothers might not have cared where they went, but to Jantalus, it was everything. Ulis was certainly not an option any longer. Returning to Marcester was equally impossible. They had a pair of names to guide them, but no place to start looking. Tyris and Stilthius seemed to know little about Peridor Finn outside of his connection to Black River, and Jantalus knew nothing of the Tassarens outside of the fragmented memories he had been able to piece together. He had no idea where to look next or who to turn to. Something told him that Durn would have some insight, but the old man was beyond them for the foreseeable future. Whatever could be done would be for the four of them to see to themselves.

He turned to look at Halonni where she lay next to him. The flickering campfire dappled her delicate face with shadows and drew angry lines on her pale skin. He had an almost desperate urge to shake her awake and ask her what she knew of the Tassarens and why they were marked as he was. He was not even sure why he suspected she knew anything, but questions raced through his mind that demanded answers. As much as the strange siblings chasing him called out for an explanation, it was not the most pressing matter on his mind. What he really wanted to ask Halonni, what twisted his gut into knots more than anything else, was the question of his magic.

Twice in the span of a single day, he had discovered strange powers he had not known he possessed. First, his magic dominated and destroyed the mind of a Sentinel on the road outside of Ulis. Then, his magic manifested as an explosion of pure force, the shockwave strong enough to send three people hurtling as if they were leaves in a gale. There had to be some explanation for that.

Or not. It's hardly the first thing about all of this that doesn't make any damn sense.

He let the matter slip away. He could ask Halonni when she woke. If she had nothing to add, there was still the promise of Drappel. Answers might wait there if he could reach the place. He glanced back to where Tyris and Stilthius were sleeping on the other side of the fire. If they had things their way, the Tassarens might have them before they went too far instead. Either was preferable to the half-existence he lived now.

He looked up at the moon the Menion brothers prayed to. Their god was one of death, war and struggle they had claimed. They seemed foolish things to waste prayers on. There were enough of all three without a god behind them. The thought reminded him of the times he had seen his mother praying all those days that he had spent unable to hear anything she had said. Perhaps there were gods that heard prayers for the ill or cursed. Perhaps there was a divine boon that cured the mark of the dead.

He shook his head at the ivory half-circle above him.

Perhaps, it was just a damn moon.

Chapter Nine

Halonni Vilcris was awake before the Menion brothers. Jantalus was just returning with an armload of firewood when he saw her ease herself up from her makeshift bed. It was already dawn, the orange ball of the sun visible through the gaps in the trees to the east. The heavy screen of evergreens blocked out whatever warmth it might have lent them, and the air was crisp and frosty. Jantalus dropped the wood he was carrying on the glowing bed of embers and remnants of logs and the campfire flared back to life in moments.

Halonni edged closer, her hands reaching out toward the flames. Jantalus watched as she blinked and stretched and yawned. She turned to him slowly, moving in such a way that suggested her neck was stiff and aching, probably owing as much to the throttling she had received from the Sentinel the previous day as the poor sleeping arrangements. She studied him thoughtfully for a long moment and then waved him over, patting the hard ground next to her. She seemed to sense his need to talk or had already planned on something beforehand.

Jantalus wiped his hands on his pants and dropped down beside her on the old blankets she had been using for a bed. Halonni squared herself to face him, folding her legs beneath her.

"How do you feel?"

He shrugged. "Fine, now. Stilthius says I slept an entire day."

Halonni nodded. "The magic you used was powerful. The more you use, the more it takes. Of course, since we know next to nothing about you, we have no idea what to expect from it."

Jantalus held up his arm. He was bruised from his left wrist to elbow where Samarus had seized him and held him fast. "Those bastards had some idea, I think."

"Do you know what those people were?"

Jantalus nodded. "The Tassaren family. I have seen them in my dreams." He stopped himself abruptly. She had not asked who they were. She had asked what they were. "That is not what you mean is it?"

Halonni shook her head. "Their name isn't one I know, but they all bore the mark like you. They are all dealers in spirit magic – Necromancers. Not Vicars, you understand, but Necromancers. You remember I told you the Vicars inherit elemental magic and that is what makes them what they are? Well, if there are any who are their sworn enemies, it would be Necromancers. The death magic they wield is the antithesis of the elemental magic of the Vicars."

He said nothing for a moment, considering what she was getting at. "If all that is true, why were they working with Sentinels?"

"Because of you, of course." She made it sound like the most obvious answer possible. "Whoever – whatever – you are, the Alliance might not be the only people after you. For some reason, you're important enough for Necromancers and Vicars to work together to find you. I would guess these Tassarens have some connection with the Vicars and that is why they are tolerated."

As was usually the case when he spoke to her, Jantalus could not shake the feeling that she knew a great deal about the working of the Vicars and the Alliance for someone who had spent so much time isolated in the little town of Marcester for so long. She knew too much about Necromancers, the mark of the dead and the relationship the Alliance had to both. She seemed conscious of the way he was studying her, perhaps sensing his doubts and looked away, watching the dance of the flames.

"Who are you?" he asked her, drawing her attention back.

He had asked her that before, several nights past when she had shown him his mark. She had spent plenty of time talking, telling him about Durn and his history, but had managed to say nothing of herself. Durn had interrupted them then and the arrival of the Sentinels who had ultimately chased them out had forestalled any further discussion on the matter. Now, there was no one to come between them. There were no pressing matters to attend to. Nowhere for her to run to.

She cocked her head at him. "Why do you insist that I must be someone of consequence? What does it matter?"

"If it doesn't mean anything, why not just tell me and get it over with?"

She shook her head. "You think I have some secret about you or what happened to you that I am hiding and I don't. I had never seen you nor heard your name before the day Durn found you alongside the road with Peridor Finn."

"But you know the mark of the dead," he pressed. "It means something to you. Something specific beyond what others see." He was right; he knew it as soon as he saw the flash of pain in her eyes as he spoke.

Halonni stared at him for a long, time, her mouth opening to speak and then closing a half dozen times. Finally, she heaved a frustrated sigh and rose. She glowered at him, her gray eyes narrowed with anger. "You remember I told you that Durn had me to turn to if he was wrong about you?"

"Yes, but-."

"I know the mark of the dead because I once hunted Necromancers for the Alliance. Not like the Sentinels or even the Vicars. I was taken from my birth parents as a child because I was born with magic that made me something the Council could not bear to have outside their control. The Vicars control elemental forces; they shape and twist the world around them to their will. Most of them have the ability to manipulate one element with some degree of skill and the rest to a lesser extent. Their magic takes great concentration and energy to use. I can do everything they can do, but I can do it quickly and my control extends to everything around me – air, water, fire and earth. Most importantly, I can sense the gift of magic in others without even trying if I am close enough. When I am trying, when I actively seek someone out, no magic of their own can hide them from me. That is why the Vicars wanted me. That is why they took me.

I was trained and tested, molded into their bloodhound they used to sniff out anyone or anything of magic they chose. Over time, they channeled my powers to eliminate those who did not willingly submit to them. I was young and did not think for myself. The punishments they used to teach me obedience were more than enough to influence such an immature mind. It made me a dutiful little servant who learned very quickly that refusing anything they asked was foolish."

She stopped talking, her hands clenched into fists at her side, her whole body trembling. She stared down at him a moment more and then turned on her heel and stalked away. He watched after her a moment and then followed. She had stopped a short distance away, her face toward the growing light of the sunrise. She did not turn as he approached.

"What did they make you do?" Jantalus asked.

She continued staring off and when she spoke, it was almost as if she were talking to someone else, far away. "When I was eleven, I was tasked with tracking two Vicars, a husband and wife, who had abandoned the order and were accused of practicing the spirit magic. I went with a group of Sentinels and a Vicar named Orlam Tate to find them. We cornered them in a small village near the edge of the Karalack Mountains to the east. They tried to hide, but my magic found them. It always did. The Sentinels and Orlam Tate never even gave them a chance to surrender. They attacked at once and killed them."

"Your parents."

She nodded and drew a shuddering breath. "I knew it the moment I saw them and did not help them. In fact, I helped the Sentinels. That was what I had been turned into. That was how far they had twisted the soul of a child. I was no better than that when Durn found me. He had come to Haven to argue his case before the council and I was there to take measure of his magic and any threat he posed. When he told his story before the Council, something about it cut through the conditioning and training. Something about it made me see what I had become. That was part of his magic, I think. Part of what Durn does has nothing to do with healing the body."

"The realization of all I had done and what I had become was devastating. I was still very young, but I understood what I was. I was broken by the truth of it, shattered. I became hysterical and uncontrollable. I was locked away. They told me it was for my own protection, but it was certainly for theirs. I spent three years as little more than a prisoner."

"Why do I doubt they let you go?" Jantalus asked.

She shook her head. "I escaped. An old Vicar who had taken pity on me helped me. He had been sympathetic to Durn as well. When he smuggled me out of Haven, he pointed me in the direction of Marcester. The Council, he explained, would assume I had gone with him and it was best we separate. I found Durn a few weeks later and he took me in. I'm old enough now that few would recognize me and Durn was always careful to keep me hidden from anyone who might. I never saw the old Vicar again. I never even knew his name."

She turned to look at him finally. "You were in our care for months, Jantalus. Months. Durn and I have helped more people than I can count, but not like that. We took in sick children until their fevers broke or we went to other villages to treat the ill, but there was never more than a week's work. I liked all of that. I felt like I was doing something right. But you? You were something more. You were constantly slipping away from us and battling back. You were…"

"Redemption," he finished for her. "More so for you even than for Durn. He wants me to prove his son was not a monster. You want me to prove that you aren't."

"Yes. I need to be right about you."

He believed her. Something about the stricken look on her face and the tremor in her voice said she needed this more than anything else. Perhaps, he thought, it was why she was with him and had not stayed with Durn. She had to see this through and know for sure that all she and the old man had endured was not the end of things for them. Jantalus had to prove to them both that they could do something better than they had managed before.

"Come with me to Drappel," he offered. She was starting to shake her head at once, but he hurried on before she could speak. "I know what you are thinking. It is too far and too dangerous for us to risk it. It is also the only option we have. Ulis and Marcester are out of the question. We have no other place to look and no allies to call on. Perhaps going to Drappel will fan the embers of my memory and something will catch fire. If not, there must be someone who knows who I am or who Peridor Finn was. Help me, Halonni."

He had no right to ask that. She had already helped him more than he could ever dream of repaying. But this was for her as well, she had admitted as much only moments before. The only alternative they had was to flee even further from Alliance lands and hope they found some refuge before Sentinels or the Tassarens caught them. To Jantalus, that was simply not an option.

"If the Tassarens know who you are," she said, "they will anticipate this."

"I know. It doesn't change the fact that we have no other choice."

Halonni looked past him at the sleeping outlanders. "And them?"

Jantalus shrugged. "They are hoping the Tassarens find us. They have a score to settle. That might make them mad men, but they would be mad men standing with us rather than against us."

"And if we do this and we learn whatever we can, what then? What of Durn? I need your word that we will not leave him in the hands of the Alliance."

Odd, he thought as she looked up at him, a mix of determination and fear mingling on her exquisite face. In a matter of days she had gone from helping him because she had been forced by Durn to do so to asking for his word to seal a bond. It was a long jump from apathy to trust in such a short period of time. The strangest part was he did not doubt her for a moment.

"My word, then," he told her. "When we have done what we can to find whatever answers are to be had, we will find Durn. If that means standing against Vicars and Sentinels and Necromancers or anything else, so be it."

The tension in her face slipped away and she nodded. She was still unhappy with the situation, that much was clear, but he guessed she was resigned to the idea that nothing more could be done in the short term. They let the outlanders sleep a bit longer and set about gathering their blankets and gear, stuffing it all into their packs and refilling their waterskins from a nearby spring. When they had done everything they could to prepare themselves, they finally shook the Merion brothers awake.

Stilthius was quick to roll up his blanket, pull on his mail shirt and boots and make ready to go. Tyris spent several minutes grumbling, cursing, and thrashing about. One boot was missing and his cloak was singed from being too close to the fire and he bellowed and shouted as if the world were coming to an end. It was entirely harmless, Stilthius advised them, and best ignored if they wanted it to end. Engaging him only encouraged the behavior and, like most tantrums, it would be short-lived.

Tyris responded to the comments with a stream of profanity and suggestions about his brother's carnal interest in swine, but eventually relented. His boot was located while Stilthius and Jantalus kicked out the fire and within minutes, they were underway.

They spent two hours working their way out of the forest, heading north and west as they made for the frontier that separated Alliance land from that of the Duke of Turgin. The forest, Halonni advised, formed the agreed upon border. The trees thinned by noon and they were soon hiking through the rolling pastures of the Censharn Valley again. Clouds gathered above them and the wind increased as the day wore on, but the promised rain never came and they wrapped themselves tightly in their cloaks and pushed on. Halonni kept them clear of roads and the small farming villages that dotted the area, assuming anyone looking for them would do so in those locations.

The settlements and roads near the frontier were the ones that the Alliance bothered to garrison with soldiers, she explained. The smaller towns and villages deeper into the valley had few soldiers as the outer ones insulated them. Those would be safer to resupply in by her reckoning. Tyris and Stilthius agreed with her logic and Jantalus had no reason to argue it.

For three days, they avoided contact with everyone and everything, choosing rougher terrain and more remote areas to ensure the smallest chance of discovery. It was arduous travel over unforgiving ground and mind numbing in its monotony. With nothing to see or do but put one foot before the other and press on, it grew tedious. Jantalus was shocked at how well he fared physically through it all. He was sore and aching, but able to keep pace with the others and actually felt stronger as time passed. His body was recovering much more quickly than he would have imagined just a few days before.

Mentally, he fared far worse. He not only failed to recall anything of substance, he actually thought he might add depression to his already fractured psyche for a time. The first day of the journey was a torture of near silent boredom. The Menion brothers spoke to each other for the most part, using a language that Jantalus had never heard before. He supposed it was their native tongue, but he could not identify it even by name much less translate it. Too preoccupied with steering them along a path that only she knew, Halonni did not notice them. Jantalus remembered nothing of the area if he ever had known of it in the first place and Tyris and Stilthius were equally lost. She focused her attention on guiding them without getting lost and avoiding contact with anyone who might give them away. She also kept clear of what she judged to be likely spots for Sentinels to lie in wait for them if they were anticipating their journey to Drappel.

It left Jantalus alone with his thoughts – thoughts that were jumbled and incomplete and maddening to contemplate. It might have driven him to breaking if the Menion brothers had not begun telling him stories. He was not sure why they began doing so except that he thought them bored with the journey and grateful for an audience to tell their tales to. Whatever their reasons, they saved him in a way all their strength, ferocity and courage could not have.

The brothers told him of their homeland. They were wealthy men once, sons of a rich merchant who owned his own trading company. The business was based in Port Abbis, a huge trading city on the western coast of Tuliny across the Dragus Sea from Kronos. A guild war had erupted in the city and rivals had killed their family while the brothers had been away. They related the events as they might a hunting expedition. Warfare was as natural to them as the rise and set of the sun. Business rivals warring with each other was the way of things in Tuliny, the way they told it.

"We killed the sorry shits that did it," Tyris explained without any indication that he thought that right or wrong. "But the family business was done. We came here to start over."

Their fluency with the Kronan language owed to the trading business. Port Abbis, they explained, dealt with Kronos almost exclusively. The brothers had been mere children when they learned the language of the people who would have been their greatest customers if not for the untimely demise of their family. The combination of speaking the language and the near constant warfare that engulfed Kronos made it an easy choice for skilled warriors in need of coin. The previous year had been their first on Kronos and a profitable one thanks to the Black River Company.

The brothers passed the days with wild tales of battles both in the field and at the gambling halls. Black River had most often been tasked with guarding trade routes in the Duke's lands against bandits and slavers that prowled the roads. When the need arose, they patrolled the border the Duke shared with the Alliance as well. The outlanders cared about the money and little else. They did not care if they were cutting men apart or drinking around a campfire. Money meant cards, ale and women and that was enough for them at the time.

"You've changed all that," Stilthius told him at one point as they were making camp for the night in the shadow of a stand of bare elms. "You and the girl. We've been drifting you see. Tyris and I have fought puny men in meaningless battles and squandered our nights drinking, gambling and humping whores. Hunnaris rewards no one with a kullar for that. We were meant to find you. I know it. These Tassarens that hunt you are meant for us as well. It is a test. Our god has set us on a path to meet them."

Jantalus looked over at Halonni for a reaction to the outlander's assertions, but she only shrugged. She had not spoken much over the last few days as the brothers shared their tales. She responded when addressed, but kept to herself otherwise. Jantalus had thought it a simple lack of experience at first. The brothers were mercenary soldiers who had lived a life of combat. Halonni had been a recluse for the last decade, hidden away from the world by Durn to keep her safe. With the exception of the short trips they sometimes took to share his healing skills, Halonni had barely left Marcester since escaping the Vicars in Haven. Her time with the Sentinels might have lent some measure of empathy for their experiences, but he doubted she would have been interested in sharing it.

In fact, it was just that subject that Jantalus thought caused her withdrawal. Halonni's isolation from them began immediately after revealing everything about herself to him. It was Jantalus's sense of things that she did not make a habit of doing so. He supposed she felt he would judge her or doubt her in light of who and what she had been.

Jantalus looked back to Stilthius and nodded. "Let's hope your god has chosen the right path, then."

Tyris and Stilthius echoed the sentiments and rolled themselves in their blankets. Jantalus had first watch for the night and the brothers took advantage by falling asleep almost immediately. Halonni stretched out on the opposite side of the campfire from them, bundled in blankets, her head on her worn old leather pack. She lay on her back staring up at the starlit sky.

Jantalus watched her a moment and then walked over and crouched down next to her. She turned slightly, gray eyes orange with firelight. Her throat was covered in ugly purple splotches still, a stark contrast to her pale skin. He looked down at her for a long moment, trying to think of something to say. He was assuming a great deal about her by attributing her distant demeanor to his stirring up her unpleasant past, but something told him he was right.

"It doesn't mean anything," he said finally. "It doesn't mean you are or aren't anything."

He thought he might have seen a faint smile cross her face as he turned her own words back on her. She reached up to take his hand and squeezed it gently. Without a word, she settled back and closed her eyes.

In moments, she was asleep.

Chapter Ten

They reached the Bame River by nightfall and followed it north by moonlight beneath a clear, calm sky. The river was a tumult of white foam and frothy spray, too wide at some points to see the opposite bank in the half-light. The flats began a gradual climb to a low, gentle series of rolling hills. At the summit of one of those hills stood a tall, slender tower of stone. The pale moonlight revealed gaps in the low wall that surrounded the crest of the hill. Spotter's Hill, Halonni explained, was an old watch post that the Free Lords' Alliance had maintained when the lands to the south were still within their grasp. After the rise of the Duke of Turgin, they had abandoned it and retreated back within their established borders. Nothing suggested that anyone was there.

They made their way up to the edge of the wall and peered through the gaps, watchful for an ambush or some creature that might be making its lair in the ruins. Several minutes of careful investigation revealed no danger. Several old fire pits and bits of refuse in different areas suggested that travelers used the place for shelter as they passed through, but the tower itself was a burned out shell with the northern face reduced to rubble. It offered three intact walls to shield them from the wind and several old sheets of canvas had been strung across the center to create a makeshift shelter. The canvas was riddled with holes that had been patched with various materials ranging from bits of cloth to wax, but the clear sky made it doubtful that they would have to test it against the rain this night.

Jantalus wandered to the edge of the riverbank as the others spread out their bedrolls and gathered what they could for a fire. They barely scraped together enough for a fire. The area had been picked clean by the steady flow of travelers over the years and no sizable stands of trees were nearby. Scraps from the last few visitors and some windblown twigs were the best they could manage. He would have checked the riverbank for anything that had been washed ashore, but the water was twenty feet down from the top edge here and the slope far too steep to navigate. A narrow wooden bridge stretched from the western-most edge of the knoll to the opposite side of the river. It was well worn, but sturdy enough by the look of it.

He walked out onto the bridge a few feet and tested his evaluation with a few heavy stomps. The construction was indeed solid.

"Hoping it will collapse?" Halonni called from behind him.

He shook his head as he turned. "Not hoping. Expecting. Things look to be going the other way for us at every opportunity."

She came forward to meet him at the edge of the bridge, leaning against the anchor post as she peered over the side at the raging river. "That depends on how you look at things, I suppose." She shrugged when he cocked an eyebrow at her. "We're still alive. That counts heavily in our favor from where I stand."

They were quiet for a time, staring together into the water that glowed silver in the moonlight. There was a steady, soothing rhythm to the rush of the river in the otherwise still night.

"You thought I would pick Marcester over Drappel," she told him, her voice nearly lost in the sounds of the river.

"Hell, I almost did. I think we both know we are not much of a match for Sentinels right now."

She ran a hand through her midnight hair. "I do. I just hated the idea of leaving Durn behind. It was easy to lie to myself and pretend he was really going to meet us in Ulis. I suppose I owe you more than wishful thinking if we are going to be in this together."

"Owe me?" He looked at her as if she were mad. "Nothing. You owe me absolutely nothing. I owe you, on the other hand, more than I could ever repay."

It was her turn to give a look that questioned his sanity. "Owe me for what? You are still lost, physically and otherwise. I am leading you to Drappel, which, for all I know, will provide no answers even if it is safe. We may spend all this time and waste all this energy and come up empty. How is that something to be grateful for?"

He shrugged. "I'm still alive. That counts from where I stand."

She held up one small, thin finger. "You have to stop that." She shook her head and sighed. "Or I do. Either or both."

He gestured to where Stilthius was waving them back toward the tower. A small fire threw orange light around the area behind him. Tyris's big bulk crouched over it.

"Are you concerned about what you might learn?" she asked him as they started back. "About who you are or who you used to be?"

He considered the question a moment. "I wonder sometimes if it will be easily reconciled with who I think I am now. Not that I have a complicated sense of myself, of course. I wonder what will change if I discover I am a cooper or an assassin or some other extreme."

She shook with a light, playful laugh. It was the first time he had seen and heard it from her. She had never looked more beautiful than she did in that moment, moonlight falling down all around her and her face alight with laughter. He found himself staring.

"A cooper or an assassin?" She shook her head and wiped at her eyes. "I hadn't thought it possible for you to overthink this. I was very, very wrong."

Tyris had prepared a small meal of bacon and the last few heels of bread from what they had stolen in Ulis. If Halonni were right and Drappel was still several days away, they had little to see them through. They had a few more strips of the salty bacon, a small wedge of hard cheese and a half bottle of bitter beer. They were not going to starve in a few days, but what was left was not going to satisfy them for even one.

They ate quickly and gathered about the dying fire for a few minutes of warmth before settling in for the night. A frosty chill clung to the air and their blankets were barely adequate. After a long day of walking, Jantalus found himself turning cold now that he was not moving, his bones aching and his fingers and toes going numb. He huddled against the corner of the tower wall, tried to think of something else to take his mind off it, and mostly failed. Tyris had first watch and was pacing just beyond the edge of the wall. Stilthius had fallen asleep with his back against a huge stone block, still armored and clutching his hammer in his hand. Everything about his posture and positioning told Jantalus that it must be beyond uncomfortable, but Tyris had thrown a few blankets over his brother and left him as he was.

Halonni shuffled over to him as he was debating waking Stilthius Menion to spare him the aching, chafing and pinching he was no doubt going to wake to. She dropped down beside him, wrapped tight in her blankets, her chin quivering and her pale face ruddy. She pulled his blankets aside, settled close against him and then wrapped them both up again.

"Keep your hands to yourself," she warned. "I bite."

He folded one arm behind his head and let her rest against his shoulder. He was too tired to answer her and too cold to care about anything but keeping her close and staying warm. After a time, the heat from their bodies mingled and made it all bearable. Halonni's weight on his shoulder left his right arm tingling and numb, but it was better than the ache of cold. Her warm breath against his neck fell into a soft, steady rhythm and he could feel her whole body relax against his.

Jantalus lay awake for a time, staring up at the clear, starlit sky, thinking. He was exhausted and his thoughts were jumbled and unfocused and refused to settle on anything specific. He chased them about until his mind was as drained as his body and then drifted off to sleep.

And dreamed.

****

Who are you?

A man was standing before him, small and thin and bent with age. He wore a long white robe that bore the device of the crossed swords and oak of the Alliance embroidered in gold thread at the breast. The old man stared at him with pale blue eyes, the lines on his face deeper with sorrow than age. More people were approaching from behind this man, a long line of them clad in the same white robes. They were all assembled in an open plaza of gleaming white stone surrounded by impressive buildings with stained glass windows and colored banners flying from slate rooftops. The sun was high overhead in the clear sky, bathing the whole place in gold.

The old man watched him without speaking as the others gathered around in a loose circle. Faces, young and old, peered out from white cowls, judging, measuring.

Accusing.

He strained to capture those faces, trying to burn the memory of them into his mind, but they were jumbled and hazy and ephemeral. Only the face of the old man was distinct and lasting. Jantalus kept his focus there, waiting for a word or a gesture. He could not speak and every attempt to move accomplished nothing. He was a spectator here, it seemed, and no amount of effort or desire was going to change that.

Where am I? Why am I here? Who are you people?

He was asking the questions over and over in his mind as if he could will them across the dozen feet between himself and the old man if he just tried hard enough. The man never reacted beyond the sad, almost remorseful stare.

A woman came forward as the last of those who formed the circle about him settled into place. She gripped the old man's shoulder with her gnarled hand and he stepped back after a moment of hesitation. She took his place, as old, stooped, and frail, but with none of the care and remorse of the old man. Her dark eyes were filled with condemnation and her creased face tight with disgust. She stared at him for a long time before raising one arm and stretching out a long bony finger his way. All around, the rest of those assembled did the same.

Jantalus turned in a slow circle to watch them. Nothing happened as they jabbed their accusing fingers toward him. They took no further action, waiting and watching.

He had decided it was all a pointless thing, a delusion and not a memory when, suddenly, a single word boomed through his mind, echoing as if shouted into a great canyon.

Guilty!

He heard himself scream, the first sound in the silent dream. He slumped to his knees clutching his head, the force of the word seeming to explode from within his skull. The ring of white robed figures took a collective step forward, tightening their circle, fingers closing in like spear points.

Guilty!

Waves of crushing pain rippled out from his very core and shook him in wild convulsions. He collapsed to his face on the hard, cold stone, gasping for breath. Everything around him swam in a haze, swirling and twisting, mixing in a muddled mess of color. He fought to rise, his instinct to get away from them all, but his body was nothing but spasmodic pain and would not respond. His fingers dug at the edges of the cobblestones, struggling for a handhold he could use to crawl, but he lacked even the strength for that. For all of his digging and pulling, he only managed to tear the skin from his hands.

A pair of sandaled feet came forward, stopping inches from his face and he arched his neck to stare up at the person. The old woman. She swayed back and forth, tilting wildly, and he could barely focus on her. She stared down at him without pity or remorse, cold, hard and unyielding. Her hands rose, fingers spread wide, and reached for him. He could feel his blood burn with new fire as she closed in, but he could do nothing to stop her or move away.

She was about to seize his face in those gnarled hands when something huge and black rose up behind her. He was conscious of the other white figures retreating from this *new arrival, and the old woman paused as it cast its long shadow over her. One gloved hand came down to grasp her shoulder and her mouth fell open in a terrified gasp. With a sudden heave, the hand shoved her aside, sending her crashing to the ground at the feet of her cohorts. Jantalus could see three people who had broken through those who surrounded him.*

Mother! Father!

They rushed forward, angry and defiant as they flanked the man in black. Each cast him a concerned glance, but focused mostly on those who surrounded them, braced for battle, daring any of them to take further action. Though Jantalus could not hear any of it, his father was shouting, face crimson and spittle flying from his mouth. His mother did not speak, tears that were more of rage than anything else running down her cheeks. He could feel his magic flare as he focused on them, sensing their power.

Between them, the man in black watched the ring of people who had attacked Jantalus for a moment, then dropped to one knee and extended his hand. Jantalus reached out with a shaking, bleeding hand of his own and took it, holding on with all the strength he had, terrified that he would be lost if he let go. With the stranger's help, he rose to his knees, panting and straining, every inch a colossal effort. The man's free hand took his elbow and prepared to pull him to his feet.

Just as he was about to rise, Jantalus raised his eyes to the face of his savior, peering into the dark cowl. The golden sunlight lit the face clearly, exposing the black eyes and matching hair.

The entire world stood still as their eyes met.

I know you.

The dark clothing. The black eyes and hair. The size and movements. Jantalus had seen the man who was rescuing him before.

You killed my mother.

****

He came awake to a rush of biting night air. The moon had slipped down from its apex, but it was still several hours from the western horizon. Halonni was still bundled in his blankets with him, curled tight against his right side, her breath warm on his neck and her head against his shoulder. His arm had gone numb beneath her and he wiggled his fingers to start the blood flowing again. Jantalus glanced across the small courtyard to find Stilthius still slumped against the far wall, fast asleep. The outlander was still in his mail, but an extra pair of blankets had been thrown over him. Beyond the wall, he could hear the sound of feet scuffing the hard ground and the whirl of something being swung about.

Jantalus eased Halonni away, mindful not to wake her. The bitter air cut through him as he rose and his whole body shivered in response. He pulled his cloak tight and made his way to the gap in the wall near Stilthius. Illuminated in the bright moonlight on a narrow flat atop the hill was Tyris Menion. Axe in hand, he executed a precise routine of steps and retreats, cuts, lunges and slashes, moving with uncanny grace and skill. The axe moved like an extension of his arms, perfectly controlled and too fast to follow.

Jantalus did not interrupt him, watching in silence until the big outlander noticed him. Tyris lowered his weapon and nodded. "Up a bit early, aren't you?"

Jantalus shrugged his broad shoulders. "When you dream like I do, sleep is not always something worth looking forward to." He gestured toward the huge axe the other held. "From the look of it, I assumed it was something crude. It seems I was wrong."

Tyris brought the weapon up a bit. "How much do you know of weapons and battle?"

He shook his head. "I remember nothing. I might have been a farm hand that never held a sword in his life."

The outlander looked him over. "You're big, strong. Someone would have seen your worth and put a blade in your hand at some point."

He held up one finger and then walked back to where he and his brother had left their gear. He rummaged about a moment and then returned with a pair of swords in battered leather scabbards. Tyris tossed his axe on the ground a few feet away and then handed Jantalus one of the swords, pommel first. Jantalus hesitated a moment and then took it.

"Fighting," Tyris explained, "is like walking. Once you learn to do it, you don't forget. You either train yourself to react in a fight or you don't. We'll see for ourselves if you were a farm hand or not."

Jantalus looked from the sword to the huge outlander and back, wondering at the wisdom of the proposal. If he had ever used a sword in his life, he could not remember it. A man twice his size with years of fighting experience was not the opponent of choice for a testing duel. Sheathed or no, a sword to the side of the head was not something he was particularly looking forward to.

Tyris laughed at his hesitation and slapped the sword against his open palm. "Trusting bastard, aren't you! I'll not split your skull for sport. If you're a farmer at heart, I'll take that sword and you can teach me to swing a hoe!"

Jantalus narrowed his black eyes at the big man and then shrugged off his cloak. Tyris had a bluster about him and enjoyed mocking, but he was no bully. If he promised only a sparring session, Jantalus took him at his word. He lifted the sword and advanced, watching the big man carefully. There was a familiarity in the heft of the weapon in his hands and the way his feet slid about as he positioned himself. Tyris saw it at once and a great toothy smile split his face as he raised his weapon in response.

The outlander began with a series of simple jabs and cuts that came out with deliberate control and unmistakable lack of speed. Jantalus slapped them aside with a nervous sweeps of his own sword, leather thumping on leather. Tyris followed them with quicker and more precise attacks, though they too were obviously lacking in effort. Jantalus deflected them as well and even managed a return stroke of his own that Tyris batted away without effort. His next series of attacks was noticeably more focused, quick and strong and Jantalus retreated as he parried them, back out of the big man's reach. Tyris pursued at once, slashing and stabbing, giving him no time to recover or room to escape. Jantalus parried the first and second, but the third slipped under his guard and the flat of the sheathed blade thudded against his thigh. He staggered a bit, but maintained his guard as he pivoted away.

Tyris retreated at once and lowered his sword. "You're better than a farmer, I'd say."

Jantalus lowered his own weapon. "No match for a certain Tulin, though."

Tyris took the sword from him and bent to retrieve his axe. "Since I was old enough to ride a horse I've been trained to fight. I've fought all over my own land and half of this one. I've stood in shield walls knee deep in mud and gouged eyes and bitten off fingers. I've carried dead men on my shoulder and charged archers under a hail of arrows. Held breaches against swarming attackers and piled bodies too high to see over more than once. Hell, I had a bastard come at me with an axe while I was taking a piss and killed him with my bare hands." He shrugged as if it were all meaningless. "It is all I do – all I've ever done. Falling short of me in a fight is nothing to be ashamed of."

It was all spoken without a hint of superiority or pride. Jantalus sensed no swell of ego behind his list of accomplishments and evaluation of his own skills. It was a statement of fact that Tyris Menion did not care for judgment on. It was as he presented it and nothing more or less.

Jantalus rubbed his aching thigh. "That seems more than a merchant son's share of warfare."

Tyris put one broad shoulder against the nearby wall. "My father, like my brother, was a man of faith. His sons, he swore, would earn the kullar that he never could. He was determined that we would not share his fate."

"What do you mean? How would your father have ever expected to earn it as a merchant?"

"He was a warrior first, as all my clan were," the outlander answered. "Tulins have no say in what they will be, that is for their parents and the elders of their clan to decide. My father was chosen by his father to be a warrior in the service of Hunnaris. He was still a young man when he lost his sight in battle. His mind was sharp and his skill with numbers good enough that he was able to assume a merchant business left to my mother when her father died, but there was no glory in that, only money. With that money, he paid the greatest of teachers to train his sons in the arts of war. When we were old enough, he pledged our service to the warlords of another clan. Stilthius and I were serving them when our clansmen were murdered."

Jantalus shook his head. "Your god would condemn him to eternal suffering for not earning his kullar even though he was blind?"

Tyris snorted and spat. "Damned if I know. I hear too much of Hunnaris that steps on what I heard last. Stilthius would say Hunnaris is the god of struggle and death as well as war. The kullar is the concern of those he chooses as warriors. Those who are not have other judgments waiting. Stilthius is the smart one. He studied, Hunnaris and other things. He speaks better than I do. Thinks faster too."

"And what do you think?"

The big man shrugged. "That I am nothing but a man. I'll leave the godly questions to the gods. Until I learn otherwise, I'll play along. After all, if I believe and discover when I die that there are no gods, what have I lost? If I deny them and then discover they are real, I'm fucked for sure." He gestured back toward their camp. "The girl speaks of a goddess sometimes, one who lives in the earth and gives magic to the people of this land. Do you believe in her goddess?"

Jantalus thought on it. "I don't believe much of anything at the moment. I'm not even sure the name I am called is my own. I dream of people I do not recognize doing things with me that I have no memory of. I am not sure who I am or where I come from. What I do know is that my mother is dead, I have been marked and a collection of assassins and Necromancers are hunting me for reasons I do not know."

He paused and looked around him. "If this world is the work of some goddess and this is how she treats her people, Halonni can have the bitch. She's no use to me."

Tyris pushed himself away from the wall. "Stand watch while I sleep. Soon enough, we will reach Drappel and see what answers we can find for your questions. Then, if whatever gods are out there favor us, these Tassaren bastards will find us and there will be a reckoning. We will see then if my brother's faith and the girl's are so much horseshit or not."

"Rushing into a fight with them might be suicide. Is it enough for your god that you fight even if it is futile?"

Tyris gave him a long look that might have been one of newfound respect. "You're a strange fuck, but don't ever let anyone call you stupid. No, suicide is not enough. If it were, we'd be running back toward Ulis looking for those assholes. Hunnaris is the god of war, but not bloodthirsty idiocy. We will fight that lot when the time and place are right. As long as we get our chance, we're willing to wait for it.

Jantalus shook his head. Tyris was a mad bastard for wanting a confrontation with the Tassarens. He would have argued the matter if there were any chance of reasoning with the outlander.

"Get some rest then," he said instead.

Tyris disappeared back inside the crumbling wall and left him alone. Jantalus retrieved his cloak and draped it over his shoulders as he began pacing to keep warm. He walked to the edge of the western side of the small hilltop, looking out across the moonlit valley in the direction of Drappel, still far beyond his sight. His hand dropped to his pocket where Peridor Finn's ring and pendant were kept. There were so many questions before and, owing to his dream, he had more.

He wondered if anyone in Drappel, or anywhere on all of Kronos, could answer so many.

Chapter Eleven

"Urs," Halonni told the three men, pointing down from the small hillock they had crested a moment before.

The town was spread out before them in little clusters of squat mud and wattle buildings, gray smoke rising from the thatch roofs into the clear, cold morning sky. They were huddled along the bank of the river to the east, small wooden docks jutting out from the bank nearby. Urs might have been a score of buildings and not half of them were the size of the single room in Durn's home where Jantalus had spent the winter. Barren fields, cold, hard, and waiting for the first plow of spring lined the edges of the tiny community. Sheep, goats and pigs dotted the faint dirt road that passed through the center of the buildings and the gentle slopes of the surrounding hillsides. A few of the townsfolk were already working, repairing thatch, herding the animals about and hanging their wash in the morning sun.

Urs had not been part of the planned route to Drappel. They had eaten all of their food, however, and had not seen a single deer or rabbit as they made their way north and west along the Bame River. They had tried fishing with no success. Tyris and Stilthius made no secret that they were neither hunters nor fishermen. Jantalus quickly decided that he had been neither in the life he no longer remembered. Halonni had suggested they try the village rather than avoid it as they had originally intended and the men were quick to agree.

She cast a look back at Jantalus. "Better be sure your face isn't seen."

He pulled his cowl low in response and they set off again, trudging down the hillside toward the waiting town. A handful of sheep scattered as they passed, but no shepherd tended them that they could see. The first person to take notice of them was an elderly woman who was bent over a barrel of water beside her little hut, washing her kettle with a lump of soap.

She looked up with a hesitant smile, all brown teeth and wrinkles. She was dressed in a worn housedress and thin cloak that had been patched so many times little of the original fabric remained.

"Morning." She dipped her head slightly.

The smile Halonni returned was warm and genuine and put the old woman instantly at ease. Jantalus had never seen anything like it. "Good morning, mother. A cold day for doing the wash."

The old woman's smile thinned a bit. "It is, but I've only one kettle and six mouths to feed."

"Six?"

"My son's four children and his widow. They used to take care of me. Now? We do what we can for each other."

"Is there no one to help you?" Halonni asked as she lowered her pack from her shoulder to the hard ground.

"None. Most of our men went to fight last fall and never came home. Every hand is a working hand in Urs now. If we don't plant, we'll not make next winter."

Halonni rummaged through her pack as the old woman spoke and pulled out one of the cloaks they had been using as bedding. She shook it out and came forward to wrap it around the old woman's shoulders. "You'll catch death out here, mother. You take this."

The old woman shook her head and tried to pull the cloak off. "I can't pay you for this, mistress. I have nothing to give you."

Halonni caught her hand and held it. "I am asking nothing for it."

The weathered brow creased. "Nothing?"

Halonni shrugged her slender shoulders. "Perhaps some information. A moment of your time."

The old woman stared at her without speaking for a long moment. "Bread. I have bread I just bought this morning. Come inside and speak with me. My son's wife and her boys are still sleeping. I can get more before they wake."

Lugging her heavy kettle behind her, she was already shuffling back toward her home before they could answer. They followed her into the tiny place, one room and no more, the floor simple earth covered in straw. A fire burned in a shallow pit at the center, the smoke rising through a hole in the roof. Four bundles of blankets with little feet poking out one end and tousled mops of hair from the other huddled around a larger fifth on the floor in front of the fire. None of them stirred as the four strangers entered. The old woman stepped carefully over them and hung the kettle back over the fire from an iron chain anchored in the timbers above.

She beckoned over to a small table with a bench on either side and retrieved two loaves of dark, hard bread from the shelf nearby and placed them on the table. She then gathered small wooden cups and poured them all a measure of ale from a wooden jug. She seated herself on a small stool, taking nothing for herself.

"Are you soldiers from the Duke?" she asked as they ate.

"The Duke?" Halonni shook her head. "No. We're just passing through. We're from Drappel. We're going home."

The old woman stared back at her, eyes narrowed. "Drappel?"

Halonni looked to Jantalus a moment, biting her lower lip. "Yes. Why?"

"The Alliance took Drappel. That's where our men went. That was where the fighting was."

Jantalus leaned forward a bit, careful to be sure his cowl still covered his face. "The Alliance? You're sure?"

The old woman nodded quickly. "Last fall. Drappel called for aid. Geften, Urs, Northshire and others marched to her, but the Alliance sent too many soldiers." She drew a shaking hand across her eyes. "Some say the Alliance will come here next and then on to Geften. Punishment, they say, for standing against them. Already, their soldiers come to talk to our leaders; they ask questions and make threats."

"What kind of questions?" Stilthius asked as he drained his cup. "What kind of threats?"

She drew a shuddering breath. "They are looking for a man, a marked man. They come every few days to ask if anyone has seen him. Sometimes they search our homes, threaten to kill us if they find such a man. We hide no one. I do not know what mark they are looking for."

Halonni looked down at the little bundles arranged before the fire and then to Jantalus. He did not miss in her eyes what she could not say aloud. He nodded to her and poked Stilthius's arm. The four of them rose and shuffled toward the door.

Halonni knelt down before the old woman and took her hands. "Thank you for the bread." She pressed a coin into her palm. "You buy more for these little ones. You take care of each other as best you can."

The old woman looked down at the coin and back to Halonni. "It is too much for bread and ale, mistress. Ten times that."

Halonni closed her wrinkled fingers over the coin. "Take it. We can manage without it. Where is this baker who sells you the bread?"

The old woman rose with her and went to the door. She pointed to the northern edge of town where two plumes of smoke rose from a long wooden building. "My lord's ovens are there. He sells the bread. You'll find beer. Meat and fish if he has any left to sell."

Halonni bent to kiss her cheek and slipped out of the hut, Jantalus and the Menions trailing. Tyris closed the door behind them and they hurried away as fast as they could without drawing attention to themselves. By Jantalus's thinking, that was next to impossible considering the outlanders were each the size of a bear.

"We probably just killed the six of them," Stilthius muttered.

"We didn't know," Halonni answered, hurrying to keep up with their longer strides. "Let's get what we need and leave before things get worse for everyone."

"They are worse," Jantalus told her.

A line of horsemen approached along the riverbank from the north, steel flashing in the sun, the oak and sword device of the Alliance flying from the pennants at the heads of their spears. He counted six, all clad in mail and carrying spears with swords strapped on their backs. He cast about for a place to hide, to disappear, but there was nothing to fade into but dirt and squalor.

Tyris was searching with him, but he looked more like he was evaluating the best place for a fight than the best place to sneak away to. "Fuck."

Stilthius pulled his hammer free from the harness on his back. "Yeah, fuck."

Jantalus watched the horsemen as they paused to speak with a pair of men who emerged from the closest building to meet them. After a brief exchange, the lead horseman stood up in his stirrups, his attention focused on the four strangers at the center of the town. Tyris stepped forward and pulled his axe over his shoulder. They had no place to run and no place to put their backs to save for the old woman's house behind them.

"Keep your hood up and stay quiet," Halonni told Jantalus as the riders started toward them.

He nodded and watched the approaching men, waiting for some reaction from his magic to their presence. Nothing, not even a hint of the fire stirred his blood.

No Sentinels. Maybe we won't die.

The horsemen reached them in seconds, drawing up into a tight half circle before them. One of the men urged his horse a few steps closer. "Morning."

"Just on our way through," Halonni told him. "We aren't looking for trouble."

The soldier pulled back his cowl, exposing a scarred, dirt-smeared face framed by black hair and a day's worth of beard. "Good to hear, girl. We're just making sure there won't be any. Where are you coming from?"

"What difference does it make?" Tyris asked. "You keeping a journal?" Halonni flashed him a warning look, but the outlander ignored it.

The man turned to look at the horsemen arrayed behind him and back again. "I'd mind my tongue if I were you."

"You wouldn't give a shit if you were me."

Jantalus turned to stare at him. That the outlanders were not afraid of a fight was something he had learned quickly enough, but now he had to wonder if courage and stupidity were one in the same to these men.

The assembled soldiers tightened their ranks a bit. Their leader dipped his spear to point at Jantalus. "Why don't you have this one lower his hood and you people can be on your way."

Tyris stepped forward, putting himself between the spear and Jantalus. "Why don't you get that thing away from us before I fuck you with it?"

The man jabbed the spear forward, the point ringing against the outlander's mailed breast. "Big words for a man hiding behind a little woman and-."

Tyris had his hand around the haft of his spear before he finished and jerked him forward, pulling him down over the shoulder of his horse. Before the man could recover, the Tulin's axe came crashing down, splitting him between the shoulder blades. He arched at the waist, his face twisted in agony, blood erupting like a fountain from his back. Tyris wrenched the axe free and turned about, the spear still clutched in his other hand, blood raining down around him as the shattered man tumbled down to the ground.

Beside him, Stilthius had stepped forward, his hammer flashing silver in the morning sun, drawing a glittering arc. It crashed into the head of the horse to the leader's left with a loud crack. The animal's legs collapsed beneath it at once, the rider pitching forward onto his face. The animal thrashed and screamed, blocking away the two men beside it, cutting them off from intervening for the moment. Stilthius seized Halonni's arm as she stared in shock and drew her back and away from the soldiers.

Jantalus saw what the outlanders had done then. They knew it was all to come to a fight. There was never any doubt about it. They had drawn the attention to themselves, clustering the horsemen near them and not Halonni or Jantalus. Tyris had disposed of the leader to stun them all into inaction and Stilthius blocked away enough of them that they did not need to fear being stabbed in the back for the moment.

Tyris had ducked under the head of the nearest horse and drove the spear upward into its neck. The horse screamed and reared back, but Tyris did not stop, driving the point all the way through until the steel head protruded up above the mane. The rider held on, but the horse pitched over backward and landed atop him, kicking and thrashing.

The horsemen to their left pulled their mounts around the dying horse that Stilthius had felled and were approaching with their spears lowered and the last rider to their right was trying to work his way around the one Tyris had skewered. Jantalus felt his blood begin to burn as Halonni's magic rose up in her, her hands reaching down to lay flat against the hard earth. A tremor shook the ground beneath his feet as the earth split and pulled apart with a sharp crack. A fissure, as wide as a man and longer than six, appeared beneath the two horsemen to their left. The horses cried out in terror and then stumbled in the hole that suddenly formed beneath them. Bones cracked and tore through skin and the riders fell from their saddles as the animals went down.

Stilthius charged at once, his hammer lifting. The first man had just gained his knees when the broad steel head crushed his face in, teeth, blood and bone mixing in a red and white spray across the ground. The second man was writhing on the ground, clutching his arm where his elbow bent at an odd angle. Stilthius turned his hammer and stabbed down, the top spike punching through the soldier's face just below his eye and silencing him in an instant.

The final enemy backed away from his efforts to get past Tyris's guard and reined his horse about. His gaze fell on Jantalus as he turned to retreat, eyes riveted to the mark of the dead. His grip slackened on the reigns and the horse came to a halt. His spear slipped from his numb fingers. Jantalus stared deep into his eyes, through them, deeper and deeper until he reached the very core of the man.

He was still a dozen feet away, too far to reach the mesmerized soldier, but he held him nonetheless. It was not the same as it had been outside of Ulis. Jantalus did not invade the man and attack him from within. Instead, his magic had reached across the space between them, slipping more subtly into his mind, drawing out the crippling fear of the mark of the dead that lay within him. Jantalus could sense his thoughts, he could taste his fears. This man knew the mark, knew what it meant and what kind of men bore it. Jantalus's magic dug deep into him, drawing out the horrors of the man's own mind, paralyzing him with panic born of his own imagination.

He was so consumed by his fear that he did not even move as Tyris came forward, axe held high, and took off his head with a single backhand stroke. Blood bubbled from the decapitated body and it slid sideways from the saddle and collapsed in a heap. The horse bolted away a moment later.

The severed head rolled to a stop against a stone on the hard ground a few feet away, the eyes still wide with horror, staring unseeing up at Jantalus.

Tyris lowered his axe and returned to where the rest of them stood. He walked to where the man who had been thrown from the horse Stilthius had killed lay. He was still on his face, his hands clutching the earth as he moaned in pain and fought to get his legs beneath him. Tyris did not even look at him as he put his foot on the back of head and ground his face into the dirt. The soldier struggled for but a moment, his hands slapping at the outlander's boot in a feeble attempt to pull it away. The hands fell away and he did not move.

Tyris wiped his bloody hands on the man's cloak. "Soft, these Kronans."

Stilthius shrugged and nodded to Halonni. "Not all. Most. Not all."

Jantalus said nothing. He was standing where he had been when it all began, his hands knotted into fists at his side, his heart hammering in his chest. He stared down at the severed head, at the sightless eyes that were still so alive with fear.

Halonni reached over to touch his arm and he flinched away from her, surprised. He drew a deep breath and recovered himself. She looked like she was going to say something, but he looked away from her and started toward the Menion brothers.

"One horse," Stilthius said, gesturing toward the animal left by the first man Tyris had killed. "If we had anything worth carrying, we could use it."

Tyris knelt next to one of the dead men and began searching him. "Check their saddle bags. There might be something worth taking." He looked up from his work when no one joined him. "Jantalus?"

He blinked at the outlander. "Their bags. Right." He went to the nearest of the dead horses and rummaged through what he found.

When they finished, what they found was too meager to warrant taking the horse, but they had found enough food to see them through several days. Tyris and Stilthius took the dead men's packs and filled them with what they had taken. When they were finished, the four of them headed out of Urs at once.

"There will be more soldiers," Stilthius said as they left the pathetic little village behind. "They'll blame these sorry shits for what we did."

No one said anything. Halonni looked over to Jantalus as he walked beside her, regret for it all mirrored in her eyes. No words would change what had happened or the fact that Stilthius was right about what would follow. He simply shook his head and kept walking.

These people are all dead because of my mark. All dead and there isn't a damn thing I can do.

To their credit, his companions said nothing about it.

The silence that followed them out of Urs almost made him wish they had.

Chapter Twelve

They pressed on through the rest of the day, keeping away from the Bame River where they were more likely to encounter any travelers or Alliance soldiers. Drappel was north and west and not along the river regardless and Halonni was confident she could find it. They screened themselves from anyone who might be watching as much as possible, moving through light forests and staying off higher ground that might silhouette them against the sky. What little relief the sun provided from the remnants of winter that clung to the wind vanished as it sank to the western horizon. They wrapped blankets around them as they walked in the growing darkness, their breath turned to vapor and the wind biting at their hands and faces.

Mindful that there would be more than just the Tassarens after them now, they built no fire when they finally stopped for the night. They hid themselves in the shelter of a huge spruce tree, its limbs wide and sagging almost to the ground. They laid out their makeshift bedrolls and bundled up with what extra cloaks and blankets they had and made the best of it.

Jantalus lay awake for some time, preoccupied by the events in Urs. The whole battle had started and ended so quickly he hardly thought about any of it as it happened. Now that it was over, it was the only thing on his mind. It was his mark that had drawn the men to Urs and his mark that had necessitated the battle. The soldiers were not going to let them leave without seeing his face and once they had, they were certainly going to attack. Tyris and Stilthius had just made sure the fight was on their terms.

"You need to let it go," Halonni told him as she knelt beside him. "There was no way you could have known those soldiers would show up when they did. It was just shit luck."

He sat up and put his back to the thick trunk of the spruce. "I had a dream at Spotter's Hill. It was real, what I saw. Not a storm of disconnected pictures and sounds like I usually see when I dream, I mean. It was a whole event; something that I am sure was a memory, not a delusion."

She folded her legs beneath her and tucked her long hair behind her ears. "What was it?"

"A trial, I think," he answered. "There were people surrounding me in a plaza of white stone. An old woman and an old man seemed to be judging me. I couldn't move or speak, almost as if some power held me fast. They announced my guilt and I was overcome with pain. Over and over they condemned me and I felt like I was being ripped apart from the inside. My parents and another man saved me."

"Another man?" Halonni asked.

He studied her face carefully before responding. She did not look surprised by what he was telling her. "A man with long black hair. I do not know his name, but I recognize him. He killed my mother. You know him?"

She shook her head at once. "Him? No. I know the trials, though. The Vicars use them to condemn Necromancers. They summon the Council members and any other Vicars present in Haven and use their magic to drain the power of the Necromancer."

"Drain it? To what end?"

She leaned forward, cupping her delicate chin in her hands. "Magic is a part of everything around us Jantalus. Everything. The water, air, earth and fire that the Vicars manipulate are all pieces of the magic that permeates this world. Their gift is the ability to touch that magic, to bend it to their will and use it. But it is not as simple as knowing about it. There is something in a person who becomes a Vicar from birth that makes them more aware, more attuned perhaps, to the magic around us. Experience and training are important, but it is all useless without the inborn gift. The magic is part of them – part of anyone who manipulates magic. Inseparable, Jantalus."

"So stealing their power steals their life."

"Yes. Necromancers choose to use their gifts to steal power from the souls of the dead instead of in harmony with the elements, but it is part of them nonetheless." She gestured to him. "It is a part of you too, no matter how different your magic might be from mine or anyone else's."

He traced circles around his black eyes. "It would seem this was earned if I was tried and condemned for it. Apparently, I was to be killed for what I was."

Her hand came up to silence him. "I was a little girl when I was in Haven, but I saw dozens of those trials. I never saw anyone walk away from one. Every single one of them was condemned. I can count on one hand the number of people I think actually deserved it. Those trials were just elaborate executions for anyone some member of the council wanted out of the way."

"I don't know-."

"That's right. You don't. Let it be until you do."

"And if I find out I am the monster you and Durn hope I'm not? If the truth is that I just sentenced the people of Urs to death and I am nothing but a soul-stealing piece of shit?"

Halonni stared back at him for a long time without speaking. Her eyes locked on his without fear, measuring him, he thought. "What do you see when you look at me?" she asked finally.

"What do you mean?"

She shrugged. "What I asked. What do you see? Who am I to you?"

He considered the question a moment. "The person who saved my life. You took care of me all winter, kept me alive in Marcester and since. I owe you my life. What are you getting at?"

She pointed past him to where Tyris and Stilthius lay wrapped in their blankets. "Those two mad bastards have been fighting and killing all their lives. They are warriors the way some men are potters or farmers. It's what they do – all they do. And you know something? I've killed more people than the two of them combined, all of them before I was twelve years old. Did I cut every throat or hack off every head? No, but I tracked men accused of being Necromancers to towns and villages that I then helped Sentinels and Alliance soldiers burn to the ground. I don't doubt for a moment that most of the people I was sent to find were nothing more than political opponents of Vicars who were better off without them around. But here I am. Am I that person to you?"

"You were a child," he answered, "warped and molded by the Vicars into something you were not to serve them. You are not that person anymore."

"I will always be that person on some level, Jantalus. We are all what we have done to one degree or another. The past is a book already written. What was – was. The point is, I made a choice to be a different person. I am who I was, but I am also the person you see now. I can't erase the first, but I can choose the second. Why can't you, assuming you even have a reason to?"

He shook his head and blew out a long breath. "None of that is going to help all of those people in Urs."

"Nothing can help those people," she said. "We don't have to like it. It's just the way it is." She dragged her pack over and stretched out on the ground next to him, using it for a pillow. "We should get some sleep."

He rubbed at his eyes. Sleep was not the most enticing idea considering what he saw every night. He pushed away from the tree and settled into his bedroll, pulling the blankets up around him. It was still except for the creaking of the tree limbs above and Stilthius's light snoring. He closed his eyes and tried to think of something pleasant, hoping it would dominate his dreams.

He was failing miserably when he felt Halonni's hand on his shoulder. He turned over to find her watching him, her pale face catching a sliver of moonlight that cut through the cover of the tree.

"If you were as terrible as you fear, you probably wouldn't give a damn about Urs, you know." She shrugged. "Just a thought."

Just a thought.

One that got him through the night without dreaming anything terrible.

By noon of the next day, the whole of the valley ahead of them was a wall of tightly packed trees that stretched as far as they could see to the east and west. It was a huge wall of black that defied the afternoon sun beating down from a cloudless sky. No road led to or from it and there were no apparent gaps in the trees to indicate trails.

Halonni admitted as soon as Tyris asked that she did not know a way to Drappel from where they were. Drappel lay beyond the forest to the north, but she had only ever approached the area from farther north and east. She had a general idea of where they were and where Drappel would be in relation, but, until they passed through the forest, she could not know for sure. Tyris and Stilthius each shrugged their indifference to the news and let the matter go. Jantalus had more reservations, but said nothing. After all, they were here because of him. Complaining about the way things were going was hardly necessary.

"The people of the Censharn call it Havenwood," Halonni told him as they walked.

"Named for Haven?" Jantalus asked.

"The other way around. When the Egunites invaded centuries ago, the people of Kronos retreated to the forest for protection. When they finally won the Censharn Valley back, they established a city nearby. Haven seemed a suitable name, I suppose. Drappel, Northshire and a dozen other towns sprang up around the forest. Most of them are what form the core of the Free Lords' Alliance."

"How much do you know about Drappel?"

Halonni shook her head and smiled faintly. "Not much, I'm afraid. I've ridden the road that passes north of it, but I've never been there. It's just a name on a map to me. From what I do know, it is not part of the Alliance proper. Like Marcester, it's a protectorate, ruled by its own lord who pays tribute, but wields no power on the Council."

Stilthius looked over at her and frowned. "Why would a man pay tribute to a lord who gives him no voice?"

She shrugged. "It's better than being burned out of your home and starved to death."

The outlander snorted and spat. "In Tuliny, a man pays tribute to a lord as a favor, not an obligation. When a man is chosen to lead, he leads by permission of his subjects. The elders of each clan choose our king and pay what he needs to rule. If that king is weak or brings shame on the clans, he is killed and a new king is chosen."

Halonni cocked an eyebrow at him. "Your kings must be nervous men."

Tyris threw his head back and laughed. "The puny shits of this land would not survive the Tulin way. They're too weak to throw off their useless kings. And your kings would not last with subjects who demand strength. Better that you stay on your island and they on theirs."

"You're here," Jantalus pointed out. The moment the words passed his lips, he wished he had swallowed them. He had not intended them as an insult or a challenge to the Menion brothers' courage. Stilthius had made it very clear that their bravery and battle prowess were what was greatest in the eyes of their people and their god.

The brothers eyed him suspiciously for a moment and then began roaring with laughter, their huge shoulders shaking. Stilthius reached out and clapped him on the back so hard he nearly knocked him over.

"You're a prick, sorcerer! An absolute prick! You should have been born on Tuliny. Hunnaris would smile on a man like you. Too many of your kind hide behind pretty words, saying things they don't mean for fear of pissing someone off. You? Fucking fearless, that's what you are!"

The brothers walked on ahead of them, still laughing as they spoke in their own language. They threw occasional glances back at Jantalus, laughing harder every time they did. For his part, Jantalus could not imagine what they found so amusing, but they did not explain and he decided to ignore it.

"I think they like you," Halonni told him as they watched the outlanders.

"I think they're mad," he responded.

It took the rest of the day to reach the edge of Havenwood. The sun was sinking into the swirl of orange and purple along the western horizon when they finally fell under the shade of the outermost trees. Tyris and Stilthius had already begun discussing the best spot to make camp with Halonni, pointing to a few stands of evergreens that might suit them and the abundance of dry wood littering the area that would make a good fire. Jantalus barely listened to any of it.

There was a strange feel to the place now that he was close to it, a sharp taste on the air, a prickling sensation that came with the gentle breeze here. He could smell nothing of the forest, but something else that he could not identify. It had a quality that suggested something burned, but he could not place it. He stood a short distance from the forest edge, watching and waiting, taking no notice of the way the others slipped in and out of the trees as they prepared their campsite.

Magic, he decided finally. He felt a presence here that was born of magic. He turned his attention to Halonni, but she was still talking with the outlanders and did not notice. Odd, he thought. The Vicars enslaved her because of her sense for magic and yet she did not seem to notice anything. He took a small step forward, closer to the forest and stopped. It was stronger here, the smell, the feeling of the wind on his skin, the taste of the magic on his lips. He peered into the shadows of the massive trees, searching for something out of place, something that might be the source of it all. Nothing. He sensed nothing at all.

He looked to Halonni again, but she was still talking to Tyris, unaware of anything he was experiencing.

Why? Why is it only me?

Stilthius called to him, but the words were muddled and slipped past him. He focused his attention on the forest and the magic he sensed within. The presence was growing in strength, but Jantalus was still standing in the same place. Whatever it was that was causing his magic to react the way it was, it was reacting to him in turn.

"Jantalus?" He felt Halonni's hand on his arm, but kept staring into the trees.

"Do you feel that?"

"I don't feel anything. What is it?"

He shook his head. "A presence. It's... calling to me."

"Just to you?" Halonni followed his black stare in to the forbidding forest. "But how could that be? If it were a Necromancer – one of the Tassarens – I would know. I would feel it too."

But it's there, regardless.

Waiting. Waiting for me.

Chapter Thirteen

He spent a restless night at the edge of the forest, sleeping in fits and starts, never comfortable, never able to rid himself of the sensation of the magic that called to him from deep in the trees. He was up constantly, pacing and watching, expecting that something was coming for them at every moment. He found he did not need sleep. Fatigue rolled off him like rain, brushed aside by his anxiety. Tyris and Stilthius each tried to convince him to rest on their respective watches, but he waved them off both times.

When the first rays of sun broke over the tops of the trees, he shook them all awake, gathered his bedroll and started off at once. They scrambled to collect their own gear and hurried after, shouting for him to wait. He ignored them. Like a signal fire on a cloudless night, Jantalus followed the pull of the strange power that called to him, making his way through the dense forest without a moment to get his bearings or consider his path. The intensity of the magic grew as he went, his own flaring in response. Halonni watched carefully, sometimes running to catch him, always an arm's length away, always aware of every subtle shift in his magic in response to what he was feeling.

He refused to stop for anything, even to rest or eat. Tyris and Stilthius shrugged it off and followed. Halonni shot him angry glances along the way, but he pressed on. The need to reach whatever this thing was that drew him on was an obsession he could not explain to them. The sensation was more powerful than thirst.

It was midafternoon when they reached the Merchant's Way. The road, Halonni warned, was the agreed upon border between what had been the protectorate of Drappel's lands and those of the Free Lords' Alliance. If Drappel had been seized, they should expect soldiers patrolling or even Sentinels watching for intruders. They found it absolutely empty and silent instead.

Stilthius bent down to examine the wide, hard packed earth of the road. "No wagon has crossed this road in weeks. I'm no tracker, but there should be ruts and holes if there has been traffic of any kind."

"No soldiers either," Tyris added. "If a battle took place near here and the Alliance won, why are they not defending their new territory? Where are the watches? The patrols?"

"This doesn't make any sense," Halonni murmured, looking down the road to the west. She pointed. "Drappel is two hours, less maybe."

"That's where it's coming from," Jantalus started down the road without waiting for them.

The Menion brothers shared an uneasy look between them and then followed, Halonni hurrying after.

Finally, the first misshapen bulks that were the buildings on the outer edge of the town began to materialize through the gloom ahead. Situated just south of the Way, Drappel was a scattered collection of squat wooden buildings nestled between the road and a small pond that lay south and east of it. No sounds came from the village, no smith's hammer on an anvil, no dogs barking, no children laughing or carts rolling through the streets. Only silence.

Stilthius seized Jantalus's arm and dragged him to a halt. "Easy now. Nothing about this is right. Nothing." He reached over his shoulder to pull his hammer free from the harness on his back. "We've come this far, pushed all day without stopping. Taking our time might keep us from walking into something we can't walk out of."

Tyris offered Jantalus one of the swords they had found, but he waved him off. He had little confidence in his ability as a swordsman and his magic was far more useful than any blade. He accepted a long knife and slipped it into his belt instead.

Tyris readied his axe and nodded to his brother. "Slow and quiet now."

"Magic," Halonni said a moment later, her words so soft that Jantalus could barely hear them. "I feel it now."

She flashed Jantalus a concerned look as they started forward, but he turned his attention to Drappel and followed behind the Menion brothers. The buildings slowly came into view as they approached, empty shells that stood silent in the shade of the trees. Most had been gutted by fire and were at least partially collapsed. The charred remnants of furniture, tools and other personal belongings were scattered about. The gate of a small pigpen swung back and forth in the breeze, clanging against the fence post in a steady rhythm. From their position behind a pair of small wooden cottages, the majority of Drappel was still hidden from view.

Tyris paused at the back wall of the building and steadied himself. He made eye contact with each of his companions, waited for them each to nod, and then turned around the corner of the home. The earthen path that wound through the place led directly to a small square at its very center. They could see little of what lay beyond, but the road before them was enough to show them what they might expect. Torn and crushed, the bloodstains on their clothing and armor faded from red to black, bodies lay strewn about. Eyes and skin had spent the fall and winter as food for insects and scavenger beasts and most were barely recognizable as ever having been human. Soldiers and townsfolk, men and women, elderly and children were among the dead. None had been spared.

"This is no town." Tyris Menion looked over it all with the composure of a man who had seen such things far too many times before. "This is a fucking graveyard."

Jantalus caught Halonni's arm. She turned to follow his pointing finger. "There," he said, indicating the far side of the town and the vague bulk of the buildings that sat back against the trees.

She nodded, her pale face lined with uncertainty. They were all watching him, waiting for him to decide their next move. He recognized nothing. He had never seen this place that he could recall. He had been so sure that Drappel must be something to him, so confident that it was where he would find everything he needed to know about himself. And yet, as he stood in the midst of the devastated town, he felt no familiarity, no sense of ever having belonged, no grief for this place and what had been done to it.

How could it be a part of me and yet I feel nothing for it?

The answer, of course, was that he had let his hopes run away with his common sense. He had been found near Drappel and Peridor Finn had last been seen here. There did not need to be a connection beyond that. Yes, he and Finn had been found together, but soldiers had come from across the Censharn to do battle here, some serving the Alliance, some from Geften and Urs and other places. He could not be sure now that he had not been one of them. In fact, Tyris had suspected and then proven he had some training as a soldier.

"Jantalus?" Halonni leaned closer.

"We'll have a look," he said. No harm in that. Probably.

Unless something is waiting to kill me here.

They picked their way through the streets, sidestepping the torn, savaged bodies that littered the place. Sightless eyes stared at them. Voiceless mouths screamed at the moonlit sky. Men lay pierced by arrow and blade, some still clutching their weapons and shields. Women lay across the bodies of their children, having tried in vain to spare them the slaughter. Pigs, goats and cattle had been hacked apart in their pens. Dogs lay decapitated near their masters. The destruction of the town had been meticulous. There was nothing living here, only the four who crept through the shadows trying not to look at it all as they passed.

They reached the town square and the dozens of hanging corpses that swung from makeshift gallows cobbled from the shattered remains of homes and wagons. A quick glance told them that these were the elders of the town and the commanders of the troops that had tried to defend it. The raven and winding river symbols were everywhere, matching the symbols that Durn had found on Peridor Finn. Shields, pennants, cloaks and medallions all bore the markings on more men than Jantalus cared to count. Every one of the bodies was a decaying mess of tattered, drooping flesh, eyes and lips pecked away by crows and feet gnawed by wolves and other beasts.

Tyris and Stilthius looked it all over with the calm and dispassion of men who had seen the like so many times that it no longer meant anything to them. If they cared for the dead mercenaries of Black River among the corpses here, they did not show it. Halonni choked back her disgust and looked away whenever she could. Unfortunately, there was no place to look that provided any relief.

The town tapered away as they moved south, the buildings giving way to gardens and small goat pastures. A few low fences, mostly broken and sagging, marked the line between homes and faint dirt paths wound back to the dark, crumbled bulk of small cottages nestled in the shade of the forest at the edge of town. Halonni caught Tyris's arm to stop him, her attention focused on one of the cottages in particular.

She looked to Jantalus. "There?" she asked, pointing.

Jantalus came forward, following the line of her pointing finger. Yes, that was the spot. At the very edge of the clearing that held the remnants of Drappel, at the point where Havenwood began again, was a small stone and wood cottage. Burned through and partially collapsed, it barely stood, the entire front half of the roof sunken to the floor of the wide porch. The little home might have been no different from half a dozen others nearby save for the single detail that had caught his eye.

In the barren front yard, the sun glinted dully on the rusted head of an old wood axe that had been sunk into a short tree stump. He knew that axe. He knew that stump.

Home.

Without a word to his companions, he turned from the road and made his way to the stump. Halonni called to him, but he did not respond. It was gouged and pitted from years of use, broad, flat, and all but stripped of bark. Two rusted wedges lay half buried in the dirt to one side. He reached down, grasped the axe handle, and jerked the tool free. The edge of the blade was still bright and keen, glinting as it caught the sunlight. He bent close to examine it, starting at the head and working his eyes down the handle inch by inch, first one side and then the next. There was no doubt about what he was seeing. This axe had belonged to his father.

He turned. The fire-ravaged shell of a cottage had been his home.

He dropped the axe from numb fingers and started for the cottage, straining to see something in the shadows. He climbed the steps to the shattered remnant of the porch, but the sagging roof blocked the door and one window. The other window was clear, the shutters torn away, and he peered inside, straining to see. Everything was a charred ruin, too twisted, black, and shadowed to make out.

The presence of magic was all about the place, clinging to everything - the walls, the roof, the floor – everything. He could not identify its source. Something about it told him there was no danger, but he could not explain why. It could have been something familiar about that presence, a magic he had sensed before. He bent his head in concentration, trying to divine the source of the power. It was like water through his fingers as he tried to grasp it. Each time his magic reached for it, it simply slipped away from him. After a moment, he came to understand why. The source of the magic was not slipping away like water through his hand, as he had first believed.

It is slipping through the holes in me – the ones in my mind. I can't catch it, because the part of me that knows it is missing.

Halonni reached him, looking the shattered cottage over. "What is it? Do you know this place?"

"Home. I need to get in there."

"Home?" She stared at him. "You are sure?"

"Very." He stepped forward and pushed on the sagging piece of roof that barred his way. It groaned and creaked but refused to move.

"That might not be wise," Stilthius told him as the outlanders joined them on the porch. "It doesn't look like there is much holding what is left of it up."

Tyris looked it all over a moment. "Step back, all of you."

Jantalus hesitated, but Stilthius had his arm in his big hand and was helping Halonni drag him backward. Tyris waited for them to stand clear, then gripped the sagging edge of the roof and heaved, shoving it upward. Burned timbers creaked and snapped and the whole thing began to shift. Tyris walked it to the far edge of the porch and gave another tremendous push. The whole section of roof gave way, sliding off to one side and tumbling to the ground. The doorway was clear and sunlight streamed in through the huge gap left above. A few smaller sections of the roof collapsed in, sending clouds of dirt and ash out in huge puffs of black. Jantalus started for the door, but Stilthius held him until the debris had stopped falling and then released him.

He hurried to the door, half tripping in his haste, catching the charred edge of the wall for support. Within, he saw the old hearth that had warmed him every day streaked with black soot. The firebox was still there, tarnished and bent, the wood within burned through. A small table still lay in pieces to one side, licked and charred by flame, the bits of metal and glass that had once been the decorative baubles atop it glinting in the piles of ash and debris. Directly across from him, at the center of the room, was his chair, still intact, covered in soot, but untouched by the fire.

He staggered inside, his feet numb beneath him and dragging along the floor. His shaking hand reached out to touch the arm of the chair, smooth and cold.

"Jantalus?" Halonni called behind him, her voice soft and small in the silence of the shattered home.

He said nothing, his head bowed, remembering. To his right, he could almost see his mother lying on the floor, her face twisted in a ghastly grin, blood drooling from her mouth as she stared up at him. He could smell the smoke, taste the ash and feel the blistering heat of the fire. His father was still grappling with the man in black, wrestling in the midst of the flames, their faces twisted in rage. He could feel himself struggling to do something – anything – to help and failing.

He sank to his knees and bent his head to rest on the seat of the old chair, his hands on his head.

I'm sorry, mother.

He heard footsteps behind him as Halonni hurried to his side, dropping down beside him. She placed her hand on his back and bent over him. "What do you remember?" she asked gently.

He sighed and looked up at her. "Nothing. Nothing but what I told you before. But I know this is the place. This is where my mother died."

The Menions were inside as well, searching about for anything to help them identify who had lived there. They found a few personal items, brushes and goblets and plates, but nothing that Jantalus remembered or that sparked any other memory. Halonni helped Jantalus up so he was sitting on the edge of his old chair, his elbows on his knees and his face in his hands. Halonni was next to him, one hand on his arm. It reminded him of sitting every day staring out the same door with his mother and he wanted to be sick for it.

"I found this in an old leather bag," Stilthius announced as he emerged from one of the back rooms. He held up an old, dirty piece of parchment. "But I can't read it. The language makes no sense to me."

He handed it to Tyris who looked it over a moment and then shook his head. "I've never seen this before." He handed it to Halonni.

"It's a letter to the Vicar Council," she told them as she read to herself. "The High Elder, Jilien Orthel, is addressed personally." She kept reading. "This person writing it is confirming an invitation to meet with her to discuss some sort of disagreement. There are no specifics, but there wouldn't be. Naming the place of such a meeting would be to invite enemies to plan an ambush for the High Elder." She read on. "It's signed."

Jantalus looked up for the first time. "Signed?"

Halonni nodded. "Joran Kathias."

He looked around at them all, blank stares looking back. That name meant nothing to any of them. Jantalus did not find that the least bit surprising.

Tyris stood across the room from him, a small tin cup in his hand as he held it up to the light that slipped through the holes in the roof. It was battered and tarnished, caked with dirt. Beside the big outlander, Stilthius was examining the leather bag that held the parchment. It was crumbling with age, dry and brittle. Halonni tried to roll up the letter she had read, but it split when she folded it over, nearly broken in half despite her gentle touch.

He ran his fingers across the thin, weathered fabric that covered the arm of his chair; it came apart in his hands, splitting to expose the dark wood beneath. Old, he realized, old and unused.

He looked up from the chair to find them all watching him, their own thoughts plain on their faces. They saw it as well. They knew. This might have been his home. The hearth might have been the one he had sat before every day and the chair where he had done the sitting. The tin cup might have been one he drank out of. The old leather bag might have been one his father had used when he traveled. The glass baubles that lay in splinters on the floor may have been his mother's decorations. But these were not things abandoned last fall.

This place had not seen use in years.

He steepled his hands before his face and closed his eyes against what he was seeing. None of it made sense. He remembered. It was, in fact, the only thing he remembered with any clarity. All those early mornings he had spent staring out the window, across the porch into the yard. His father had been there, cutting wood and playing with the hounds. His mother had sat right where Halonni was now standing, feeding him, washing him, holding his hand. They had to have been recent to be so clear.

Or did they? Is another void in the mess that is my memory really so hard to believe?

He had no reason to think all of those memories were from the previous fall. Yes, it had been autumn when he had seen his mother murdered, but he had no evidence that it had been the previous one. The battle between the Alliance and the men who stood with Drappel did not have to have coincided with his memories. He had drawn a conclusion without any proof that the events were linked.

Halonni knelt down in the ash, soot and debris before him. All fatigue and bruises and scratches, her face caught the light of the sun as it flooded through the gaps above. Her eyes were ringed in black and bloodshot. He could scarcely remember the last time they were not. Her throat was still mottled with finger shaped bruises inflicted by the Sentinel outside of Ulis, turned all purple with hints of yellow. Her long, midnight hair was matted and filthy. The hands that reached out to take both of his were scraped raw at the knuckles.

"The magic here is strange. It surrounds this place, flows around it, over it, and even through it. I can't find a source for it, though."

He nodded. "I know. It eludes me as well. I recognize it, but I don't know why. I am beginning to think I never will."

Her hands squeezed his. "Don't say that. We've come this far. We can keep trying – keep looking."

"Where? Drappel was the only place we had to look." His hand knotted into a fist and hammered on the arm of the chair. "Why was I drawn here if I was to find nothing? What good is a burned out old house and a name I have never heard before?"

She caught his hand again, closing her fingers around his fist. "You're exhausted. We all are. A night's rest might clear our heads."

He closed his eyes and heaved a sigh.

All of this for nothing. I know less than I did before I came here.

"She's right, sorcerer," Stilthius was saying. "It's been a hard day. Let's find a place to sleep, start again tomorrow."

Jantalus's eyes slipped open. "Sleep here?"

Tyris shrugged. "There has to be a building in town with a door we can lock behind us."

Had he anything close to the energy to even walk into the forest and make camp he would have. Instead, he simply nodded and pushed himself up out of the chair, drawing Halonni up with him. He glanced down to his left at the edge of hearth. His mother's staring eyes looked back, her gaping mouth drooled blood. Her hand reached out for him.

Or maybe not. Maybe none of that was real either. Maybe I'm just mad.

Chapter Fourteen

The woman came to him without a sound.

She drifted across the rough-cut planks of the floor without touching them, floating on air as easily as a wind-blown mist. She was a translucent thing, an ethereal approximation of a girl, a faint white and blue glow drawing her in muddled lines against the black wall behind her. A tattered robe hung about her almost skeletal frame, trailing behind her as she came, rippling as if blown by a gentle breeze. Her long hair flowed down about her slender shoulders like a white veil.

Jantalus sat up on the bed in the little cottage they were using for refuge. One of Drappel's few intact buildings, it had a solid door they could bar and an undamaged roof overhead. There were two beds for them as well. Tyris and Stilthius slept back to back on one while Halonni was huddled up against him in the other. They built no fire in the hearth for fear of being spotted. They had simply locked the shutters on the windows and rolled themselves in their blankets against the night air.

But Jantalus was not cold. In fact, he was not even awake.

He knew it at once. His body was alive with magic, the surging power directed toward the apparition that advanced on him. But, the air was no longer bitter. No vapor passed from his lips. Beside him, Halonni was still and quiet and did not breathe. What he was seeing was not real. It was something akin to a dream, but not entirely of his making. It was not a memory like the dream he had experienced at Spotter's Hill. This was a mixture of his mind, his magic and something from without.

The ethereal woman stopped at the foot of the bed, her ghostly face lifting. "Jantalus Kathias."

"How do you know me?" he asked.

Their words were not spoken aloud. Their lips were not really moving. Everything was a proxy, a substitution for reality created by his imagination as a medium for their interaction that was taking place only in his mind. The room they were in was a place he had created because it was the foremost location in his mind owing to its being the most recent. His own appearance was as he had been that day, worn and ragged, dressed in rumpled clothing that was stained with dirt and sweat. Halonni appeared as she had when he had last seen her just before slipping off to sleep.

"*I have waited for you,*" *the woman answered.*

He rose from the bed and approached her, his movement nothing more than a visual representation of his mind and magic rising up to meet hers. "I do not know you. I'll ask again how you know me."

Her head bowed slightly. Submission. Her power was limited. She was no threat. She had come with no intent to challenge him. "I am called Khessa Rhenn. Do you know that name?"

He shook his head. "I recognize no names. My own sounds strange to my ears. Why are you here? Are you the magic that called me through the forest?"

"*I am. I have little time, Jantalus Kathias. Your presence has awakened me from my sleep and now that I have come, my magic slips away. Listen to me while there is time."*

He said nothing, waiting.

"*We knew each other once, but not well. Your father, Joran Kathias, and my grandfather, Addicus Malshere, were great friends. When the Alliance attacked Drappel, my grandfather sent men to defend it. I was among them. We failed, as you have seen. The battle and everything around it does not matter, not now, at least. What you need to hear is what happened after the battle. When the Alliance soldiers came, they brought Vicars and Sentinels with them. One of those Vicars was a man named Mordoc Tassaren. He and your father battled all throughout Drappel, wielding magic that few could even imagine. Alliance soldiers and Sentinels fell on the defenders of Drappel while they fought, wave after wave hammering steel against steel. When it was over, the dead were even more than you see here, for the Alliance bore theirs away. Drappel was broken, but your father and a few men who rallied a final defense remained. The Alliance withdrew their soldiers and Mordoc fled."*

"*Fled? He did not withdraw with his men?"*

Khessa Rhenn shook her ghostly head. "No. He could not. He had something that they would not accept among them. He took to his side a horror so terrible, a power so beyond controlling that the Vicars of Haven would have cast him out."

"*What was it?" Jantalus asked.*

"*You."*

"*Me?"*

"*Mordoc headed north, into the Tijian Mountains, with you. Your father and those who remained, my sister included, gave chase. None returned. Addicus came to find us and found only the remains of Drappel. He summoned my spirit from the realm of the dead and left me to stand watch until he — or you — returned. He then left for the Tijian, seeking my sister, Mira, and the others who chased after Mordoc.'*

"But who was I that this Mordoc would take me? What power was he after?"

Khessa Rhenn faded almost into nothingness for a moment and then reappeared, the bluish glow that formed the apparition gone dull. "Only a fragment of who I was remains here, Jantalus. My memories are not complete. Addicus made me only as whole as I needed to be and no more. The magic he used to sustain me is fading. I am slipping away. Go to the Tijian. Seek Addicus and your father and the rest. The answers to who you are and why this came to pass are with those who hunted Mordoc Tassaren."

She was fading away again and he reached out to stop her, his magic thrusting forth to entangle hers, trying to drag it back into his mind and hold it. In the proxy dream state of their interaction, his hand passed through her. Nothing was left of her to hold onto, no magic to snare.

He thought he might have seen a faint smile on the fading face as it melted into the darkness of the room. "I am sorry Jantalus. Good luck. Enyara watch over you."

His hand grasped for her again, but she had faded. He caught nothing but emptiness.

The burning sensation that had been the call of her magic slowly cooled, dying away. Leaving him alone.

Chapter Fifteen

Jantalus woke to silence.

The little wooden cottage around him was dark and still, a tomb in the graveyard that Drappel had become. The faint light of morning outlined the edges of the door and the nearby window, allowing enough through that he could see they were both still barred against anything that might approach from without. A frosty edge to the air turned his breath to vapor that curled away from his mouth and vanished into the gloom. To his right, Tyris and Stilthius were still asleep atop the old bed that looked comically small with the two giants stretched out atop it. To his left, Halonni slept with her back to him, nestled close and curled up like a child.

All real. No ghosts.

He closed his eyes a moment and then opened them. Nothing changed. He might have been able to dismiss the shade of Khessa Rhenn as a simple dream or even a resurfacing of one of his fragmented memories, but that would have been lying to himself. He knew better. What he had seen was no trick of his mind. The spirit of the dead girl had come to him in his sleep and delivered the message she had been left to give. The brevity and lack of detail was maddening, but he let the anger and frustration slip away. It was more than he had come with after all, even if it made for a thin thread of hope that more waited to be discovered.

He reached over and shook Halonni's shoulder gently. She came awake at once, her body tensing, her eyes snapping open and darting about the room. When it was clear they were in no danger, she heaved a sigh and lowered her head back to the balled-up cloak she had been using as a pillow. She closed her eyes and rubbed at her bruised neck with one hand.

"I was comfortable, dreaming." She yawned her way through each word. "A legion of Alliance soldiers and Sentinels had better be on their way. Anything else and I'll kill you for waking me up."

"Who is Addicus Malshere?"

Her eyes snapped open, all of the playfulness and sarcasm draining away in an instant. "He was a Vicar once, many years ago. He was in Haven while I was, but I don't recall ever meeting him. His kin are the lords of Northshire. Durn says Addicus abandoned Haven and the Vicar Council to go home. He said Addicus was disgusted by what the Vicars had become and refused to be a part of them any longer."

She paused. "How do you know that name?"

He turned a bit, lying on his side with his head in one hand and his elbow propped up on the bed. He related the encounter with Khessa Rhenn in its entirety, watching her for some reaction. Halonni remained silent throughout his story, waiting patiently, nodding occasionally to indicate she was listening. When he was finished, she simply looked at him for a long time.

"They may all be dead," she said finally. "Why else would only you and Peridor Finn have escaped?"

Jantalus shook his head. "I'm more concerned with what it was about me that this Mordoc was so interested in. If my dream about the trial in Haven was real, he saved me from execution by the Vicars. If he then came to Drappel with the Vicars and battled my father, what happened between the two events? Why would he take me away after that? If Khessa Rhenn was right, he hid me from his allies in the Alliance as well."

She put a finger to his lips. "You're getting too far ahead of yourself. You are assuming the dream was completely accurate. You're assuming Khessa Rhenn was who she claimed to be and told you the truth. You don't know any of that."

He brushed her hand away. "You listen to me. I understand why you insist on things the way you do. But you have to stop. At some point, I have to choose something to believe. I have to stand on something solid if I am to take a step. I might step the wrong way, but at this point, it's better than standing still. I believe the dream I had. I believe Khessa Rhenn too."

She sighed and nodded. "All right. Let's assume you're right. Too much of this still makes no sense. That house you remembered must have caught fire years ago. It certainly hasn't been just one winter since someone lived there. And yet the town was sacked in the fall to be sure. So how many times did Mordoc Tassaren attack you here? How could he have burned your home last year if it has been abandoned for far longer? Can't you see why I have to doubt what you think is real?"

"I know it doesn't fit," he admitted. "I'm confused. But maybe I need to accept that this isn't going to end in a way that validates what you and Durn were hoping for. How far do I have to take things before I let go of any pointless hope I have that everything will prove to be the opposite of what it seems? I've already walked across the whole damn valley only to find more questions instead of answers. Do I go north and try to find my father and Addicus Malshere? Is there any point to that?"

Halonni frowned. "Will you be able to live your life without regret if you walk away now and know you didn't try? The outlanders think your path leads them to a destiny spelled out by their god. I think your magic is something I have never seen. It is not the magic of a Vicar or a Necromancer. It is something different, strange. I think there must be a reason for it and that reason will define who you were – who you are."

"What if I am nothing but an accident, a freak that was marked and condemned for a reason?"

"You wouldn't have come this far, tried this hard, if you believed that." She met his black gaze. "And neither would I. It is always worth trying, Jantalus. Better, don't you think, to at least try and not regret?"

Unless I regret trying.

He kept the thought to himself. Halonni was not going to listen to any suggestion that he give up. She was prepared to see this through. He supposed that was for herself as much as for him. She had made her own stake in his good end clear enough. There was more to it than that though. She believed. Why she bothered was beyond him. What he was sure of was that she was willing to hold onto the hope that he was something worth all the effort, even if he was beginning to doubt.

"One more," he told her, finally. "One more look. We'll go north and see if there is anyone that knows anything. If we find no answers or simply more questions that complicate it all, I'm done."

Halonni's hand reached out for his, quick, impulsive. "We will find something, Jantalus. If it isn't what we hoped for, we'll make it right somehow."

She cared - more than he did, he realized in the moment. It seemed insane to him that she did, but it was plain enough. Her own experiences had been powerful, formative in a way he could not fully understand.

Perhaps he would when his own past became clear, but he doubted that. She had a need to see something good come of his search for himself, something to assure her that he was not who he feared he had been.

Because if I am something better than I was, she can be too.

He rose from the bed and began gathering his things. "Wake them." He gestured to the Menion brothers. "I want to leave as soon as we can."

Havenwood stretched north for a time, surrounding them still as they pushed on. It was thinning throughout the day, though, and by noon, they had left the bulk of it behind. Before them, the Tijian Mountains rose up like a great rock wall, dagger points tipped in white thrust deep into the blue spring sky. The trees gave way to the rolling terrain that led to the foothills of the mountains, rough, steep, and slow beneath their aching feet.

Tyris and Stilthius had made no comment on the decision to press on. Halonni had explained everything to them regarding Jantalus's dream and his hope that men from Drappel had run north, but the outlanders might not have been listening for all the reaction she got out of them. A shared shrug and a gathering of their gear was the whole of it. Jantalus had assumed from the start that they would lose their patience, but he had been proven wrong so far. Tyris could claim what he wished about his own beliefs, but it was clear that he deferred to his brother in this and Stilthius Menion's faith was unshakable. Their destiny, he believed, was caught up in Jantalus's fate and he was going to walk the same road as long as he felt led to it.

Halonni was not as familiar with the area as she had been with the valley below. She knew, mostly by what she recalled from maps she had read, that several settlements dotted the edge of the Tijian. She had forgotten the names and most of the exact locations. It was more than Jantalus or the Menion brothers had to offer and so they followed without complaint.

When they finally sighted the faint glow of watch fires as the sun dipped below the mountaintops, Halonni could not be sure what town they were looking at. It was still a distance from them, partially screened by the rolling hills they were hiking, small and squat and shadowed. The promise of a warm fire and the safety of walls was enticing, but they decided to wait for dawn before approaching. The town, for all they knew, could be under Alliance control and they might not be able to see well enough in the dark to make that determination before they had put themselves in a dangerous position. Instead, they found a small defile hidden back in the hills, away from any sightline to the town. They built a small fire behind a screen of trees and huddled in their blankets while their food cooked.

"It won't be long," Stilthius said, breaking the silence that had settled over them all.

"What?" Halonni managed in the midst of a yawn.

"The Tassarens," he explained. "They will have followed us to Urs and from there, Drappel." He looked to Jantalus. "We're ahead of them, it seems, but they don't have to have much imagination to know where we're going. There were two score or so in Ulis, by my count. If they lost a handful to us and a few more fighting their way out, I suppose, we still have thirty or so chasing us. They'll move slower for that number, but not too much slower. They'll catch up and it will be soon enough."

"Then we need to move faster and for longer," Halonni insisted. "We'll reach that town and that should keep them off us for a bit."

Tyris rubbed his big hands together as he leaned close to the fire. "Those fucks don't seem the kind to care a shit where they are. They attacked us in the middle of a street in Ulis. They won't be stopped by anything or anyone between us and them." He stared at Jantalus across the shimmering haze above the flames. "You are that important to them, I think. Whoever Jantalus Kathias was – or is, whatever you want to say – you have made the worst kind of enemies."

The sorcerer nodded. "So it seems. But who could I have been? My parents didn't live like the wealthy or powerful."

"Oh, I think they were important in some way," Stilthius said, drawing all eyes to him. "That little house in Drappel was not their home. There was nothing in that place, nothing at all, that belonged to anyone." He held up his big hands when Jantalus tried to stop him. "Listen to me. Yes, they owned things. I am not disputing that. But a home has things that are treasured. An old heirloom or a craftsman's touch to the building of it. That place was just another cottage in just another town. It was almost like they were trying to be just another family."

"Hiding?" Tyris nodded along with the suggestion. "It makes sense."

"Hiding from the Vicars," Halonni said, continuing the thought. "That explains why they would have a letter written to Jilien Orthel. You say your father battled Mordoc Tassaren. He may have been a Vicar who left the council or he possessed magic and would not submit to them. They might have chosen Drappel as a place to hide with you."

"No," Jantalus said, realizing at once what must have happened. "Not hiding with me. Hiding me. Why else would so many be after me? If it were about them, why come after a man who remembers nothing? What difference would it make if I went on as I am - not knowing a damn thing?"

Stilthius poked at the fire with a scrap of wood. "You are either a threat to them or you know something that is. Could be they fear you will remember what that is."

"And the Vicars?" Halonni asked. "Are they behind this or was this all Mordoc Tassaren's doing?"

They shared a long look across the fire and let the question float away on the mountain breeze. There was no answering it, not now. Maybe the answer was in that town nearby or another. If not, all that remained was the inevitability of a confrontation with the Tassarens. Given their recent history, Jantalus did not like his chances of learning everything he needed no matter where they wound up, but he liked their chances against the Tassarens even less. For now, he decided, they were doing what they could with what they knew.

He gestured to Tyris. "Take first watch. Stilthius, last. I'll stand middle watch. You two have been as tough as old leather and dependable as the sunrise. You earned some sleep, I think."

Stilthius pulled his blanket up over his shoulders. "You're all right, sorcerer. I sure as hell hope we don't find out you're an evil prick."

Tyris let loose a roaring laugh and went to stand at the edge of their shelter where he could see the faint bulk of the town beyond the ridgeline, his huge axe resting on his broad shoulder. Jantalus wrapped himself in his own blanket and stretched out beside the fire, his head in the crook of his arm. The fire was dying down as they had hoped, but the ember bed was deep and hot. The shelter of the rocks would keep the worst off them when the embers finally went cold, and not having a signal beacon for the Tassarens was more important than comfort.

Halonni rolled herself in her blankets and lay down near him, her head close to his and her feet pointed away. She propped her head up on her elbow and looked down at him, questions mixing with firelight in her gray eyes.

"I don't know," he told her, unprompted.

117

She raised an eyebrow at him. "I didn't ask anything."

"You were going to ask me if the idea that my parents might be hiding me from the Alliance changes my thinking. It doesn't. Perhaps they hunted me for a reason. That, or I was just a convenient target like so many others. It still answers none of our questions. I know you don't like that, but I have to keep my expectations in check. It would be too simple to believe in the best possible scenario for myself."

A small smile tugged at the corner of her mouth. "Fair enough."

It was his turn to be surprised. "No lecture?"

She sighed and lowered her head into her crossed arms. "I'm too damn tired and cold. Right now, I'll settle for you at least leaving the question open to possibilities."

"One of those possibilities might be an evil prick."

She yawned and pulled her blanket up over her shoulders. "Go to sleep or I'll put the two blocks of ice in my boots on your bare back."

He suspected the threat was more truth than fiction and let the matter go.

Chapter Sixteen

Ailen.

The faded word was chiseled into a tall, flat-faced rock a hundred yards south of the gate that split the tall stone block wall that closed the town off from the dirt path that curved around it and continued up into the Tijian Mountains. Rows of iron spikes topped the wall below the pennants and banners that flapped in the mountain breeze. Jantalus recognized none of the symbols, but took note of the fact that none of them was the oak and crossed swords of the Alliance. The braziers that had burned atop the gatehouse all night had settled to smoldering embers, thin columns of dark smoke twisting up and away from them to vanish into the clear, cold sky.

The portcullis had been raised and the iron bound wooden gates had been pushed open. Seven men stood atop the wall, all armed with bows and carrying signal horns that hung from their belts. Four more guards stood at ground level, watching carefully as a handful of men filed out, leading mules and carts behind them. The men turned south, stumping down the trail, casting disinterested glances toward the four who came north and then went on their way without comment.

"Trusting bunch," Tyris muttered, gesturing to the guards at the gate. "They'll ask questions...."

Halonni nodded, looked in Jantalus's direction and sighed. "We should try at least."

He looked the wall and the guards over a moment before shrugging. Even if they were allowed in, he doubted this place was going to prove to be worth their time. Everything about it said it was the wrong town. If the remnants of the defenders of Drappel had run here, they would probably have been turned away at the gate. Certainly, no one with any sense would have let Mordoc Tassaren or Jantalus himself in. Two men bearing the mark of the dead would have to have had miraculous luck to slip in unnoticed. To have spent any length of time in the town and avoided discovery would have likely been impossible.

He turned his attention away from the wall and the gate to the wide, rough trail that meandered up the mountainside beyond. The climb was a gradual one, but the slopes beyond were steep and blanketed with snow and ice. The Tijian was a jumbled collection of ridges and peaks, cuts and defiles that could swallow you up and never let you free.

Which is likely exactly what happened.

Jantalus looked back to Halonni. She was looking up at him from the cover of her cowl, her pale cheeks burned red by the wind, her matching nose dripping. Any argument against the hope of Ailen being any source of information died before it reached his lips. The first thing she would say to his contention that everyone was lost to the mountains and not coming back would be that he and Peridor Finn had. He could debate the merits of that argument, but he had no desire for it. Another night in the cold, huddled around a tiny campfire for fear that a larger one would invite someone to come cut their throats, and eating spoiled food with numb fingers was one more night too many. If Ailen had nothing more to offer than a warm bed and a decent meal, that would be enough until he decided on what to do next. There was no reason Halonni or the Menion brothers had to freeze their asses off while he figured things out.

"They'll ask about me covering my face," he said finally. "One look and being turned away is the best we can hope for. A volley of arrows is the reaction we're bound to get."

Tyris Menion held up one finger and then dropped his pack to the cold earth and began rummaging through it. He pulled free one of their spare cloaks and cut a long strip from it with his knife. When he was finished, he wadded up what was left of the cloak in the pack and tossed the strip to Jantalus.

"Cover your eyes," he told him. He gestured to Halonni. "She is traveling north. We are her escort and you are her blind brother. The pass is snowed in, so we're here to wait until it's clear."

Halonni cocked an eyebrow at him. "And who am I that I have servants?"

The big outlander shrugged. "Shit if I know. Ask your brother. I'm just the hired help."

She sighed and rolled her eyes at him. "Asshole."

Tyris smirked and Stilthius laughed. She ignored them both and helped Jantalus secure the blindfold. It worked almost too well. Other than a sliver of the ground visible through a small gap at the bottom edge of the cloth, he was completely blind. He reached out and caught the edge of Halonni's cloak as she started away from him, nearly tripping as he did. She caught his arm and settled in beside him, guiding him along the trail as Tyris and Stilthius led them toward the gate.

He heard carts rolling by and shod hooves pounding on the hard packed earth. The stink of oxen and mules lingered after they were gone, mixing with the acrid smell of the braziers that burned near the gatehouse. Leather creaked and metal fastenings jingled as the soldiers shifted about. Halonni guided him with two hands on his arm, steering him along at a slow and steady pace until finally dragging him to a halt.

"Morning," a voice called from in front of Jantalus. "Where are you lot from and what's your business here?"

He heard Halonni draw a deep breath. "I am from Opelin, to the north. I came last summer to the Censharn and will be going home. I can see the pass is still blocked. I was hoping to find lodging here until we can make our way."

The man paused a moment before he responded. "And these three?"

"My brother and our guardsmen."

"A pair of outlanders and a blind man saw you through Agron Pass and a winter in the valley? You're either brave or stupid, girl."

Jantalus tensed at the insult, but Halonni's hands clamped down on his wrist in warning. "If you won't let us in, say so. I'll head back south and spend my money elsewhere."

A collective chuckle rose up from the soldiers at the gate. "Easy, girl. Just making sure you aren't trouble. Go ahead, just keep to yourselves and don't stir up any shit."

Jantalus heard another shifting of men and Halonni tugged at his arm, urging him on. They walked for a short time, the sound of people passing them by all around. Boots thumped on stone, hooves pounded and wagons rolled along. Children laughed and ran, men shouted and cursed and pipe music floated on the crisp spring air. He felt a maddening familiarity to the quasi-awareness that the blindfold created, the darkness all too familiar and stifling. He fought the urge with each step he took to tear it away.

121

Finally, Halonni stopped and pulled the cloth away from his eyes. "Keep your cowl low," she warned. "There are people everywhere – plenty of opportunity for someone to get a glimpse of you."

He nodded and looked about, careful to keep his head slightly bent and his eyes downcast. They were standing on a wide street that cut the town of Ailen down the middle. Before him to the east, past a densely packed collection of stone buildings, he could make out the broad market square at the center of it all. Most of the people and carts were headed toward it, though a few small stalls stood along the way. Most of the buildings in the immediate area seemed to be garrisons for the town watch and a few small private homes.

"Where to?" Tyris asked. "Food and beer, I hope. Somewhere warm."

Halonni rubbed at her eyes. "To bed, if I have my way."

Tyris looked back at her with a shake of his head. "No, no. You're a nice girl, but I like my women tall and dark, fiery. Angry almost! Tits too, I like those." He paused and shrugged. "Not to offend, but you're small all around."

Stilthius's fist hammered into his shoulder. "Shut up, you dumb shit! She isn't asking you to bed. She's tired."

Tyris rubbed his arm as he looked from Halonni to his brother and back again. After a moment, his eyes went wide. "Ah. I see. Sorry about that." He gave a helpless shrug. "About the tits bit, too. I'm sure another man would be happy enough-."

Halonni stared daggers through him, her hand coming up to silence him. "Just shut up."

She turned on her heel and started off toward the market square. Tyris hurried after, desperately trying to explain the Tulin ideal of beauty and why she was so far from it through no fault of her own.

"Where is she headed?" Stilthius asked as he and Jantalus fell in a few steps behind them.

The sorcerer shrugged. "You want to go ask her?"

"And get dropped into a hole in the ground or whatever else that little witch can conjure up? I'll stay here with you. Black eyes and shit attitude aren't near as dangerous as that." He gestured in Halonni's direction.

Jantalus shook his head. Tyris was still trying to explain himself as they walked, but he might as well have been talking to the road as Halonni. She completely ignored him as she looked over the buildings they passed. More than a few of the people that wandered by turned to look at the enormous outlander as he hovered over her, pleading his case like a little boy desperate to please his angry mother. If Jantalus had anything resembling a sense of humor left after the last few weeks, he might have laughed at the spectacle of it.

"Why is she here?" Stilthius asked, breaking the silence.

"She needs to know almost as much as I do," Jantalus answered after a moment's consideration. "She needs to be sure she spent all that time and effort helping someone worth helping."

Stilthius looked him over a moment and then shook his head. "No. It's more, I think."

Jantalus failed to stifle a yawn. "I think too many days without good food and a soft bed have made your mind play tricks on you."

The outlander snorted. "That it?"

Tyris found them a half-filled tavern to drink and eat in that was close to the market square. For all of his hovering over Halonni and pleading, he had noticed it first, a fact Halonni attributed to his blocking her view half the time she was looking. The place was old and small, looking like it had been cobbled together with the scraps of other buildings to shore up years of rot and degradation. With most of the people in Ailen working or preparing to in the early morning hours, the four of them shared the taproom with only a handful of heavy eyed soldiers who had spent the night on watch and were finishing their last round before returning home to sleep. Halonni grudgingly spared a few coins from what Durn had given her in Marcester for food and beer, and they ate and drank until they were satisfied.

As soon as they finished eating, Tyris and Stilthius rose from their table and approached the soldiers at the other side of the room. Jantalus could not hear them as they spoke. After a few moments, the brothers dropped the swords that Jantalus had used to spar with at Spotter's Hill on the table and pulled up chairs. The soldiers threw in coins and jewelry and Stilthius produced a deck of old wooden cards from his pack.

"Unbelievable," Jantalus muttered as he watched them.

Beside him, Halonni leaned back in her chair, her head against the rough wall and closed her eyes. The heat of the nearby fireplace washed over them and filled the air with the scent of hickory. Jantalus put an elbow against the tabletop and his head in his palm. He was exhausted, but sleep was not an enticing idea. The nightmare from Spotter's Hill flashed through his mind whenever he closed his eyes and he had no desire to relive it. If that dream was too scattered to haunt him, he had the apparition of Khessa Rhenn or the almost nightly revisiting of the death of his mother.

He wondered more than once if forgetting the whole matter was his best option. The dreams might disappear in time and he could imagine himself latching on to Halonni's suggestion that who he had been could be left behind for who he wished to be. The answer to who and what he was might not be worth discovering, after all.

A quick, vivid picture of his mother's death mask always whisked the lure of such a decision away when he closed his eyes. That, if nothing else, would haunt him forever. He would settle that score, and, if it were not in his power to see that done, at least have an explanation for it all. He might not like the answers he found about himself, but he would have them one way or another.

Despite his best effort, he found himself dozing when the clamor of coins hitting the table snapped him awake. Tyris Menion stood over him with a satisfied grin. A handful of silver coins were scattered before him.

"Easy money from these fools," he announced. "Take these and get us a place to sleep for the day before we start losing." He was gone again before Jantalus could answer, rushing back to the card game like a child running off to play.

"Where did you get those?" Halonni murmured, her eyes half open as she watched him pick up the coins.

He jerked a thumb at the Menion brothers. "Their gambling." He slid the coins to her. "Why don't you see if you can buy us a bed for the day?" He paused and looked up at her from beneath his cowl. "I meant the four of us, not you and me."

She sighed and took the coins. "Of course. You all like them big and fiery, angry-."

"I never said-."

She waved his words away as she pushed herself to her feet and crossed the room to where the innkeeper was stacking wood near the hearth. She spoke to him for a moment, motioning to Jantalus and the Menions as she did. He watched the polite give and take between them. Finally, Halonni handed him a coin, leaned up and kissed him on the cheek.

She made her way back to Jantalus with an impish grin on her delicate face.

"New friend?" he asked as she picked up her cup to finish the last of her beer.

She took down her last swallow and wiped her mouth on her sleeve. "He said I was too sweet to charge a full day's board for the only room he had left. His sons are away for the week and he let us have their room for the day. It's in the rear, off the kitchen."

Jantalus pushed his chair back and rose. He gathered their packs as well as those of the Menion brothers and followed her though the kitchen to the room. Halonni crossed to the far side, opened the shutters on the window to allow light in while she found a pair of candles, and lit them. The room contained only a pair of chests secured with heavy iron locks and a single bed that would hold two of them at best and only if neither of those was Stilthius or Tyris. A series of hooks along the wall held bags of clothing and other personal items, but the innkeeper's sons either owned very little or had taken most of what they did with them.

Halonni placed the lit candles atop one of the locked chests and then closed the window against the biting air and latched it. She wrapped herself in one of the blankets and dropped down on the bed with an exhausted groan. Jantalus stood where he was and eyed the bed with a growing sense of dread. He would have to sleep sometime, he told himself. Now or later was the only question. It made sense, but it did not move him from where he stood. Sleep meant dreams and he was tired of those dreams and what he was beginning to believe they meant for him.

Halonni pushed herself up on her elbow and looked at him. "Sleeping standing up?" She sighed and rolled her eyes at him. "Self-conscious now, are you? I know you weren't trying to get me into bed, I was just pissing about Tyris and his big, reeking mouth."

Jantalus pushed back his cowl and ran his hands through his hair. "I know. It's not that. I just…" he shook his head as he trailed off.

She sat up, drawing the blanket over her shoulders as she repositioned herself. "What is it? You're not still obsessing over that dream from Spotter's Hill, are you?"

"Obsessing? There's a difference between fixing on something and having it following you. If I could make it – or any number of other things I see – go away, I would."

She held her hands up, palms facing him. "Easy. I'm sorry. I didn't mean it that way." She patted the bed next to her. "You have to sleep, Jantalus. The Tassarens or Alliance soldiers or Sentinels or anyone else could come looking at any time. Better that you have your strength."

He heaved a heavy sigh and stripped off his cloak before climbing in next to her. For all the heat of the kitchen on the other side of the door, the room was uncomfortably cold. The shutters were ill-fitting and rattled in the mountain wind. The wall was dotted with gaps in the masonry, decades of neglect allowing slivers of cold daylight through. Halonni put her back to him and inched closer. He let her settle against him as he wrapped himself in his own blanket.

"Hands to yourself," Halonni mumbled, repeating her warning from Spotter's Hill.

Jantalus looked around the tiny room. "What about Tyris and Stilthius?"

"You can grope them all you want."

"I mean where are they sleeping?"

She yawned. "They want to gamble, they get the floor. Go to sleep."

He did not respond and after a time, he felt her go limp against him. The cold nipped at his nose and ears, stung his fingers. He wondered at the coin they had traded for the room and what difference another night under a tree would have made by comparison. He considered how long the Menion brothers had been gone and whether they were winning or losing. He thought about the Tassarens, where they were and when they would finally catch them.

Anything but sleep.

Chapter Seventeen

Caleb Tassaren stood with his brothers in the shadow of an enormous oak tree as they peered out from the fringes of the forest of Havenwood into the city beyond. The moon was high overhead and shone down from the cloudless sky like a great white beacon. The night was hushed and still and cold. Behind them, a score of fighting men huddled in blankets, gathered close for warmth. No fire burned before them and they passed jugs of spirits to take the edge off the frigid night.

They were late. Despite a hard ride throughout the night, they had been unable to catch their prey before they entered Ailen. The sorcerer's use of magic in Urs had given away his position and stopped Caleb before he wasted time searching elsewhere. He had hurried as much as he had been able in the dark, but, ultimately, missed his prey by a matter of hours. Now, he waited in the dark and cold while they decided what was next.

Caleb glanced over at his men, his lean, handsome face devoid of sympathy. These were hard men, and a night in the cold would not be the end of them. To build fires would invite prying eyes and he was not ready to tip his hand. He had missed Jantalus Kathias in Urs, but he might yet catch him unaware in Ailen. If they had any chance at continued secrecy, he was not about to squander it. They had enough drink to warm their bones. Besides, it was not as cold as it might otherwise have been for an early spring day in the Censharn Valley.

He turned to his left and then his right, watching his brothers. Both focused on Ailen, watching, waiting. They did not wait for the same things.

To his right, Samarus stood tall and straight, his eyes closed and his blocky face taut with concentration. He was a tall, heavily built man, much bigger than Caleb, but lacking the agility and grace of his middle brother. While Caleb had trained extensively in the arts of war, Samarus's primary devotion was to the magical arts of the Vicars. No stranger to a sword, he was nonetheless far more practiced, and deadly, with the control of the elemental powers he had inherited from their father. Samarus might have been Mordoc Tassaren twenty years ago. He had the same black hair and eyes, and the same silent intensity about him.

To his left, Rossin was everything that the eldest of the Tassaren men was not. Smallish and whip thin, he had a tight, pinched face that resembled that of rat with small, penetrating eyes. In contrast to Samarus's calm, Rossin was a man in constant motion. He fidgeted and twitched with anticipation as they waited, his face split wide by a maniacal grin. A huge scar split his face from left eye to right lower jaw. His lips were mangled, rotted teeth showing through the gaps of ruined skin. Long the outsider among them, Rossin was the son of Mordoc's mistress by whom he had also sired their younger sister, Dianan. He shared his sister's auburn hair and black, lifeless eyes as well. He shifted constantly, shuffling his feet and rubbing his hands together or caressing the pommels of the twin swords that rested at his hips. He glanced over at Caleb expectantly and looked almost hurt when his brother simply shook his head.

It was not yet time.

Samarus's eyes snapped open. "If Jantalus Kathias is in Ailen, I cannot locate him. There is no reason to believe he is even in Ailen. He might be elsewhere. If not, he is either intentionally foiling my scrying or his power has grown to the point that it resists mine without effort."

Rossin laughed, an eerie cackling that drew uneasy stares from the men assembled behind them. "So strong is he? Oh, no, brother. No, no, no. Perhaps you are not looking hard enough. Perhaps you are not so strong as you believe."

Samarus stiffened as he turned to the madman. "I know my own power, bastard. And let me assure you, Jantalus is stronger than you might think. Too strong for the three of us."

Rossin stepped forward, one long, gloved finger stabbing toward his brother. "Nonsense. He is a man and he can bleed. He will die like any other if you put a sword through his heart."

Samarus stared down the length of his nose at the little man. "So simple is it? Why don't you go try it? We will wait here. If we are fortunate, he'll be waiting for you."

Rossin sneered, but Caleb came between them before he could

respond. "We wait for Shantara. She will come for us soon. When she has considered the situation, we will all decide together what is next to come."

Rossin turned to him, his fingers lacing together and his head dipping slightly. He looked almost as if he were begging. Only the wicked, twisted smile on his face spoke otherwise. "Let me go to Ailen. I will find them and come back to you. I'll tell you where they are. When Shantara comes, we will be able to act quickly." He turned to look out at the city again, his face almost pleading. "At least let me watch them. Let me watch."

Samarus frowned at Caleb. "You cannot be considering this. If Jantalus is there and this maniac alerts him to our presence, Shantara will kill us."

Caleb bent his head to the side, his ear to his shoulder, and cracked his neck. Samarus was right, of course. Shantara would be furious if Rossin were discovered. However, Rossin was an excellent hunter. He knew how to hide himself, regardless of his surroundings. He was as adept at disappearing into a shadowed alley or a crowd of revelers as he was a dense forest. If he could find the sorcerer and verify that he was in Ailen, it would save them all precious time. Better yet, if he could find the exact location of Jantalus Kathias, it would make everything so much easier for them all.

He took another look at the madman that was his half-brother. The weight of the insanity that danced in the other's eyes crushed every hope of an advantage he might gain by allowing Rossin to go. Samarus was right. He was a fool for even considering it.

"We wait for Shantara," Caleb repeated.

A quiver shook Rossin, his face slackening with shock. Obviously, he had taken Caleb's moment of contemplation as a positive sign. "Watch and listen, watch and listen." He sneered. "Always smarter than me, aren't you? Do as you do. Listen to what you say. Yes. Yes. I'm the fool, the madman. So smart the two of you are. But you are just a pair of fools who wipe Shantara's ass for her when she asks for it."

Caleb raised his hand, his face contorting in anger. He hated that mouth. He hated the nonsense that spewed from it. To silence it, if but for a moment, would be worth almost anything. Samarus caught his arm before the blow could fall.

"Enough," the big man said. "Shantara comes."

The three men turned back toward Havenwood and watched as their sister made her way through the ranks of the cutthroats that huddled together. As she passed, the men bowed their heads, their eyes fixed on the ground. Shantara ignored them as if they did not exist, continuing her advance. Behind her, Faylor limped along, bundled in her dark cloak, small and frail and ever the faithful hound at her side. His sisters were hardly close in the sense of normal siblings, but Faylor never argued with Shantara, never questioned what she was told. They both possessed magic of staggering power, Shantara the greater, but Faylor's something twisted and insidious and unpredictable. It made her useful to her older sister and Shantara was careful to keep Faylor under her thumb.

Shantara stopped before her brothers, Faylor, head bowed, a step behind. Shantara was tall, as tall as Samarus, with a square jaw and short, spiky hair. Thickly built and strong, she was a physical match for most men. She fixed her brothers with her black eyes, staring them down as she might unruly children.

"Have you found Jantalus?"

Caleb met her gaze without flinching. "No, but we know he is within the city walls. He is resisting our scrying, I think."

"You think?" Shantara laughed. It was a deep, gravely sound that carried no indication of humor. "That, dear brother, is something beyond the three of you for the most part. I will do the thinking. Your talents lie in action."

Caleb took a step forward, his lean frame tense. "Try impressing someone else, Shantara. Get to your plan and let us have what we came for."

His sister stared at him, her face a cold mask of anger. "Very well. First, we will need someone for gathering information."

Rossin thrust forward, his eyes alight. "At last!"

Shantara dismissed him with a wave of her hand. "Not you, bastard. Not alone, at any rate. They will catch you before you can learn anything of value. What will you do then? Beg for mercy?"

Rossin's face went calm in an instant. He straightened and his mouth twisted into what might have been a wry smile. "Like you did when Joran Kathias had you on your knees pissing yourself in the fall?" He shot a look at Caleb. "Or you when Peridor Finn schooled you like a child and sent you running with your ass stinging? Or you, Samarus? Did you not beg Khessa Rhenn for your life? I seem to recall being the only one who needed no mercy. I retreated because father commanded me to."

Caleb's hand closed on the dagger at his hip. In that instant, he almost killed Rossin. The urge was not new. If not for his almost miraculous ability to prove himself useful in the most unlikely of scenarios, Rossin would have expended what little goodwill sharing a father afforded him. If not for Shantara's insistence that she needed him for her plans, Caleb would have killed him years ago.

The madman was looking at him, his wild eyes shifting from the dagger to Caleb's face. "Do it." His voice was soft, inviting. "Do it. Draw on me, Caleb. We can find out what you've been wondering since we were children, since the first time I refused to take a beating without fighting back. We can find out which one of us is the best."

Shantara stepped between them and shoved them apart. "You do as I tell you, when I tell you to do it. We all know what is at stake here. I'll not have the two of you comparing the size of your cocks. We need to focus. When we are finished, feel free to kill each other." She looked to each of them in turn. "Agreed?"

Caleb stared. "Agreed."

"Rossin?" Shantara pressed.

He shrugged it away, the wild grin returning. "Whatever you say, Shantara."

"Good." She indicated herself, Faylor and Samarus. "I say we wait. For now. Our magic is potent enough for Jantalus to sense if he is even a fraction of his old self."

Samarus crossed his arms over his broad chest. "And what do we do about finding out what is going on in Ailen?"

Shantara flashed him a crooked smile. "I said the three of us are too strong to get near him. Not Caleb and Rossin."

"And if he finds us?" Caleb challenged her. "I'd rather not have my neck stretched out for him."

His sister shrugged. "Like all of us, you are expendable." She laughed as if she did not mean it. They all knew better.

Caleb watched Samarus turn away. He kept silent, but the look he gave them said he had little faith in Shantara's sense of humor. He did not trust her any more than Caleb or Rossin did. A good thing, Caleb decided. Shantara was the most powerful of them, but the least predictable. As long as the three brothers shared a distrust of her, the balance of power would not swing too heavily in her favor, Faylor notwithstanding.

Caleb was something of gambler and, in this game, three against two were even odds.

Dead even if I am not careful, he reminded himself. But then, was any game worth playing without high stakes?

He snatched a handful of Rossin's cloak. "Come on, you fucking idiot."

Rossin cackled like a maniac.

Chapter Eighteen

"Twenty-nine," Tyris Menion announced as he spread his cards on the table for all to see.

A chorus of curses sounded from the handful of angry men who gathered around the table. Cards slapped down against the rough-cut wood and coins slid in the direction of the huge outlander. Tyris gathered them up with a sweep of his great arms and laughed at his good fortune. Money had been a concern only a few hours ago. Now, he and Stilthius would dine on roast fowl and work off several weeks of frustration with the finest whores the inn had to offer.

"A cheat if ever I saw one," one of the men opposite him muttered. "No man takes three in row so handily. If I could figure out your game, I'd have your filthy black ass for it!"

A tense silence fell over the table and the other players slid their chairs away from the speaker. Tyris stopped counting his coins and looked over at his brother. Stilthius was sitting next to him, keeping out of the game while he drank down his third bottle, his chair leaning back against the wall and his feet propped on the edge of the table. He glanced sideways at his brother and shrugged one shoulder before going back to his mead. Shit for help there, Tyris thought.

He turned his attention back to the man who had challenged him. He was drunk like the rest of them, his red-rimmed eyes staring over the tops of three empty tankards, narrowed and accusing. He was half a man next to either one of the outlanders and the whole half dozen of them probably would not have been enough to threaten the hardened warriors in a fight, but mead had a way of making just about any fool invincible. The pity of it was the way it always seemed to make the smallest of men feel so big.

Tyris rolled his head around on his neck until it cracked. The man watched him without blinking, his hands curled into white knuckled fists on the tabletop. Tyris took a great swallow from his mug of mead and tossed it aside, empty. It was the best he had tasted since coming to Kronos and he figured if he was about to get thrown out on his ass, he might as well have the whole of it.

"Cheater you say?" The man nodded without taking his eyes off the giant. "All right then. If you want your money back, you have two options. One of them involves you playing better cards and walking out of here. The other one involves you trying to take it and going out of here broken into little fucking pieces. I could give a rotten shit which one you pick, so you go ahead and think it over. I'll be counting my money while you decide if you have more brains than balls."

The gambler snarled and started to his feet, but a gloved hand seized his shoulder and forced him back into his chair.

"You looking to make widows and orphans of your kin you stupid bastards?"

Tyris Menion looked up to find the speaker was a smallish, wiry little man with a face so scarred it hardly resembled anything human anymore. A great, wide gash of pink stretched from left eye to the right corner of his jaw, splitting his lips along the way. His broken lower teeth were visible through the gap, a long steam of saliva drooling out to wet the front of his tunic. At his shoulder stood a slightly taller man with short black hair and the same black eyes, all menace and fearless intensity.

Rossin and Caleb Tassaren? Jantalus had told them several times about the people chasing them, but Tyris paid more attention to what they were than whom. Their magic and skill were the threat. Their names meant shit.

"Cheating bastard stole my money!" the drunken gambler insisted, struggling without success to get free.

Caleb Tassaren grabbed him by the neck and shoved him half across the table toward Tyris, his face close. "Take a good look. A hard look. You see that man? Can you miss him? He's seven feet of heartless killer, you fucking moron. The wenches will be cleaning you up with their ale rags when he's done with you." He yanked the man back into his chair. "The lot of you get out of here before someone caves your damn heads in."

The surrounding gamblers hurried from their seats and headed for the door, dragging their more vocal friend with them. The drunkard shouted insults and accusations of cheating as his companions pulled him away, his cries fading away as he was forced out the door into the street beyond. Rossin squared the man's vacated chair around and seated himself opposite the Menion brothers. His brother stood at his back, cold and silent, black eyes watching. Careful, this one, Tyris thought as he looked him over. The smaller brother might be mad, but this one was cold and deliberate, dangerous in a way Rossin probably couldn't comprehend if his mind was in the same state as his face.

"Looking for a game?" Tyris asked as Rossin leaned forward, his elbows on the table.

The scarred man slid one of the departed gambler's cups over and helped himself to a swallow. "For a friend."

Stilthius looked up from his mead. His hammer was just within reach, leaning against the wall beside him. "Sorry, our circle of friends is exclusive and full. We just don't have the time for any more."

The cup lowered to the table and slid aside. "No, no, no. Jantalus. This is about him, not you. Just tell us where he went and we can all walk away from this." He wiped the drool from his chin. "So. Where is he?"

Tyris resumed counting his coins. "Didn't ask. Figure if it was our business, he'd have mentioned it."

Caleb's eyes narrowed at them. "You want to think about all this again and come up with another answer?"

Tyris scooped up his money and deposited it in a small leather bag next to his chair. "No. I like the answer I gave."

Caleb Tassaren leaned forward over the back of his brother's chair. "Well I don't."

Tyris met the cold, hard eyes without flinching. "I don't give a shit what you like. Why don't you and your woman get out of here while you still can?"

Rossin pushed back from his chair. "Bad, bad mistake."

Tyris was on his feet in an instant, his huge axe slamming down on the table, sending cups and cards scattering. The tavern went still. All eyes turned to the four men. Rossin had shrunk back into a defensive crouch, his hands on the twin knives at his waist. Caleb had one hand on his brother's shoulder and the other on the hilt of his sword. To Tyris's right, Stilthius had lowered his feet to the floor and closed his hand around his hammer, but was still sitting.

"Mistake?" Tyris leaned over the table toward the two men. "Looks to me like the mistake is yours, asshole. What the fuck did you think? You were going to come threaten us? I will fucking end you, little man. I fear no one, not you, not your brother or the rest of your litter. We welcome this fight. Here? Outside? Choose, woman. I care not where you die."

Caleb took a step forward. Stilthius rose to his feet drawing up beside Tyris with his hammer in his hand. "Please."

Caleb's hand caught Rossin's shoulder and eased him back from the table. "We'll see you again, outlanders."

Tyris spat at them, barely missing adding to the sopping mess that was Rossin's chin. "The sooner the better, ladies."

The Tassaren brothers backed away, shuffling to the door without ever taking their eyes off the brothers. Caleb elbowed a man aside and dragged Rossin out, the two of them disappearing back out into the street.

"We should have killed them here," Tyris muttered.

"Patience," Stilthius answered. "The time will be right and we will know when it is. No good could have come from a fight here. Too many people to interfere and a city full of soldiers ready to get between us."

"I suppose." He still would rather have split their skulls than let them slip away.

His brother clapped him on the shoulder. "We'd best wake Jantalus and Halonni – let them know what's happening."

Tyris began collecting the spilled coins. "Suppose so."

Stilthius made no move to help him. "You were quick to challenge them. Do you feel it too?"

"Feel what?"

"Hunnaris's call. His promise that this is our destiny."

Tyris snorted and shook his head. "I feel like I need another drink and a pretty face attached to my cock."

"Then why challenge them?"

Tyris shrugged. "I was getting bored."

Stilthius sighed. "You stupid bastard."

Chapter Nineteen

Jantalus waited no longer than the time it took to wake Halonni and gather their things to leave the tavern behind after the Menion brothers told him about their confrontation with the Tassarens. It occurred to him only after they were deeper into the center of Ailen and mingling with a crowd of late-day market goers that they had fled without a plan for their next destination, but being away was enough for now. He feared being spotted in the open, but it was preferable to being cornered. He agreed with the assessment Tyris had made a day earlier that the Tassarens were not going to be deterred by the presence of others. Still, he found a small measure of reassurance in the idea that they had the chance to see them coming rather than being killed in their sleep.

They kept their cloaks tight and their cowls low, but it seemed a foolish precaution beyond himself to Jantalus's mind. Avoiding the curious gaze of a citizen of Ailen was fine considering his mark, but the Tassarens or anyone else actively looking for them was not about to miss the pair of black-skinned monsters who accompanied them. Tyris and Stilthius were as subtle as piss in fresh snow, a head taller than and twice as broad as almost every man they passed.

"We could ask if anyone has seen Addicus," Halonni suggested after they had paused at the end of a line of merchant's stalls along the road. They had been wandering for a time, silent and searching for some idea of what to do and where to go.

"Ask who?" Tyris shook his head.

Stilthius turned away from them all, looking north at the snow-capped mountain peaks that loomed over the town. "A guide."

His brother shot him a sideways glance. "What? A guide to where? We have no idea where we are going."

"No, not us. I mean Addicus or Finn and the others before him. Think about it." He turned to Jantalus. "Those mountains are nothing but ice and beasts and canyons waiting to swallow you up by the look of them. I don't give a shit who your father or any of the rest of them were. Unless they lived here, how the hell could they know where they were going? They would need someone to help them through."

Jantalus thought on it a moment. "If they vanished, their guide probably did too."

Stilthius shrugged in return. "Someone here would still know he went. They might also know where."

Tyris still looked unconvinced. "Awful lot of someones around here to just start asking. We'll draw attention too. That will have those black-eyed fucks back on us." He glanced in Jantalus's direction. "No offense."

The sorcerer dismissed the comment with a wave of his hand. "So who do we ask? Who would know?"

"They'd need mules," Halonni said stepping into the little circle they had formed. "If they were here late in the fall or early in the spring, there would be too much snow and ice for horses. Someone must have provided them."

That someone was a horse trader named Kitmen Zherm. They found him shoveling mud and shit out of a corral not far from the central market where Halonni had suggested the idea. He was a small, wiry man, bald and wrinkled, his face set with deep lines that owed as much to hardship as hard work. He looked up from his task as they approached and nodded, leaning heavily on his shovel. He introduced himself as a trader in horses and other animals, but gave no indication of enthusiasm for his work in any of it.

"Went into the mountains, did they?" Stilthius asked, pressing the trader about the people he claimed to have seen.

Kitmen Zherm spat in their direction, his dark, squinting eyes turning toward the high jagged peaks. "They did. Fucking mountains."

"Last fall?" Halonni insisted. "A man bearing the device of a black bird and several others?"

Kitmen Zherm cocked an eyebrow at her. "What's your interest in all that, pretty girl?"

"They were friends."

The horse trader shook his head. "Were is right. Nobody came back from that. Every last one disappeared in the Tijian."

"Some came back," Jantalus told him, his head bent beneath his cowl.

Kitmen Zherm scowled at him. "What is it you folks want? I'm busy and, like I said, I have nothing to do business with even if I wanted to."

"We need to know where they went," Halonni told him. "We are looking for more survivors."

Zherm stared at her, his eyes flat and dull, his face devoid of emotion. "Little young to be throwing your life away, pretty. Best you let this alone and go back where you came from."

"Then you know who they were and where they went?" she asked.

"I told you to forget it, girl."

Tyris took a step forward, his big hands knotted into fists. Halonni caught his arm and backed him away with a shake of her head. She flashed Kitmen Zherm a small smile. "Why don't you let me worry about what I should and shouldn't do? We can pay you for information if that is your concern."

"Money?" He snorted. "You can shove your money up your-."

Tyris came forward again, crossing the space between them in one quick step. "Watch what you say. You show a little respect or I'm going to hit you as hard as I can, little man."

Kitmen Zherm swallowed hard and nodded. "Not looking to get hurt, mister."

"Dead," Tyris corrected. He dug into his pocket and produced a handful of silver coins. He took the trader's arm, turned it over and pressed the coins into his palm. "We'll keep this business. You tell us what you know and you get the money. You make another comment I don't like and I'll knock your ugly fucking head off of your shoulders. Do we have an agreement?"

Kitmen Zherm gave a hurried nod.

"Answer the nice lady's questions then."

"I'm not looking for trouble. I just-." He looked Tyris Menion over carefully. "You folks aren't looking to hurt anyone? Anyone at all? Just information?"

"Some of the missing are family," Jantalus told him.

The horse trader gave them all a final measuring look and sighed. "All right then. You all follow me."

"Follow you where?" Tyris asked without moving.

Zherm jerked a thumb toward the building behind him. "To see the only man who knows where that lot you asked about went."

"And how does he know?" Halonni had not moved either.

"He went with them."

Kitmen Zherm's home was large and comfortable, twice the size of any other on the street and warmed by two huge hearths. A young woman was sweeping the stone floor when they entered, her eyes flicking over them without any sign of concern. Zherm dismissed her with a wave of his hand and she turned away, disappearing though a doorway. He led them to a collection of chairs arranged in a small circle before the larger of the two fireplaces and invited them to sit. Halonni and Jantalus took a pair of chairs closest to the fire, but Stilthius and Tyris stood where they were.

Kitmen Zherm, silent throughout the short walk from his corral to the home, looked as though he regretted bringing them. His hands clasped and unclasped as he paced a small section of floor, his eyes on his feet as if he feared to meet their gazes. Finally, he stopped and lifted his head.

"Dareth Sya is an old friend of mine. We have known each other since we were children. He was a tracker, a guide who helped people through the mountains. The route for merchants and the like is simple enough – you head north through Agron Pass and stay on it until you come out the other end. Dareth helped people who might not want to be spotted by Alliance patrols or anyone else looking. He knew the secrets of the Tijian, the forgotten trails from the miners who abandoned the area long ago and the cave networks that honeycomb the mountains."

"He took the people we're looking for into the mountains?" Halonni asked, edging forward in her seat.

"He did. Only he came back and I am not sure he should have. There's not much left of him now. How he survived to get back here, the gods only know. He rarely leaves his bed and never goes out of the house. He says evil spirits still look for him and he is afraid they'll find him. I am not sure his mind is any better off than his body. I'll see if he will talk with you, but even if he does – and I can't promise he will – I am not sure how much help it will be."

"But you brought us here," Jantalus said. "Why? You could have told us whatever you know and sent us on our way."

Zherm straightened a bit. "I owe Dareth Sya. What and why probably wouldn't mean much to you folks, but I do. Maybe you know something that will put those fears of his to rest. If not, maybe you'll find it in whatever direction he points you. He shouldn't be here, you see. His body and mind are too far gone. But I think he's waiting. I don't know what for, but maybe you do. Maybe that's what he needs to let go."

Jantalus nodded once. "Fair enough."

Zherm turned toward a door at the rear of the room. "Wait here."

A moment of hushed, indistinct conversation followed by shuffling feet and a creaking sound that might have been an old bed reached through the thin walls. Halonni gasped and shrank back into her seat as Kitmen Zherm emerged from the shadow of the doorway, all but dragging a second man into the firelight. Dareth Sya was something only vaguely human. One arm was drawn across Zherm's shoulders, holding him upright. Opposite it was only an empty sleeve. He shuffled his feet as he moved, his legs twisted at odd angles and barely supporting him. One eye was sewn shut with small black stitches, the face above and below deeply scarred. His skin was mottled and loose, drooping from him as from a corpse. His hair was yellowed and thin, hanging like a filthy veil.

Kitmen Zherm steered him to the nearest chair and eased him down opposite Jantalus and Halonni. Dareth Sya all but collapsed into it, his body trembling, his head lolling back. His hand clutched at the arm of the chair, fingers thin and curled like the talons of hawk. His body quivered as he drew trembling breaths. Finally, he lifted his head and turned to Zherm.

"Cold," he muttered.

The other man retrieved a blanket and draped it over him. Dareth Sya pulled it up under his chin with a shaking hand and fixed his good eye on the four visitors. "Who are you?"

Halonni leaned forward in her chair again. "We've come from-."

"Not you." The shaking hand lifted, one bony finger pointing at Jantalus. "You."

The sorcerer hesitated. A long silence hung in the space between them, broken only by the crackling fire and the rattling of Dareth Sya's breath in his chest. Finally, Jantalus reached up and drew away his cowl.

Dareth Sya hissed air through clenched teeth. "The mark of the dead." His finger jabbed out again. "You bring evil spirits. You come for me. You will have my soul!"

Kitmen Zherm took a step toward the door, his face gone ashen. Stilthius barred his way at once, shaking his head slowly. Dareth Sya was thrashing about in his seat, desperate to rise, but lacking the strength to do so. The serving girl they had seen earlier poked her head out from the doorway, her eyes wide.

"Enough!"

All eyes turned to Jantalus as he gained his feet, his black eyes sweeping the room, catching the light of the fire and gleaming like polished onyx. Zherm retreated to Dareth Sya's side and the stricken man stilled himself.

Jantalus shook his head at Dareth. "I don't know you. I'm looking for my father and Peridor Finn. If not them, a man named Addicus-."

"Malshere," the wasted man finished for him. He was calm again, more composed than he had been at any point. "I know them all." He drew a rattling breath. "Knew them all…"

"Then they are all dead?"

"I don't know." He ran his shaking hand through his filthy hair. "Maybe. Probably. Watched most of them die. Watched Mira die…" He trailed off with a choking cry.

"Mira?" Jantalus lowered himself back to the edge of his seat. "Mira Rhenn?"

Dareth Sya nodded and wiped at his single eye with his single hand. "She was among them when they came to me in the fall. They were chasing two men into the mountains and had lost their trail. I told them to forget it. The snow was already starting and the trails outside of Agron Pass are dangerous at the best of times, but they wouldn't hear it. They offered steel, coin, even jewels. I refused it all. What good is wealth when you are dead?" A gruesome smile twisted his ravaged face. "If only fate had been kind enough to grant me death."

He said no more for a time, staring into the flickering hearth, one thin tear slipping from the corner of his eye. When he spoke again, he did not look at any of them. "Joran Kathias was their leader. He was a magician of some kind, wielded power I can't begin to describe. The men he was hunting were his son and the man who had taken him. There were others. Soldiers, some of them. Mercenaries too. Peridor Finn was their commander, a nobleman turned sell-sword from what the others said. Hard lot, that bunch. But it wasn't their strength that convinced me any more than the money. They never did threaten me, but even if they had, I wouldn't have cared."

He leaned his head back against the chair and sighed. "It was Mira I went for. She never said a word when they met with me, but she convinced me just the same. My beautiful Mira. Odd, isn't it, what a pretty girl can make a man do with a smile? She had one too. That smile of hers could have melted the ice off the peaks of the Tijian. But you know what? It didn't. She was pretty enough." He gestured to Halonni, his good eye settling on her. "Not so beautiful as this one, of course, but prettier than a man such as myself should ever dream for. But it was not that sweet smile that drew me."

Dareth pulled the blanket up around him once more. "Tears. More powerful than any smile. When we are children, how do we draw our mother's attention? It is a lesson some of us never forget. I refused them thrice and was prepared to see them gone when I saw her tears. They were not for me to see, I think. It was no plan to manipulate me. They were pain and frustration and loss and too many days and nights spent chasing this man they were after. Her smile must have drawn me to her, I suppose. But the need to wipe those tears away caught me up, bound me, and never let me go. And so, I took them north, into the Tijian and to their doom."

"What happened?" Jantalus asked when he did not go on.

"Mordoc Tassaren happened," Dareth spat. "We followed him for weeks, always a step behind, always a moment too late. He left things for us, dark, dangerous things. He had a way of twisting the beasts of the mountains to his will, forcing them to serve him. They would wait in ambush and take a few of us at a time. He summoned spirits from another world as well, misty things that killed with a touch. Once, when we passed an old mining town, he used his power to summon the dead from their graves nearby and sent them against us. We never saw him, never. But soon enough, there were only six of us left. Six. When we left Ailen, we numbered almost thirty."

"Joran still led us. Peridor Finn was there too, of course. That bastard was impossible to kill. Myself and Mira remained, she because she had the magic like Kathias. Me? I must have been too stupid or too in love with her to know I was outmatched and far beyond my abilities. Cirrin Ravensbourne and his cousin, Kennis, were the last. They were noble men from Geften, related in some way to Finn, though I never paid much attention to how. Cirrin and Peridor were cousins maybe? Bah! What did it matter? We followed Mordoc to a place called Sentry, an old mining town on a mountain called Kiranon. He made his stand there. I saw Mira die and was wounded myself. I never saw any other. How I got here, I don't even know. Not alone, that's for sure. The men at the gate say two men brought me, dropped on the pass outside and turned north again."

He sighed and shook his head. "That's all I know. All I remember, at least. Best you all go. Go back where you came from and forget this matter. If the spirits don't kill you, the mountains will. Damned cold and wind will freeze a man to death. Slip once on the ice and you'll fall a thousand feet into some gorge. The people of the mountains – the Avaruns – have no use for outsiders either. Some of them would kill you just for trespassing. That's if a Valsen doesn't have you."

"Valsen?" Tyris asked from behind them.

"A cave bear," Kitmen Zherm explained. "Huge and strong. Fast too, can out sprint a horse over short distances. They blend with the rocks and ambush people and animals along the trails. I've seen them tear a horse in half in seconds."

Dareth was nodding beside him. "Best you leave it all alone. Just go home."

"I can't," Jantalus told him.

Dareth Sya's single eye narrowed at him. "Why? What is so important that you'd throw your life away for it?"

"I am Jantalus Kathias."

Dareth's breath caught. He struggled to straighten himself in his chair, his hand clutching at the arm as he pulled himself upright. "Come closer."

Jantalus pushed himself back to his feet and crossed the space between them. He paused a moment and then dropped to one knee before the twisted wretch, single eye and black eyes level. The twisted claw of a hand stretched out to him, stopped just short.

"You have your father's face."

"I need to find him. I need to know what happened – who I am."

The hand fell away. "Kitmen. My maps."

The trader turned and disappeared through the door that led to Dareth's room. A few moments later, he returned with an armload of scrolls, books and parchments. He dropped them on the seat of a chair nearby and held them up one at a time to the stricken tracker. Dareth pointed to those he wanted and waved away the rest. When they were finished, he gestured to Jantalus.

"Give them to him." Kitmen Zherm complied, handing a small stack of scrolls and papers to him. "The last time I saw your father or any of the rest was atop Kiranon. My maps will show the mountain and the town called Sentry. You cannot reach it from Agron Pass, not now. You need to climb the pass to where it meets Greylock Pass. Greylock Pass leads to the base of the mountain of the same name. The pass ends at a town there called Zantizan, another old mining place. Of all the old mining towns, only Zantizan remains. The remnants of the old guilds run it now. Cutthroats and thieves the lot of them. They might help you – if you can pay. Mount Greylock has many mines and tunnels. Some pass right through to the other side. Beyond Greylock is a valley and the peak at the other end of the valley is Kiranon. The trails and cuts are on the maps."

His hand caught Jantalus's as the sorcerer began to back away. "She's still up there."

"Mira? You said you saw her die."

"Her spirit waits. I do not know why. I know it does, because mine waits for hers."

Kitmen Zherm's hand settled on the thin shoulder. "Easy, Dareth. That's foolish talk and you know it."

Dareth shrugged the hand away with a snarl. "A fool now am I? She waits. I wait with her." The hand tightened on Jantalus's. "Perhaps, she waits for you."

The sorcerer knelt down before him again. "What do you know of me? What did my father say?"

The ruined face leaned close, fetid breath filling Jantalus's nostrils. "Mordoc coveted you. Coveted what you possessed. Magic. Power beyond controlling. Power enough to stand against the Vicars." He shook his head. "I understood little of what he and Mira talked about. I know only that you were important to them both not only for who you were, but what you could do."

"And Addicus Malshere? What role does he play here?"

Dareth frowned, his ruined face exaggerating the sag of his cheeks. "He was Mira's grandfather. She spoke of him often. He came here weeks ago, asking what you ask. I sent him to Kiranon too. No maps, though. He claimed his magic would guide him. An hour? Less? And then, he was gone. I never saw him again."

He slumped back into his chair. "I remember no more."

Jantalus rose. "You remember enough."

Kitmen Zherm adjusted the blanket around his friend. "He needs to rest. You should go."

Jantalus gathered the maps under his arm and waved his companions to the door.

"Sorcerer."

He looked back to find Dareth Sya's single eye staring up at him. "When you reach Kiranon – reach Mira..." He swallowed a lump in his throat. "If she is there still, if she suffers..."

Jantalus nodded. "I will do anything I can for her."

A small sigh escaped him and Dareth Sya sagged back into his chair again. His eye closed. His thin lips twisted into what might have been a smile.

Chapter Twenty

Caleb Tassaren opened the door without making a sound. Beside him, Rossin was grinning like a fool, drooling a long line of clear saliva down the front of his tunic. The rest of his siblings were a dark presence behind him, their impatience a palpable annoyance. Rossin leaned forward to look inside and Caleb swatted at him. It was still daylight and there were enough people about that being quiet and unseen was the best choice.

They were too late. They all knew it, but something remained to be learned here. After their confrontation with the outlanders, Caleb and Rossin had returned to Shantara, reasoning that their quarry would flee the city at once. As it turned out, they had been in something less than a hurry. By design or dumb luck, they had managed to melt away into the citizens of Ailen, leaving no trace.

None but the horse trader and his home.

He shot Rossin a warning glance and slipped inside, padding across the stone floor without a sound. A girl was hanging wet clothes on a line that stretched across the front of the room, her back to them as they approached. Two men sat in the chairs near the fireplace. One of them was slumped over sleeping and the other was facing away from them, a thin ring of pipe smoke rising up around his balding head. Two hearths blazed to either side of them, throwing enough heat to make it all a bit uncomfortable for Caleb's taste.

He crept up behind the girl while she was working and clamped one hand over her mouth and nose the other seizing her throat. Her eyes bulged and her body went rigid, her head twisting slightly to look at him. Caleb held her tight, waited until she blacked out, and lowered her to the floor without a sound. As he started for the man with the pipe, he saw a knife flash in Rossin's hand, his mad, wild eyes fixed on the girl. He held up a hand to stop him, shaking his head.

Rossin could do as he pleased, but not until the situation was firmly under their control.

With a look might have been disappointment, his half-brother lowered the knife and waited. Caleb's eyes flickered to the door for a moment, Samarus, Shantara and Faylor barely visible as indistinct shapes crowded at the threshold.

Less to worry about there, he told himself. They were all eager, to be sure, but none of them was as foolish or impulsive as Rossin.

He reached down to his boot and slipped his dagger free, stalking to the back of the chair, pipe smoke mixing with the scent of ale as he approached. Fluid, silent, perfect. He waited for the man to pull the pipe from between his teeth before reaching around in a blink, his hand tight against the coarse stubble of his lips and chin. The gleaming blade of the dagger pressed against his exposed throat as Caleb put his lips to the man's ear.

"No sound or I'll make you a pretty red necklace. Understand?"

The man managed a slight nod.

Caleb eased his hand from the quivering chin and patted him roughly on the cheek. "That's a good lad." He motioned his siblings forward without turning away. "We're here to talk, my kin and I."

The man's eyes darted to the four who crowded around him and then back to Caleb. "What do you want?"

Caleb reached down to the small table beside the man and lifted his glass, helping himself to a swallow of ale. "You met with people today?"

"Yes."

"And you know where they are now?"

The man shook his head. "They left a few hours ago."

Shantara leaned forward and took the man's chin in her strong hand. "Left for where?"

"The mountains. They are looking for someone." He licked his lips. "Please. I'll tell you anything I know. Just don't hurt us."

Shantara gestured to the scarred man in the next chair. "Who is this?"

"A friend." His eyes widened again. Fear. "Please."

Faylor stepped around the chair beside her and drifted over to the sleeping man, a wispy, empty thing in her black cloak. Her thin hand reached out to touch the weathered face, fingers trailing over the stitched eye and down the ruined face. She raised her hand to her lips and licked her fingertips.

"Magic," she whispered, her voice something thin and weak like a child's. "Not his. He has been touched by another."

"Kathias?" Samarus asked.

Faylor shook her head from within her cowl, her face all shadows. "A Vicar, and…" She looked back at the sleeping man. "Father."

"Father?" Shantara's eyes snapped to the slumped figure in the chair. "Then he was there?" The black eyes narrowed. "I don't remember him."

Rossin crept closer. "I do." He raised his knife and traced the scar that ran down the man's brow, through his damaged eye and trailed along his cheek. "I know my work when I see it."

"Leave him be!" the other man called, surging forward in his chair.

Shantara shoved him back, hard. "Be still or he'll look positively handsome by comparison when my brothers are done with you." She turned to Caleb. "Have a look around."

He nodded and left them, searching through the remaining room so the home for anything of use. In the rear of the building, he found piles of books and maps that had been shuffled through with some obviously missing. Caleb skimmed over what was left, a clear pattern emerging at once.

"Kiranon," he announced as he returned to the parlor. "They came here for information. They might have taken maps with them."

Shantara cocked an eyebrow at the man seated before her. "Did they?"

He nodded quickly. "Yes. They needed to know the way to Kiranon. We gave them maps and Dareth told them about the men he led there in the fall. Then, they left. They did not return and I don't know where they are now."

Shantara was shaking her head. "Needed to know the way to Kiranon?" She looked up at Caleb again. "How is that possible?"

He shrugged. "It isn't." He bent over the man she was talking to and caught a handful of his tunic. "This piece of shit is lying to us."

The man's hands came up at once, fingers laced together, his whole body trembling. "It's the truth, I swear on my life."

Caleb jerked him forward, their noses nearly touching. "That's exactly what you are swearing on, asshole."

Samarus gestured toward the sleeping man. "If he was at Kiranon, I could look inside his mind and learn what he knows."

Shantara waved him off. "Why? We were there. We know as much as he – or more." She tapped a thick finger on her square jaw. "Why would Jantalus Kathias need a map to get to Kiranon?"

Rossin shrugged and flashed his fool's smile. "Maybe he forgot the way."

Samarus snorted. "Mad bastard."

"No." All eyes turned to Faylor as she spoke. "He's right. He's exactly right."

Caleb waved a dismissive hand at his younger sister. "Like hell. Rossin's just shitting out his mouth as always."

Faylor held her ground, her faceless cowl fixed on Shantara. "Think. Jantalus has wandered about without purpose. He returned to Drappel even though he knew it to be destroyed. He stopped here – of all places – and we missed him only through bad luck. Why? If he knew what was going on – if he remembered everything – why come anywhere near here? Because he doesn't remember. He is not himself. Something happened, something to alter his memory of things. He's stumbling about blind."

Samarus cursed and put his hands to his hips. "Stumbling right into Addicus Malshere if we aren't careful."

Shantara whirled on the man in the chair, her big hand latching on to his face, knuckles white. "Addicus Malshere. Do you know the name?"

The man nodded, eyes riveted on hers.

"Does Jantalus Kathias?"

He nodded again.

She thrust him away. "He cannot be allowed to reach Addicus. We will have to stop him in the mountains." She rose, looking them all over carefully before settling her gaze on Rossin. "I need him alive. Alive."

Rossin spun his long knife through his fingers. "How alive?"

Shantara shrugged. "Any little bit will do."

Caleb seized a handful of hair from the quivering man who sat before them. "And these bastards?"

Shantara shrugged. "Are no threat to us. Do what you will with them."

She straightened, beckoned to Faylor and walked out the door with her diminutive younger sister at her side. Samarus looked the room over a moment, shrugged, and followed after.

"Are you going to kill me?" the man asked, staring up at Caleb. His face was ashen and glistening sweat.

Caleb patted him on the head and smirked. "No."

The man heaved a sigh of relief.

Caleb stepped away and nodded to Rossin. "But I'm afraid he is."

Rossin threw his head back and laughed like a jackal.

The screams had already reached a high-pitched shriek by the time Caleb made it to the door. He heaved a sigh as he shut the door behind him and joined the others in the street.

"I'm sending Faylor back," Shantara told him as he joined his siblings. "The four of us should be more than enough to track down Jantalus Kathias with the men we have. After we have him, we'll regroup and decide our next move."

Caleb nodded. It was Shantara's decision to make. Father had been clear about who he trusted in his absence.

Samarus gestured toward the door and the shrill cries that sounded behind it. "This is a waste of time."

Caleb sighed. Samarus was right, but there was no changing things now. Rossin was so hard to keep happy sometimes.

Mad bastard.

Chapter Twenty-One

Jantalus and his companions did not debate leaving Ailen.

Dareth Sya's information coupled with the maps he had provided gave them a sense of direction and purpose that spurred action. The fact that the Tassarens were near and hunting them erased any lingering doubt about timing or further delay for preparation any of them might have harbored. Staying in Ailen was no better than lighting a signal fire for their pursuers to follow. The town was simply too small to hide in. Choosing the shops that lay away from the market square kept them from the majority of prying eyes, but they had no sure way to remain hidden. They simply gathered what they needed and set out as soon as they were able.

Jantalus remembered as they headed for the gate that Tyris and Stilthius had not slept the previous night. Their gambling and drinking had lasted until dawn and the arrival of Rossin and Caleb. Neither of the outlanders seemed to be suffering for it. They were laden with the bulk of their gear – canvas shelters, heavy cloaks and extra blankets – as well as their own weapons and mail, but carried on without complaint. Dawn was only two hours past by the time they were ready. A steadier flow of men and wagons was coming and going, offering a chance at concealment. They joined a small cluster of men and beasts that were headed out and tried their best to blend with the rest.

Nothing shielded them from any watching eyes here. Those they had left Ailen with turned south toward the Censharn Valley and Havenwood leaving them alone. There was no help for it, so they began their trek north, casting constant glances to the trail behind them. After a time, the pass began to climb, rising up into the knife edged peaks of the Tijian. The wind howled down from the north, funneled by the walls of stone around them, bitter and numbing. They wrapped themselves tight in their cloaks, bundled their hands in their sleeves and bent their heads against it.

True to Kitmen Zherm's word, no beasts of burden were to be had in all of Ailen. The few traders they had bothered to ask confirmed this for them. It was the same every spring, they advised. Until the merchant caravans began to move through the area, there would be no stock to sell. The traders in Ailen had fat purses from selling everything off in the fall, but had to wait for something to spend it on in the spring. That meant slow moving and heavy loads for Jantalus and the Menion brothers.

They struggled along the trail, hampered by a layer of snow and ice that clung to the hard ground. They slipped and stumbled constantly, fighting for every inch in the steepest places. They rested when they could, finding rocky outcroppings and huge boulders along the path to break the wind and offer respite. Always they watched the trail below them, expecting at any moment to find the Tassarens in pursuit. The companions never caught any sign of them, however, and relief turned to suspicion as the day wore on.

As the day wore on, they were too cold, tired and battered by wind to force themselves on. They chose a nook in the side of the pass that offered some protection from the wind and settled in to rest.

Nobody spoke, but Jantalus could feel the tension. The Tassarens were chasing them along a path that took no effort to follow. The wonder of how they had gone so long and so far without seeing the enemy was worse than knowing they were being chased. They wrapped themselves in heavy cloaks and blankets and stared out at the pass together.

None of them slept. They were moving again in a few hours, struggling up the trail in the wind again, hardly rested, but determined to press on. Still they remained silent aside from muttered curses when they slipped and dashed their knees on the hard ground or twisted an ankle trying to get a foothold in the ice and snow. All the while, the mountains rose up ahead, challenging, mocking. The pass behind remained empty.

As the sun was slipping away to the west, they came to Greylock Pass. It opened from Agron Pass in a great wide split, wedge shaped and flat, snaking around the outer edge of the mountains towering above it to the north. Like Agron Pass, this trail was well used and wide enough for wagons, but without the upward slope that had made footing so difficult. The mountain to the north blocked away the worst of the wind and blowing snow. They paused for only a moment to survey the area before turning into Greylock Pass and continued their journey to Zantizan.

The walked for hours, keeping a slow, steady pace, less concerned with the footing here, but careful not to take chances. The last rays of sun beat down on them from the clear sky and provided a measure of warmth in the absence of the wind. They shared a sense of comfort in the easier going and much of the tension slipped away. Tyris and Stilthius took to telling tales about battles and adventures and women that Halonni shook her head at, but laughed along with their boasts regardless.

Jantalus kept to himself for the most part, responding when spoken to but remaining silent otherwise, his attention focused on the path ahead and his mind wandering back to what might be close behind. To think they would stay ahead of the Tassarens forever was foolish. In fact, the more he considered the situation, it seemed nothing short of amazing that they had managed to avoid them for so long.

He was mulling it over when Tyris stopped him. The outlander pointed southeast, down the slope of the mountain below. They could see the lower reaches of Agron Pass and Jantalus recognized it as the spot from which Tyris had first seen Greylock Pass. It looked far less formidable from this distance, small and empty.

"We've made more progress than I would have thought possible," Jantalus said as they stood together at the edge of the path.

Tyris nodded, his face lined with a deep frown beneath his cowl. "Good progress considering we spent a few hours resting down there. Too much good fortune is usually a sign that it's about to start raining shit, my father used to say."

Jantalus turned to face him. "Meaning?"

The big hand lifted toward Agron Pass again. "Thirty men, by my brother's count, should be after us. So where the hell are they? Hiding? Not unless we are blind. So they are either so far behind us that they're too incompetent to be worried about or-."

"They're ahead of us," Jantalus finished for him, anticipating his point. "But how?"

The outlander shrugged. "Agron Pass was the only way into the mountains Dareth Sya knew – not the only way at all. If the Tassarens know where we are headed, they might just be waiting there or somewhere on the way."

"So we might be walking into an ambush."

Tyris snorted and turned away to join the others. "Might be?"

Chapter Twenty-Two

Every step became a cautious one after Tyris shared his suspicions with the rest of their little company. Regardless, they had no choice but to go on. They could not return to Ailen, even if they had wanted to. There was every reason to think the Tassarens had sent someone to watch for them in the event that they should discover the ambush or simply decide the climb was too much for them. The best option they had was to stay vigilant, spot the ambush before it was sprung and do what they could to slip past it. If escape was not possible, detecting the Tassarens first might still give them an advantage that Jantalus or Halonni could exploit through their magic.

Dusk had settled on Greylock Pass when good fortune, despite Tyris's dire prediction, finally favored them. They were winding through a snaking section of the trail where huge boulders lined the floor of the gap, creating something of a forest of stones. The cliff face above was jagged and uneven, all shelves of rock and small goat trails. Black holes, like a dozen eyes along the gray face of the mountain stared out across the Tijian. They took them at first glance for mine entrances, but the lack of suitable paths for men or beasts to reach them seemed to indicate they were caves. They were in the midst of a conversation about the idea of using one for their night's shelter when Jantalus spotted a small orange flare in one. It came and went in an instant, but he was confident in what he had seen.

He beckoned his companions back a bit to where the rocks shielded them from anyone looking out from the caves. "It was a signal," he told them. "It had to be. The ambush is here."

Stilthius dropped his pack and kicked it aside, his hammer gripped in his big hands. "There will be some behind us then, to cut us off when it is all sprung ahead."

Halonni glanced back, but the trail was dark and empty. "How many?"

The outlander shrugged. "A few. Enough to put a sword in the back of anyone who looks like they are turning to run from the ambush."

"And we walked right by them without seeing?" she asked, her eyes darting about in search of the hidden enemy.

"It's the right way to set an ambush," Tyris answered, sounding disturbingly carefree about it all.

Jantalus bent his head around the corner of the huge boulder at their backs searching for any sign of activity. "Do we have anything we could call a plan?"

Stilthius tapped the head of his hammer against his gloved hand. "The way I figure it, those black eyed bastards – no offense – will be ahead with most of their men. The handful waiting behind us will just corral us if we run. You and Halonni stay here and watch our backs and the two of us will go cut these fucks up."

"And if this all goes to hell?" Halonni asked, looking more than a bit concerned about the simplicity of it all.

Stilthius shook his head. "Girl, once the dying starts, it always goes all to hell." He paused, lifting his eyes to the sky. He raised his hammer up toward the moon and bowed his head until it touched the steel haft. "Hunnaris, grant us strength."

A moment and he was done and moving though the rocks, retracing their path, Tyris at his side. Jantalus watched them until they vanished from sight. He glanced up at the faint moon in the evening sky and wondered just how much help it would be to them. Better a wasted breath than no hope at all, he thought and then turned his attention back to the trail ahead, watchful for any sign of movement. Halonni crouched next to him, her cowl pulled back from her pale face, her black hair hanging loose about her shoulders. She did not look at him, her eyes riveted to the shadows ahead.

They waited and watched, knowing it all had to turn to chaos, and anxious for it to begin just to break the tension. When it erupted into mayhem, it was Tyris's bellowing roar that sparked it, a massive shout that echoed through the pass. A high-pitched shriek and the clash of steel followed. Jantalus risked a quick glance behind him, but saw only darkness.

Halonni was tugging at his arm as he turned back, one thin finger pointing. A dozen men, cloaked and hooded and stealing through the shadows of the half-light like they belonged to it, approached. In the instant he saw them, his blood began to burn. It was all familiar enough to him now. He knew what the warning meant.

Necromancers. The Tassarens.

The first of the black cloaked men, naked sword flashing silver in the dark, was upon them when Halonni struck. The man had slipped between the boulders, his attention focused on the darkness beyond and the sounds of battle he heard. Halonni side-stepped the cover of the huge rock and thrust one hand out, a burst of wind tearing through the air between them and hammering into the unsuspecting man. The wave caught him, lifted him from his feet and slammed him with bone shattering force against a boulder. He collapsed without a cry, but the shockwave of the magic and the sound of the body striking the rock alerted all of the men.

Two more men rushed toward them and Halonni's magic hurled them away as well. The rest scattered, seeking cover behind the huge rocks and waiting. Waiting, Jantalus knew, for the Tassarens to even the odds. There was no sign of the Necromancers, but Jantalus could still feel their magic. He stayed where he was, still partially concealed by the boulder, Halonni pressed against him.

One of the men who had taken cover peeked out and pointed, shouting to someone unseen. Halonni reached a hand down and dug her fingers into the hard earth. As Jantalus watched, great tendrils of stone erupted from the ground beneath the shouting man, clamping down around him as they formed a huge fist, and pulling him down flat against the ground. He screamed and thrashed, but the stone hand held firm and with a final, brutal surge, it crushed the life from him and left him a broken, bloody heap. A pair of his companions broke cover and ran, shouting in fear.

Any hope that the rest would follow was quickly dashed by the appearance of the Tassarens. They approached as one, Shantara at their head, tall and broad shouldered like a man, strong and imposing as she stalked up the trail to the battle. Samarus was behind her to the right, bigger still than his sister, all sinister darkness in his black cloak and hood. Rossin and Caleb were to her left, smaller and quicker, moving with grace and speed the other two lacked, steel flashing in their hands. The remainder of the host followed, two dozen or more, a mass of black cloaks and flashing blades. The two retreating men stopped their flight at once and turned back to the battle.

Jantalus started to back away, thinking to fall back to a better position, to join forces with his friends to make a stand, but Halonni caught his arm. He turned to where her eyes were fixed to their left and saw a knot of men already working their way around. Tyris and Stlthius would have their backs to these if they were not stopped. It meant committing to a stand here, with the Tassarens and better than a score of men coming right for them. Jantalus knew what those odds meant. They meant death. Sacrificing their companions was not an option though.

"I have them," Halonni told him, her lips pressed against his ear. "Keep the rest off of me for a few moments."

He nodded and turned away without comment, stepping out into the open to face the Tassarens and their men. He gave no thought to how he would do as she asked, he simply acted. Tyris had told him at Spotter's Hill that fighting was like walking – once you learned, you never forgot. Magic, he learned in the few seconds it took for the men who approached to see him, was the same. Instinct overrode the blanks in his memory, shoved aside the doubt and the questions and made him something more than he could have been through conscious effort.

One of them loosed a bolt from his crossbow, but the invisible wall of magic Jantalus had already formed deflected it harmlessly away. Shantara and her siblings slowed at the sight of him, taken aback by his bold move. The hesitation lasted only a moment and then they were moving again, Shantara and Samarus coming directly for him while Rossin and Caleb split, one circling left and the other right.

Jantalus tried to watch them as they rushed for the concealment of the boulders, but Samarus and Shantara had their arms outstretched, black fire roaring forth. He summoned more magic, stiffening his defenses and his shield of magic caught it, the impact of it rocking him like a fist to the face. He staggered but held firm, his magic raging like a caged animal. The victory was illusory, he knew. The Necromancers did not even need to overpower him. If they could hold him in place, Caleb and Rossin or any of the others would simply run around and put a knife in his back.

Halonni's magic was tearing apart the earth behind him, crushing the life out of screaming men and hurling them across the pass into the cliff face beyond. She returned to him just as a pair of men rushed his flank, swords lifted. Her hands stretched out and a great burst of wind roared forth, hurling them back and away, sending them tumbling through the darkness. She turned her attention to Samarus and Shantara next, kneeling down to slam her palm against the earth at her feet as she had done against the horsemen in Urs. The ground beneath the two Necromancers heaved up and threw them back and away, their black fire flaring and then dying.

Rossin and Caleb appeared from their flanks just as Jantalus dropped his protective wall of force, black cloaked men a step behind them. Hemmed in, Jantalus seized Halonni's arm and charged forward toward where Samarus and Shantara had been, narrowly escaping the trap closing around them. The men gave chase and Jantalus swung about to send a rippling wave of force fanning out toward them. It knocked the closest men sprawling and rocked the rest, halting their advance. Movement behind him and to his left brought him back around in time to see Samarus emerge from the darkness, black fire spurting from his hands. Jantalus threw up a hastily formed shell of magic, but the Necromancer's magic hammered into him and sent him crashing backward.

He landed heavily on his back. The breath blasted out of him and he gasped for air, struggling to right himself. Samarus advanced, charging like some great, shambling bear. Black fire wreathed his hands as he dove atop the sorcerer, reaching for his face. Jantalus caught the thick wrists and tried to hurl him away, but Samarus was heavy and strong and bearing down with all of his fury, his face twisted in rage and his black eyes fixed and staring. The black flames that burned along his hands inched closer, the numbing cold prickling Jantalus's face. Already, he could feel his strength waning in the presence of the draining magic. With a cry, his magic flared, exploding out of him without focus, a desperate, panicked last resort. The shockwave blasted Samarus free, tearing his wrists from Jantalus's strong grip, and sent him tumbling away. He slid across the hard ground and stopped against one of the boulders, unmoving.

Jantalus rose to his feet, his body shaking with weakness and exertion. His vision swam for a moment and he shook his head to clear it. A knot of black cloaked men rushed him from his left, weapons lifted as they shouted to their fellows. He turned toward them, but his every action was somehow exaggerated and he could not focus his magic. The sound of battle roared in his ears, overwhelming his own voice as he tried to force himself to concentrate and defend himself.

The men were a dozen feet from him when Stilthius and Tyris appeared, hammer and axe hacking. Three men were down before the other four knew what was happening. They tried to turn about to face their new attackers, but, as they did, Stilthius stabbed one through the throat with the top spike of his hammer. A moment of hesitation cost another his head when Tyris tore it off with a brutal slash of his axe. The remaining two began to backpedal.

Jantalus searched about for Halonni, but it was too dark and the trail too littered with the massive boulders to see much of what was going on. He looked back to where Samarus had fallen into a crumpled heap, but he was gone. Jantalus stumbled forward, searching the shadows cast by the towering rocks.

He found Halonni between a pair of massive boulders, her hands outstretched and weaving an invisible pattern in the air. Shantara stood twenty feet ahead, her own magic flaring about her. The ground shifted around and beneath them as first one and then the other tried to twist it into weapon. Each of them was able to counter the other at every turn, locking them in a stalemate.

He rushed forward to help just as Halonni gained the upper hand. She summoned a great stone fist like the one she had used earlier, drawing up from the ground at Shantara's feet. It was smaller than the one she had used before, and Shantara turned her magic against it and forced it back into the earth. A distraction, Jantalus realized. Shantara had assumed it a full attack and used a great surge of power to force it back, leaving her unprepared as Halonni struck with a more forceful assault. Her hand thrust out, and a great torrent of wind exploded forth, whirling about Shantara in a rush. It lifted her, spun her in violent circles and then vanished, dropping her to her face upon the hard earth. Shantara hit with a dull thump, her head lifting a bit and her hands reaching out, but she collapsed again with a cry.

Halonni might have finished her if not for Samarus. He charged at Halonni from the shadows. Jantalus shouted a warning and Halonni turned, but Samarus was already on her, his hands reaching, the black fire flaring. Halonni shielded her face with her hands, fighting to push him away. Jantalus reached him at the same time, summoning his magic in a protective shell about himself to ward off the fire as he grappled with the big man. He managed to pull him away from Halonni, one hand on his dark cloak and the other with a handful of cowl and the hair underneath. Samarus tore at him, his hand clutching at Jantalus's face, but the shield of pure force he had encased himself in held for the moment, keeping the black fire from draining his strength.

His magic thwarted, Samarus was still a powerful man and he pressed Jantalus backward, trying to throw him to the ground. Back and forth they struggled, each fighting to overbear the other and create an opening. Jantalus felt his strength waning, his head still swimming from his first encounter with the Necromancer. His vision was blurred and doubled, but he held fast to the other man, refusing to be pushed away. Halonni came at the Necromancer from his left, a rock the size of Tyris's fist in her little hand. She raised it to strike, but Samarus kicked out at her as she did. His heavy boot came down on the side of her knee and Jantalus heard a loud popping noise. Halonni screamed, the rock tumbling from her hand and fell to the ground.

The kick had drawn Samarus off balance and Jantalus yanked him to the side, slamming him hard to the ground. Samarus landed on his face with a groan and immediately tried to push himself up on his hands. Jantalus fumbled for the rock Halonni had dropped, snatched it up, and threw himself on the Necromancer's back before he could rise. He brought the pointed edge of it down against the back of Samarus's head with a crunch, blood bubbling up over his hands. A second time and then a third he hammered, blood spattering his face and tunic.

Footfalls thudded against the earth behind him and he turned to see Rossin Tassaren charging. He scrambled from Samarus's back, nearly tripping over his body as he did, and rose. Rossin was on him before he could summon his magic. Sword and long knife lifted toward him, flashing in the pale streams of moonlight. Jantalus raised his arms to defend himself, his shell of magic still intact but weak and unfocused. The sword slashed down against his forearm, turned aside by the protective magic but jarring him backward. The knife came for his face and he threw a hand up to stop it. His magic was crumbling, his focus too scattered and his strength drained. The knife broke the last of his defenses. Through the palm of his hand and out the back it plunged, smooth, easy, almost effortless. Blood cascaded down his wrist and forearm in a rush, and he jerked his hand free, the blade tearing more flesh as it pulled away. He clutched it to his side and lifted his free hand, a burst of magic, weaker and less focused than he had hoped, rippled forth, staggering Rossin back.

Too weak, he cursed himself, too little to stop the madman. Worse, Caleb Tassaren had just appeared at his brother's back, twin swords ready. As feeble as the attack had been, it ultimately saved his life.

The moment of hesitation by Rossin gave Stilthius Menion the time he needed to insert himself between them. His hammer whirling in a deadly circle, he charged the two men with an ear-splitting cry, every bit as quick and graceful as the smaller men. Rossin tried to stand his ground, sword lifting to defend himself, but the sheer force of Stilthius's attack knocked the sword away and sent him sprawling. Caleb attacked at once, cutting at the outlander from his flank, but Stilthius turned about in time to meet it, slapping both of the scything blades away and jabbing back at him with the spike atop his hammer. Caleb shuffled back, circling around, trying to find an opening, but Stilthius matched him step for step, jabbing at him to keep him from moving to his flank.

Rossin recovered as the two men feinted and jabbed at each other, rushing back to the fray. Jantalus lurched forward, trying to stop him, but stumbled to one knee, dizzy and unsteady. Stilthius had seen Rossin and pivoted away, retreating to where he could put his back to one of the huge boulders, keeping the brothers in front of him. They pressed him from both sides, pulling him one way and then the next like wolves bringing down a deer, but Stilthius was patient and controlled and did not expose himself by overcommitting. Caleb's sword slipped through his defenses and scored a grazing slash across the outlander's thigh, but Stilthius thrust at him with his hammer and drove him back without so much as a pause.

Jantalus tried again to rise, but his legs had lost all strength and he could not make them work. He looked beside him to find Halonni crawling forward, one leg dragging uselessly behind her, her attention focused not on the battle between Stilthius and the Tassaren brothers, but where Shantara was staggering to her feet.

Shantara's bloody face lifted toward them, her black eyes fixed and her lips curled. She ignored the battle between her brothers and the outlander and stalked forward, shuffling along with a pronounced limp. Jantalus tried to summon some bit of his magic, thinking only that he needed to stop her, but he had nothing left. He braced his arms against the ground and pushed, forcing his legs to move beneath him, struggling to his feet. He teetered and nearly fell, but steadied himself with an effort. He stooped and took Halonni's arm with his good hand, his head pounding with the effort, his vision dimming for a heartbeat before refocusing. She pushed herself up with one leg, the other bent at the knee and unresponsive as she sagged against him. Jantalus retreated as Shantara continued to advance, gaining on them despite the limp. He all but dragged Halonni along, all of her weight on him as she gripped his cloak in her hands, her face twisted in pain, air hissing between her clenched teeth.

Jantalus dragged her behind the closest boulder and put their backs to it, gasping for breath. He thrust his bleeding left hand under his right armpit and pressed down, but the blood continued to flow, soaking his tunic and running down his pant leg. He closed his eyes and tried to think. Shantara was coming and neither he nor Halonni had the strength to match her magic now. That left Tyris, but he had not seen the outlander since he had saved him from the Tassaren's men and could not be sure he was even alive. Stilthius was battling two men and could not last if more joined the fray. Certainly, none of them was a match for Shantara.

He turned his attention to the rough face of the mountainside above them. The black holes of cave entrances stared back at him, cold and empty. His strength was nearly gone and his magic with it, but up there, in the dark with no room for Shantara to move and use her elemental magic, he might snare her. He needed to get close enough, to force her into a tight space. The cave or a narrow spot in the trail would serve his purpose. He was a fool to try as weak as he was, but if he could draw Shantara away, he would at least be giving the rest of them a chance, small as it might be. He looked down at Halonni and her injured leg and wondered at his own sanity. The thought that he would be able to drag himself up one of the steep, narrow trails to the nearest cave, some twenty feet above them, was laughable. To think he could all but carry her as well was nothing less than stupid.

And yet, a moment later, he had his cloak off and balled about his bleeding hand, his good arm around her waist to support her, and was staggering toward the faint goat trail that began at the base of the cliff face. He stumbled and tripped, catching himself against the cold, hard rocks to either side of the uneven path, his feet finding every knot and hole in the dark. He lost track of Shantara and he could not see anything of what was happening below from where he stood. He pressed on, dragging Halonni along, hoping Shantara was following and not turning her attention to their companions. The trail turned sharply, cutting across the face of the slope and he looked back, finding himself with a clear view of the pass below. He dropped to one knee and leaned on the rocks, one arm still around Halonni as he watched.

Stilthius was still backed against the huge boulder, Caleb and Rossin lunging and feinting, trying to break his defenses. Stilthius drew Caleb in, pretending to slip, and the Necromancer took the chance to commit to a wild slash with both blades. Stilthius surged forward, his broad shoulder lowered and crashed into him, lifting him from his feet and charging the boulder behind Caleb. He slammed the helpless man into it, crushing him between his shoulder and the stone and dropped him in a heap.

How the outlander sensed Rossin was at his back, sword and knife lifted, Jantalus never knew, but Stilthius spun about, his hammer lifted and blocked the attack. He pressed the smaller man back, the great steel weapon spinning and thrusting, hard, jarring blows pounding against Rossin's hasty parries. The scarred man shuffled backward, trying to twist away, but Stilthius gave him no room to move. Finally, one thunderous blow knocked the sword from Rossin's hand.

Rossin smiled like a fool and simply vanished from sight. Stilthius retreated at once, placing his back to the nearest boulder, his hammer lifted and ready. A moment of calm and silence allowed him to catch his breath and then Rossin appeared again, slashing with his long knife from the side, aiming for Stilthius's unprotected head. The outlander raised an arm to ward it off, the blade tearing his cloak but skidding off the mail beneath. Stilthius launched a mighty swing of his hammer. Rossin danced away and promptly vanished.

A second time he blinked into view again, this time on the opposite flank, the dagger jabbing at Stilthius's face. Stilthius twisted aside, the knife glancing harmlessly against the boulder and kicked at him. Rossin was spinning away and vanishing again before the blow could connect. Twice more he flashed into view and twice Stilthius's mail turned aside the knife blows as he shielded his head with his hammer. Rossin vanished away each time and Stilthius put his back to the stone once more.

Instead of waiting for him to come back, Stilthius was moving, dashing forward from the protection of the boulder toward a patch of empty ground. Rossin blinked into view before him, crouched low, the fallen sword in his hand. Stilthius, Jantalus realized, must have seen it move and realized what was happening. The hammer lifted, crashing down on the half-raised blade and knocking it from his hand once more.

Rossin tried to recover at once, stabbing forward the long knife at Stilthius's face, hoping the outlander would retreat. Stilthius caught the little man's wrist in one huge hand and jerked the arm out wide. Rossin only had time to throw his free arm over his face in a futile gesture of defense before the steel hammer came crashing down, shattering his head like a glass bauble.

Stilthius thrust the ruined body away from him and raised his hammer to the moon, his massive head thrown back in a wild scream. "Hunnaris!"

Jantalus could not see who he was screaming to, but at the call, Tyris came running from the dark shadows at the other end of the battle to join him. Dark shapes trailed after him, a dozen or more, pressing around them to create an island near one of the huge boulders. The outlanders put their backs to it and waited, weapons ready.

Still alive at least, Jantalus thought. He scanned the area, searching for any sign of Shantara. Caleb still lay in a heap where Stilthius had left him. Jantalus thought he might have moved slightly, still alive, but no threat. Samarus's body lay forgotten and alone a short distance away, a crimson stain at the end of his black cloak all that was visible. He caught sight of Shantara at the far edge of the trail as she searched for them among the more densely packed boulders. Stilthius's shout snapped her attention away and she started back to where her men had them corralled.

Jantalus searched about until he found a sizeable stone and heaved it toward her. He missed her completely, but it struck a nearby boulder, drawing her black stare to him. He straightened and stared back, standing tall atop the trail, his arms wide in challenge. She called out for her men and started after him at once, still limping as she broke into a lumbering run. Jantalus waited long enough to see her men abandon his companions and then pulled Halonni up again and continued his climb.

He heard Tyris shouting and looked back to see the big man urging his brother after Shantara and her men. Jantalus shouted back, waving them off. They stopped, staring up at him in confusion. He risked a glance back at Shantara. She was closing on the base of the trail and some of her men had gained it already. A wild, foolish plan formed in his mind. It was so mad that he would have laughed at the stupidity of it had he time to think it over, but it was all he had.

"Run!" he shouted at his companions. "Run!"

Tyris hesitated, Stilthius pulling at his arm. The older brother understood, Jantalus realized. Perhaps he could not guess the plan down to the every detail, but Stilthius had an idea as to why he was being told to run.

Tyris still stayed where he was, his eyes fixed on Jantalus and Halonni. Jantalus shouted to him again, but the big man was rooted in place. Finally, Stilthius seized him from behind and began dragging back. Tyris resisted for a moment and then finally turned and ran.

Jantalus watched them for a heartbeat and then stumbled on, the black cloaked men closing. He feared for reaching the cave before they caught him, all the while wondering what difference it made. Halonni was panting next to him, her good leg weak and trembling as she hopped along, still clutching his cloak. He wanted to say something, to explain that he had a plan, as insane as it was, or that he was going to see them through, but, instead, he tightened his grip and dragged her on, hoping he knew what he was doing.

He was a dozen yards from the cave entrance, the trail so steep that he was sliding with every step he took, when he felt his blood burn. He turned to see Shantara, halfway up the trail already, her men charging ahead of her, her arms raised toward her prey. The wall of rock next to him warped and shifted, fingers of stone reaching out for him. The whole cliff face shuddered in response, huge chunks of rock above shifting and tumbling away. They fell wide of the trail, crashing down around Greylock Pass back where Tyris and Stilthius had surprised the men tasked with sealing the ambush. Shantara withdrew her magic at once, the fingers of stone melding back into the rock without ever reaching Jantalus and Halonni.

Just as I suspected.

He hurried on, skidding along the steep trail, straining to drag Halonni with him. He was halfway to the cave when he finally fell. They slammed against the rocks littering the path and began to slide back toward their pursuers. Halonni cried out in pain and Jantalus struggled for a hold on something, his injured hand all but useless wrapped in the bulky cloak.

Finally, his foot caught the edge of a huge rock next to him and he braced himself to keep from sliding further down the trail. Shantara's men were close. Spurred on by his fall, they rushed forward. He stretched out his injured hand, blood dripping from the soaked cloak and summoned what feeble magic he had left. The surge of force he managed was weak, but it buffeted the closest of their pursuers and knocked them back. Two men lost their footing and went down, cutting the legs out from beneath those behind them. The lot of them went down in a heap. Jantalus released Halonni and the two of them crawled the remaining distance to the cave entrance.

He was at the very edge of the black opening when a warm, putrid puff of air blew into his face. He arched his neck, looking up into the cave when the red eyes appeared from the dark, and the low rumble sounded. He slowly crawled backward, his good hand locked on Halonni's arm as the massive muzzle inched forth, the huge shaggy head took shape and the white fangs flashed in the half-light. Huge and black, the beast filled the whole of the cave entrance, all black fur and claws, white fangs and red eyes.

Kitmen Zherm's tales had not done the thing justice. The Valsen was quite simply the most massive beast he had ever seen.

Jantalus's plan evaporated in an instant. He had hoped to gain the cave, trapping his enemies on the narrow pass, and use what little magic he and Halonni had left between them to let loose the massive rocks above them. The question of whether or not he and Halonni retained the strength to accomplish that aside, it was a plan that had relied on a great many things to go his way. The first of which, he realized, should have been the cave being empty.

The Valsen rose up on its hind legs and roared, the cry echoing through the pass and stopping Shantara and her men where they stood. Jantalus tried to retreat, but his feet slipped on the loose rock of the steep trail and he began to slide again. The Valsen dropped back to four legs and started after him, its huge head thrashing back and forth, fangs bared. It lunged and he summoned his magic, knowing it was useless to even try. The blow never fell. Halonni's hand thrust down against the trail, her magic flaring. Her strength spent, she had nothing resembling the force she had mustered against Shantara, but it was enough.

A wave rippled through the ground between them, creating a small ridge at the Valsen's feet. It tripped and sailed over them, crashing down the slope of the trail in a raging mass of fur and claws. It landed in the midst of the black cloaked men, crushing one under its great bulk. It twisted about and regained its feet in an instant, huge paws lashing out, claws rending leather and flesh. Men thrashed and screamed, blood spraying from severed limbs as the beast tore into them. The foremost were sacrificed as the rest quickly retreated, leaving their comrades to be slaughtered like cattle.

Jantalus watched the savage frenzy for only an instant before grabbing a handful of Halonni's cloak and pulling her up as he scrambled to the cave entrance. She cried out in pain as he jerked her along, her injured knee dashed against the hard ground. He dragged them both into the cave where she collapsed, clutching her leg in agony. Jantalus grabbed hold of the cave wall and pulled himself to his feet, his whole body shaking with the effort. The Valsen had finished the men it had trapped and was watching the rest as they fled.

In their midst, Shantara stood watching the beast, her black eyes fixed and unafraid even as her men abandoned her. The Valsen rose up on its hind legs once more, roaring a challenge. The Necromancer answered at once, her hand stretching forth, black fire erupting from her fingertips. It struck the beast about the face and head, drawing a shriek of pain and fury. It stumbled back and fell back. It hesitated only a moment and then swung its huge head around, seeking the safety of the cave.

The cave Jantalus was standing in.

A new roar went up from the Valsen and it came forward at once, scrambling up the rocky slope, quick and sure-footed. Jantalus had no time to think of what he was doing. He had to react or he and Halonni were dead. He stumbled free from the edge of the cave entrance and thrust his hands high over his head, sending a desperate surge of force up at the rocky mountainside directly above them. The surrounding stone shuddered as the power of his magic slammed into it and then, in a thunderous roar, it began to slide. The Valsen, paused, great head upturned. Somehow sensing what was happening, it launched itself down and away, springing toward the trail below in a powerful leap. Jantalus saw Shantara, her face twisted in anger as she raised her hands high, the power of her magic sending a searing surge of fire through his veins.

He turned to see Halonni struggling to her knees, her eyes fixed on the collapsing mountainside, her mouth hanging open in shock. He dove at her, tackling her away from the cave entrance as tons of earth and stone crashed down, sealing them inside and burying everything.

He tried to twist as they fell, thinking to cushion her fall with his own body, but barely turned at all and landed heavily atop her. The roar of the collapsing mountainside muffled her cries as they struck the hard floor of the cave.

He managed to slip a hand under the back of her head, saving her skull from the impact with the rock beneath them, but their heads clashed into each other's and everything went dark.

Chapter Twenty-Three

He woke to impenetrable blackness. For a moment, he panicked, believing himself back in the emptiness that his mind had retreated to for so long. It was the same darkness, the same isolation. Was it the magic he had used? Halonni had warned that there was a price to be paid. Maybe that was the reason for the pathetic existence he had lived for so long before. It could have been that he had used so much power, damaged himself to such an extent that it had taken years to recover and the price had been his memories. The possibility of being trapped in his dreams again stole over him so completely that he nearly despaired. He would not be like that again. Whatever his life was now, it was better than the cruel joke it had been.

And then, pain reminded him of where he was and why.

His senses returned as if he were emerging from a fog. It was still black as pitch and he could not see his hand in front of his face, but he knew for a fact it was there. Throbbing, stabbing pain reminded him with every beat of his heart. He could feel blood still leaking out from under the cloak he had wrapped about it, rolling in a thin, warm line down his arm as he lay on his back. His head pounded and he reached up with his good hand to dab at the slow trickle of blood from above his left eye. The rest of him ached and the rock floor of the cave dug into his back and shoulders.

He rolled onto his side and felt about in the darkness. "Halonni?"

No answer. He moved his legs to either side, but his boots only kicked rocks and dirt. He rolled over to the opposite side, his hands searching. He felt cloth under his fingers and rounded flesh beneath. He shook Halonni gently and called to her again.

"That's my ass," came the mumbled response.

He slid over toward her and felt for her hand with his good one. She clasped it and sighed. "Are you all right?" he asked.

"No."

He gathered his legs under him and struggled to his knees. They needed light, but his flint and steel was in his backpack and he had dropped that in the pass as soon as the ambush was sprung. He dug through his pockets, knowing as he did that he had nothing of use. He could feel the dagger Tyris had given him still tucked in his boot, but all of his other gear was gone. He reached down, feeling about until he found Halonni's hand again.

"Halonni?"

She mumbled something back at him.

"We need fire to see."

Halonni hissed in pain as she shifted a bit. "I can't create. I only manipulate what's already there."

He settled back down beside her, trying to gather his thoughts. Staying where they were was going to end predictably, but not being able to see made moving impossible. He was assuming, of course, that there was anywhere to move to. He felt around for a few small rocks and threw them in each direction, listening for the sounds they made. There were walls close to him to his right and directly ahead. The one to his left was further away and the stone he had thrown behind them fell to the floor before hitting anything.

"Can your magic give you a sense of the cave around us?"

She did not answer him.

He squeezed her arm gently. "Halonni?"

She stirred slightly. "What?" Her hand clutched at his. "Sorry, I blacked out."

He blew out a long breath and said nothing. Her magic was not going to help them here. He knew without asking she did not have the strength to use even the smallest amount. Anything done to help them was his to do. He thought about crawling along the cave floor behind them to see if he could find anything, but decided against it. If Halonni lapsed into unconsciousness again and could not call out to him, he might not find his way back to her. Worse, he had no idea what was in the cave. He might fall down a hole, strike his head on a rock or crawl right into some waiting beast that could see him in the dark.

He might try to use his magic to clear the rockslide from the cave entrance, but he brushed that idea aside as soon as it came to him. Aside from the fact he was not even sure which direction the cave entrance was, he doubted he had anything close to the strength he needed to move so much rock and earth. Of course, even if he did manage to move it, he risked bringing down even more of the mountainside that was resting atop it. It was something to consider if he felt no other options remained, but he had another question to answer first.

He bent down over Halonni again and shook her. "Awake?"

"Yes."

"I need your magic, just a touch of it. Can you manage it?"

He heard a shuddering sigh. "I can't Jantalus. I can't."

"Just a touch," he insisted. "If there is another entrance to this cave, there has to be fresh air. Can you tell? Can your magic do that?"

She did not answer him for time and he feared she had lapsed into unconsciousness again. He squeezed her hand and she squeezed it in turn. "Yes."

"Yes, you can do it?"

"Yes, there is another entrance. Behind us, but I have no idea how far. It could be as big as that Valsen or small as a coin."

It was enough either way, he decided. A chance, no matter how small, was better than he expected. What remained was finding a way to take advantage of that chance. The problem of stumbling about blind was still the pressing matter. Halonni's magic was no use to them in that, even if she had the strength left to use it. That left his, and he was not sure if it would do them any more good than hers. He sat in silence for a long time thinking it over, Halonni's hand still in his, reassuring both of them.

He toyed with the idea of using his magic as a buffer to protect himself while he staggered around in the dark. He might escape injury, but the idea of stumbling and falling for hours on end and possibly making no progress in those hours decided him against it. There had to be another way, he kept telling himself. He would not accept that for all he had been able to do to this point, all the obstacles he had overcome, that he would be defeated by mere darkness.

He was nearly to the point of admitting defeat, when the answer came to him from pure nothingness. It was a theory, a hypothetical use of his magic that he would need to test first, but the very possibility of it gave him a rush of energy. He squeezed Halonni's hand again and then released it, crawling a short distance from her toward the wall he knew to be somewhere ahead of them.

He held one hand out before him and summoned a tiny fragment of his magic, releasing a gentle wave of force out from him. He concentrated on the magic as it floated out in the inky blackness, feeling its movement through the cave. It struck the wall so gently it made no sound, rebounded and drifted back until he felt its gentle touch brush against him. A rush of victory washed over him, but he calmed himself and tried it again, this time widening the pulse of force, top to bottom and side to side, his total concentration on the magic as it traveled out. In his mind's eye, he drew an image of all of the things it touched and rebounded from, forming a crude three-dimensional picture of their surroundings.

The wall before them was what had been the cave entrance. He could visualize the huge boulders that had rolled just inside the mouth of it, missing them by mere feet. He stretched out the ripples of magic, sending them off to the sides as well. The far wall of the cave was some twenty feet away to his left, rocks and debris littering the floor between them. To his right, his magic rebounded off Halonni where she lay, a vaguely human shape in his imperfect use of the magic, the echo approximating her form. Beyond her was the third wall of the cave, some six or so feet away. He rose to his feet and turned about, sending a wave out to the vast expanse behind him. The magic flowed out until it faded away, vanishing without touching anything. He could not be sure how far it went before losing strength. More than twenty feet, he decided, based on the distance to the wall to his right.

He continued to release his magic in small pulses, creating a constant image of his surroundings for a few feet in all directions. He took a few testing steps, fearful that his magic was not sensitive enough to find small rocks or holes that he might trip over. His fears were well founded, but only partially true. Small cracks and bits of debris were still invisible to him, but he found that if he shuffled along, he could avoid tripping over them.

He returned to Halonni and crouched down over her. "I have to get you up," he told her.

"Up?" He saw her head shake as his magic echoed off her. "I think my leg is broken."

He bent and slipped his arms under her. He lifted her as gently as he could, but she still cried out softly as he jarred her injured leg. Cradling her like a child, he pulled her close and rose. "Too much?" he asked.

"N-no," she muttered through clenched teeth. "I'll be all right." She slipped her arms around his neck. "How do you plan to keep from falling on your face?"

He strengthened the pulse of his magic, drawing a mental image of the cave again. "I can see."

Her face turned towards him and he could only imagine to look she was giving him, but she said nothing. He started forward, sore and aching from their ordeal but driven by the need to be free of the cave. He shuffled ahead, careful not to trip or stumble, mindful of jarring Halonni or, worse, knocking them both down. His shoulders and back began to burn from carrying her despite how light she was, but he pressed on, doing his best to ignore it. His throbbing hand was harder to put out of his mind and he wiggled it out from under Halonni's thigh and put her weight on his forearm instead. It did little to alleviate the pain and he set his teeth and pushed on.

The cave began to narrow as he went, forming a passageway deeper into the mountain. He kicked aside small bits of material on the floor as he went, hollow little sticks that he imagined were the bones from the Valsen's prior meals. They crunched beneath his feet as he went, sending small rodents scampering away. He could hear bats along the roof of the cave as he went, but the ceiling was so far above him he could not even see it and they stayed where they were. He lost any sense of time as he went, fighting though pain and fatigue, but never losing hope that he would be free. His magic, minor as the use of it was here, was beginning to wear on him as well, exacerbating the ache that already ran through him in waves. He stubbornly pushed through it until he was numb, but continued to concentrate on the passage.

Finally spent, he put his back to the wall and slowly slid down to sit on the hard floor, Halonni cradled in his lap. "That's it," he told her. "I have to rest."

Her hand came up to his face as his magic faded away, plunging him into darkness again. "You did more than I imagined you could have," she told him. "We can try again later."

Her head sank down against his shoulder and he pulled his injured hand out from under her and laid his arm across her lap. The pain was almost unbearable, but he was so exhausted he felt himself drifting off. His last thoughts were of what might be in the cave with him, but he did not even have the strength left to worry about it.

He woke without knowing how long he had slept. His left hand was a pulsing bit of agony at the end of his arm and his back was cold and sore from the rock behind him. He summoned his magic again, drawing an image of the passage in his mind once more. Halonni was still slumped against him, her breath soft and warm on his face. He managed to slip his arm back under her legs and struggled to his feet without waking her. Nothing remained to him but determination and the hope that they would be free of the cave. He shuffled forward again. He was so thirsty his throat hurt and his stomach was an aching hole that grumbled at him as he went.

Halonni grew steadily warmer as he plodded on, her face beaded with sweat and the heat of her body uncomfortable against his. She stirred a handful of times but did not wake. He considered waking her, but decided against it. Instead, he adjusted her weight as best he could and forced himself on with a new sense of urgency.

He smelled the fresh air before he finally rounded the corner of the passage and saw the sliver of light that leaked in. He had not even bothered to try counting the hours it had taken to get them there, but the sight of the hazy rays of sun actually drained his sense of urgency and seemed to suck the last of his strength. He slumped to his knees and laid Halonni against the cold floor. He knelt, his head lowered and his aching hand clutched to his abdomen and questioned his strength to reach the end. Finally, he crawled forward, bent his head around the corner and looked. His breath caught and he slumped down against the wall as he turned away.

The crevice at the end of the passage was narrow, too narrow to squeeze through. He would need magic, his own or Halonni's, to escape. He sat back, too tired to crawl to Halonni and wondered if he would have the strength even to try.

The sound of Halonni's hoarse, strained voice calling to him snapped him awake. He bolted upright in a panic, confused for a moment. He had blacked out he supposed. He looked immediately for the streams of light from the nearby crevice and saw it still shining from around the corner. He looked back for Halonni, barely visible at the edge of that light. Propped up on one elbow facing him, she trembled like a newborn foal.

She sighed when he turned toward her. "I was afraid-." She drew a deep breath. "Never mind." She lifted her face to his again. "Light. You found the exit."

He pulled himself up, one hand gripping the wall behind him and made his way back to her. "A crack - too small for either of us to squeeze through. We'll have to make it wider and I don't think I have it in me."

She reached a hand up to him. "Then I'll have to."

He put his arm around her and pulled her up on one leg. She was shaking and burning with fever and nearly fell, but he caught her and lifted her off her feet. She put her head against his shoulder and heaved a heavy sigh. "I'm sorry."

For what he could not imagine, but he simply nodded and carried her around the corner of the passage to the tall, narrow gap in the rock. The sunlight burned his eyes and he looked away for a few moments until they adjusted. An icy wind blew through the opening, a welcome relief to the warm sweat that bathed his face. Halonni held one hand up to shield her eyes from the light as she studied it.

"Get me close enough to touch it," she told him. "Once it begins to open, get us through as fast as you can. I have no idea how long I can hold it open, or even if I can move it at all."

He moved them closer and waited while she readied herself. Her feverish face taut with concentration, she closed her eyes and took deep, steadying breaths. Finally, her trembling hand reached out, fingers pressing against the cold stone. Jantalus felt his blood burn as her magic rose up. Her delicate face twisted with the strain, her jaw tight. For a moment, nothing happened and Jantalus thought she was too weak. Then, the edges of the crevice began to draw back from each other like huge stone curtains parting. A low rumble shook the rock around them as the wall of the cave folded back on itself, grinding and scraping.

Jantalus did not wait for any signal from Halonni, surging forward with a burst of energy born of his need to be free. He nearly slipped and fell as he gained the broad flat shelf of rock beyond, righting himself just as Halonni's magic faded away. He backed them away from the opening just as the wall realigned and collapsed in on itself, the rock above shifting slightly to settle down over the newly formed gap. It was over in a thunderous crash and a great belch of dirt and air. Behind them, the crevice was completely sealed.

Jantalus turned them away from it and looked out from their perch. The noon sun lay across a long, wide valley before them, ringed all about by tall, snow-covered mountains. An endless carpet of evergreens lined the lower slopes, forming a deep, dark green ring around the valley floor below.

A river snaked through its center, rolling down off the mountains at the near end of the valley in a great waterfall and disappearing into the forests at the other end. The mountainside below the great terrace of rock they stood on sloped gently down to the forest floor, all firs and spruce as far as they could see. Jantalus lifted his face to the cold, biting wind and breathed in a great gasp of fresh air.

Lost, wounded, and bereft of anything but what they were wearing was the truth of it.

But alive.

Chapter Twenty-Four

They paused for only a brief rest near the collapsed cave entrance before moving on. The wind was brutally cold and they found nothing to use for shelter from it. Jantalus struggled down the slope of the mountain, nearly slipping on the uneven ground and sending them both tumbling, but managed to keep them upright and get clear. Once they reached the trees below the ridgeline, the rock gave way to earth and better footing. The trees sheltered them from the wind but blocked out the sun and he was soon numb with cold and shivering.

He could not help Halonni. Her skin covered in a damp sheen, she was still feverish and sweating through her clothing. Shelter and warmth were what she needed, but Jantalus doubted his chances for either. The evergreens here provided little to use for shelter and less to use as fuel for a fire. The oaks, elms and maples closer to the valley floor looked more promising and they needed to reach the river. He had no idea how long they had been in the cave above, but his thirst was consuming him and he had a crushing headache to add to his list of maladies.

The day wore on without relief and by the time the sun was edging toward the mountaintops in the west, Jantalus was convinced he would never make the river before his exhaustion or thirst got the better of him. He was sitting on a fallen spruce tree, Halonni across his knees, her head slumped against him, thinking he was finished when he spotted the eagle that saved them. It was flying in a slow circle almost directly above them, descending slightly with every pass until it finally dove down below the tree line. Had he not been too exhausted and hurt to be up and moving, Jantalus might not have bothered to watch for its return. When it rose back up above the trees, he caught the silver flash of a fish clutched in its talons.

Jantalus was on his feet at once, shifting Halonni's weight away from his injured hand as he started to where he had seen the eagle disappear into the trees, fearful that he would misjudge it if he gave himself too long to think it over. He wove through the forest, cutting across the slope of the mountain, pushing himself hard, the promise of water his only concern. He heard it before he saw it, little more than a gentle babbling sound, but water nonetheless and that was all that mattered.

The evergreens parted ahead and he found himself on the bank of a small stream dotted with bare elms. The ground was covered in a carpet of old, dry leaves and deadwood that promised a fire if he could manage to light it. The eagle had shown him food if he could manage to catch it. He had water for the taking. It was precious little in any other situation. Now, for the two of them, it was the difference between life and death.

He eased Halonni down on a bed of leaves and went to the stream. On his knees, he bent down and scooped handfuls of cold, clear water into his mouth. The dried blood and grime dissolved away as he splashed his face. He knelt over the stream a moment, letting the cold water drip off him and the wind kiss his skin. He let his eyes close and heaved a heavy sigh. So much more needed to be done that the thought of it was overwhelming, but this moment was something to hold on to. A moment and no more, he reminded himself.

He unwrapped a short length of the blood soaked cloak from his hand and cut it free with the knife tucked in his boot. He wrung out all the blood he could and then plunged the scrap of cloth into the river. He wrung it out several more times, cleaning it as much as he could and then soaked it again and carried it back to Halonni. He put a hand under her head and eased her up a bit, shaking her gently and calling her name.

She blinked awake, her eyes glassy and unfocused as they settled on him. He put the wet cloth to her lips and she sucked the water from it one hand lifting to squeeze it. When she was finished, he wiped her face with it and pressed it against her forehead. She closed her eyes and settled back into the bed of leaves, her head in her hand. He sat with her, waiting while she drew deep breaths. Finally, she opened her eyes again, fully awake.

She reached out and gently took his arm, pulling his injured hand closer. "Don't take that off," she told him, looking the makeshift bandage over. "Until we have something to replace it, you'll be doing more harm than good." She released his arm and lifted her fingers to his face, inspecting the gash over his left eye. "That looks worse than it is. Where else are you hurt?"

He reached up to take her hands and gently pulled them away from his face. "Everywhere, but none of it is going to kill me. I'm more concerned with you at the moment."

She sat upright with a groan. "Help me pull my pant leg up."

He pulled it up over her injured knee as gently as he could. It was swollen to twice its normal size and bruised from the midpoint of her thigh to her shin. She bent forward to inspect it and immediately reached for her back with a gasp of pain. She settled back with a wince, her face lined with frustration. Jantalus circled behind her and pressed gently against her ribs on her left side. She cried out again and flinched away. With his help, she pulled her cloak aside and lifted her tunic so he could see her lower back. Bruises covered her there too, from her left hip up to her armpit from front to back, a mix of red and blue, dark and ugly against her fair skin.

"Broken?" she asked as he probed along her back with his fingertips.

He lifted his hands away fearing he would do more harm than good by prodding. "I'm not sure." He looked around them with a shake of his head. "I'm not sure of much at the moment."

She caught his arm as he pulled back, drawing him face to face with her. "You saved our lives, Jantalus."

He shook his head. "I pushed too hard, grew too eager for answers. Solving the riddle of Jantalus Kathias became more important than using common sense. We should not be in these mountains, not now. We certainly should have turned back when we knew there was an ambush waiting."

"And who is to say that ambush would not have simply been sprung at another time and place, perhaps one that found us less prepared?" she insisted.

"You are asking me to rationalize my stupidity with a fantasy scenario."

"We all knew what we were doing," she shot back. "You twisted no arms in this." He tried to speak, but she pressed her fingers to his lips. "I'm tired, Jantalus, too tired to fight about this. Whatever happened and why no longer matters. It's over. Let's worry about where we are now and what we are going to do about it."

He sat back on his heels and looked up at the afternoon sky. Clouds were slowly edging in from the west as the sun continued its slow decline.

Daylight was slipping away from him and he had decisions to make about how to spend that time. A fire would be best, he knew, but he doubted his ability to make one with what he had. The mechanics of it all were simple enough, but the time and effort required were what concerned him. If he spent hours trying to start a fire and failed, they were going to be no better off than they were now and colder and hungrier as well. Food was a concern, but they had water which was more pressing and, as uncomfortable as his aching gut had become, a few days without food was not going to kill him.

That left the question of shelter. If the approaching clouds were bringing rain, it would probably be the end of them. Halonni was already ill and getting drenched and then freezing cold again would only make matters worse. The forest provided enough material here for him to build something that would at least attempt to keep them dry and a bit warmer as well. As strong as the desire for a fire pulled at him, he decided that a shelter should be his priority.

He helped Halonni wrap her cloak back around herself and eased her down on the bed of leaves once more. He made her as comfortable as possible, then went to the fir trees behind them, and cut the densest boughs he could find, gathering them in a huge pile near the riverbank. It was a slow, frustrating process, his work hampered by his useless left hand, but the fading sunlight was a constant motivator and he forged on. When he had what he deemed an adequate supply, he searched the forest floor for long, straight branches to use as poles, cutting them from the nearby elms when he had to. He trimmed them and arranged them like the frame of a tent over a thick bed of evergreen boughs. He kept the structure small, just enough room for the two of them. He laid the rest of the limbs he had collected from the fir trees along the sides and top, layering them to provide as much insulation as possible. Finally, he finished the shelter with a thick layer of leaves and debris, filling the gaps in the branches and piling as much extra as he could find atop it all.

He was aching and exhausted when he was finished, spent from the ordeal. The sun had finally set when he leaned against the trunk of a nearby oak and surveyed his work, bringing a frosty chill to the air. Still lying in the bed of leaves a few feet from his finished shelter, Halonni had drifted off to sleep again as he worked. He wondered again if a fire or food would have served her better. As if to answer his silent question, a few droplets of rain spattered against his face from the gathering clouds above.

"All right then," he muttered to no one in particular.

He went to Halonni and lifted her up, groaning with the effort. She did not stir as he carried her to the shelter and eased her down on the ground in front of the small entry hole he had left for them. He crawled in ahead of her and then slipped his hands under her arms and dragged her inside. The shelter was low and narrow, and he could barely sit up enough to turn and crawl back to the entrance and gather in armfuls of debris to block it off. When he had closed it as best he could, he wiggled back to where Halonni lay on the bed of spruce branches. She lay with her back to him and he edged close, wrapped one arm about her and buried his cold nose in her hair.

The rain beat a pattering rhythm against the roof and he stared up at the ceiling of pine needles and leaves expecting it to begin leaking at any moment. The rain remained light but steady and his work proved enough to keep it off them. He lay with his eyes closed listening to the sound of it for a time before sleep finally claimed him.

The rain had passed by the time he woke. He was cold and more than a little wet. His shelter had performed beyond his expectations, sparing him the worst of the weather, but it had been far from perfect.

He could still feel the heat of Halonni's fever as she pressed against him. Cramped and sore, but better off than he would have thought possible for having slept on a pile of branches, he stretched his legs a moment. A small hole near the entrance of the shelter let a pinpoint of morning light through. He was surprised to think he had slept through the night and even more surprised that some creature had not come to disturb them.

Luck, he decided, had owed him one anyway.

He was thirsty and hungry again and food was going to be the first order of the day. He could spear fish in the river and attempt a fire. After that, his intention was to head for the larger river he had seen from above. If anyone lived in the area, he imagined it would be along that river. He might find no one of course, but Dareth Sya had told him that the Avaruns lived in many of the valleys of the Tijian. They might not be pleased by the arrival of outsiders, but the tracker had suggested that they were not all in the habit of simply killing them either.

He tried to pull his arm free of Halonni, but her hand caught his and held it fast. Jantalus leaned over her to see her face. "I haven't been this warm in a week," she mumbled. "If you try to move, I'll bite your fingers off."

He indulged her for a bit and then finally slipped away as she fell back to sleep. He left the entrance of the shelter open a bit so she could see if she woke as he surveyed the area. His plans to build a fire evaporated at once. The rain had done thorough work, turning every bit of scrap wood in the area soggy and useless. Even a search beneath the thick cover of the evergreens turned up only a tiny bit of useful tinder. The promise of not having a fire put his plans for food in doubt as well. He made a cursory search for any plants or roots he could identify as edible, but it was a pointless exercise. Most of what he saw meant nothing to him. He was as likely to ignorantly choose something poisonous as not.

He leaned against a tree and stared down the length of the stream for a time, thinking instead of what was left to them. The river offered the most likelihood of finding help. It was also dangerous. They were taking the chance of running afoul a Valsen or worse if there were such a thing.

His thoughts turned to the Menion brothers and he wondered for a time what had become of them. He had watched them run, but he knew Tyris's mind. The outlander would have come back to see what had become of them and Jantalus feared that the Tassarens or the Valsen or both would be waiting.

He let the matter drop, accepting that there was nothing more he could do. His focus was survival first and finding his companions second.

Halonni called to him, breaking his moment of reflection and he went to her, helped her wiggle free from the shelter and took her to the river to drink. She washed her face and hands in the cold water, stripping away blood and dirt, her pale face chilled red. Cut, scraped, and bruised in every place imaginable, she made no complaint as she worked. When she was finished, she took another long drink and nodded to him that she was ready.

He bent to collect her, drawing her up without effort. She slipped her arms around his neck as he lifted her, her face pulling close. Before he could even think to realize what she was doing, her lips brushed against his, soft and still cold from the icy water. She said nothing as she broke the kiss, but lay her head against his shoulder and closed her eyes.

The fever, he decided and started walking.

Chapter Twenty-Five

He followed the stream as he headed north into the valley, reasoning that it likely ended at the river. The clouds blew east as the morning slipped by and the sun reappeared. It was warmer than it had been, but not enough to be comfortable. Small animals scattered through the trees as he passed them by, but nothing threatened to bar their way. Halonni slept in short intervals as he carried her. She never seemed comfortable enough to settle into something more, but she did not complain. In fact, she did not speak at all, merely nodding when he would inquire if she was all right or offer her water from the piece of cloth he dipped in the stream. Jantalus let her alone with her thoughts and did not press her on her silence.

It was noon when he saw the column of smoke rising into the sky along the edge of the stream ahead. Halonni had just fallen into one of her fitful naps and he chose not to wake her. He hoped he had found a village of Avaruns at first sight of it, but as he closed on it, he realized the smoke could not be from a fire of any size. Still, a fire was a sign that someone was close and it spurred him onward.

He was still too far to see the source of the smoke when he spotted a horse drinking from the stream. He was so startled by the sight that he stopped in midstride and stared. The animal's ears twitched and it looked up at him for a moment before returning to the water.

Jantalus retreated a few steps to the nearby trees and shook Halonni gently. She woke with a start, her gray eyes snapping open. She looked about in a panic for a moment and then heaved a sigh and lowered her face to his shoulder in relief.

"There," he said, nodding his head as he stepped out from the cover of the trees.

Her eyes went wide when she saw the horse and she blinked as if expecting it to vanish. "Any people?"

"Not yet." He returned to the trees and lowered her to the ground. "I'm going to leave you here and go see-."

She clung to his neck. "Like hell you are. You have no idea who or what might be out there."

He gently pulled her hands free. "True, but I'll have a harder time defending myself if I'm carrying you."

She started to argue and then stopped, clearly unhappy with his decision but fighting to fault it. "Just be careful."

He pulled the long knife from his boot. "I intend to. Stay here. Don't call out, it will give you away."

He waited for her to nod before turning away and starting along the riverbank. The horse looked up at him again as he approached, but did not move. It wore a saddle and halter, the reins hanging down into the stream as it drank. He approached slowly, mindful of spooking the animal and giving himself away. The column of smoke was rising from a spot in the trees further downstream, but he could not see its source. He noticed the horse favoring one of its hind legs as it shifted back and forth. He saw no wound, but it was obvious the animal was unable to bear much weight on it.

Jantalus circled around it, continuing along the bank, watching the trees for any sign of movement and listening for any sound to indicate who or what was causing the smoke. There was nothing. Focused on the trees, he nearly missed the cloak that flapped about at the edge of the stream. He turned as it caught his eye, shuffling toward it with the knife raised. A hand protruded from beneath the cloak, resting across a flat stone along the edge of the river. He peered down over the bank and found the hand belonged to a man lying face down across the bank. Dried, black blood from a deep gash on his head pooled at the corner of the rock.

He stepped over to the motionless man and nudged his hand with the toe of his boot. The hand slipped off the rock and into the water and Jantalus bent to take the man's shoulder and turn him over. The man's head lolled to one side, eyes fixed and staring into the sky. He was small and dark, with skin the color of chestnuts and dark eyes. He had been dead for hours by Jantalus's guess, his body tight and rigid and his lips and nails tinged blue. Jantalus looked him over a moment, debating what to do. Finally, he stripped the man of his cloak and wrapped it around his shoulders. It was doing a dead man no good. He searched the body and found a good knife in his belt, but nothing else useful. As he rose, he spotted a spear lying in the water a short distance away and reached in to take it.

He found no sign of struggle or battle here. The horse, he decided, must have lost its footing and thrown the man to the rock. The smoke, he assumed was from the man's camp, but a campfire could not have burned for so long on its own. That meant he was not alone. It also meant that any companions had not found his long absence troubling.

Jantalus thought on it a moment and then retraced his steps back to Halonni. She had pulled herself up against a nearby tree, watching for him. A look of relief lit her face for a moment as he came into view. Odd, he thought. He had been gone for a matter of minutes.

"People?" she asked as he joined her.

"A dead one so far." He related what he had found and his concerns about no one having come looking for the man on the rocks. "The camp is a bit farther downstream. I didn't want to leave you this far away."

He carried her closer, moving cautiously, watching and listening as they went. He left her at the edge of a tree line not far from the dead man and, spear in hand, stalked through the forest toward the source of the smoke. A small camp was nestled in an open space among a stand of elms with a large fire pit at the center. A canvas sheet had been hung over a low tree branch forming a crude tent. A mule was tethered to a nearby tree and a man sat atop a log that had been dragged close to the fire. He was small and dark like the man at the river with long, black hair shot through with streaks of white. An Avarun, Jantalus surmised. The man tossed a piece of wood into the fire from a small pile beside him and looked about as if expecting some sort of response.

Jantalus waited to see if anyone else was about and then crept forward to the next tree, trying to get a better look at the camp. The man near the fire turned toward him at once and reached down to snatch up a long staff from the ground at his feet. He began shouting in a language Jantalus could not understand.

Jantalus stopped where he was, the spear gripped tight.

The man's head cocked to one side and the other, listening. He did not move from where he stood, the staff quivering slightly in his hands. The shouting resumed, but again, it was gibberish to him.

Jantalus watched him a moment more before he realized why the man had not approached or fled. He was blind. He was searching with his ears, listening for the slightest sound, but his eyes almost never turned toward Jantalus.

"Ord!" the man called, a word he had repeated throughout.

Jantalus broke cover and approached, slow and careful, making no movement that might frighten the man further. "I am not Ord." It was an assumption, thinking the word a name, but crouching in the trees all day was not going to resolve anything.

The man focused on the sound of Jantalus's voice, his empty stare fixing. "Who are you then?" The man changed languages with ease.

"I am called Jantalus. I am lost here and saw the smoke of your fire."

The man held the staff out before him, his hands shaking still. "I am not alone."

Jantalus stopped at the edge of the fire opposite the man. He could see the milky white eyes clearly now. Strange markings covered the man, scarred into his skin, his entire face decorated in elaborate patterns. More symbols marked the thick, rough hands that gripped the staff. He was dressed in dark leathers with sturdy boots and a heavy cloak. This was not a man thrust into the elements unprepared, but one who had been traveling by choice by the look of him and his gear.

"I am afraid you are alone," Jantalus told him. "I found your companion down by the river. He was thrown by his horse and struck his head."

"Dead?" the stranger asked.

Jantalus nodded, realized the futility of it and then said, "Yes."

"So you think that leaves you and me?" the man asked. Nothing about him suggested he was shaken by the death of the man called Ord. "Not so, stranger! The spirits are with me, here."

Jantalus thrust the point of his spear into the ground beside him. He had no idea what spirits the little man was referring to. "You needn't fear me. I won't hurt you."

"No?" he was almost amused by the idea.

"No. If you let us share your fire, I might even be able to help you."

"Us?" the man asked. "You are not alone?"

A foolish mistake, Jantalus thought at once, but dismissed the notion. There was no harm in it here. "My companion is hurt. I left her hidden by the stream while I looked for your camp."

The man's scarred face creased as he thought the matter over a moment. "No harm in sharing a fire. Fetch your friend, then."

Jantalus went for Halonni at once. He paused long enough to tell her everything that had transpired and then carried her back to the camp. The strange man was sitting on the log again, his staff propped against it beside him. His head turned toward them as they approached, cocked slightly to the side as he listened. Jantalus stopped on the opposite side of the fire again and lowered Halonni to the ground as gently as he could. She stretched her hands out to the fire and inched closer, shivering.

"Does your friend have a name too?" the scarred man asked.

"Halonni," she answered after a moment of hesitation.

The cloudy eyes turned toward her, a crooked smile breaking the dusky face. "Pretty name. You are lowlanders?"

"We are," Jantalus answered. "And you are?"

"I am Devoc of the Suledane," he answered. "Why are lowlanders here, in the Valley of the Sacred? Only the Suledane are allowed here. It was made known when we made peace with your people."

Jantalus dropped down beside Halonni and hunched over the fire. "We are not here by choice. We got lost in caves to the south and wound up here. And I know nothing of the Valley of the Sacred or the Suledane."

Devoc turned his face to the sun. "The spirits live here, the spirits of the earth, sky and water. I am one of the Suledane – the spirit talkers – I come every spring to ask their blessing and guidance for my people."

Halonni raised an eyebrow at Jantalus before looking back to Devoc. "Just two of you? That seems dangerous considering the beasts that hunt the mountains."

The little man shook his head. "I fear nothing here. The beasts will do no harm to one of the Suledane, not here. No harm will ever come to me here from one of my own or a creature of the mountains."

"And Ord?" Jantalus asked.

"The spirits called him home," Devoc answered. "His kin will be honored that he was chosen to die here in the most sacred of places. I am pleased for him."

"Your people are far from here?" Jantalus asked, trying to decide for himself if he wished they were or not. Devoc's people might be able to aid them, but, if they considered them trespassers on their holy ground, they might just kill them instead.

He shook his head. "Not far. At the end of this valley is a pass that leads to another. My people camp there, waiting for me. The spirits, it seems, have sent you to guide me home."

Halonni blew out a long, exhausted sigh. "I blame a few dozen cutthroats, a Valsen and a rockslide."

Devoc set his staff against the ground and rose. He shuffled around the edge of the fire and approached them, the staff clocking against the hard ground as he came. He stopped when it tapped Halonni's boot and knelt down before her. He sniffed about her like a dog for a moment.

"Who are you?" he asked again, his face screwed up in a mask of curiosity.

"We told you who we were," Jantalus answered, rising to tower over the smaller man. He did not like the sudden courage the man was showing or the bold approach he had made. Halonni raised a hand to calm him and waved him back.

Devoc's hands lifted toward her. "May I?"

Halonni bit her lower lip and looked to Jantalus. He shrugged. "All right," she answered, not quite sounding confident in the choice.

The scarred, calloused hands reached out for her face, stubby fingers brushing her pale skin. "Beautiful," he murmured. "I could see once. I sacrificed the sights of this world for those of the next. Few have the times been that I have wished for my old eyes back as I do now."

He traced invisible lines from her temples to her jaw, back up and over her nose, gently caressing her forehead. Then, he gasped, cupping her delicate face in his hands.

"Fire-caller," he whispered.

His head bent, his white eyes closing.

"Earth-melder."

He drew a deep breath.

"Water-walker."

He exhaled slowly, his head tilting back.

"Wind-bender."

The sightless eyes fluttered open. "Magic."

Halonni's hands came up to pull his away, her face lined with concern, her gray eyes flashing fear. "How do you know that?"

"I am Suledane," he answered as if that explained everything. "We speak with the spirits of the earth. The same spirits you call upon." He reversed his hands, grasping hers. "Your presence honors me, child of the elements. You are blessed of the spirits."

Halonni shook her head. "No, I'm not. I'm the daughter of two Vicars whose magic is an aberration, a mistake."

Devoc shook his head and waved his hands at her, dismissing her words. "Lowlander speak, that. The spirits do not lie." He rose again and approached Jantalus, his hands reaching.

Jantalus took a step back. "Spirits or no, I prefer to be left alone."

The hands pulled back. "As you wish." He shuffled back to his seat. "We'll need wood and water if we are to make this night. There's food in my bags and a place to sleep. In the morning, we will leave and return to my home. You will be my guests, sent to me by the spirits."

Halonni and Jantalus shared a look that said the blind man was mad, but Devoc was smiling up at the afternoon sun with a look of sheer joy.

"I thought I was here to die when Ord did not return." He was still staring up at the sky as he spoke, as if not addressing them at all. "But now, you are here and the gift of the spirits is clear. Forever will I be in your debt for your help, lowlanders. Forever will I honor the will of the spirits by serving you."

Jantalus walked to the canvas tent nearby and searched until he found a few blankets and some food. Devoc heard him and called for him to take whatever he wished. He found nothing to drink, but spied two empty wooden jugs with stoppers. He gathered them as well and returned to Halonni, wrapped her in the blankets and gave her the hard cheese and salted meat he had found. Devoc refused food but reminded them that he was thirsty and his fire wood nearly gone.

Jantalus took the jugs to the stream and filled them. Ord's feet were visible around the gentle bend of the riverbank and his horse still wandered about further upstream. Best to leave it, he decided. The horse was useless to him and some predator would have it eventually. Burying Ord might have been a decent gesture, but he did not have the energy to spare. Devoc had not been concerned about it, and Jantalus let the matter go. He brought the water back to camp and then set about gathering more firewood. Everything was still wet from the night's rain, but Devoc's ember bed was deep and hot and Jantalus tossed the driest of what he found in and stacked the rest close by.

When he was finished, he moved Halonni to the log beside the strange man and sat between them. Halonni handed a portion of the food he had given her back to him. He took it without comment and devoured it, still hungry when he was finished but no longer aching from it.

"How far a walk is it to where your people wait?" he asked Devoc as the old man sat mumbling in his strange language.

He shrugged. "A long way, but an easy walk. Sunrise to sunset. You should sleep."

Jantalus took a long drink from the wooden jug of water Halonni handed him. "You sleep. I'll keep watch."

The old man snorted and laughed at him. "The spirits keep watch. You can sleep." He felt around on the ground before him until he located his blankets and then slid down in front of the fire and wrapped himself up so that only his scarred face showed. "Sleep. Nothing will harm us here. Nothing at all."

Between Necromancers, Valsen, rockslides and falls from horses, Jantalus had more faith in his own eyes than the old man's spirits. Besides, he reasoned, the spirits might protect the old man, but he was a stranger in this land and those spirits owed him no debt.

Halonni leaned over to rest her head on his shoulder and was asleep in minutes. Alone with his thoughts, he stared into the fire and wondered what match the old man's spirits would be for Shantara Tassaren.

Chapter Twenty-Six

Tyris Menion barely glanced up at the horsemen that rode out from the iron gates of Zantizan and turned east on Greylock Pass to intercept the intruders. Along with Stilthius, he had spent an entire night searching the rubble of the massive rockslide for Jantalus and Halonni and come away with only bruised and bleeding hands to show for it. Stilthius had been quick to point out that they had not found bodies either. When that did not improve his brother's spirits, he offered that both Jantalus and Halonni possessed magic beyond their comprehension – magic that might have allowed them to escape.

There were plenty of corpses sticking out of that rubble to look over, twisted limbs, shattered skulls and bodies bent at all kinds of impossible angles. None of them was Jantalus or Halonni, and the brothers might have found some hope in that, but they discovered no sign of where their friends had gone. Given what he had seen of them in the mess of the ambush, he doubted they had gotten far. One of the caves, maybe. That was Stilthius's suggestion, a little bit of hope about him when he made it. It sounded reasonable enough if you were looking for a reason to get out of the wind and go collapse next to a warm fire, he supposed. Tyris preferred reality to conscience-soothing horseshit. Even if they had managed to reach a cave, it was blocked now and there was only so long Jantalus and Halonni could survive.

That was him, though. Always trying to look at things with the horseshit wiped away first.

Stilthius had finally talked him into abandoning the search. His brother was not the kind to give up. As much as it tasted like shit to him, Tyris had to swallow the truth of his brother's take on things. Nothing the brothers could offer was better than what Halonni and Jantalus were able to do for themselves if they were lost in the mountains.

That left a long hike through Greylock Pass to Zantizan. Their discarded packs were among the mess of blood and mangled flesh buried beneath the mountainside. That left them with no blankets, no food and water and none of the money they had won in Ailen. How they were getting into Zantizan was anyone's guess. Not that it mattered, really, he reminded himself. If they were turned away, they were dead. If they never tried, they were dead.

Dead was dead, after all. No one gave a damn how or why you got there.

The horsemen closed on them, hooded and wrapped in heavy cloaks to ward off the cold. They pulled up short a few yards ahead, spears pointed toward them, steel glinting in the morning light. Eight and all armored, carrying long spears and mounted was the crux of the situation. That meant no hope of a good end if it came to a fight. They were either going to come up with something to convince these men they should be allowed into Zantizan or they were going to die in the Pass.

"That's far enough," the lead rider told them. "You don't look much like merchants and no one else but brigands travel these mountains."

Tyris gestured to the bloody bandages he and Stilthius had fashioned from the cloaks of the dead. "That's what we are, fucking thieves."

One of the men in the rear of the group snickered, but the leader shot him a look that shut him up. "You wouldn't mind telling us what you're doing here, then."

"Looking for lost friends," Stilthius answered. "A man and woman. Seen them?"

The leader shook his hooded head. "No one in months, outside of supply runs, before the lot of you. What were your friends doing in the mountains this time of year?"

"Does it matter?" Tyris asked.

The man leaned forward. "Don't care much if we let you in or not, that it? I'd watch my mouth if I were you."

Tyris shrugged. "Last asshole that pointed a spear at me and said that got his fucking back broken for it."

"Tyris," Stilthius muttered, his eyes narrowing at his younger brother.

"Tyris?" the horseman echoed. He kicked his horse forward a bit. "Fuck me! Tyris Menion? Stilthius?"

Tyris stared at the man, one hand reaching slowly for his axe. How someone in the middle of a remote mountain range knew him was beyond him, but he had to think it was for the wrong reasons.

One gloved hand came up to pull the hood away from his head, revealing a gnarled, pitted face with a short red beard and a long braid of matching hair. The thin lips split wide in a gap-toothed grin as he threw his head back with a tremendous laugh that echoed through the pass.

"Shaddix?" Stilthius was staring like a fool. "I'll be damned! I haven't seen your puny ass since Turgin. What the hell are you doing out here?"

"Long, that story is!" the other man responded. "Why don't we go crack a barrel and share a few tales?" He turned to his men, barking orders over his shoulder. "Get you sorry asses down and let these men ride. Move you lazy shits!"

A young man in finely crafted mail and embroidered cloak pushed to the fore, drawing his horse alongside Shaddix's. "What is this, Captain? Who are these men?"

Shaddix gestured. "Derek Ravensbourne. Tyris and Stilthius Menion."

"Ravensbourne?" Stilthius's eyes snapped up to the boy. "You were in the company of Peridor Finn and Joran Kathias?"

The young man drew back his hood, revealing a lean, handsome face shaded by a day's worth of beard that he had not long been able to grow. "How do you know that? Who are you?"

Shaddix reached out and laid a hand on the boy's arm. "Relax. These boys are Black River. Your uncle and I fought with them in the border towns north of Turgin. They're evil fucks, meaner than a rabid wolf and tougher than week old steak, but I trust them as much as I trust any man."

Tyris looked the boy over. "Peridor Finn was your uncle?"

"My mother's brother." He paused. "Was? Then he is dead?"

Tyris nodded and said nothing.

Derek Ravensbourne spat on the hard ground. "We assumed as much, my brother and I. What brings you here, then?"

"Jantalus Kathias," Stilthius answered. "We were in his company until last night."

Derek flinched as if struck, looking as though he might fall off his horse. "Did you say Jantalus?"

"I did."

"Where is he? What did-?"

Tyris's big hand came up. "He is one of two we are missing. If you don't mind, I'm freezing my balls off here and bruised more places than I care to count. We need rest and food if you can offer them and then we plan on going back to look again."

Derek shouted for horses to be brought forward and then turned his men back toward Zantizan. He said no more to Tyris and Stilthius, riding ahead of the others, hurrying on to the town.

"Kathias, eh?" Shaddix asked as they pulled themselves into the saddles of the provided horses.

"What do you know about it?" Tyris asked.

"Less than I should. More than I want to," the mercenary answered.

"That bad?"

Shaddix shook his head and kicked his horse forward. "Worse. A lot fucking worse."

Tyris and Stilthius shared a long, exhausted look and then followed him up the winding trail to Zantizan.

Within the hour they were wrapped in heavy blankets and drinking ale in front of a roaring fire. Shaddix had taken them through the gates of Zantizan without being challenged and led them straight to a small stone building that served as an infirmary for the soldiers of Zantizan. Their wounds were bound, clean clothing provided and food and drink brought at Shaddix's word. When they were warm and fed, he took them to a small room at the rear of the building, ordered the two men who were lounging before the hearth out and gathered them all around. A few of his men came with them, but they were more interested in the food and beer than acting as any kind of protection to Shaddix. For his part, the mercenary settled in without a care, even tossing his weapons into an empty chair as they made themselves comfortable.

They saw no more of Derek Ravensbourne. Tyris asked about the boy, but Shaddix simply shook his head and shrugged.

"All of that will have to be sorted out soon enough. Eat and rest while you can."

Stilthius leaned forward a bit and swallowed the food he was chewing. "What the fuck is going on Shaddix? Why are Black River men here? This place is in the middle of nothing, on the way to nothing and filled with nothing."

"But you were headed here?" Shaddix pointed out without answering the question. "What the hell for? The only thing to see out here is snow. The gods know there isn't enough silver left to waste your effort on."

"Jantalus Kathias, we said," Stilthius answered. "He was searching for family. We were with him."

Shaddix snorted ale through is nose and choked. "With him? Why the hell would you be with him? You boys looking to get yourselves killed? Half the Censharn is looking for him – Sentinels, Alliance soldiers, Vicars and worse. The price on his head is so high, I'm not sure it could actually be paid."

He paused as he wiped ale out of his beard with the back of his hand, the smile draining away. "You're fucking serious."

The brothers stared at him without moving. Tyris Menion had known the mercenary well enough for the few months they had fought together. Shaddix was many things – a gambler, a thief and a drunk – but he was not one to be loose with his talk. If he thought something serious, it generally was. As a man in trouble more than out, he was well aware of what constituted serious business and what did not.

He pushed his cup aside and leaned forward on his elbows. "You two listen to me. You listen real good. I don't give a shit for most, Black River or no, and you boys know it. I wouldn't piss for the next man unless he paid me to. But you two? I owe you. I don't forget that. Let me repay a bit of that debt. Get out of here. Go back to Turgin or wherever you were and leave this shit behind you. You want nothing to do with it. Trust me."

Stilthius propped his arm up on the table and rested his cheek against his huge fist. "We walk the road we feel led down, Shaddix. Hunnaris sets our path here."

Shaddix scoffed and waved his hands at him. "Don't start all that with me again. I deny no man his gods, but how many times are you being led to glory by your war-god? First, it was that siege in Corak. After that, you charged a shield wall at Borlon Fields. Lucky to be alive is what you are. You two mad fucks ever stop to consider that you're just bigger, faster, stronger and meaner than everyone else? Maybe that's why you cut through men like farmers cut wheat."

"This is different-."

"Shit it is. You'll be humping whores and playing cards inside of a week dreaming about the next battle your god calls you to."

Tyris laid a restraining hand on his brother's shoulder as he saw Stilthius's jaw tighten and heard his knuckles crack with the clench of his fist. "Why don't you let us worry about our reasons and tell us what's going on?"

Shaddix heaved a defeated sigh and refilled his cup from a nearby pitcher. "Your asses, I suppose." He took a long drink and smacked his lips. "My boys and I were late to the whole thing, you understand. When Finn called Black River to Drappel, we were a week away, south of Turgin mixed up in a mess with some deserters from the Duke's army. By the time we reached Drappel it was a smoking mess of a place. Tracker with us said men went north so we followed. Stopped in Ailen first and word there pointed here. We were hoping to find Finn and whatever men were left, but there weren't any. The mountains swallowed them up and no one found a trace. We settled in here because the snow was flying. Offered our swords to the local lord in exchange for a winter's stay and he agreed. We figured on moving out of here as soon as the first spring wind blew through."

"But here you are," Stilthius said, relaxed a bit, but still regarding Shaddix with a cold stare.

He nodded. "Here I am. A man came through the pass a few weeks ago, right through a snowstorm that a Valsen wouldn't chance. Just an old man and his horse. I figured he was part of some group of fools trying to navigate Agron Pass that got lost. Turns out, he's an old Vicar and he's looking for this Kathias fellow you're mixed up with. Evil old bastard, make your blood run cold just by looking at you. Word spread that he's a real Vicar, like the tales say. You know, magic and all that. Anyway, he starts asking around about Finn and the others, says he's looking for people. Not much we could do with the snow blocking everything, but he doesn't care. He settled in and started going over old books and maps and asking questions of anyone he can get the ear of."

He paused and took another drink, gulping beer. "That included me. I met Peridor Finn a few times, years ago, and that interested him. Wanted to know what he looked like, said it had been even longer since he saw him last. Asked about the men Finn had with him too, but I couldn't help him much. I pointed him to the Ravensbournes and the old man took to them like flies to shit. Wouldn't call them friends, but the three of them are working together, looking for the missing men. They leave me out of it, so I just keep my head down and try to stay out of the way. If that had been the end of it, I'd have been fine with it all."

"But it wasn't?" Tyris asked.

Shaddix shook his head. "No. A few days after this old man shows up, a bunch of Alliance Sentinels come knocking. Now, Zantizan is its own place and doesn't answer to anyone, but it isn't in the habit of pissing off the Alliance or the Duke of Turgin or anyone else who can field enough men to make an issue of things. The old man? Well, let's just say he's less careful about stirring shit."

"The Sentinels come asking for anyone who can point them the way of a black-eyed man by the name of Kathias. The old man has black eyes, you see, so a few fingers pointed his way. When the Sentinels tried to round him up, he fought back with magic."

"Ran them off, did he?" Tyris asked.

"Killed them," Shaddix answered with a grim smile. "All of them. Six men in as many heartbeats. I was there. I saw. Not too proud to say I would have pissed myself, but I was too scared to even do that. The old man did them in, walked away from it all and went right back to his research and meditating or whatever else it is he does. A few days after that, a group of bounty hunters shows up saying there's a reward for the same man the Sentinels were after. The old man gives them a pile of money to go into the valley on the other side of Mount Greylock looking for this Kathias bastard. Their heads came back, dropped off by the Avaruns who live in the valley. Not much for trespassers, that lot."

"Avaruns?" Tyris asked. He remembered Dareth Sya mentioning the name.

Shaddix shrugged. "The people who live in the Tijian. They claim the mountains are the home of their gods. They allow Agron Pass to be used and leave Zantizan alone, but the rest they defend with swords. As luck would have it, this is their holy time. Their magicians, the Suledane, declare it every spring. It lasts weeks sometimes. Those men the old Vicar sent into the valley went to the wrong place at the wrong time. Not that it stopped anyone. More bounty hunters have trickled in and a few men I think were Sentinels sniffing around. No one has the balls to challenge the old man now, not even the baron who runs Zantizan."

Stilthius leaned back in his chair, rubbing his chin. He thought it all over a while and then shrugged one shoulder at his brother. Tyris didn't know what to make of it all ether. Shaddix didn't seem to be making it all up, but he left plenty of holes in the story that needed to be filled in. He had the sense that Shaddix was telling what he knew and what was missing was due to his ignorance. The warning he had given was probably worth heeding if they were going to be smart about it all. Running back to Ailen and forgetting the whole affair was probably their best chance of avoiding a bad end here.

Of course, that wasn't going to happen.

"This old Vicar have a name?" Tyris asked.

Shaddix looked up from his cup. "Yeah. Addicus. Addicus Malshere. Why?"

Tyris blew out a long breath and turned to Stilthius again. They knew that name too. Whether that was a good thing or not remained to be seen. Best, he decided, to stay away from him until he knew for sure.

"And this Derek Ravensbourne and his brother?" he asked.

"Half-brothers," Shaddix corrected him. "Lorum and Derek – nobles from Geften. They went with Joran Kathias along with their older brother and their father – and Peridor Finn, of course. Two of them are all that's left from a whole damn family that vanished last fall. What of them?"

"We should speak with them. See what they know."

The mercenary rubbed his eyes with the backs of his hands. "You two are just not going to be talked out of this are you?"

Tyris put his feet up on the edge of the table and lifted a cup. "Sooner would be better than later. We'll be headed back to Greylock Pass to have another look for our friends."

Shaddix pushed himself back from the table and rose. "Right."

He walked away from them without another word, shaking his head as he went.

Chapter Twenty-Seven

The squeal of the rusty hinges as the door opened woke Tyris. He was still sitting at the table where he had eaten, his head resting on his arms. Stilthius had moved to more comfortable chair in the corner by the fire and was shaking off the fog of sleep as well. Tyris straightened, his shoulders tight and his neck clicking as he turned to the door. His hand slipped down to his axe where it rested against the side of his chair, more instinct than any expectation of danger. His hand retreated when Shaddix stepped inside, his mouth drooping in a deep frown beneath the chaotic jumble of red beard.

"You bastards have done it now," he announced as he pushed the door shut behind him.

Stilthius stretched and yawned. "Did what?"

The mercenary jerked a thumb over his shoulder. "I went to the Ravensbournes like you asked and they told Addicus all about you straight away. They're on their way here to talk to you – all three of them."

Tyris glanced over at his brother at the news, but Stilthius only managed a slight shrug between his stretches and yawns. As usual, Stilthius didn't give a fuck.

Tyris passed the shrug along to Shaddix. "We'll have this all talked out sooner rather than later, then."

"I'd watch what I say if I were you," the other countered. "The Ravensbournes seem like a decent sort, but remember what I told you about the old man. Don't antagonize him. I know that's asking a bit much of you pricks, but take my advice on this."

A door opened from without and footfalls sounded on the stone floor. Tyris turned his chair to face the door and Stilthius made his way back to the table. He lifted his hammer from where it stood on end near Tyris's axe and laid it across the chair next to him. Careful as always, Tyris thought.

They waited in silence for a few moments before the door creaked open again. A man stepped into the firelight from without, tall and strong, older than the Menion brothers, but not by much. His dark hair was flecked with gray and his face was lined with troubles beyond his years. He wore a black patch over his left eye, the pink edges of a scar rising up through his brow and down his cheek. Behind him came a boy who teetered on the edge of manhood. Derek, Tyris recalled. He was nearly as tall as his brother, somewhat awkward in his body as if he were too big for his feet to keep up with him. The dark hair was identical save for the lack of gray and the face was a younger, less weathered version that lacked only the missing eye and scars. They were clad in matching mail with broad swords swinging at their hips. The blue cloaks they wore carried the symbol of a black bird.

Addicus Malshere followed them in. There was no mistaking him. Shaddix had offered little beyond calling him old and unnerving, but nothing else was necessary. The Vicar was a wrinkled, white-haired, wisp of a man, nearly lost in his gray cloak. He stood straight despite his years, his head nearly equal with those of the younger men who preceded him. His hands were tucked into the sleeves of his simple tunic. He stared down at the outlander along his long, hooked nose, black eyes searching.

"You do not fear the mark of the dead?" he asked without any introduction.

Stilthius snorted. "I've yet to see it stop a hammer from caving a skull in. You'd be Addicus, then. Shaddix says we might be looking for the same person."

The old man looked them over a moment before answering. "Perhaps." He indicated the men with him. "Lorum and Derek Ravensbourne. They have an interest here as well."

Tyris looked at the one-eyed Lorum. "Derek tells us your mother is Peridor Finn's sister."

He nodded. "She is one of his many sisters."

"Peridor Finn is dead."

Lorum Ravensbourne stiffened a bit. "So my brother told me. You are sure of this?"

"Very. I trust the person who told me that. She would not lie."

Lorum simply shook his head. "We suspected as much."

"Which leaves the question of Jantalus Kathias," Addicus Malshere broke in. "Where is he?"

Tyris leaned back in his chair and folded his arms over his broad chest. "If I knew, I'd be on my way there now. We told Shaddix-."

The old man waved his words away. "I was told of the rockslide. If he survived, he did not come here. Where was he headed?"

"We figured you'd know better than we do," Stilthius said. "His father disappeared here. I imagine he'll be focused on that if he can't reach us here."

Addicus looked them both over for a long moment. Lorum and Derek seemed to grow more uncomfortable as the silence that hung across the room deepened, but Tyris and Stilthius watched the old man without concern. Whatever was so important to him was lost on them.

"Why would he look for his father?" the old man asked finally.

Tyris hesitated a moment, turning to his brother. Stilthius turned his palms up and shrugged. "His father is missing. When there was no sign of him at Drappel, we kept moving north. Some girl said men went into the mountains."

"A girl?" the old man asked. "Or the echo of a girl?"

"Echo?" Tyris cocked an eyebrow at him. "You mean a ghost? Jantalus says he saw her in a dream. He says she was left there by you."

Addicus Malshere shook his head. "Not by me. By him."

"Who?"

The old Vicar stared at the brothers again, measuring them as he might an opponent readying for battle. "You have no idea, do you?"

Tyris crept forward in his seat a bit. He liked the whole affair less with each passing moment. Something about Addicus Malshere went beyond his being intimidating or simply strange. He had a smug condescension about him that made Tyris want to crush his skull. Deeper than that, seemed to be assuming they knew far more about what was going on than they really did.

"Why don't you stop glaring at me like you think I'm pretty and tell me what the fuck is going on?" Tyris suggested.

Addicus let out a sigh that spoke to man trying to be patient with a matter he found tedious. "I left no ghost behind in Drappel. She was there when I arrived. I called her soul to me, but it was Jantalus who condemned her, trapped her between this world and the next. I tried to speak with her, tried to set her free. I failed."

Stilthius dragged his chair a bit closer, scraping it across the floor. "Why would he want to do that?"

"He didn't say?" Addicus asked in return.

Tyris smirked at him. "Seems like you might be the one who doesn't have any idea what's happening. Jantalus is completely lost. He knows just about nothing outside of his own name. He didn't even know your name until that ghost told him."

Addicus looked down his crooked nose at them. "I do not believe you."

Tyris snorted and rose, lifting his axe and setting it across his shoulders. "I don't give a shit what you believe. You obviously can't help me and I have two missing friends that aren't getting any closer to being found while I sit on my ass."

The old man held up a hand. "I have more questions."

The outlander met his black stare, looming over him like a giant. "Get out of my way, old man. I'm done with you. You have nothing that I want."

The old man stood his ground. To either side of him, Derek and Lorum Ravensbourne crowded closer. Stilthius was on his feet to Tyris's left, his hammer lifting. Something was brewing now and it was not going to good for any of them. The old Vicar was likely powerful like Halonni, but being an arm's length from Tyris was going to be the end of him before he could do much of anything. That meant a dead Vicar, but it left Tyris exposed to the men with him. Stilthius would never be able to stop them both before he had a sword in his belly.

Nearly forgotten by all, Shaddix took a step forward. "Let's not do anything stupid here." He eased himself between the outlander and the old man. "Now, Addicus tells me that he has a sense for folk with magic. He might be able to figure out if this friend of yours is even alive. Maybe you can tell us exactly where he was the last time you saw him and give Addicus a place to start looking."

Tyris stayed where he was, his attention focused on the old man even as he spoke to Shaddix. "And if we find out he is alive?"

Addicus returned the fearless stare. "Then we go to him together. If he doesn't remember me, he might think me an enemy. Without you to tell him otherwise, I could end up a ghost myself."

Tyris considered his words a moment, measuring them against the angry lines around the black eyes and the deep creases that framed his mouth. The two did not agree. Of course, most people lied most of the time by his experience. Either they had half the balls they needed to say what they really meant or they had to twist what they were saying to be sure you never heard what they really meant. Either way, Tyris had learned that half of what he heard was horseshit from an early age. Picking which half that was made for the hard part.

He gestured to the Ravensbournes. "And these two?"

Lorum folded his arms across his chest. "I'll know more about my father if there is anything to know. We've another stake in this as well. I lost men far beyond Peridor Finn in Drappel."

Tyris glanced back at his brother. Stilthius lowered his hammer with a slight nod. It was all shit, but they were looking at an impossible situation and the offer they were entertaining was probably the only one they were going to get. Their resolve aside, they were not going to sift through an entire mountainside looking for their friends. If Addicus Malshere could confirm Jantalus as dead or alive, it was too much to walk away from, no matter how little they trusted the old man.

"All right," he said finally. "How soon can you know if he is alive or dead?"

Addicus shrugged. "I'll have Shaddix bring a map. You can point me to his last location as precisely as you are able. Once I have that? An hour or less."

Shaddix turned and started for the door without further prompting. He paused before leaving, looking them all over as if he expected them to be back at each other as soon as he left. With a shake of his head, he let himself out and disappeared.

"So what do we do while you look for Jantalus?" Stilthius asked.

Addicus snorted softly and turned away. Lorum Ravensbourne came forward, seated himself in an empty chair, and motioned his brother toward another. "You listen."

"Listen?" Stilthius cocked his head at the one-eyed man.

Lorum rested his arms on the table and nodded. "I have a very long story to tell you. I don't think you are going to enjoy it."

****

Caleb Tassaren picked his way through the rubble-strewn waste that had once been Greylock Pass, stepping over torn and shattered bodies with their fixed, staring eyes and mangled limbs. He paid none of it any more attention than he would dust on the floor of his bedchamber. These men were nothing, hired swords that served for the promise of pay and plunder, useful, but replaceable. That was the way of those born without the gift of magic. They either served or they were broken and forced to serve. These men had served and died. They were worth nothing more and received nothing more than they were worth. It was a simple truth of the difference between the gifted and the ordinary.

He paused atop the split remains of one of the boulders that had once stood tall in the Pass. The tremendous avalanche of earth and stone that had rained down from the mountain above had shattered it. He surveyed the whole area, searching for his kin. Everything had changed with the rockslide and he needed a moment to get his bearings once again. His magic had healed his wounds, straightening twisted limbs and shattered bone, closing gashes and rent skin. He had spent the night in the trees at the edge of the Pass, lying motionless as the men who had traveled with Jantalus Kathias searched the area. They missed him in their search, too concerned with their friends to notice.

He dropped down and made his way to where a collection of bodies lay strewn among the remaining boulders standing in the Pass. He went first to where he had seen Samarus. His oldest brother was face down on the hard earth, his head crushed in from the back, dark blood pooled all about him. The blood stained rock lay to one side. Too little remained of Samarus to salvage and Caleb let him be and moved on.

Rossin lay nearby, slumped against the ground with his eyes open and staring up into the cold morning sky. One side of his head was shattered, bone and flesh torn away and gray brain showing though. Twisted fuck, Caleb thought. Even now, his face was warped into a hideous smile as if there were something to laugh about here. The outlander had been quick and smart and beaten Rossin at his own game. Caleb would keep that in mind when he avenged his little brother.

He left Rossin where he was as well. His brothers were beyond help. He had suspected as much, but it had cost him nothing to be sure. He turned his attention to what was left of the mountainside and began climbing up the rough, rock strewn slope. More bodies littered the pass here, broken, shattered and buried in the rocks. All of their men were dead or had run away in the face of the collapse. It was just Caleb now.

He paused, catching sight of the ragged black cloak flapping in the mountain breeze. Sunlight flashed on something silver. No, not just me, he thought. Not if my luck holds.

He scrambled over the nearby rocks until he reached the fluttering cloak and stopped. It was Shantara. She was staring up at him, her face all torn skin and blood, one eye socket collapsed and her nose flattened against her broad face. She gurgled blood as he approached, broken jaw useless, her one good eye blinking rapidly. Her legs and one arm remained buried under the massive rocks. Her free arm was twisted at an odd angle, the bone broken through the skin at the elbow. Her hand flopped uselessly at the end of it, trying to reach out, her silver ring the sparkle he had seen in the light.

He hunched down next to her, his face close to hers. "There will be a price for my help. A price for the years you have been strong and I the weaker. You will pay that price or I will leave you here. Do we have a bargain?"

The hand writhed against the rocks, the eye blinked even faster. Her shattered jaw shook, blood bubbling up in her mouth. "Yesh..."

His hands reached out to touch her shattered face, his magic rising. "Stupid bitch, you should have at least asked what I wanted."

Shantara gasped as his magic flooded through her, arm straightening, bones mending. Her jaw realigned and the skin on her face melted back together. Her free hand stretched out to touch the earth, her own magic flaring. The rocks pulled back from her like a blanket kicked off the edge of a bed. She rolled over and gained her knees, her body continuing to twist itself back into shape. Finally, Shantara Tassaren rose, pulling herself up to her full height.

"I am owed," Caleb told her as their black eyes met.

She scowled. "And you will be rewarded. First, we have business to attend to. Jantalus Kathias is still alive."

Caleb snorted. "I doubt it."

"That is why you follow orders rather than give them." She started down the slope toward the remnants of the trail. "We have to reach Sentry before he does or all of this is for nothing."

"As opposed to how well it's all gone to this point?" He smirked at her when she looked back at him. "It looks to me like you've fucked this up about as thoroughly as possible."

Shantara stopped and stared black daggers into him. "Then stay here and celebrate how smart you are. When Jantalus reaches Sentry and learns the truth of everything, I'm sure he won't come looking to tear you to pieces. Don't forget what we were told. There is no one to stop him but us."

Caleb was looking down the mountainside, ignoring the stern looks she gave him, his attention focused behind her. "Shantara."

Below them, back at the center of the collection of huge boulders that littered the pass, a man was crawling across the rough ground, scraping his way through the rubble. He made no sound as he came, dragging his broken body along without any cry of pain or call for help.

Rossin. Caleb shook his head. He should have checked his half-brother more carefully, but enough of his head was missing that Caleb had assumed the madman dead.

Shantara started down the slope toward him, beckoning Caleb on after her. They picked their way through the debris until they came to him, stopping a few feet ahead of the ruin of a man. Their half-brother raised his shattered face to them, saliva dripping from his ruined lips, madness lighting his eyes. He tried to speak, but no sound came and he vomited on the dirt before lowering his face back to it.

Shantara squatted down next to him and seized a handful of his bloody hair, jerking his head up again. "Caleb could fix you or I can end this."

Rossin panted, eyes bulging, saliva, puke and snot running down his face. His mouth trembled and twisted but no words escaped. Finally, he reached out with a shaking hand and pointed to his brother.

Shantara released him, dropping his face back to the puddle of vomit. She cast Caleb a cold glance. "Do it."

"I can't fix his mind," he told her. "It will probably be worse than before. He might not be worth it."

Shantara's black eyes did not waver. "Do it."

Caleb shrugged and came to kneel beside Rossin. He gripped the shattered head in his hands and summoned his magic once more. Rossin screamed then, his back arching as he convulsed. The wound in his head shifted and cracked, bone sliding to cover brain and morphing his skull into something grotesquely misshapen. His face scarred over around his right eye and cheek, skin knitting together into ghastly, mottled ridges. When he was finished, Caleb released him and stood, taking a step back to rejoin Shantara.

Rossin lay on his face a moment, panting, and then pushed himself up, rising to his knees. His ravaged face lifted toward them, catching sunlight, a gruesome distortion of a man. The right side of his head was a fist sized hollow where his skull had been crushed and the reformed skin on his face below was a maze of folds, creases, and raised scars.

Shantara grimaced. "Fuck."

Caleb scowled back at her. "My power is not limitless and I used no small measure restoring myself and then you."

Rossin ran a shaking hand over his face and head, finger probing. His small, dark eyes widened as he felt the depression above his right ear and traced the lines along his face. He repeated the process a half dozen times, a slow, drooling smile widening as he went.

"It doesn't matter." He shook his head, saliva and puke dripping from his chin. "Was an ugly shit anyway." He held up his hands and flexed his fingers. "These work. They can still cut. That matters."

Caleb and Shantara stared at him for a long time, watching the way he grinned at them, looking from one to the other, his head all odd angles and scars, blood, drool and puke. He was looking at them with wide, mad eyes, the sick smile still splitting what passed for his face. He watched them in turn. And waited.

Like a fucking dog, Caleb thought.

Shantara waved a dismissive hand and turned away. "Find his blades or whatever else is lying around. We have to move."

"To where?" Caleb asked, ignoring Rossin.

"Sentry," Shantara called back. "We still need to find Jantalus. I assume you agree?"

As if I have a choice, he thought. She was walking away from him expecting him to follow. Rossin was watching him, waiting to be told what to do. He had gone from having leverage over Shantara to assuming the role of a nanny to what was left of Rossin while she carried on like the lady of the house as usual.

Any advantage he had hoped for disappeared into the wind. Any promise of payment he might have secured from her was a lie. She was the stronger and he had been a fool to think otherwise. Even so, it would have been a mistake to deny her. As much as he hated her, hated her power, she was right about Jantalus. If the sorcerer learned the truth of his past at Sentry, he would come for them and there might be no stopping him. Together, they might ambush him before he reached the place. Failing that, they would certainly need each other against him.

"To Sentry," he said, grinding his teeth in frustration. It seemed he and Shantara were together by necessity even if they both wished otherwise.

She stopped where she was and called back to Rossin, patting her hip to draw him to her side. Like a faithful, slobbering hound, he hurried after her, cackling like a mad man. He was hers. She would have Caleb keep watch over him when she was bored with him, but Rossin looked to her. Of course he did, Caleb thought. She always treated him like a pile of shit.

Shantara called again, beckoning to him in a way only slightly less insulting than how she had called to Rossin. Caleb followed, curiosity overruling anger for the moment. Best, he decided, to see what she was planning. It might just work to his benefit as well.

And if it did not, he could always wait for his next opportunity and kill her.

Chapter Twenty-Eight

It was almost dark by the time Jantalus caught sight of the Avarun camp. As Devoc had promised, it had taken all day to cross the Valley of the Sacred to the short pass at its western end. They had found the river he had seen from above two days before and followed it until it ended in a large lake. At that point, they could see the pass well enough and skirted along the water's edge to it.

All of Devoc's supplies had been loaded onto his mule and the old man alternated between riding along with his things and walking beside the animal, one hand on its thick neck to guide him. The lead rope was wrapped around Jantalus's hand as he carried Halonni. She had tried riding the mule herself for a time, but the odd positioning and rocking motion hurt more than it helped and she abandoned the idea quickly enough. Between carrying her and fighting to keep the mule moving, Jantalus wondered how he had made any progress at all. They were in the pass though, the worst of the journey behind them, looking out at a collection of dozens of tents and fires that dotted the near edge of the valley. Horses milled about in the open fields and children chased goats as they strayed from the herd.

Halonni's head lifted from his shoulder, her ashen face beaded with sweat, and looked out across the camp with him. A sigh slipped between her lips. "I'd feel better about going there if I was sure we were welcome."

Devoc shuffled forward, his staff clicking on the rocks. "You are. Trust, girl. Just a bit, now. Old Devoc will see you safe. I am Suledane and my sister, Gyun, is the Elder of the tribe. No one will harm you. No one will cross the spirits."

Halonni looked from the old man back to Jantalus. "If they see the mark-."

"Mark?" the old man leaned close. "What mark?"

Halonni bit her lip. "She means me," Jantalus answered. "I bear the mark of the dead."

Devoc cocked his head to one side and tucked his staff under his arm. His gnarled old hands reached out for Jantalus's face and the sorcerer did not stop him. Rough, calloused, the fingers trailed over his skin, pressing at the temples and cheeks, searching. The old man's thumbs went to his eyes, brushing over the eyelids. He let out a hiss that might have been pain and the hands jerked back.

"Demon!" the old magician breathed. "You carry the magic of another world."

"Jantalus saved your life!" Halonni protested.

Devoc scratched at his chin. "The spirits do not lie. If a demon is to save me, then a demon is meant to save me. I do not question the spirits. I do not pretend to know all." He set his staff against the ground once more. "Come. My people will let you pass on my word. I will speak to Gyun about this mark you bear."

Without waiting for a response, the old man tapped his way forward, guided by the sounds of the camp and leaving the mule for Jantalus to lead on. He gathered up the lead rope and followed for lack of another option. Down the gentle slope of the pass they came, the trail flattening against the valley floor and then disappearing into the hard, barren fields. A knot of men approached them as they neared the camp, all bearing great, broad-headed spears and long knives like the ones Ord had. Devoc stopped when he heard their approach and raised a hand in greeting. The men approached a few more steps before recognizing him, at which point a great, whooping cheer went up among them. One of their number turned to race back to the camp, shouting the news of Devoc's return.

Jantalus stayed safely behind the old man for a time as he conversed with those who had come to meet them. They spoke the strange language of the Avaruns and Jantalus could follow none of it. He glanced at Halonni, but she looked as lost as he. He saw the men all turn to look at them, faces twisted in fear and anger. The Avarun men were all sharp outbursts and gestures, but Devoc pounded his staff against the hard earth and they fell silent. He spoke to them once more, his voice even and controlled and the men nodded along with his words, although they looked no happier with him.

Devoc waved Jantalus forward. He took a deep breath and complied, leading the mule as he came, shifting Halonni's weight a bit to relieve the pain in his back. The men speaking to Devoc stared at him, a few even retreating as he came to stand at the old man's shoulder.

"These men," Devoc told him, "will take you somewhere and let you rest. I will go to my sister to speak with her and send someone to help you. These men will not harm you. I have explained that you have been sent by the spirits and their souls are at risk if their fear should win out over their sense."

One of the men extended a hand for the mule's lead rope and snatched it away as soon as Jantalus handed it to him. He led the animal away as fast as he could. Another man came forward to speak with him, but his words were gibberish to Jantalus and Halonni.

"He asks if you wish for him to carry your woman," Devoc translated.

Halonni's arms tightened on his neck as she shook her head. "No." She paused, her eyes meeting Jantalus's. "I mean, if you can carry me."

Jantalus shook his head at Devoc. "Tell him I am fine."

Devoc waved them after him, promising to send someone and to be along himself when he was able. They exchanged uncertain glances and then followed their guide. He led them through the camp without speaking or even looking their way. The Avaruns stared as they passed, children gathering around to watch before being shooed away by their mothers. A few caught sight of Jantalus's black eyes and cried out in horror, but a few shouts from the man who guided them sent them away.

They were taken to a large canvas tent decorated with strange symbols. The man pulled the flap away and pointed inside. Jantalus bent down as far as he could while holding Halonni and peered into it. No one was inside, only piles of bedding, clothing and other personal items. He looked back at the man who simply pointed into the tent again and grunted. Jantalus stepped inside and the man followed. The Avarun went to a pile of fur bedding and pointed, his dark face intense.

He was telling them to stay, Jantalus realized. He nodded in response and the man returned the gesture before leaving them.

Jantalus took Halonni to the pile of furs and gently placed her atop it before dropping down beside her. She leaned back against the soft bedding with a groan and closed her eyes. "So we wait?"

"I suppose so," he answered. "There doesn't seem to be another choice."

He pulled a pair of heavy blankets over her and then wrapped one around himself and settled back next to her. They could hear the Avaruns without, tending to their animals, going about their chores and calling to each other in their strange language. Jantalus could also see two pairs of feet near the tent flap. Guards, he assumed, watching to be sure the strangers stayed where they were supposed to be. The idea of it might have made him angry any other time, but he was so tired and aching that he closed his eyes and ignored it.

He felt Halonni gently lift his arm from his side, and slip under it, her head resting against his shoulder. She was still too warm, her face glistening sweat even as she shivered beside him. Halonni cradled his injured hand in both of hers and looked it over. His fingers were stained with dried blood and purple where the tips poked out from the filthy cloak he had wrapped the whole mess in.

"You didn't say anything," she told him after they were quiet for a time.

He waited for her to elaborate, but she simply lay with him, holding his hand. "About what?"

"Me kissing you."

He put his free hand behind his head and closed his eyes. "Don't let it bother you. I didn't let my imagination get the better of my sense."

She shifted slightly, her head tilting up to look at him, one hand coming up to touch his face. He opened his eyes and looked back at her, trying to read the emotion behind the way she chewed her bottom lip and the way her eyes held his.

"I spent more time taking care of you than anyone else but myself I suppose. I told you what I thought of that, how many times I wondered if it was right or wrong. We were walking the streets of Ulis, lost and hunted and I was still wondering. But things have changed, Jantalus. Maybe you have, maybe you haven't. My perception of you has, I know that. You speak to me of owing so often, but you really don't owe me anything. We chose to take you in. We chose to risk it. Even Durn made a choice when he sent you away and faced those Sentinels alone in Marcester. I was honest with you when I told you that taking care of you was as much about Durn and myself as it was you. Do you remember that?"

"I do."

She drew a breath and let it out slowly. "I suppose I told you that because I wanted you to know that something besides yourself was at stake. It was selfish, but more than that, I think it was a test. I think I wanted to see how you would react. If you were what that mark says you are, what I wanted wasn't going to mean much. But something happened between Marcester and here, Jantalus. I stopped taking care of you and you started looking out for me. Why? Not because you owe me. You really don't. So, why?"

The tent flap moved aside before he could answer and Devoc entered, his staff tapping against the canvas flooring as he ducked through. A woman as old as he followed, taller and grayer, without the markings on her face and hands, but unmistakably his kin. Jantalus eased Halonni away as they entered and sat up to face them.

Devoc tapped his way over to them. "Gyun, Elder of the Wydant."

"Wydant?" Halonni asked as she placed a hand on Jantalus's shoulder and pulled herself up a bit.

"Our tribe," the old magician answered. "She would speak to you." He bowed his head to his sister and retreated a step.

Gyun took his place, pulling a small wooden stool over to sit on as she squared herself before them. Jantalus could not guess at her age, though it was obvious she was no longer young. Everything about her defied the passage of time. Her hair had grayed, but her skin was still tight and smooth, marred only by the slightest lines around her eyes and mouth. She moved with an easy strength that suggested she was still sound of body as well. The dark eyes that measured them were bright and clear and burned with life.

"My brother says you saved his life." A halting cadence to her speech spoke to a lack of practice rather than knowledge of their language. "My people are in your debt for that. He also tells me you each bring magic to our camp, one the power of the spirits, the other the mark of dark, evil things."

Halonni shook her head at the old woman. "You do not have to be afraid. Jantalus is no danger to you. We are only here because we had no choice in the matter. We had no intention of trespassing on your sacred lands."

The Elder nodded. "That may be true, but the fact remains that you have. Ordinarily, my people are peaceful unless we must defend ourselves.

This, however, is the first full moon of spring and the most sacred time for us. Outsiders are forbidden and the penalty for trespass is death."

Jantalus leaned forward a bit, his black eyes boring into hers. "That is a judgment you may regret trying to enforce."

She stiffened at his words, her chin lifting. "My brother thinks you are here for a reason. He claims the spirits sent you and that your presence is not a bad omen, but a sign. Because of his belief and the fact that the Suledane know the spirits better than I, I have agreed to hear your reasons for being here before I make any decision."

Jantalus nodded. "All right, then. Men came into the Tijian before winter and vanished. One of them might have been my father. I am searching for him and those who vanished with him. They are said to have come through the mountains. I was headed to Zantizan looking for information about them."

Gyun stared at him a moment and then turned to her brother. "You knew this?"

Devoc shrugged. "The spirits did not ask. If they do not, I do not."

She turned back to Jantalus. "These men you speak of went to Kiranon – the mountain to the north of this valley. The Valley of the Sacred is where the spirits live, but Kiranon is where they are born. The oldest tales of our people say the mountain was once a great pillar of fire from which the spirits sprang to life. Deep inside it are the spirits who have left this world and those who have yet to enter it. If the spirits live in the valley, they sleep in the mountain. It is why we forced your kings to remove their men who dug holes there. They defiled our sacred places and risked awakening spirits who wished to be left alone."

"Do you know anything of the men who went there in the fall?" Halonni asked.

Gyun nodded once. "They came from the east, through what your people call Agron Pass. One of the Avarun tribes, the Kokanan, tried to bar their way, but these men you speak of cut them down with magic the like of which our people have never seen. Your people reached the mountain fortress and did battle with each other. None of them left the mountain that we know of, but there are things on Kiranon still, left behind in the wake of their madness."

"Left behind?" Jantalus turned to Halonni, but she shrugged her ignorance. "What do you mean? There are survivors?"

"What is left up there is not alive," Devoc answered for his sister. "Up there, the dead walk. Some have bodies like you and I. Others? They are nothing but mist that kills when it brushes against the living. Dark magic rules that place now. Dark and evil." He pointed to Jantalus. "The spirits say you have come to destroy it."

Gyun's hand came up sharply. "So you say, brother. I am not yet convinced. I have called a meeting of my most trusted advisors and sent word to the Haudeno. I would speak to the Suledane among them as well. For now, you will stay here. I have women with me who can tend to your wounds and provide water to bathe. Food will be brought. Devoc will let you use this tent as long as you need it."

"And Kiranon?" Jantalus asked as she rose from her seat.

"I will speak with the Suledane," she answered. She did not wait for further comment before speaking a word in her own language to her brother and ducking back through the tent flap.

Devoc clapped his hands and rubbed them together. "This is good." He smiled like a madman.

"Good?" Halonni asked with a raised eyebrow. "How so?"

The grin never slipped. "You are still alive." He tapped his way back to the tent entrance. "I will send Gyun's attendants; we will speak again while you are tended to and rested."

He opened the canvas flap again and called to people without, his gnarled hand waving them in. A trio of young girls entered, none as old as Halonni. They carried towels, clothing and basins of water and small bags hung from their shoulders. Devoc spoke to them briefly, pointing at Jantalus and Halonni as he did. Two of them went to Halonni while the third hung a blanket from the long poles that braced the outer shell of the tent and stretched it across to cut the space in half. Devoc beckoned Jantalus to him while Halonni stayed with the two girls on the far side of the tent.

"Sit," Devoc told him, tapping about for one of the nearby stools.

Jantalus guided Devoc to a seat first and then took one for himself. The remaining Avarun girl approached slowly, her eyes darting to the old man, though he could not see it. She reached into her bag, pulled out several wooden jars and bandages and knelt before Jantalus. She hesitated a moment and then spoke to Devoc.

The old man answered with a laugh. "She asked me if your blood will turn her into a demon. I told her only if she does her work poorly."

Not the best answer he could have given, Jantalus thought, but said nothing. The girl took his injured hand, her eyes avoiding his, and began unwrapping the filthy old cloak. He hissed air though his teeth as the fabric clung to the dry blood and the girl poured a measure of water on it to loosen it before finally lifting it away from the wound. He examined it with her as she looked it over. His palm and the back of his hand were a brutal mess of torn flesh and blood. A flap of skin covered the hole on the back, but his palm was nothing but a gaping wound. He steeled himself as she began to wash it, her hands practiced and gentle. The flesh beneath the dirt and dried blood was mottled with bruises and his fingers were purple and swollen. He tried to wiggle them, but only the first and last moved. The two in the middle twitched slightly. It hurt enough that he decided not to try again.

The girl smeared a white paste on two pieces of cloth and pressed them into both sides of the wound before wrapping his whole hand in a clean white cloth. When she was finished, she cleaned the cut over his eye and then turned to Devoc, speaking again.

"She wants to know if you have other wounds," the old man translated.

"Nothing she can treat," he answered.

The girl spoke again and the old man grinned. "She wants to know if she needs to wash you."

"I think I can manage that myself."

The girl produced a small cup, scooped some water into it and then crumbled a few dark leaves in it. She held it out to him. He made no move to take it, watching her carefully. She waited a moment and then spoke to Devoc again.

"It will ease your pain and help you sleep," the old man told him. "Its effects are slow and subtle. It is not dangerous."

Jantalus took the cup, sniffed the contents and then drank it down. It had almost no taste. "Thank you."

Devoc translated and the girl answered briefly before collecting her medicines and bandages and slipping though the screening blanket to help those who tended Halonni. "She is not disappointed you will bathe yourself," Devoc told him with a laugh. "You must be ugly as well as marked by demons."

"Do you think your sister will allow us to go to the mountain?" Jantalus asked as he stripped off his clothing.

"She may. She may not." The old man shrugged. "She is wise and fair, but this is a sacred time and she must not appear to our people to be allowing outsiders to defile our blessed lands. For many years, our people have rejoiced that no outsiders walk the sacred mountain. There was once a mining town, and before it, a watchtower. Sentry, your people called it. Your kings gave it up when our peoples made peace. But now? Already outsiders have shed blood on Kiranon and summoned the souls of the dead. This makes things difficult for her. Difficult for you."

"This Sentry is where the other outsiders went?"

Devoc nodded. "That is where they did battle. That is where the souls of the dead are so restless."

Jantalus soaked a towel in the water basin and began to wash, discovering scrapes and bruises in places he had not realized before. He recalled no name on the map, but he remembered seeing a town marked on the mountain that the Avaruns called Kiranon. He wanted to ask something more about it, but he sensed Devoc was not much more comfortable with the thought of outsiders there than his sister had been.

"Who are the Haudeno?" he asked instead.

"Another tribe from the southern end of the valley. We stay in the north. Here, near the Valley of the Sacred, is neutral land. All have access to it. We are not enemies with the Haudeno, but our peoples have differences. The Wydant live under the shadow of Kiranon, a sacred place. The Haudeno demand access to it. Gyun does not think any but the Suledane should tread there, not even herself."

Jantalus said nothing for a time as he washed his face and hair, rinsing clean with the remaining water before dressing with the provided clothing. They were loose fitting and comfortable, deerskin he assumed, but perhaps made from another animal from the Tijian he did not know. When he was finished, he took his seat beside the old magician again.

"How long before the other tribe and their holy men come?"

"A day or two," Devoc answered. "It depends on how eager they wish to seem. If they hurry, they look like they are coming as Gyun commands. If they are slow, the Suledane among them will be angry when they discover that this concerns the spirits. A day or two will satisfy all."

One of the women called from the other side of the curtain and

Devoc responded. "They have finished. They will be back to build a fire. When you have rested they will return and bring you food."

One of the women took down the makeshift curtain while the other two gathered their things and left. Jantalus rose and walked back to Halonni where she sat up on the great pile of furs.

His breath caught when her face lifted to meet his. All the dirt, blood, and fatigue had covered her face so long that he had nearly forgotten. Dark circles still stained her face under her eyes and she had a small cut at the top of her forehead near her hairline where their heads had clashed, but she was more stunning than he ever remembered seeing her. Her long black hair had been washed, dried and combed, hanging loose over her shoulders except for a pair of small braids at her temples. Her old, filthy clothes were gone, replaced by a long, loose doeskin dress.

She stared back at him a moment, a puzzled look on her delicate face. Finally, a slow, shy smile curled the corner of her mouth. "What? Is it the clothes? They feel strange."

He shook his head as he crossed the tent to her. "The clothes are fine. How do you feel?"

She pulled up the hem of her dress to expose her bruised and swollen knee. "It still hurts, but they gave me something to drink that one of them indicated would help me sleep." She winced as she straightened the leg. "I'm starting to doubt that."

He knelt down and pulled her blankets over her. "Try to get some sleep. Gyun is meeting with others to decide what to do about us."

"I know. I heard. What if they decide we are trespassers after all?"

He shrugged. "Then we will need our strength. Now rest." He gathered a few blankets and spread them out a few paces away, preparing a bed for himself. As he worked, the women who had tended to them returned. They did not speak, but began arranging wood in a shallow pit at the center of the tent. They lit the small pile and added more as the fire began to grow. When they were finished, they brought in several more armloads of logs and left, closing the tent flap behind them.

"Friendly," Halonni muttered as the girls departed.

Jantalus shook his head and finished building a thick bed for himself out of the furs. The fire warmed the tent quickly enough, the smoke rising up through a small hole in the top of the canvas cover. He added more wood to be sure it would last for a few hours while they slept. He stripped off the tunic he was wearing and then settled into bed and pulled the blankets over himself.

"Devoc interrupted you before you answered me," she said as he closed his eyes. "I asked you why you take care of me the way you do."

He drew a deep breath and turned on his side to face her. She was watching him carefully, her gray eyes holding his again, her bottom lip pinned nervously beneath her teeth again. "I didn't have an answer anyway. His timing saved me." He looked back at the tent flap. "No luck, now."

"So I get no answer?"

He threw off his blankets, crawled to her and reached up to take her face in his good hand, her skin warm and damp against his. "I don't know the answer. I'm not trying to slip out of answering. I'm not playing a game. Things are just never... right, I suppose. In my head, I mean. Every thought, every feeling, comes with a little fractured piece of memory attached to it. Have I seen, heard, or done something before? Why and with whom? Nothing is simple. Nothing is right or wrong. Everything is a question. Does that make sense?"

She nodded slowly. "I think so." She shook her head. "No."

Of course it doesn't. How could it?

"You tell me at every turn how I have to keep an open mind. You tell me to believe that I will be proven someone worth all of this effort and suffering. But what if you're wrong? What if I am everything I don't want to be? Better that you keep me at a certain distance until we are sure."

"But-."

He bent and kissed the top of her head. "Get some sleep. We can talk later."

He pulled away from her and retreated to his own bedding. He pulled the blankets up around his shoulders again and turned away from her. Sleep, he told himself. He was too tired and his mind spinning too fast with everything to think all of it over. He would sort it all out when he was rested. The warmth of the fire spread over him and he let the tension ease away.

He might have dozed off for a moment before he felt her come to him. He stirred at her touch, his eyes slipping open. Halonni was next to him, propped up on one elbow, her face hovering close to his, her dark hair all about him like a veil. He tried to speak, but her little hand came up, her fingers pressed to his lips.

"Don't say anything, you don't have to. What you've done says all I needed to hear."

She leaned down to kiss him, her lips soft and sweet, the smell of her filling the breath of air between them. She slipped his blankets off of him with one hand, rolling gingerly into his embrace. She let out a soft groan as she set her injured knee against his leg but did not break their kiss. One hand pulled the hem of the dress up and she shrugged her slender shoulders out of the top. Damp with sweat, her warm skin pressed against his.

He reached for her with his good hand, but the web of purple and black along her ivory skin stopped him. She took his wrist and pulled his hand to her. "You won't hurt me."

Jantalus broke away, staring up at her as he gasped for air. "Halonni-."

She shook her head. "You won't," she told him again.

He pulled the blankets up around them both and spoke not another word.

Chapter Twenty-Nine

Jantalus woke as the fire was dying down, its embers barely more than an angry flare in the darkness. Halonni was curled up next to him, skin to skin, her legs tangled with his, breath soft and warm on his neck. He stroked her feverish face absently, staring past the glow of the embers, past the shadows of the far side of the tent. Everything about him was silent. The Avaruns were asleep, he assumed. No animals were being herded about, no children laughing and playing. There was only him, Halonni and the glow of the fire.

For the first time since he had awakened in the back of Durn's cart, staring up at the old man in the cold autumn sun, he began to doubt the worth of pushing on. Pain and exhaustion had been the whole of his search for who and what he was. Sentry, the best chance at any answers to all of his questions, was an entire mountain and possibly a camp full of Avaruns away. Already he had been beaten and separated from his companions, one hand crippled. Halonni could not even walk on her own. What more lay ahead for them and what price would they have to pay?

It would have been simple enough to walk away from it all. He would find Devoc, tell him they had no desire to reach Sentry and should be clear of the Avarun's lands as soon as possible. Zantizan was close by and Tyris and Stilthius had likely gone there to wait for them in the hope they had survived the rockslide in Greylock Pass. In a matter of hours, they could leave it all behind and start over somewhere. They would have to see to Durn, of course, but that was for when they were stronger.

His impulse was to wake Halonni, tell her it was all over and he was willing to forget the past and settle for who he was. The harder he looked into who he had been, the less he liked what he saw. Where was the harm in wiping it all away and moving on?

He almost convinced himself of it, but every time he closed in on the decision, he saw the same image in his mind that haunted his every hour. It was his mother, shrouded in the smoke of his burning home, her neck bent at all the wrong angle, her eyes frozen and staring, blood dribbling from her mouth, one hand stretched out as if reaching for help her son was too weak to give. That image shoved aside all thought he gave to giving up his search for the past. He still owed someone a debt in blood for what had happened to his mother. Mordoc might be dead and that reckoning was not his to see through. But his father was missing as well. If he were alive, at least Jantalus could do something he was unable to do for his mother. If they were all dead, if every step from Marcester to the moment he faced failure was a waste, at least he could start the new life he dreamed of with no tether to the past.

He looked down at Halonni, his fingers tracing the fine lines of her exquisite face. Enough, he told himself. His path led to Kiranon, to a confrontation with where he had been and who he used to be. Halonni was done with this journey. She had given enough, physically and otherwise, to see him though. What was left to do was for him.

He eased his arm out from under her and pulled away. She stirred slightly, one hand reaching up to touch his face. He closed his own over it a moment and then gently pulled it away. She settled into their blankets and fell back to sleep in moments. He bent to kiss her soft black hair and then rose. He found his pants and tunic and his worn old boots and dressed. Ord's cloak lay across a stool where he left it and he wrapped it about his shoulders. He gathered up a bag and shoved a few spare blankets inside. He took a wooden jug full of warm, bitter ale and wrapped it in a spare cloak, also placing that in the bag. He searched about for something to eat, but found nothing.

A small matter, he told himself. He would live a few days without food if that was what it took. He went to the tent flap to listen a moment and then slipped it open a crack to peer outside. The camp was asleep, watch fires blazing on the perimeter, but no one other than the single guard outside his door was about. He retreated and looked about for a moment before deciding on one of the fist-sized stones that served as a barrier around the fire pit at the center of the room. He threw a few pieces of wood on the fire and took the rock.

His black gaze settled on Halonni for a moment and he felt an ache in the hollow of his stomach. Would she understand? If he survived this, would she forgive? He steeled himself and hefted the rock. It had to be done. She had endured enough. But then came a moment of doubt. A flash of conscience said he was rationalizing leaving her by blaming her. He shook it away. His decision had been made.

He hit the man guarding the tent just hard enough to render him unconscious. One arm wrapped about the man, he dragged him to the side of an adjacent tent and left him there.

He allowed himself one last glance at Devoc's tent and then slung the old leather bag over his shoulder and started north out of camp. One watch fire stood between him and the mountain, Kiranon. Already, he could see the man posted there leaning casually against a nearby tree, his spear hanging loose in his hand.

Slow and quiet, using the surrounding trees to mask his movements as much as possible, he slipped by the drowsy sentry.

No one saw him go as he vanished into the darkness.

"I think he's lost," Stilthius Menion muttered to his brother.

Ahead of them, Addicus Malshere stood on the slope of the northern face of Mount Greylock, staring over the deep, wide valley that separated it from the peak called Kiranon. Derek and Lorum Ravensbourne flanked him, wrapped in heavy cloaks over their mail, swords at their belts and leather packs across their backs. Shaddix and a handful of Black River mercenaries waited a few paces away, the dark looks they cast the way of the old Vicar saying they wanted nothing more to do with him than necessary.

"I don't think he knew where the fuck he was going in the first place," Tyris answered without any mind to how loud he was. Lorum looked over at him and Tyris spat in his direction, a wad of phlegm falling far short.

The lot of them were together because they had to be and for no other reason. Addicus had retreated to his quarters to search out Jantalus Kathias with his magic, leaving Tyris and Stilthius with the Ravensbournes and Shaddix the whole night. Lorum had spun a tale about Jantalus Kathias, his family and the events surrounding the slaughter at Drappel that was hard to believe at the time. A full day to think it over had left him no closer to believing it or not. He and Stilthius had discussed it for a few moments while preparing to leave Zantizan and Tyris got no sense that his brother had a clear opinion of it all.

Addicus insisted they waste no time and they had barely finished packing supplies when he rushed them all out of Zantizan. The old mining tunnels in Mount Greylock were extensive and a few had been bored from one side to the next, making for the fastest route into the valley beyond. It was there, along the eastern edge, that the old man claimed to have sensed Jantalus's presence. He shared, when pressed, that he was not alone, though Addicus could not identify the second source of magic he felt. It was strong, the old man told them, but he knew no more. When they were closer, the old man advised, he would try again.

The source must be Halonni, the brothers had decided to their shared relief. Their faith had not been misplaced.

He looked back to Addicus. The old man was looking from one end of the valley to the other and back again, settling on neither. Agreeing to follow the old man had been more a matter of lacking other options than trusting him. The outlanders' ability to find Jantalus on their own was limited at best. Addicus, in turn, needed them. The risk the old man would have taken approaching Jantalus alone was very real. Without Tyris or Stilthius to assure him there was no danger, the sorcerer would probably kill any marked man he saw without hesitation.

"We moving or camping here?" Tyris asked finally.

Addicus Malshere turned toward him slowly, his black eyes glinting in the half-light of the new dawn. "There is another presence in the valley. Someone else has come. Jantalus is to the east. The new magic I sense comes from the west and is headed this way."

"Not Halonni, then," Tyris told his brother. "Not unless they got separated."

Addicus Malshere's black eyes narrowed. "Who?"

"Our other friend we told you about. She was with him."

The old man's expression did not change. "She wields magic as well?"

The outlander shrugged. "You're asking the wrong person, old man. I know less about magic than I do knitting. What difference does it make?"

Addicus sneered and turned to Stilthius. "And you?"

Stilthius shrugged. "Could be the Tassarens. Some of them probably escaped the rockslide. Whatever they're after, they're not the kind to give up."

The black gaze settled on him. "You have no idea. We must reach

Jantalus Kathias before they do or this is all for nothing."

Tyris nodded. He had heard the whole tale and knew what the stakes were. "The longer we stand here, the harder it's all going to be. Keep moving old man."

Lorum Ravensbourne scowled at him. "Carefully, remember? The Avaruns here will have our heads if they find us in the valley. They are unfriendly enough even when it is not their holy time. They'll attack on sight now."

Addicus was moving before Tyris could respond, beckoning them all to follow. Derek and Lorum joined him at once, a step behind as always, a pair of constant shadows. Shaddix and his men trailed, Shaddix himself slowing his pace a bit so that he fell behind with the Menion brothers. He had spoken little throughout the night, though his expression had never changed from the black frown that had settled under his moustache the moment Addicus had announced he was to join them. The mercenary and his men had not been asked. If he thought he would have been allowed to, Shaddix would no doubt have walked right out of Zantizan and disappeared back to Ailen or beyond. He was afraid of Addicus though, and probably with good reason.

"Sorry for all this," he muttered to the brothers as they walked. "Sorry you got all caught up in this shit. Even sorrier for myself."

Tyris shook his head. They had no other way to go now. Being sorry for where they were was pointless. He gestured toward the old man. "What do you think his part is here? You're here because you were afraid to say no. We're here for our own reasons. The Ravensbournes think they might have family and friends stranded out here. But Addicus? He was careful not to say much beyond being friends with Jantalus's father."

Shaddix shrugged his thick shoulders. "That not enough for you? I get your god and your glory and all that, but this Kathias is your friend, isn't he?"

Stilthius nodded. "He is. But Addicus? That son-of-a-bitch was never anyone's friend in his life. Ever. I'd bet my black ass on it."

The mercenary looked them over a moment. "I could find a few hundred people to say the same about you two. Same about me, too." He waved a dismissive hand. "Fuck it. We're here. Guess we just do what we have to and get on with it, eh?"

"Guess so," Tyris agreed.

Shaddix shook his head, set his frown securely in place across his mouth and stomped forward to join his men.

"That old man is playing a game," Stilthius said when no one but his brother was close enough to hear. "I don't know what it is, but he's up to something. He was all for rushing ahead when he thought he had found Jantalus and could reach him without trouble. Now? Learning about Halonni pissed him off. The Tassarens – or whoever else it might be – being close pissed him off even more. Why? If his interest is just in finding Jantalus for the sake of being friends with his father, what fucking difference does it make if Halonni is there? If the Tassarens are coming, wouldn't having Jantalus with us be a help? Halonni too, for that matter. So what the hell is going on?"

Tyris nodded without responding. Stilthius had made good points all, but Tyris had nothing to add to them. Everything smelled like shit, but the old man's boots were clean so far.

They walked in silence for the remainder of the morning, following the others down the rocky slope of the mountainside as it gently melted away into the trees that lined the valley floor. The spruce and pine blunted the force of the wind, but they deflected the warmth of the sun as well and a frosty chill settled over them as they walked.

"How much of it do you believe?" he asked Stilthius after a time. "Of what Lorum told us, I mean."

Stilthius seemed to chew on the matter. "I'm less concerned with the truth or if I even give a shit one way or the other. Maybe he's everything they say he is. Maybe he did things like they say he did. Do I care? Did he do any of it to me? The way I remember the last few weeks, he and that girl saved my ass as much as I saved theirs. Who he was can stay forgotten in the past for all I care. I'll worry about today."

"You know what I think?" Tyris asked.

His brother shrugged. "No. Don't give a shit either." He flashed a toothy smile.

Tyris snorted. "I think it's mostly horseshit. I think Lorum and Derek believe it. I think part of it might even be true. All of it, though? No fucking way. Not the Jantalus Kathias I've known for the last few weeks. I think there's something behind all this and someone benefits from him being some kind of twisted bastard."

"Benefits how?" Stilthius asked.

"I don't know," he answered. "But I'll find out before any of these shits lay a finger on him or Halonni."

Stilthius smirked and clapped him on the back. "Hunnaris set us on this path for a reason. I still believe that. We'll see this through. And he'll see us through it."

Tyris reached over his shoulder to touch his axe. "This will see us through."

Stilthius shoved him and let out a booming laugh. "A gift from Hunnaris, that. Show some respect you heathen fuck!"

"Keep your voices down!" Lorum hissed at them from up ahead. "There could be Avaruns near."

Tyris waved him away. "Piss off, asshole!"

Lorum glared more fiercely.

Stilthius laughed even harder.

Tyris shook his head at them both and prayed to the long faded moon that he was right about Jantalus Kathias.

EDWARD K RYAN

Chapter Thirty

Kiranon was tall and rough, all jutting rock ledges capped with ice and snow that glistened beneath the light of the moon. The lower slopes and their concealing evergreens had given way quickly and Jantalus huddled in his dark cloak in the frigid wind and hoped he was not visible from below. The light of dawn would silhouette him against the snowcap, and he moved as quickly as his aching body would allow. Every part of him not aching from his injuries was numb with cold, but his determination drove him beyond it all. His sense of direction was limited to climbing higher and nothing more. In the dark, nothing looked familiar compared to the maps he had studied before they were lost under the rockslide in Greylock Pass.

He glanced back down at the watch fires of the Avarun camp a few times during the first few hours, but now stayed focused ahead. Nothing but doubt and regret came of trying to pick out Devoc's tent among the little black specks along the valley floor. He had wrapped one of the blankets he had taken around himself and torn another into strips to protect his hands and face. It was not keeping him warm, but it was keeping him alive.

He located the old trail used by the miners years before as the sun broke over the mountains and lit Kiranon with a fiery glow. The path was faded from the years of neglect since the Avaruns regained the place, strewn with rock that had tumbled down from above, but it was far easier to navigate than the rocky mountainside around it. He climbed for hours. Rockslides had buried parts of the path over the years and he was forced to climb over them, dragging himself across the ice-slicked stones, slipping and sliding as he went, tearing the skin from his hands and bruising every inch of his body. His injured hand was bleeding again, crimson staining through the bandages beneath the wraps he had made from his blanket.

At one point he halted, wrapped in his remaining blanket in the sun in the center of the trail, soaking in what heat it provided, resting as much as possible. Rocks along the trail ahead blunted the force of the wind and made it almost bearable. He managed a short nap, but nothing substantial and growing frustrated enough to simply pull himself back to his feet and keep walking.

It was late in the day, the shadows long across the trail, when he came to the spot he remembered most from Dareth Sya's map. The path continued ahead of him, but he knew from the map that it simply rose higher into the mountain before descending the other side. It was the trail to his left that was important. It cut across the face of the mountain and wound to the top. It would lead him to Sentry - assuming he could make the climb, of course. What the maps had not shown him was that the trail was buried under huge rocks, leaving no sign of a pathway ever existing.

He dug the toe of his boot into a depression in the massive boulder next to him and began climbing.

The rocks were frosted over and he slid and fell as much as he climbed. He was aching and bleeding by the time he pulled clear of the patch of jagged stones, standing once more on a trail that led deeper into the mountain. This one was even more faded than the last, just a depression in the thin layer of snow that remained along the length of Kiranon. Above him, broken fingers of rock stretched into the clear cold sky, blocking out what was left of the sun and plunging him into near darkness.

He trudged on, shaking and limping along on bruised legs. Soon, he told himself, one way or another, it would be over. Desperate for food, his gut twisted and groaned as he went. Every pounding step sent shockwaves of pain through his feet. His face was raw from the wind and the cold mountain air seared his throat. His back ached so much he walked with a hunch. His heartbeat pounded in his ears. He had exhausted his supply of ale and had filled his wooden jug with snow and placed it under his tunic to melt, turning his skin to ice against it.

Jantalus thought of Halonni as he walked, trying to distract himself from the pain and cold. He lost count of how many times he told himself he had done right by leaving her behind. The Avaruns would not harm her, he reminded himself over and over again. Devoc believed her touched by the spirits and his sister had been far more concerned with the mark of the dead and the possibility of Jantalus treading on sacred ground than Halonni.

They might refuse to let her go to Kiranon, but she would stay with them as long a Devoc advocated for her. He owed her more than to abandon her in the night and strike out alone, he supposed. Much more, in fact. Keeping her safe, ending the insufferable running and fighting, and ensuring there were no more days without food and sleep were all he had to offer. She might not understand or agree, but at least she would benefit.

His thoughts turned to the Menion brothers. That they were alive was an assumption he had made soon after being separated from them. Samarus and Rossin were dead and Caleb might be as well. Shantara's magic might have saved her from the rockslide, but her interest was in Jantalus and no one else. The outlanders had no information that would benefit her. She was well aware that Sentry was the ultimate goal and needed no one to tell her that. No, she would have no use for Tyris and Stilthius Menion. They might come looking for him, but he hoped against it. If not for Devoc's belief that Halonni shared her power with his spirits in some way, Jantalus believed the Avaruns would have killed them for violating their sacred time and place. The outlanders would have no such protection.

Time drifted away from him as he turned every possibility and question over in his mind hundreds of times. The moon was rising in the sky again when he finally stopped and took notice of it. Hunnaris, the outlanders believed, was the god of the moon. A god of war. Of death. Of struggle. Jantalus drew a deep breath and stared at the ivory hole in the curtain of black. He could use some help with his struggles. If that came from a god he had no faith in, he figured to take it anyway.

In the end, he could not be sure if it was his stubborn refusal to feel pain, cold and fatigue or some divine aid, but he found himself staring up a wide, sloping path at a collection of crumbling buildings that had once been the old Alliance mining town. A flat ledge of rock lay across the mountain above him, the empty shells of ancient stone structures scattered along it. Behind it all, rising up like a black giant against the pale moon, was the single tower of the fortress from which Sentry took its name. Older than the buildings beneath it, the tower was in better condition than the rest, tall and strong against the wind.

As he stared up at the black, empty windows Jantalus felt the cold hollow in his stomach fade away, replaced by the searing fire of his magic. Something called back to him, something powerful. He closed his eyes and concentrated on that power. No, he realized at once. Not one thing. Many.

Magics of all different intensities permeated the place, some barely perceptible and others brutally strong. Among them, he found one that felt familiar. It was the strongest, the most intense in provoking a response from his own magic as he sought it out.

He had faced this level of power before. Both times, Halonni had been at his side to do battle with it.

Now, injured, exhausted and shaking with cold, he would face it alone.

A rough, calloused hand on her shoulder brought Halonni Vilcris awake with a start. She recoiled, clutching the heavy blankets to her naked body. Devoc was standing over her, his staff tapping all about, searching. Light seeped into the tent from the open flap at the entrance and she could hear men shouting without. She turned to ask Jantalus what was happening, but he was gone.

"Where's your friend?" Devoc asked a moment before she asked him the same question.

She searched beneath the blankets for her clothing, finally found a handful of the doeskin dress and pulled it over her head before someone besides the blind old man wandered in. "I don't know. He might have gone to-."

The words froze in her mouth. The stool across the room caught her attention as she looked about. Jantalus's cloak, the one he had found on the dead man at the river, was gone. His boots had been close to it and they too were gone. He was not out relieving himself or looking for food for them from the Avaruns. He was gone.

"No one's seen him?" she asked the old man, struggling to sit up. Every movement of her knee sent sharp, stabbing pain up and down her leg.

Devoc knelt down in front of her, his milky eyes staring past her. "You listen, girl. He cracked the guard's head with a stone and left by the look of it. You need to tell me what you know before Gyun asks herself."

"What I know? Nothing, that's what. I was sleeping. You woke me, didn't you?"

The old magician nodded. "I did." He held a hand out to her. "You must come with me."

Halonni made no move to take the proffered hand. "Why?"

"Gyun will speak with you. She is not pleased that her guard was injured or that your friend is missing. She is not pleased with the other outsiders either."

She shook her head, trying to process it all. "What other outsiders? What are you talking about?"

He thrust the hand forth again. "Come with me and we will find out together."

She took the hand finally and let him pull her up. Leaning heavily on the old magician, she directed him around the shelter while she gathered her cloak and her battered old boots. Forcing her left foot into the cold, stiff leather was agony, her swollen, aching knee sending lancing pain through her as she wiggled and pushed and pulled. She could hear men outside as she worked. They called to each other in gruff, angry tones, though she understood none of what they said.

When Devoc finally led her through the tent flap, she found a half-dozen men gathered around one of their fellows as he sat back on a stack of firewood. The sitting man held a bloodstained cloth to the back of his head, his face contorted in pain. He looked up as Halonni and Devoc emerged, one finger pointing as he barked what she could only guess were insults at her. The others gathered about turned and added their own angry words, but a shout from Devoc silenced them all.

The old man led her away from them, weaving through the collection of tents toward the central fire pit. Dozens of men and women were gathered, and Halonni could make out Gyun's slender form atop a wooden platform that stood close to the fire. She staggered into their midst, Devoc all but dragging her. Her whole body was a weak, shivering collection of aching muscles and throbbing injuries and her face glistened with sweat from her fever. A murmur went up among the assembled Avaruns as Devoc brought her to the center of the circle, stopping opposite the fire from Gyun as she stared down from her seat like some sort of monarch from a throne. A handful of others, men and women of similar age, flanked her, their faces grave and their eyes judging as they looked down at her.

Gyun raised a hand and the crowd around them fell silent. She locked eyes with Halonni and spoke to her in the Avarun language, the words meaningless, but the tension in her pinched face and the anger in her hard eyes clear. When she was finished, Devoc leaned close.

"She says she showed extraordinary kindness and restraint by allowing you here. She credits me with her good will toward you. You have betrayed her trust, insulted her hospitality and defiled our holy time and holy lands. She demands to know where your friend has gone."

Halonni stared at the old man in confusion a moment and then looked up at Gyun. "Your brother woke me. I did not know Jantalus was gone until then."

Gyun rose to her feet in an instant and shouted something. She paused a moment. "Liar!" she translated without waiting for her brother. "I have suspected you from the first. You are no sign from the spirits. You are like the rest who have come to defile our lands. I think your man has gone to Kiranon. I think it was his plan to leave you in our care and go from the first."

Halonni shook her head. "No."

Devoc held a hand up to his sister. "These people saved my life, sister."

"You defend her?" Gyun's dark eyes narrowed. "Against me? I am Elder!"

The old man pounded his staff against the ground. "And I am Suledane! I know the will of the spirits! I have heard their words. This girl did not come to harm us!"

They continued back and forth, all harsh words and angry gestures as they slipped back into their own language again. Halonni was lost through it all, fighting without success to interrupt them. The assembled Avaruns did not so much as whisper among them, many of their faces stunned by the sight of their Elder and their holy man raging against each other. Finally, Gyun's hand came up sharply and Devoc fell silent. She turned to one of the men standing beside the platform who had been shouting at them through it all, trying without success to get their attention. He and Gyun spoke for a moment before the man bowed his head and left them. Halonni tried to ask the old man what was happening, but Devoc shook his head, listening instead to what Gyun was whispering to the elders assembled behind them.

Finally, he stepped back, drawing Halonni away a few steps. "Men have entered the valley, a dozen or so from Zantizan. Our scouts spotted them this morning, but did not challenge them. One of them bears the black mark like your friend."

Halonni drew a steadying breath. "A woman? Big and strong like a man with short black hair?"

Devoc cocked his head at her, his milky eyes blinking. "A man, old and frail they say. He travels with soldiers and a pair of black giants."

Her hands tightened on his arm. "Black giants? You are sure?"

"You know these men?"

"No. Not all of them. Certainly not the old man. But the outlanders, I know. You must bring them to me."

The old magician shook his head. "Gyun has ordered twenty men to go lay an ambush for them. They are to be killed."

"Killed!" She yelled the word loud enough that it drew the attention of those around them. Halonni caught Gyun's stare and hobbled forward, all but dragging Devoc with her. "You must allow those men to come to me."

"Must I?" The old woman glared at her, cold, angry and defiant. "I'll litter the valley with their corpses."

"You have to-."

Gyun's hand came down on the arm of her chair with a sharp crack. "No! I'll do nothing for you. That you are not joining them is the only charity you can expect. If not for my brother's insistence that you are someone touched by the spirits, you would be dead already."

Halonni straightened in an instant. She set both feet against the hard ground, grinding her teeth against the pain in her left knee. One hand still gripped Devoc's arm, but there was only Gyun for her now. The old woman seemed to sense the change in her and recoiled a bit. Devoc was talking, but Halonni ignored him, his words slipping by her like leaves in an autumn wind. All about her, the world had gone still. She no longer saw or heard the movement of the assembled Avaruns. The bitter spring air no longer nipped her skin. The glare of the sun falling down around her from the clear sky did not sting her eyes.

Beneath her, the earth magic that permeated the whole of the world pounded out a steady rhythm that only she could hear, a raging heartbeat that grew more intense as she immersed herself in the power. Beside her, she heard Devoc gasp and he pulled away from her. Without his support, her left leg buckled and she sank to her knees. The pain stabbed at her, but she ignored it, ignored Devoc, her focus Gyun and nothing else. There was a weight to the air that hung between them as it turned to a shimmering haze. The old woman felt it, her face gone slack and her dark eyes wide.

"I would be dead?" Halonni asked, her voice barely carrying above the murmur that went through the crowd. "Twice you have threatened me. The first time, Jantalus warned you that you would be sorry for any misstep. You should have listened to him. There will be no more chances for you."

Gyun raised her chin, tried to summon an air of courage about her, and failed. "I am Elder-."

"You are no one to me," Halonni told her, her soft voice cutting through the old woman's words. "You hold no power over me and make no demands. I decide who lives and dies here. I do."

She laid her hand flat against the earth and it began the tremble beneath them, shaking the wooden platform the elders sat on. The assembled Avaruns cried out in fear and confusion, stumbling back, tripping over each other as they gathered up their women and children and tried to get away. A pair of men with spears advanced on her, shouting at her in their strange language, faces twisted in anger. Halonni's free hand stretched out to the fire that raged in the great pit at the center of the assembly. At once, a jet of flame formed and flowed back to her like water. It wreathed her hand, spinning and crackling, raging like a caged animal. She thrust it toward the men, her fingers spreading out, and it encircled them in a whirlwind of flames. It spun and raged, not yet touching them, but stopping them where they were.

Halonni's eyes never left Gyun. "Bring them to me. Now."

The old woman could not answer her, stunned dumb by the display of magic, helpless to act in the face of her fear. It was Devoc who tapped his way forward, one trembling hand reaching out to settle on Halonni's slender shoulder.

Halonni did not even turn. "Get away from me."

"I may still be able to reason with her," the old man protested.

She leaned close, her eyes boring into his. "Now, or I'll kill you to keep my friends safe."

She shoved him away before he could answer, moving him more because he was not expecting it rather than any strength she could muster. Her body ached, shaking with fatigue and nearly at the point of collapse. Her heartbeat pounded in her ears, her knee was on fire and she was sucking air through clenched teeth. Gyun had to see, she kept telling herself, she had to understand that Halonni was the one who controlled things here. Tyris and Stilthius Menion's lives depended on it.

She dug her fingers into the hard earth, tearing skin as she curled them into a fist, mashing dirt between them. In response, great stone fingers erupted beneath the dais, splintering wood and shattering it apart. Men fell away as it began to collapse, dropping them all forward onto the ground. They fell in a heap before the fire pit, eyes wide with terror as they stared across the empty stone ring at Halonni. Gyun was on her hands and knees as well, her people too terrified to help her, hair tousled and hanging free, her voice a desperate wail as she called out in the Avarun language.

"Bring my friends to me," Halonni repeated, her voice worn and strained, a faint croak.

The fingers of stone rose up, looming over the Avarun Elder, threating to crush her like an insect. The old woman did not even see them, her dark eyes fixed on the girl. She finally tore her gaze away and began waving her hands at her men and shouting. A group of them hesitated only a moment and then turned to run. Gyun shouted something to Devoc and he responded.

He shuffled forward and bent down beside Halonni, his hand fumbling for her shoulder again. His face closed in, his lips against her ear. "She has sent for them. She promises they will not be harmed."

Halonni did not respond, did not even look at him.

The old man's hand tightened on her. "She knows, girl. She understands, at last, that you are who I said you were." He turned her shoulder a bit, forcing her to face him. "She believes."

Halonni relaxed her fist and slowly drew her bleeding fingers out of the earth. The huge pillars of stone she had summoned slid back into the ground with a piercing grating sound. The shaking slowly died away and the earth was still once more. She watched as Gyun pushed herself to her feet, a pair of her attendants rushing to aid her. Halonni turned to the men trapped in the swirling fire she had called from the pit. They were huddled together at the center of it, arms over their faces to save them from the blistering heat, shaking and crying out. With a wave of her hand, she drew the fire back to herself, held it in a raging ball of orange and crimson on her palm and then gestured toward the central pit. The fire flowed to where it had been, the smoldering logs flaring up again.

She was shaking, fatigue, cold and rage overwhelming her. Still, she watched the crumpled dais where Gyun was watching her in turn. "How long?" she asked Devoc through quivering lips.

"Soon," he assured her. "They are close. Come, I will take you somewhere warm. You can wait for them there."

"Right here," she answered. "I am not leaving until I see them."

"But it could take-."

"Right here," she repeated.

The old man gave a hurried nod. "As you wish, Mistress." He sank down to his knees beside her. "I'll wait with you."

He drew off his tattered old cloak and wrapped it around her shoulders. It smelled of campfire smoke and untold weeks and months of sweat and dirt, but she was cold enough not to care. The pounding in her head was maddening; everything was spinning before her eyes. She felt she was going to get sick but managed to contain it, forcing deep, even breaths and closing her eyes. Conscious of how much danger she might find herself in if she showed weakness, she managed to stay upright as they waited. As long as they feared her, she was safe. If they knew she was on the verge of collapse, if they suspected she had no strength to summon another lick of magic, it would all be for nothing.

She lost all sense of time, her mind and body gone numb to all but the excruciating pain of her knee and even that finally faded to something dull. Devoc spoke to her throughout, but she heard little and remembered even less. Nothing he said penetrated the cloud of fatigue and pain. It was reduced to a buzzing in her ear and no more.

Gyun was finally moving, helped to her feet by her attendants. She approached slowly, taking each step with the care of a mouse crossing before a sleeping cat. She stopped before Halonni and joined her brother as he knelt with her.

"You see now?" Devoc asked her. "You see she is blessed of the spirits? Do you believe me?"

The old woman nodded once. "I believe, Devoc. Praise the spirits, I believe. Pray, brother, that I live long enough to earn their forgiveness." She turned to Halonni, her eyes imploring. "I beg for yours, child. Forgive me."

Halonni was struggling for something to say, fighting the haze that clouded her mind when she caught sight of movement behind the old woman. She watched as the crowd of people who still stood watching parted and a knot of men pushed their way through, Avarun warriors leading them.

Halonni's hand reached out toward them. "Tyris."

"Who?" Gyun asked, turning to follow her stare.

The outlander was there before she could respond, Stilthius and several others she did not know a step behind. The brothers shouldered their way through like massive towers of steel and muscle that loomed over the tiny Avaruns. Tyris dropped down before her, his big hands taking her and holding her up. She heaved a sigh that shook her whole body and hugged him impulsively, her feverish face against the cold steel of his mail.

"Sent by the spirits!" Devoc was saying, repeating it over and again, laughing like a mad man.

Stilthius seized the old man's cloak and lifted him away from her. "Back you mad bastard or I'll cave your damn head in."

Halonni lifted her head from Tyris's shoulder and reached out a shaking hand. "No, don't. He tried, Stilthius. He tried to help me." She licked her dry lips and drew a breath. "Jantalus. We have to find him."

"Find him?" Tyris asked her, one hand coming up to her damp cheek. It felt like ice against her skin and she flinched away.

A new face trust forward, old, wrinkled, framed by wispy white hair. A pair of black, lifeless eyes stared down at her. "Where is he? Where is Jantalus Kathias?"

"Gone," she told him, shaking her head. Everything was growing hazy around her and beginning to spin. "Gone to Sentry."

"Sentry?" the old man asked.

He spoke more, but his words were nonsense to her. Everything was fading and spinning and drifting away. She had held on as long as she could. Just enough, she thought.

The last thing she remembered was Tyris's arm coming about her as she slipped down against him and the world went black.

Chapter Thirty-One

Sentry was as desolate as Drappel.

Jantalus approached the dilapidated buildings slowly, his feet scuffing along the coat of snow that covered the ancient stone street. Nothing moved in the old town but snow blown by the mountain wind. The only sound was that of old iron gates hammering against the low stone walls that they once guarded as the wind tossed them open and then shut again. With a growing sense of familiarity, he picked his way past the metal scraps that had once been framing for carts and wagons and the rubble of buildings that had finally given way to time.

He followed the curve of the street around the hollow buildings until he looked on the old market square. It was nothing but a wide, snow-covered plaza. Devoc claimed there had been a battle and Jantalus expected to see its aftermath. He expected to see something not unlike Drappel. But Sentry was different. No corpses littered the streets or hung from makeshift gallows. He detected no stench of rotting flesh, saw no gnawed remains left by scavengers. There was nothing but cold emptiness. Nothing at all.

Nothing but memories.

They were his first that he had been able to catch hold of since the day he woke in Durn's rickety old cart staring up at the sky wondering where he was and who he was. He had remembered his mother's name, but that had been no more than a word he had been able to place an image to. Everything else had been dreams – visions of times and places he had felt no connection to, events that might have been someone else's experiences for the lack of emotion tied to them. He had reason to question them all. Nothing had been clear or direct.

Until now. He saw people he knew, events he recognized. This was not the first time he had set foot in Sentry. It was simply the first time he had been here alone. Gaps remained in what he saw and what those people and images meant, but he knew the things that were clear to him now were real.

In his mind's eye, he placed Cirrin Ravensbourne against the wall of the building to his left, one hand clutching at the socket of his missing eye. The white robed figure of Mira Rhenn was beside him, head split wide, blood pouring onto the street. At the center of the empty plaza, his fractured mind added Peridor Finn, sword raised, bloodied face angry and determined. His father stood at Finn's left, hands raised, his body alive with the crackling power of his magic.

Before them was Mordoc Tassaren, black hair shot through with silver, dark cloak swirling as his magic turned aside steel and sorcery, a great rock against the tide of battle. No one moved in his conjured scenario, frozen in place like a painting of the events had been made in an instant. He saw nothing of himself in this memory. Perhaps it was because it was his hand drawing the picture and it had taken place as he stood in the very spot he now found himself in. He turned about, shuffled to one side and then the other and walked a short distance through the empty plaza in which he had inserted the images. His movement sparked no such motion in his memory. It was a picture, frozen at a specific moment. For a reason he did not understand, he could move no sooner or later in the events he was seeing.

He forced the memory away and the images vanished. Peridor. Cirrin. Mira. Mordoc. Joran. One by one, they blinked away, leaving him in the cold emptiness of Sentry. He scanned about, but saw nothing. It was a collection of broken old buildings, sagging fences and bare earth. He was alone except for the presence of the other magic.

He lifted his face within his cowl, black eyes searching. They settled on the tall, slender tower from which Sentry took its name.

He stared up at it, watching, waiting. After a time, he came to feel eyes upon him. Things hovered at the edge of his vision, watching and waiting as he did. The walking dead, Devoc had warned. Spirit things too, he had said, things without bodies that killed by their touch. He could feel them, but he could not see them. Something was holding them back. Did they fear him? Did some power restrain them? He did not know and he did not want to risk finding out.

He resumed walking, headed for the tower. The strange power that permeated the place grew stronger as he approached. It became a buzzing in his ears that drowned out even the sound of the wind. He climbed the short set of steps to the twin doors of the fortress and shoved with his shoulder. The doors groaned and creaked and then slowly swung open. He was in a long, narrow chamber that stretched to the back of the tower and the staircase that spiraled up into the darkness. He took a moment to inspect his surroundings and then went to it and began to climb. It ended at a small platform with a trap door above him. He hesitated a moment before thrusting it open and climbing through.

He stood in an open room with empty arched windows from which the glass had been broken. The wind and snow whipped through the circular room, cutting through his cloak and the blanket he had wrapped about him. At the center of the room, burning without any source of fuel and shedding no light, was a column of black fire. The flames threw no heat and caused no harm to the stone blocks of the floor and ceiling. The wind that howled through the empty window frames did not sway the fire even as it made his cloak flap about him. Something stood at the center of it all, a muddled shape that he could not identify. Something lay on the floor to one side. Two things, he realized as he studied them, vaguely human shapes wrapped in dark cloaks.

He inched closer, wary of the strange pillar of fire, trying to see what burned within and what lay on the cold stone floor near it. Beneath the tangle of the dark cloaks were two corpses, one man and one woman. The woman was small and slight, her skin gray and loose, hanging from her skeletal frame. Her hollow eyes stared up at him, her mouth gaping. Beneath the thinning hair, the skull was exposed, cracked open like an egg. The dirty white robe was stained black with old blood.

Mira Rhenn.

Too little remained of the other body to identify it. Shrunken and withered, he looked as if someone had sucked the very flesh out from beneath his skin and left it hanging off his bones like wet laundry draped over a line. His face was a twisted ruin, all torn and sagging, white bone showing through at his cheeks and forehead. His eye sockets were empty, two dark holes staring upward at the stone ceiling.

There was nothing to identify him. He wore no ring or pendants; no mark adorned his simple clothing. Jantalus stepped back from them once more and looked them over from several paces away. Mira was closer to the fire and seemed to had fallen with her back to it. The other corpse had been facing her, opposing her, he supposed. She had placed herself between the ring of black fire and the unidentified man and died keeping them apart.

He felt certain of the analysis without evidence to support it aside from his hunch. He sensed he was right, but could not be sure why. Was he remembering something or was he simply confident in his guesswork? He shifted his attention to the pillar of black flame. He would have his answer there if he were to have any answer at all.

He came forward again, closer to the dark fire without touching it. He leaned in, trying to identify the shape that the magic obscured. It was a man, he realized as he studied it. The features were still indistinct, blurred by the roar of the strange magic around him. The man was his size, that much he could tell. He wore clothing that was still intact despite the strange fire. He did not seem conscious, or at least he had no awareness of Jantalus's presence judging from the lack of reaction. His feet hovered several inches off the floor, but Jantalus could see nothing that suggested what might be holding him up. His body hung limp and loose, his arms dangling free. His head was thrown back, and Jantalus could not see enough of his face to know if he was awake or asleep.

He drew a breath and steadied himself. He had to know who this man was. The magic that he had felt as he entered Sentry, the drumming heartbeat of power that called him on came from this spot. His search had led him here and nowhere else. What he learned here might be something he wished he had not or he might find nothing. Still, whether there were answers here, more questions or simple emptiness, he had to see for himself and have an end to his search.

His hand stretched out, his magic flaring, building like water raging against a dam. The air about him shimmered with power, the very stone of the chamber shaking. His magic surrounded him, armoring him against the black fire, preparing him for whatever effect it might have when he touched it. The ring of flames sputtered and hissed as his magic brushed up against it, flaring angrily, but his own power held firm and kept him safe.

"Jantalus."

The sound of the word was such a surprise he started, his magic stuttering and nearly dying. He looked all about him, but no one was in the room with him. He took a hesitant step toward the ring of fire and peered inside once more. The man remained as he had been, frozen in his silent scream, his body stiff and still. He looked down at the corpses beside him, but they had not moved either.

Not that they could.

He looked behind him at the trap door he had entered through, but no one was there either. For a moment, he questioned his own sanity. He was exhausted, wounded and spent emotionally. It would have been a simple thing to dismiss what he had heard as a trick of his mind. That was the problem with it, though. He had not heard anything. The word had not been spoken aloud.

He stepped away from the fire again, a cold dread spreading over him. There was more here than first appeared. The eyes he had felt on him in the town below, the odd man in the ring of fire and the voice in his mind were all adding up to some game being played. Yes, he told himself, it was all too easy. He had walked through the town unopposed despite Gyun and Devoc warning that spirits and dead men haunted Sentry. He had come to the tower and climbed to this room to find nothing to stop him but a fire that did not burn and a mute, defenseless man waiting for him. It was all perfect, everything arranged just the way he would have asked for it to be.

He let his magic fade, cooling the fire that burned through his veins.

As his magic vanished, a new one replaced it. He felt it at once, a faint, struggling, shimmering of power that was separate from the overwhelming force that was the pillar of black fire. It rose up from Mira's corpse and swirled about, a silver-white mist that drifted up and out, molding itself into a vaguely human shape between Jantalus and the ring of flames. He took a step back as it sharpened before him, a translucent figure of a small, delicate woman. She faded in and out, magic surging and retreating, alternating between a vivid image and a barely perceptible one. Much like her sister, Khessa, Mira came to him as a blue-white ghost of an image, an ethereal mockery of the person she had once been.

"Jantalus." The ghostly face looked almost relieved. "Finally."

He stared at her, stupefied. All these days, all the distance, toil, and pain, and finally, in a word, he had a reason to believe it had not all been a waste. A thousand questions raced through his mind, a million emotions on top of them, swallowing them up like a great wave, and yet, he could not speak. His breath caught in his throat, his palms grew damp and his legs turned to mush beneath him.

"Jantalus," the apparition called again. "I am glad you returned."

He swallowed hard, regaining his senses. "Why? Who are you to me?" He drew a steadying breath. "Who am I?"

The spectral face looked strangely sad. "Who are you? You don't remember?" She shook her head. "I see. I wondered why you had returned. Of course, this is why. Why else?"

He reached out for her, impulsive. His hands grasped only air, but he did not notice. "What do you mean? Why would I not come back here? I am searching for my father and those who disappeared with him."

Her head cocked to one side. "Are you? I don't think so. I think you are searching for Jantalus Kathias."

"But I am-."

"No," she said, cutting him off. "I don't think you are. We wondered what would happen to you, how you would respond to what was done. We should have listened to Addicus all those years ago."

"I don't understand. Tell me what has happened. Tell me who I am."

The ghost hand reached out, passing through his face without the slightest touch. "I can't. I do not know the man before me. I know your face. I know your voice. But what lives inside you now is not who you were. That man is no longer whole. What you are is what they created when they tried to change Jantalus Kathias into someone they could all live with. What you are is a piece of a whole, the remainder of a man torn down to his very soul and rebuilt with the parts they all found palatable."

"Who?" he demanded. " Who did this thing to me? Answer me, damn you!"

Mira Rhenn gestured to the withered corpse of the man that lay beside her own. "Your father." She turned back to him. "Addicus Malshere. Mordoc Tassaren. Your mother. All of them had a hand in what you are now – in what was taken from you."

"And what was that? My memories, you mean?"

The apparition shook its head slowly. "What would they gain from simple memories? No, Jantalus. Magic. They stole your magic. Power far beyond anything you now possess. Power worth fighting over – killing over. Power worth going to war over. And they did. Mordoc, Addicus and your parents. All of them vying for what it was that made you who and what you were."

He took a step back from her, shaking his head, his hands held up before him as if to ward her off. "And what was I?"

"Something the like of which none of them had ever seen. Something beyond comprehension. Beyond controlling. And isn't that what all who wield power fear? A power greater than their own that they cannot contain?"

"But what am I that I held such power?" he asked, trying to make sense of it all even as it felt as though he never would.

"What are you?" She shrugged her thin shoulders. "A freak. A mistake. An accident of birth."

He stared at her.

"Would you have me lie?" she asked. "Joran and Aralyn Kathias were Vicars, born of elemental magic. It stood to reason that their son would be born with the gift as well. But you? You possessed nothing of the sort. Something about you was twisted, warped from what it should have been. What it was who can say? And even if we knew, what would it matter now?"

Jantalus ground his teeth, his hands clenching so hard his fingers ached. He wanted to seize her and shake the answers he wanted from her. He wanted to force her to stop dancing away with her words, answering in muddled pieces of information that did not make a whole. But there was no one to throttle, no neck to squeeze in his big hands. She was only smoke and a whisper of magic.

"I need to know more," he told her, forcing down his impatience. "I need so many answers I do not know where to begin."

The ghostly hand lifted, one translucent finger pointing to the ring of black fire behind her. "Your answers are there. All of them? Like as not, no. There is no Jantalus Kathias anymore – not as a whole. Like a window shattered, reassembling the pieces will still never make it clear. Always there will be fractures. Always the view through it will be warped."

He looked past her to the muddled figure inside the pillar of flames. "Who is that man?"

"The man is you."

"Me?" He shook his head. "That's impossible."

"No, it isn't." His attention snapped back to her. She gestured to the savaged corpse that lay near her own. "That, is Joran Kathias. But is it? Or is it just so much rotting flesh?" She turned back to the ring of fire. "That man is Joran as well."

Jantalus glanced down at the body once more. No emotion stirred in him at the revelation. Perhaps the condition of the corpse, the utter lack of anything about him even remotely recognizable as a man, let alone a specific man, was making it hard to see a person. Still, it was his father, she said. Should he not feel something for that? The identity aside, her contention that the single man trapped in the ring of fire beside her was both himself and his father was even more unbelievable.

"How can one man be two? How can I be both the man who speaks to you now and the man in there? How can my father be lying there and also be standing in the flames? You speak riddles, ghost."

"I must. You are, after all, quite a riddle yourself, Jantalus Kathias. A pity we did not know each other well. I am here because of you and you alone. Your magic created the fire, trapped the thing that exists within and holds me here. It was you who bound my sister as well."

He shook his head. "I know neither of you. I remember doing nothing to you. Why would I?"

Mira Rhenn's shimmering face leaned close. "Perhaps the part of you that did this was not Jantalus Kathias. You, as I said, are not simply you. You will soon see what I mean. The only question that truly remains is that of understanding. And if you are able to comprehend it, what will you do about it?"

Jantalus looked from her to the fire and back. This was a pointless exercise. The apparition was either refusing to answer him directly or was, as Khessa Rhenn had been, too small a piece of a whole to be of real use beyond what she had provided. That left the strange figure in the fire.

"How do I-?"

"You created it," she told him, cutting him off. "You must know it will do you no harm."

But I don't. I don't know a damn thing.

He took a step toward the fire and then paused again, looking back at the apparition. "Why did I do this? What purpose does this serve?"

"Protection," she answered at once. "Mordoc had you and was trying to break you, twist you and make you his own. You and your father battled him, but he was too strong to defeat. You drove him off, but your father was dying and you were wounded – not in body as much as in spirit. Mordoc's magic nearly destroyed you from within. You had to save your soul and your father's." She gestured. "You saved them both by locking them here."

"But why then did I leave this place? Why have I been gone so long and forgotten so much?"

Mira Rhenn shook her ghostly head. "You assumed, as I did, that your mother or another with the power to aid you would come. But no one like that came. We remained here, you and I, and began to fade. My wounds were too great and I passed to the spirit world. You were found. Barely alive and unable to speak to tell what had happened, but alive. Peridor Finn found you and bore you away, never knowing that what you truly needed to be healed was right here the whole time."

Jantalus stared at the flickering black fire. "You should have told him."

"No. I am a spirit now. Only those with magic can see me and hear me. Peridor Finn never knew I was anything but a corpse. Peridor Finn could not even see the ring of fire you and I see."

He did not look at her as she spoke, his black eyes riveted to the black flames. It was all there. Everything he wanted to know. The answer to every question he had. He had but to take it, from what Mira was telling him. He did not remember how, if he had ever known at all. But he would try. All of the running and fighting and suffering through pain and cold and fatigue had led to the ring of black fire and the spirit things trapped within.

"If I can reach…those spirits…what of you?" he asked.

"The fire burns because a window to the spirit world is opened here and the energy of that world feeds the flames. It sustains me as well. If you close that window, I will rest. Forever."

He looked at her finally. "You wish for that? For an end to what you are now?"

"I beg for it."

He nodded and turned back to the ring of fire. "Then hope I am strong enough to do this."

He stepped forward and reached out with his good hand, fingers spread. The black fire flared and spit like something angry at his approach, but as his hand came near, it seemed to recoil. He pressed forward taking a step, his hand still leading, magic rising up in him. He thought to summon a defense against the fire even though he felt no heat from it, wary of what effect it might have on him. If it were the same black fire Shantara and Samarus Tassaren had used against him, it might drain the very life from him. The flames rolled back by inches as he crept ever closer, receding as if pushed by some unseen force. Finally, they drew apart like a curtain and opened a corridor to the shimmering, faceless figure that hovered above the floor at the center of the dark circle.

Jantalus paused and flashed Mira Rhenn a quick, questioning glance. The spectral face was alive with wonder and excitement. "I told you, Jantalus. It was of your making. It obeys your will."

He said nothing in response, taking a step into the space created by the retreating fire. It burned to either side of him but caused him no harm and came no closer. He took another step, his hand reaching for the thing in the center that Mira claimed was both himself and his father. It was all faint white light that resembled Mira Rhenn's ghost-form, but without any attempt at approximating human features. It had no mouth, no ears or eyes or nose. The body was a simple outline in the shape of a man and nothing more.

His hand closed on the glowing line that mimicked a shoulder, resting on something solid but not strong.

He felt a tremendous surge of pain, a shockwave of force that felt like a horse kick between his eyes. He opened his mouth to scream, but the pain was too intense for him to summon enough breath. He heard the rush of the flames around him as they flowed back into the shape of a ring, trapping him inside with the glowing figure. An image flashed in his mind, sharp, clear and unmistakable.

His father's face appeared, stricken with panic, blue eyes wide with fear and anguish. "No! Get away!"

But he had nowhere to go. The fire was everywhere and the pain froze him in place regardless. He could not move. He could not breathe. His teeth clenched and his body rigid, he stood like a statue in the ring of fire, the shimmering figure still before him, and his hand resting on its shoulder.

Through the haze of the flickering flames, he saw the shade of Mira Rhenn drift close, peering in at him. The glowing face twisted into something that might have been sorrow.

"I'm sorry, Jantalus. But this is for the best. Best for us all."

Chapter Thirty-Two

Halonni Vilcris woke to cold, thin fingers against her face.

Her eyes snapped open. Her breath caught in her throat. The world was a hazy, murky clash of color before her eyes. Her own heartbeat hammered in her ears, drowning out all else. She reached up to grab the hand that clutched her face, closing around a small, frail wrist. She tried to push it away but it would not move. She could feel the rush of magic all around her, flaring against her own and turning her blood cold in her veins. A dark shape bent over her, tall and thin, a blur of pale skin and gray robes.

Addicus Malshere?

His magic hammered into her, shattering what meager defense she could muster and overwhelming her in an instant.

The world went black once more and all she knew was the sensation of falling into an endless darkness.

"I am sorry for this."

She was standing in a simple tent that might have been any one of the many that formed the Avarun camp. The place was colorless, only black and white and shades of gray. No source of light illuminated it all, but she could see just the same. She heard no sound but the voice that had spoken to her. No animals or people outside the tent. Not even her own breathing.

Because, of course, she was not breathing here. She was not here at all.

Addicus Malshere stood before her. She knew him at once even though she had only glimpsed him the day before. He was tall and spare and lost in the great gray cloak that hung about him like a shroud. This was his doing. He ruled here. All that she saw and heard was his invention. He had drawn both of their conscious minds to a plane that existed only as thought and the projection of that thought - the tent, the furnishing within it, Addicus and even what she saw of herself - were only images drawn by her imagination to represent the interaction of their magic and psyches. Physical objects were simple to understand and served as relatable proxies for magic far too complex to be explained otherwise.

"Sorry?" she asked, incredulous. "Why? What is it you intend to do?"

The old man shrugged. "Whatever I wish, of course. You are mine to do with as I please."

He was not being smug nor was he bluffing. Halonni had no strength to fight him. The surprise and ferocity of his attack would have overwhelmed her even if she had not been completely spent before. "What do you want, Addicus?"

"Jantalus Kathias."

"You know he went to Sentry. Everyone in this camp knows it."

The old man nodded. "But I need to know more. I need to know what he knows."

She hesitated a moment. "About himself you mean? About who he is?"

"Yes."

"So you can be sure of how strong he is before you try to kill him?"

"Kill him?" Addicus shook his head beneath his cowl. "He is no use to me dead."

"And just what use is he to you?"

"That is my concern." He lifted his hand toward her, his fingers curling into a fist. "Tell me what I want to know or I'll take it. The first will be far less painful than the second. Play with me and I'll leave you a drooling idiot for the rest of your life."

He is bluffing, she thought. At least a bit. She had no doubt he would destroy her to get what he needed, but something held him back. His power was staggering, but he was conserving it. He was anticipating a battle with Jantalus, she mused, and was being careful about how much of his magic he committed to his attack on her. If she was clever and careful, she might be able to parlay that hesitation into a way to survive here.

"Jantalus's memory is fragmented. He remembers almost nothing. He dreams of things he cannot be sure are the past or just tricks of his imagination. He sees faces without names sometimes. Other times he puts faces to names but does not know anything more about those he sees. He knows his parents' names, but they do not mean anything to him. He knows the faces and remembers some events, but he feels nothing for it."

Addicus took a quick step toward her, his black eyes narrowing as they stared down at her. "His magic! I don't care about his memories. I need to know how much of his magic he wields!"

Halonni shrugged one shoulder, trying to appear dismissive about it all. "I don't know him as he was. Only as he is. His magic is strong. Very strong. He was a match for Shantara Tassaren. More perhaps."

His hand reached out to grasp her throat, dragging her close, a proxy for the way *his magic coiled about her mind and drew them closer. "You will show me."*

Helpless, broken, she submitted to him, her memories bared. He drank them all in, absorbing them like rainwater vanishing into the surface of a pond. He closed his eyes as they flooded into him, his face creased with concentration that slowly turned to concern and then fear as it all came to him.

When he was finished, he thrust her away, sending her sprawling. She collapsed and lay before him without the strength to rise. He had broken down her mind and taken her memories by force, leaving her dazed and reeling. It had cost him though - cost him something more than a touch of his own strength and magic. By making direct contact between his thoughts and hers, he had allowed her a small glimpse into his own memories and intentions.

Halonni knew why Addicus wanted Jantalus Kathias. She also had seen who and what Jantalus had been and why he was the man she knew now.

"He is strong." Addicus was not even looking at her as he spoke. "His power has grown far beyond what I had imagined it would in so short a time. I will need all of my strength and I may have the Tassaren bastards to deal with as well."

He fell silent for time and then raised his black eyes to Halonni again. "What I need, girl, is an advantage."

He came for her again, hands lifted, black eyes cold and filled with purpose.

Halonni watched him come without even the strength to cry.

****

Tyris Menion stormed into Devoc's tent with the same ferocity with which he had charged shield walls. Men scattered as the black giant thundered through the tent flap. One man held up his hands and jabbered at him in the Avarun tongue. Tyris hooked one huge hand under the man's arm and heaved him aside with all the effort he might have needed to swat an insect away. No one else even looked at him.

At the far side of the tent, Gyun and Devoc bent over the pile of bedding atop which Halonni Vilcris lay. The girl's eyes were closed and her pale face had gone whiter than the snowcaps of the surrounding mountains. Her lips were tinged blue and her breath came in shallow, ragged gasps. Gyun was shaking her shoulder and calling her name, but Halonni was not stirring. Devoc was kneeling beside her, mumbling what might have been a prayer.

"What the hell is going on here?" Tyris demanded as he stopped at the bedside, looming over everyone and everything like a wall of steel.

Devoc's milky eyes lifted toward him. "We came to see if she was awake and found her like this. Something has changed since this morning. She was weak before, but not like this."

Tyris hunched down, his big hand reaching for her pale cheek. It was cold to his touch and damp with sweat. "Your healers-."

"No." Devoc shook his head. "There is something not of the living world at work here."

"What the fuck does that mean? Speak plainly, old man."

"Magic," he answered at once. "Evil spirits."

"Piss on your spirits."

Gyun glanced up at him sharply, but he ignored it.

A commotion behind him drew his attention and he turned to find Stilthius and the Ravensbournes hurrying in. Stilthius shouldered his way to the front of the gathered men. Derek and Lorum trailed.

"What happened?" his brother asked.

Tyris gestured to Halonni. "She won't wake and she looks half in the grave. The old man says evil spirits are responsible. Where is Addicus?"

"Gone," Stilthius answered.

"Find him!" Tyris insisted. "If this is about magic, that old prick is the one we need."

"Tyris. I said gone. Gone completely."

The big outlander shook his head. "Gone where? There's nothing here." He stopped and looked back down at Halonni. "Nothing but Sentry."

Stilthius joined him, one hand settling on the girl's shoulder. "He needed something from her. He took it and went after Jantalus."

"For what?" Tyris muttered.

Stilthius shook his head. "Damned if I know."

Tyris looked up from Halonni and turned about to face Lorum and Derek. His face flushed with anger, his eyes narrowing dangerously. "You know."

Lorum raised his hands. "Addicus kept his own council."

"Filthy fucking liar!" Tyris was on him in an instant, shouldering Derek aside and knocking him away. His huge hand caught Lorum's throat as he bore him back, burst through the tent flap, and drove him onto his back in the dirt without. He groaned with the impact, barely able to make any sound at all as Tyris's hand squeezed tight. The outlander bent over him, eyes wide with madness. Lorum struggled against the crushing grip but he might have been trying to bend steel.

"What does the old man want?" Tyris demanded. "Tell me or I'll tear your fucking head off and then I'll move on to that snotty little cunt of a brother of yours."

"M-magic," he managed. "He wants Jantalus's magic. It's what they all wanted."

"Leave him be!" Derek called from behind. Steel scraped against leather and Tyris half turned to see the boy advancing at his back, sword ready.

Stilthius was on him before he realized it, twisting the sword out of his hand and pitching him forward into the dirt. His huge foot slammed down on the boy's back before he could rise, pinning him. "Stay there and shut the fuck up or I'll kick your fucking head in."

Tyris turned back to Lorum Ravensbourne, bending over the straining, purple face. "Why Halonni? She had nothing to do with this."

"Don't know," came the choked response. "Never heard of her until I met you two."

"And you two? What did he promise you? Magic? Power?"

Lorum shook his head as best he could. "Our father. He vanished in the battle at Drappel. He says Jantalus and Mordoc took him, used his life to fuel their magic. If I can find him-."

Tyris released him and he drew a sharp, wheezing breath, coughing as he reached for his throat. The big outlander waved Stilthius away from the boy. "You dumb bastards. It was all shit. All of it. That old bastard used you. He needed you to watch his back and run his errands and he hung your missing father in front of you like a carrot in front of a horse."

"You don't know that!" Derek called as he rose to his knees.

"The hell I don't. I've spent weeks with Jantalus Kathias. I've seen his magic. He used no one for it. He's not one of those...Necromancers... or whatever you call them."

"He bears the mark of the dead!" Lorum insisted.

"So does Addicus, fool!" Stilthius shouted back.

The Ravensbournes went silent, staring up at the outlanders, waiting like men facing judgment. All about them, Avarun warriors stood with spears in hand, watching them and the Ravensbournes, trying to make sense of what they were seeing and when or if they should intervene. Tyris turned in a slow circle, watching them all, staring back at them with the promise of death should any man move against him. He crossed the space between himself and his brother, passing by Derek Ravensbourne where he still knelt, staring up at the huge outlander with wide eyes.

"You know what is left now," Stilthius told him.

Tyris nodded. "Us. As always happens. Just us."

"It's a tall mountain."

"They are good friends. Our only friends." He shrugged. "Unless Hunnaris is showing you some other road."

Stilthius clapped him on the shoulder. "No. He still has me following after a black-eyed, soul-stealing prick with nothing but an unbelieving, asshole brother for help."

Tyris looked around them at the assembled Avaruns. "We'll need a guide."

Lorum Ravensbourne gained his feet and straightened. "I know the way. I have seen enough of Addicus's maps that I can't forget it."

Stilthius snorted. "You? I don't trust you enough to tell me which way the wind is blowing without checking."

"I don't trust you either," he replied. "But it does not change matters. You want to find your friend and find Addicus to help the girl. I need answers still. We're traveling the same road. Safer to walk it together, don't you think?"

"Shaddix likely knows the way too," Tyris told him. "I'd rather have him at my back than-."

"Gone," Derek told him, cutting his words off. "No one has seen him or his men since Addicus disappeared. We were looking for them all when your brother brought us here."

That didn't sound much like Shaddix, but Tyris did not argue the point. Considering the old man's magic, it was very likely that Shaddix and the others were not with him by choice.

Regardless of why they were together, it made things harder still for Tyris and the rest. A dozen men and the old sorcerer were too much for the four of them assuming he accepted the offer Lorum was making. If the old man had been telling the truth about another presence in the valley, they might have the Tassarens involved as well. Adding the story Devoc had told them earlier about dead men and restless spirits haunting the mountain and they were up to their ears in shit.

"If we go," he told his brother, ignoring the others, "we're leaving

Halonni behind with these people."

Stilthius blew out a long breath and nodded. "They think she is some sort of servant of the spirits they worship. I don't think they would hurt her." He shook his head. "I'm more worried about her making it through until we get back."

"And if you die?"

They turned to see Devoc and Gyun standing at the entrance to the tent, watching them all. The old magician tapped forward a few steps, his gnarled staff scratching jumbled patterns in the dirt as he came. He paused and cocked his head to one side listening. After a moment, he lifted his face to the wind and drew a deep breath through his nose.

"The spirits are angry, angry with this old man who works his demon magic. The spirits order our people to aid you."

"Devoc!" Gyun called.

The old man shook his head without turning back to her. "They order it! Wydant warriors will stand with you. Those who defile the sacred mountain will feel the wrath of the spirits."

"And Halonni?" Stilthius asked. "You will watch over her until we return?"

The old man closed his eyes and spread his arms wide, humming a series of strange words that might have been a prayer. "No." He waved away their words as they tried to protest. "No. She is not to stay here. You must take her to the mountain. You must take her to the spirits. What can be done to save her must be done there."

"Madness!" Lorum was shaking his head as he spoke. "We've enough to worry about without carrying that half-dead girl up the mountain."

Tyris jabbed a finger at him. "No one even asked you to come, asshole."

"She cannot stay," Devoc insisted, cutting off further debate. "The old one took a piece of her with him. She is not strong enough to survive without it. If you leave her here — even if you are able to find him and force him to return it — she will die before you return."

"How do you know this, old man?" Derek Ravensbourne asked him.

"The spirits," he responded with a shrug.

Stilthius leaned closer to Tyris. "Are you willing to risk her life and ours on the old man's ghosts?"

"We've risked as much or more on the whispers you hear from the moon," he replied.

Stilthius said nothing. Behind him, Devoc and Gyun waited for his answer as well. He turned to find Derek and Lorum Ravensbourne watching. How it all came to fall on him he couldn't figure, but there it was. None of was right. He'd followed behind horses on a road march and smelled less shit. He could hardly remember how many people he and Stilthius had walked away from when things started taking a bad turn. The brothers were alive more for knowing when a fight wasn't worth the fighting than from their ability to carve their way through it. This one looked like the kind a smart man walked away from.

But he knew he'd be carving soon enough.

He nodded to Gyun. "Get your men together. We'll move as soon as we can." She nodded and took Devoc's arm, leading him away. Tyris turned back to the Ravensbournes. "If you're coming, your asses are mine. You cross me and I'll cut you into little pieces and sprinkle you across the mountain."

Lorum inclined his head slightly. "Agreed." Derek said nothing.

"We're going to fucking die," Tyris muttered to his brother.

Stilthius, to his surprise, nodded. "Probably."

Chapter Thirty-Three

They were moving within the hour.

Lorum and Derek were there to depart the Avarun camp with them as promised, neither looking the least bit trusting of the Menion brothers, but committed nonetheless. Tyris took them at their word, the more he thought on it. A missing father was reason enough to hunt a man you thought responsible. More than enough next to following your brother's belief that your god willed it, he supposed. If the Ravensbournes wanted to learn whatever Jantalus knew about him or what had become of their father, that was simple enough. If they thought they were going to have some sort of vengeance, that would be another matter. Best, Tyris decided, that they worry about such things when the time came.

Gyun had provided them with an escort of some score of Wydant warriors. They were an enthusiastic bunch, Tyris had to admit. Devoc had advised them all that guiding the lowlanders up the mountain and doing battle with those they found there was the will of their spirit gods and this task would earn each man favor. The promise had brought out nearly every man in the camp and the cries of disappointment from those turned away were louder even than the shouts of triumph from the chosen. It might have made them brave men. More likely, as Stilthius suggested, it made them fools.

The most surprising addition to their number was Devoc himself. Stilthius, especially, had argued hard against him. They were already facing opponents with power they could not counter and a force of hardened killers in the mercenaries of Black River that had gone with Addicus. Adding a blind man who could not fend for himself was not a complication that was going to benefit them. Devoc had made a strong case for himself in the end.

The spirits of the mountain would grant them passage if one of the Suledane was among them, he promised. That had meant nothing to the Menion brothers. The old man claimed he could summon the spirits of the mountain to protect Halonni as well. She was fading from them, slipping away with each passing minute, her magic and her very life drained away by what Addicus Malshere had done to her. She was one with the elemental forces of the spirits of the mountain, Devoc told them all. What she was losing, they could restore.

It might have been so much horseshit and Tyris suspected it was, but any chance to help Halonni was one he was willing to take. If the old man could summon his spirits to protect her until they found Addicus or Jantalus or both, they had to try. And if the old man was simply mad, at least she was not suffering any further harm for it.

Tyris was carrying Halonni as they started north out of the camp, crossing the light forest of the valley floor as they headed for the mountain the Avaruns called Kiranon. Wrapped in a huge bundle of wool blankets, only her face was visible. Her eyes were closed and her breathing so shallow and ragged that Tyris was constantly lifting her up to feel her breath on his face for fear that she had slipped away. Her pale skin was slowly turning gray, a subtle shading around her eyes and the hollows of her cheeks. The veins in her neck and forehead had gone black beneath white skin, a dark angry web. Her lips had faded from blue to gray.

Devoc walked beside him, guided by a short, rawboned warrior he called Chanok. The old man would reach out, tapping about with his hand until he found Halonni's face every few minutes, muttering prayers to his spirits in his strange language. Each time he would simply shake his head and offer no explanation for what he had done or might have learned. After the first few times, Tyris decided that the old bastard wasn't learning anything at all and that was what was troubling him.

The sun was already sinking toward the jagged mountain peaks to the west when they reached the base of the mountain. The Avaruns paused as they gained the slopes, looking up at the huge, craggy wall of snowcapped rock that loomed over them, their faces alight with wonder and reverence. Devoc tapped the one called Chanok on the arm and waved the outlanders close. They produced a map drawn on a piece of hide and spread it out on a flat rock nearby.

Chanok guided the old magician's hands as he spoke, first in his own language to the warrior and then to the others. "Your friend, we think, went this way." He traced a line with his gnarled finger that climbed up the eastern edge of the mountain. "There are old trails from when the lowlanders dug holes in the mountain. It is a long climb, but not very hard. It would have taken him many hours. The old one followed him that way, the spirits say."

"Addicus's maps showed those trails," Lorum said. "I remember seeing them."

Devoc spoke to Chanok again and their hands slid across the map to the center of the mountain face. "We are here. Ahead of us, hidden among the rocks where only my people know, is another path. The Suledane used this path to climb the mountain and pray to the spirits. When I was young, I climbed it many times. The men who guide us were chosen because they are strong. The path is hard, but shorter than the rest."

"Our best chance to catch Addicus, then." Stilthius looked to Tyris. "We can share the burden of the girl."

Tyris shook his head. "There's hardly anything to her now."

"She will not fail," Devoc told them, drawing their attention back to him. "I have asked the blessing of the spirits. They watch over her here. They watch over us all."

"Are your spirits stronger than Addicus Malshere?" Derek Ravensbourne asked. "Can they stop his magic from killing us?"

The old man shrugged, showing no anger at the challenge. "I do not question them. They provide in ways only they understand. I think they have chosen all of you to defeat this demon-man."

Lorum snorted. "He'll tear through us without stopping to blink." He looked up from the old man to Tyris. "We had better hope Jantalus Kathias can help us or the girl comes around."

Stilthius hefted his hammer. "Sorcerer or no, his skull can be crushed like any other man. If we've no one else to aid us, we'll have to be faster, smarter and more careful than that old fuck. We've faced his kind before and walked away."

Lorum shook his head and turned away.

"Keep us moving," Tyris told Devoc.

The old man rolled up his map, slipped it into his belt, and then shouted to his warriors. They responded with a cry and started forward, picking their way through the rocks and thinning trees as they began the ascent. Tyris and Stilthius let the rest go ahead, walking together at the rear of the procession. The Avaruns led them to a small footpath that wound along the face the mountain, slowly climbing through the scrub and trees. It was easy enough here, but the slope of the mountain above made it clear that the worst lay ahead for them.

Stilthius offered to carry Halonni but Tyris refused and the brothers walked in silence after that. Tyris sensed an understanding between them that he figured had always existed. They knew what they faced and what the likely outcome was. They had been in enough trouble over the years to recognize when things were likely to turn out all wrong. Skill, courage and brute strength had seen them through enough of those times, but neither one of them was stupid enough to discount luck. If anyone else had asked they would have called the notion horseshit, but they knew better than to think any man survived the things they had without it.

By Tyris's way of seeing things, Stilthius liked to call that luck Hunnaris. He wasn't above it himself at times. Spirits, gods, luck or whatever else it was had kept them alive so far. Tyris was just hoping it didn't decide to leave them now.

The climb turned torturous within the hour. The little footpath led to a ridgeline that turned them north along a rough, boulder-strewn slope so steep that some men resorted to using their hands to help them climb. Chanok was all but dragging Devoc along, the old magician pushed far beyond his physical limits. Tyris refused all offers of aid and struggled on, stubbornly hammering one foot down in front of the other, willing himself to ignore the burring in his legs and the aching in his back. He stumbled and slipped, knees dashing against the hard earth, but forced himself back up each time, Halonni cradled safely against him, and struggled on.

They reached a small, flat shelf of rock better than halfway to the summit where the Avaruns stopped to rest. They had no time to squander, Stilthius reminded them all, but consented to the break nonetheless. Men collapsed to the ground, put their backs to the jagged rock of the mountain and took what respite they could. Tyris eased himself down near a huge boulder, Halonni across his lap, and waited. A few feet away, Stilthius knelt next to Devoc and Chanok, reviewing more of their maps and discussing things Tyris could not hear.

He put his head to the cold stone behind him and closed his eyes.

"Tyris."

His eyes snapped open and he looked back to where his brother still gathered with the Avaruns. None of them was even looking at him. To his left, Derek and Lorum had their backs to him as well. He glanced down to find Halonni staring up at him. Her face had gone grayer in the last few hours, the dark lines more pronounced beneath her skin. The same black tendrils streaked her eyes as they found his.

"I'm dying, aren't I?"

He shook his head. "No. The magician says his spirits will protect you until we find Addicus or Jantalus."

Her eyes closed a moment and she drew a breath that rattled in her chest. "You cannot challenge Addicus. His power is too strong. He is a too much for you – stronger even than the Tassarens. Throwing more lives away accomplishes nothing."

"Then Jantalus…"

Her eyes snapped open, shining with tears and his words slipped away from him. She knew. Everything the old man and the Ravensbournes had told Stilthius and himself – she knew. The old man might have told her or what he had done to her could have revealed it to her somehow. Tyris did not know how or why, but it was clear that she knew it all.

"I'm sorry, Halonni." He wished for something more to say and felt like a fool for not being able to think of it.

She blinked away the tears before they could fall and drew another shuddering breath. "Addicus took a part of my magic, Tyris. My magic and my very life are entwined, like the metals forged together in a sword, they cannot be separated without destroying the whole. He thought to cripple me to use the promise of my death to bargain against Jantalus."

"For his magic?" Tyris asked. "Addicus wants his magic?"

She nodded. It seemed like a titanic effort for her. "He took memories from me when he took my magic - memories of Jantalus so that he could know what he faced. But when he did, he showed me his own. I know what was done and why. This is a fight that you and Stilthius and the others have no place in. What you need to do – all you can do – is try to reach Jantalus before Addicus and warn him. Tell him what you know. Try to stop him before he makes a choice he doesn't understand. The man he is now, the one we know, may choose not to return to being the man he was."

She struggled for a moment before working her hand free from the blankets wrapped about her. She held it up and examined it. It was as gray as her face, spider webbed with black lines, her nails gone the color of slate. She turned it over, studying it, and then let it drop with a sigh.

"I will be like the ghost that haunted Jantalus's dream in Drappel. I will fade until I am more shadow than human." She paused. "Leave me. There is nothing more to do for me. I am too weak to use my magic and you have no way to aid me. I slow you. If all that is left is to give Jantalus a chance, then do that."

Tyris gathered his legs under him and pushed himself to his feet, lifting her up again. "Stilthius!" His brother turned to him at once. "We move."

Halonni's hand clutched at his cloak, gray, shaking, and weak. Worn with fatigue and the strain of the magic that ravaged her, her voice was so soft he could barely hear her. "No, Tyris. This is a waste."

He raised his eyes to the mountain above him. Somewhere, hidden among the crags and snow and cliffs, Sentry and Jantalus Kathias waited. "You are my friends. I have no others."

Stilthius was at his side in a moment, his eyes widening at the sight of Halonni awake. "What is it?"

Tyris shook his head. "While we walk."

Stilthius gathered up his pack and started ahead once more, Tyris a step behind. Chanok called after them in the Avarun tongue, but they understood none of it and ignored him. Derek and Lorum were scrambling to their feet and the exhausted Avaruns stared at them as if they were mad.

"Our men are not rested!" Devoc called after them, milky eyes casting about.

"Then follow when they are!" Stilthius called back.

The Ravensbournes hurried to them, falling in beside them as they walked. Tyris paused for only a moment, looking them over.

Lorum stared back at him with his one good eye, his face lined with determination. "Do you think our father means less to us than your friends to you?"

Tyris bent his head in acknowledgement and gestured for Stilthius to continue. The four men and the stricken girl fought forward, challenged by the mountain for every step. They had not made a dozen yards when they heard the Avaruns behind them. Tyris turned to see Chanok once again dragging the old magician along while the warriors clawed their way on behind them. A score of dusky faces stared back at the outlander with iron determination.

"Mad bastards," Tyris muttered to his brother.

"Their spirits guide them," Stilthius reminded him. "The power of faith is strong. You should know that."

Tyris turned and resumed walking. Halonni was asleep again, her head against his shoulder, her body limp in his arms. "You are the one with the faith."

"In Hunnaris? Yes. You have it too. I just don't think you recognize it for what it is."

He was wrong. Stilthius had always been wrong about that. Hunnaris might be a god. But there was no gain in believing. Jantalus had told him once that the goddess the people of Kronos worshipped was of no use to him if she let her people struggle in vain in a world that forgave nothing. Tyris found the god of his people no better. Praise for a god that did nothing to earn it were the words of a fool.

He glanced down at Halonni, at the dark magic that was slowly changing her over and destroying her.

Fuck this world. Fuck the gods. Fuck everything.

His faith was in the axe strapped across his back. Addicus Malshere, Shaddix, the walking dead of Sentry, the Tassarens – it made no difference to him. Someone – all of them if needs be – would answer for what had been done. Let others worry about magic and faith and spirits.

Tyris Menion would deal in blood.

Chapter Thirty-Four

The black fire numbed his hand as soon as he touched it. For an instant, he felt only a tingling sensation across his fingertips and then the pain began. Like claws, the magic of the strange fire pierced his skin, digging deep into him, hooking around his magic and raking it out of him. He screamed, his legs collapsing beneath him, his knees hammering against the cold stone floor. A bright light flashed before his eyes as his head felt like something was trying to split it apart from within. He was paralyzed by the pain, his scream choking off as he failed to draw another breath. His body convulsed, his eyes bulging, everything starting to disappear into the blackness that crowded his vision.

When he was sure he was going to die, when his lungs felt ready to burst, a hand seized Jantalus Kathias from behind and pulled him back.

He crumbled to the floor, still surrounded by the ring of black flames, but no longer touching it. He gasped, his face pressed against the stone, his chest all knots and fire. He could hear his heart pounding in his ears and his hands shook too hard for him to push himself up. He lay still for a time, his eyes closed and his body quaking, trying to gather himself. He tried to think around the excruciating pain in his head. He could not focus, not even for a moment. He experienced no relief, no moment of calm. Only pain.

He lost all sense of time. He drifted, losing consciousness, he supposed, though he could not be sure. He was still lying on the floor when he opened his eyes again and realized the pain was subsiding. He pushed himself up, still shaking and uncertain, wary of doing anything that would bring on the rush of agony once more. He managed to turn himself over and sit up, his elbows on his knees.

The featureless man he had found inside the ring of fire was staring at him. He had tried to communicate with the man several times, but he had gotten no response. Mira Rhenn's ghost had drifted away and not returned and the black fire allowed only distorted glances of the room beyond. She might have faded away completely for all he knew. Jantalus had asked, pled, and even demanded for the strange man to speak with him, to tell him what was happening, but the thing remained mute. It simply stood, stared, and waited.

It was infuriating. When Jantalus had first stepped into the fire, the man had spoken to him. Why not now?

His frustration had grown to the point where he had abandoned the attempt and concentrated on finding a way out. His single attempt to pierce the ring of fire had nearly killed him. Communicating with his fellow prisoner seemed worth another try.

Jantalus leaned back on his elbows and considered the odd man a moment. The creature knew him, that much was clear. He could think of no other reason for the creature's initial warning for him to stay away. Since then, the flat, expressionless eyes it had formed never left Jantalus, and the black hole of a mouth it had created to scream with earlier made no more sound. Yet, the man had saved him from his failed attempt to escape. Jantalus tried to find something about the man he could recognize, but failed. The thing had no hair and average features. It bore no distinguishing mark or trait. The eyes and mouth showed no hint of personality or emotion.

But here you are, trapped like I am. It can't be a coincidence that it is you and I.

Considering what he was seeing and what his reaction to it should be, he stopped himself.

Not trapped like me. Trapped by me. Because you are a part of who I was.

The words of a shade that had betrayed him, he knew, but he thought he had heard a ring of truth to them. Jantalus found that both impossible to believe and impossible to ignore. Mira Rhenn had tricked him, imprisoned him. Trusting her word was beyond foolish.

But something told him he had to.

She had been sorry. It was not only the words she had spoken to that effect that convinced him. It was something about the ghostly face, something about the pain in her ethereal voice. She may have tricked him into imprisoning himself, but not everything she had told him might prove to be a lie.

The question of why she felt it for the best that he be held here was one for another time. Why was immaterial next to the fact that he was. He needed to escape and the only help he had in that was whatever the strange being staring down at him could offer.

Mira had told him that battling Mordoc Tassaren had cost him much of his strength, and that the ring of fire was protecting his soul from the death of his body. His father, too, was trapped, part of the creature as well. Peridor Finn had nearly doomed Jantalus by removing his body from this place. If not for Durn, his body would have crumbled, leaving only the shard of magic trapped here. Jantalus Kathias had been split into two people. That, he surmised, was the reason for his fractured memories and lack of control over his magic. His power and part of his very essence were trapped in the fire, and took the form of the odd man.

But that is all it is. It is not really a man at all.

He struggled to his feet and squared himself before the thing. If he were wrong, would it be just like touching the fire? Worse? He was trusting the word of a ghost that had betrayed him. Everything she had told him was suspect. For all he knew, she had been his enemy in his past life and was having her revenge and he was misreading everything about her that he thought was remorse for what had been done. He might be compounding trickery with stupidity.

Or I could be talking myself into standing here doing nothing until I starve to death or something comes along to kill me.

He raised his hand, his arm still weak and shaking, and touched the expressionless face. The surface of it felt nothing like skin. It was a barrier of some kind, a plane of pure magic that had formed a shape resembling a face. The blank eyes stared back at him. It did not react for a long time. The thing did not move. Jantalus felt no pain. No magic stirred between them. It was as if he had reached down and touched the cold, lifeless stone beneath his feet.

And then, slowly, so slowly that he could have stopped it at any time or simply stepped aside, the strange man's hand lifted for Jantalus's face. He watched the fingers stretch out toward him, felt the cool, smooth palm against his own face. He made no move to stop it, his body tense with the need to get away, but his mind forcing it to remain still. Black eyes met blank ones as they stared into each other across the little space they shared amid the deadly ring of fire, watching, waiting.

The magic was subtle at first. Jantalus felt it as a he might a soft spring breeze floating through an open window. It brushed against him, prickling against his skin so gently that it was barely noticeable. It rose up from the strange creature that he held and held him in turn, washing over him in a light sheen before intensifying to a wave, pulsing, drumming against him, its power growing in surges. It caused him no pain, but it had a sense of weight about it. It exerted a pressure that was not an attempt to overpower so much an urgent need to reach him.

Jantalus forced away his fear and doubt and opened himself to it, willing his magic to accept it.

He closed his eyes and left himself to the mercy of what was coming.

When he opened his eyes again, the summer sun was on his face, bright and warm and filled with the promise of life. Trees, bright with green leaves, swayed in the gentle breeze all about him. A tendril of smoke floated past him, hickory mixed with maple. He turned to find the source. It was a wood and stone cottage in a small grove set back against a thick forest. The smoke rose up from the hole in the roof, vanishing into the blue summer sky. A pair of old, gray hounds lay on the front porch, shading themselves. Pieces of split firewood surrounded the familiar old stump between him and the porch. A pair of iron wedges and an old axe, the handle worked smooth by years of use, lay atop the pitted surface.

Home.

"Your last true memory?"

He spun back around at the sound, body tensed to fight, magic rising. A man was standing where none had been before, older than he by the gray that marked his temples and the deep lines that creased his handsome face. He was tall and broad at the shoulders, long-limbed and strong from years of hard work. A dullness in his green eyes spoke to sorrow and hardship, a broken spirit hidden in a whole body.

Jantalus knew this man. "Father."

The man shook his head. "No. It has been a long time since I was anything close to what a father should be to anyone. I am what is left of Joran Kathias, but I am no father to you."

Jantalus looked around them. "Where are we? What is this place?"

Joran Kathias took it all with a great sweep of his arms. "This? Nothing. A place built by imagination. A picture used to tell a story. A lie."

"Whose lie?"

Joran pointed. "Yours."

Jantalus looked about them at the green trees, felt the warm sun and gentle breeze, and breathed in the sweet hickory smoke. "I don't understand."

The other man cocked his head to one side. "What if I told you that you might not want to? What if I told you that the answers you are looking for are ones you could be better off never knowing? You should not have come here, Jantalus. You should have taken the new life you found and forgotten about what was. It would have been better."

Better. The same word Mira Rhenn had used. Jantalus found he did not like what it implied. "Better for whom?"

Joran frowned back at him. "Everyone." He drew a long breath and let it out slowly. "I suppose that is beyond us now. Here we are, you and I, trapped together."

"Then there is no way out?"

"That depends."

"On what?" Jantalus pressed.

"How far from who you are now you are willing to retreat to make yourself free of it."

"That would depend," he said, "on just who and what I was before." He paused. "On what you are willing to tell me. You say I might not want to hear it. Perhaps. Perhaps not. I am still trying to decide if you are who I think you are - if I should believe you at all."

Joran Kathias gestured to the cottage behind them and the grove around it. "Is this not your home? Did your imagination not draw these images for us? If it were not real, why would it be the comfort your unconscious mind sought? Do we all not turn to home when we feel lost? Is it not where we feel safest?"

Jantalus folded his arms across his chest and narrowed his black eyes at the thing that appeared as his father before him. "Is there no better way to relax a man's defenses than to make him comfortable?"

A slow, wicked smile creased the lined face. "You are not as much changed as I thought, boy. Something of who you were persists in that muddled mind of yours. Maybe what I am going to tell you will not shake you as hard as I suspected."

"Then you will tell me who I am?"

"You know who you are. You are Jantalus Kathias. What you were is what matters here. That is why you and I find ourselves trapped." The smile drained away. "Last chance, boy. If you have sense that you might be happier for not knowing this, say so now."

"And stay here? Waiting for what?" Jantalus shook his head. "I'll take my chances. Tell me who Jantalus Kathias is — or was."

Joran Kathias smirked and snorted, all disgust and contempt. Nothing in that face showed warmth for a son lost. "What you are, I don't know. You know it well enough, I suppose. What you were? Dark. Twisted. Cold. Ruthless."

He paused and shrugged. "You were everything we made you."

"You and Mordoc and Addicus?"

Joran cocked an eyebrow at him. "Learned a touch of it, did you? I promise you, it is far worse than you can imagine. What we did – what I did – were things no father should have the capacity for. But to you? They seemed so… necessary. I suppose the blame was always mine – your mother's too, but mine chiefly. We knew from when you were a child that you were something that should not have been. We were Vicars in the service of the Council at Haven then, powerful, respected, and even feared by our opponents. Mordoc Tassaren, Addicus Malshere and Jilien Orthel – the High Elder herself – swore allegiance to us. We were a coalition like no other in the history of Haven. We wielded power unchallenged. Our will was the will of the Council. Who would stand against us? Fools, perhaps, but no one sits on the Council if he is too stupid to pick his battles."

He waved a dismissive hand, as if it were all easily cast aside. "It was good for a time. Until you, that is. You were born with magic; it was clear from the first. From the time you were old enough to walk we could sense it, feel it around you. Jilien, especially, was hopeful. You would be the first of the next generation of Vicars. Our work would pass to one of our blood when we were gone and sustain what we had done; sustain Haven for another generation, at least. Soon after you began to show sign of the magic, Mordoc's eldest daughter was born with the gift as well. Addicus Malshere's granddaughters came next. After the magic had skipped his sons, it was a sign that everything was falling into place."

"Your training began first, of course, for you were the eldest. You mastered the simplest of things, as would be expected of any with the gift for the elemental magic. But you became stubborn, unyielding, as soon as we tried to move on. Your skills were minor at best and showed no signs of improvement. Months of training passed with no results. Soon, Mordoc's children began to surpass you despite being younger. We pushed you, tried to force you through the training, hoping to draw out more of your magic and force you to tame it. Nothing worked. The decision was made to stop your training. We were mistaken, we decided. You had only a minor gift, a gift too weak to waste time pursuing. Your mother and Elder Jilien were disappointed. I, of course, was disgraced by your lack of focus and effort. I turned my efforts to the Tassaren children and their training."

He shook his head and sighed. "If only I had spent a bit more time with you, this all could have been avoided."

Jantalus waited for his father to go on as the other seemed to collect his thoughts. He felt a strange sense of disconnection. His own father was detailing his disappointment with his son, his wish that he had been someone or something else, and yet Jantalus felt nothing for it. This man, by his own admission, was no father to him. It did not agree with the fragments of memory he had of the man, of the hardworking husband and caregiver who had seemed so concerned with his invalid son and stricken wife. But Jantalus could not deny the lack of emotion when he looked at the image before him and what it represented.

"Left to yourself, you proved a better teacher than I and every other who wasted so much time and effort on you. Without my knowledge or any other's, you explored your own power and learned its secrets. One of the many things I came to learn about how I had failed to teach you was the fact that your power was not the elemental magic of the Vicars. It was a twisted, corrupted and, ultimately, wholly different thing. It was also nearly impossible to detect by use of my magic unless you allowed it. For that reason, it took many years for us to even realize your power continued to grow on its own. By the time we realized our mistake, you were almost a man, capable of your own decisions, your own direction. You were also, understandably given the circumstances, rather less than trusting of your parents and the others around you. It made our efforts to deal with you somewhat challenging."

"You mean it made me hard to control," Jantalus said. "That is what this has all been about, isn't it? My magic was not what you wanted it to be, so you abandoned me as a son. When I proved to have power very different from you, it was your inability to control it which led you to go even beyond abandonment."

Joran Kathias shrugged. "What good is power you cannot control? If you were not ours, you might stand against us. We would have been fools to allow that."

Jantalus stared into the dull green eyes, into the unflinching confidence and remorseless pride Joran Kathias felt for what he had done. His father had done what he needed to do to preserve his privilege and position and made no apology for it. It was as logical a choice as putting down a lame animal that could no longer work for you, or, perhaps more to the point, a rabid dog that posed a threat, no matter how loyal it had been in the past.

"You stole what I was – who I was," Jantalus said finally. "You stripped me of what made me what I was so that I could not be used against you. You broke me to keep me under your control."

"Yes."

"Without remorse. Without regret."

Joran shook his head. "I have one regret."

"One?"

"I should have killed you when I had the chance."

Chapter Thirty-Five

"There is a gorge," Devoc told them all as they gathered around him under the cover of a huge, overhanging rock, his maps spread out on the ground before them, barely visible in the fading light.

The worst of the mountain was below them, a steady climb of agony and frustration that few would ever forget. To a man, they had struggled up, pushing themselves to the end of their strength and yet still finding enough to help those who had no more to give. Battered, frozen to the bone and exhausted, they found little enthusiasm for celebrating the accomplishment. Sentry was close, but more obstacles stood before them.

"There was a bridge over that gorge when last I climbed here," the old magician continued. "Now? Only the spirits know."

Stilthius peered up the winding path before them, all shadows and sharp turns among the rocks. "When was the last time you were here?"

Devoc shrugged and laughed like an old fool. "I was your age, I think."

Stilthius groaned and glanced over at Tyris. "So the bridge is about a thousand years old."

Tyris shook off his pessimism. "How far, Devoc? To the bridge and then Sentry, I mean."

The old man spoke to Chanok a moment and then looked back to him. "The bridge is close – a short walk from here, but around many turns. Sentry? We should be able to see it from the bridge. An hour? Less, I think."

Lorum Ravensbourne leaned forward a bit. "We could send scouts ahead to check – keep us from wasting time."

Tyris nodded. "If the bridge is gone, where do we go, old man?"

"No scouts. No need," the old man answered. At his prompting,

Chanok traced a line on the map with his finger. "We follow the gorge west. It narrows after a time and eventually disappears. We can climb up the rocks there. Not easy, outlander. Not easy at all."

"Then we had best hope for a bridge," Derek put in. "We don't have the strength for another climb."

Tyris glanced down at Halonni where she lay across his lap as he knelt on the trail. They did not have the time, either. She was worse than only an hour ago, her breathing more erratic, the dark stain that spread over her skin growing. Devoc had counseled patience as they climbed, insisting the spirits he prayed to would watch over her. His spirits, Tyris thought, might be watching, but they were just watching her die.

He gathered her up once more and stood. Stilthius watched him a moment and then held out his hands to help. Tyris shook his head. If they were close to Sentry and things soon to turn to shit on them, Stilthius was not the pair of hands he wanted tied. He cast about a moment until his gaze settled on Derek.

"Come here, boy."

The young man stopped in mid-step and stared back at him. "Me?" Lorum inched a bit closer to his younger brother, his face grim and his eyes flickering a warning.

Tyris ignored the look. "Yes, boy. Have you ever drawn a weapon against a man?"

Derek lifted his chin. "Yes. Many times."

"In battle?"

"I fought at Drappel last year. I bested two men that day."

"Two!" Stilthius roared. "And on the same day! Hunnaris has sent us the finest warriors this land has to offer!"

"Come here," Tyris told him again. "I'm putting your skills to work."

Derek shot his brother a questioning glance. Lorum nodded once, his face relaxing a bit. He knew, Tyris thought as he watched him. It made sense to him as well. The boy came forward.

"This girl," Tyris indicated Halonni with a nod, "is precious to me. I am a Tulin. Do you know what that means, boy? It means when I swear myself to someone, I will die for them. I will kill for them. I have two friends in this whole shitty world. She is one. The other is in Sentry. With my brother at my side, everything that means anything is here. When the fight comes, I will be fighting for everything I have. Do you understand?"

Derek hesitated a moment. "You must not be burdened carrying her. But, I am the least among us. If I cannot fight, I cost us nothing."

Tyris stretched out his arms, passing Halonni to him. The boy eased her down to his shoulder and shifted her weight a bit. He was big, strong. She would not slow him much.

Tyris reached out and gripped the boy's shoulder. "Takes balls to be honest, boy. Most men don't have them."

Derek stared up at the big man with a surge of pride that lifted his chin and nodded.

Tyris released him and started ahead, Stilthius at his side. His brother leaned closer as they started down the trail, huge boulders looming over them at either side. "I might have been wrong about some of the people of this land."

Tyris did not look at him. "That so?"

"That boy, at least, has some balls."

Tyris simply shook his head and kept walking.

They snaked through the walls of stone that bordered the trail, twisting and turning their way to the promised gorge. The sun was vanishing quickly, casting everything in deep shadow as it retreated below the surrounding mountains. It gave them a sense of walking through a tunnel. The trailed turned sharply as they neared the gorge, the surrounding rocks thinning. Tyris and Stilthius led them all, Devoc tapping along behind them while Chanok guided him.

Tyris cleared the last of the huge boulders, turning to his right to face the chasm and stopped where he was. Three people stood at the edge of the long, wide split, all cloaked in black. They turned at the sound of approaching footsteps, swords and knives flashing free of scabbards.

The Tassarens.

Tyris stepped to one side, giving Stilthius space as the brothers pulled axe and hammer from their harnesses. The rest of the Avaruns filed out from the trail behind them, spears and swords ready. Caleb and Rossin dropped into crouches to either side of their sister, watching and waiting. Shantara stood tall between them, her face lifting so that her black eyes glittered in the half-light.

"Look, lads, the outlanders." She looked them all over. "You seem to be short one black-eyed sorcerer."

Stilthius gestured with his hammer. "You all seem short more than

273

that." He nodded to Rossin. "Sorry I didn't hit you harder."

The scarred face did not even turn to him, his eyes wide and unfocused, spittle dribbling down his chin as he stared ahead.

A cry sounded from behind him and Tyris turned to see Lorum Ravensbourne charging forward, sword in hand. His face contorted in fury. His good eye focused on Rossin. "Filthy bastard! I'll have both of your eyes!"

Tyris caught his cloak from behind as he rushed by and yanked so hard he toppled to his back and landed heavily. The outlander stomped down on his cloak so that he could not move. "Stay there. She'll kill you without trying."

Devoc pawed at the air before him, his milky eyes flickering back and forth. "Demons. There is evil magic here."

Shantara snorted at him. "If you only knew, you old fool." She turned back to Tyris. "Perhaps we should try to resolve this, outlander. I doubt you all want to face me, and I am not foolish to think I can best all of you in such a small space."

Tyris did not lower his axe, holding it before him like a shield. "You could get the fuck out of my way."

She smirked back at him and indicated the gorge with a wave of her hand. "Even if I wanted to, you wouldn't go far. The bridge is old. It collapsed a long time ago"

He shrugged back at her. "Then maybe you should give this up and go home."

"We both know that is not going to happen." She put her hands to her thick hips. "We might strike a bargain."

"I doubt it."

She shifted her gaze, looking past him and into the knot of Avarun warriors at his back. "The girl? Injured is she? My brother, Caleb, can heal all sorts of wounds." She gestured toward the twisted, misshapen ruin that was Rossin's face.

Tyris stepped to his right to block her view of Halonni. "Her wounds are deep, witch. Not the kind caused by a blade or arrow."

"No?" She cocked her head at him. "Magic, was it? Then the sorcerer finally turned on you."

Tyris spat at her. "The fuck he did. She was attacked by another."

"Another?"

"Addicus Malshere," Derek called before Tyris could silence him.

Shantara's blocky face went black. "Addicus? You are certain of that?"

"We are," Stilthius called back. "What difference does it make here? We will not retreat. Get out of our way or we'll do what we must."

Shantara did not seem to have heard him. "Where is Addicus?"

Tyris pointed with his axe. There was no sense hiding anything now. "Sentry by now. We're following him."

Caleb came forward and put a hand on his sister's broad shoulder, but she slapped it away without looking at him. "He must not reach Jantalus Kathias. Help me get across the gorge and I will help you stop him."

Caleb came forward again, seizing her arm and jerking her about. "Addicus will tear us to pieces! And these useless fucks will be of no help at all."

Shantara pulled her arm away and whirled back to the outlanders. "Addicus goes to Sentry to rob Jantalus Kathias of his magic and make it his own. More magic waits there as well, much more. Jantalus imprisoned his father in Sentry and he too holds great power. If Addicus reaches them, he will drain them of their magic and kill them. We cannot let that happen."

"Because you want it for yourself?" Stilthius asked, his finger stabbing out at her.

"Only what part of it belongs to the Tassarens," she answered. "Only what was taken from our father. We would see him restored. If Jantalus Kathias agrees to that, we can go in peace."

Stilthius turned to Tyris, switching to the Tulin language so that only the brothers would understand. "She's lying. Everything she says is a lie."

Tyris nodded. "Do we have a choice?"

Stilthius set his jaw and shook his head, but said no more. It was a pile of shit they were jumping into, but it was the only place to land. Tyris nodded back toward Halonni. "What can you do for her?"

Shantara stared at him for a long moment and then started forward. Rossin and Caleb started after her, but she motioned for them to stop and came on alone. Tyris steeled himself as she approached, expecting some trick, some sort of clever ambush. She stopped just short of him, her hands held out to her sides in a gesture of peace. He watched her, measured her, and noted the distance between them and how simple it would be to split her in two before she could even blink. He beckoned over his shoulder with one hand.

Derek came forward slowly, Halonni still cradled against him. He stopped next to Tyris, his youthful face flushed with fear as he looked upon the black-eyed Necromancer. Shantara ignored him completely, bending down over Halonni. She studied her for a moment and then pulled off one of her gloves. She held up her empty hand for Tyris to see and then slowly reached out to place it against Halonni's face. The Necromancer's eyes closed and her face creased with concentration. After a few moments, the black eyes slipped open again and her hand lifted away.

"Addicus has taken a piece of her soul away. In its place, he has left a quite sinister bit of magic. He has created in the void left by her magic a connection with the spirit world. Rather than the elemental forces that the Vicars draw on for their magic, the girl calls on the forces of death from the netherworld to sustain her. Magic and life are intertwined for those of us with the gift. The spirit world is slowly making her part of itself. She will fade until she is nothing but shadow."

"Can you cure her?" Tyris demanded.

"No." She shook her head. "Only Addicus can give back what was taken. I can slow the process though. I already have." She looked up at him again. "Another reason to help me, outlander. If we find Addicus, we may yet save the girl."

"I doubt that old prick is just going to cure her because we ask," Lorum muttered as he pulled himself to his feet.

Stilthius hefted his hammer. "It all depends on how you ask."

Shantara looked them all over. "We have little time. The girl has less than most. Do we have a bargain or no?"

Tyris watched Stilthius shake his head. He didn't like it, but, then, there was nothing to like. No good could come from this. It was also their only option.

"What do you need from us?"

Shantara turned and pointed to the gorge. "The bridge was tethered here by two lines and two lines on the other side. Both supports have collapsed on this side and the bridge hangs from the pair across the chasm. Caleb, enterprising boy that he is, managed to hook the bridge, but it is too heavy for us to pull up so we can secure it here and cross."

Tyris lowered his axe and beckoned to Stilthius. The outlanders crossed to the gorge, watching the Tassarens as they went. Rossin looked up at them for the first time, eyes empty and staring as they settled on

Stilthius. One hand lifted, his finger tracing the depression in the side of his head and the folds of scarred skin below it. Tyris watched him a moment until he was sure the madman was staying where he was.

"Broke my back, you know," Caleb muttered to Stilthius as they passed each other. "Took more than a bit of magic and some pain to heal that."

Stilthius shrugged at him. "I'll try harder next time."

Caleb took a step toward him, but a shout from Shantara stopped him. "Soon," he hissed through clenched teeth. "Very soon."

They reached the edge of the gorge to find a rope tied off to an old stone anchor set deep into the ground. The other end had an iron hook that was wedged between the wooden slats of the bridge where they dangled from the supports on the other side, some fifty feet away. Between the wood, the heavy chain that formed the handrails and the metal hooks and eyes that held everything together, Tyris did not doubt that the Tassarens had been unable to move it.

He turned back to his companions. "Lorum. Chanok." He gestured to Caleb Tassaren. "You too, unless you want to stand here forever."

The five men took hold of the rope and heaved, dragging it up hand over hand. The bridge creaked and swayed in the mountain breeze, jerking back and forth as they pulled. The iron hook threatened to slip free with every sudden movement, but held. When at last they had it at hand, Chanok gave a cry and a handful of his warriors came forward with ropes and lengths of cord to bind the broken chains to the supports that remained. When they were finished, Tyris released the line and motioned for the rest of them to do the same.

The bridge held, still swaying a bit, creaking and popping as the wind rocked it back and forth. Stilthius came forward and stepped on the first of the old wooden slats. He hammered his feet down on it to test it.

"Wait here," he told the rest.

Without another word, he took the chains that served as handrails and made his way across, the bridge swaying and groaning in protest as he went. He reached the far side and immediately turned back.

"Strong enough," he announced as he rejoined them. "I would go in pairs, though."

Tyris clapped him on the shoulder with a sigh of relief. "Derek!" the boy scrambled forward. "You take Halonni over first. Caleb and Stilthius can follow. Devoc, you send your people over in pairs after them."

"And me?" Shantara asked with a mocking smile. "Do you leave me here alone or trust me on the other side with your brother and the girl?"

Tyris returned the smile. "When the rest are safe, you can walk across with me."

The smile twisted into a sneer. "What makes you think you can trust me?"

He shrugged. "I can't. But that bridge is very narrow. You do anything stupid, and I'll throw you off before you can blink."

The look she shot back at him was full of arrogance, fury and pride. It also told him that she knew he was right.

Chapter Thirty-Six

Jantalus stared at the figment of his imagination that represented his father, trying once more to see something about it that made him feel a connection. The absence of emotion and recognition beyond the physical appearance of him was an unsettling thing at first. His father's admission that he wished his son were dead at his own hand turned it somewhat darker than merely unsettling. He felt a rise of anger at what Joran Kathias was saying, but still no feeling for the man who said it. Jantalus was as furious with his father as he might have been with a stranger for suggesting it.

Something he could not fully grasp and hold to told him he should feel something more for hearing it from his father.

"Killing me for your position and power on the council is what it should have come to?" he asked after a long silence between them. "Were you so addicted to it all?"

Joran Kathias shook his head at his son as if he were still but a child spouting foolish thoughts. "The Council? Oh, I loved my power, the respect I had, and the good life it provided. But to kill for it? Only if necessary, and not a son. No, it was what came after the sudden development of your bastard magic that made me hate you. I fought for you see, fought to shield you from all of them. We could not hide of course; your power was too great for that. Even though the Vicars' magic could not sense yours, you were young and careless about concealing it. They learned. They all learned. How could they not? Shantara and Caleb and Dianan and the rest of Mordoc's children were your friends. You told them everything and they told their father. Mordoc was a good friend. He kept your secret and ordered his little bastards to do the same. There were loose lips about Haven, however, and word spread. Rumors and unproven accusations were the start of it. We dismissed them for a time, but we knew the truth would find its way out."

Kylar and Telena Thel soon learned what you were and demanded you be brought before the Council. When it was determined you were a danger, the decision was made to strip you of your power. Mordoc and I were away at the time and they almost had you. We returned to halt the trial and the theft of your power."

Jantalus stared at him. "So the dream I had of the trial at Haven and the Vicars judging me was real. Was Mordoc Tassaren killing my mother real too?"

His father frowned, his face turning all ugly lines. "It might just as well have been you killing her. My losing her was, ultimately, your fault."

"You blame me for her death? Is that where all of this hate comes from?"

"Hate?" Joran snorted. "You've no idea. After barely saving you from the wrath of the council, Mordoc and I met with Addicus and tried to reason with him. Addicus was a friend, a mentor even. I called on the years we had spent at each other's side, pled for him to listen to me. You were my son and I a respected member of the council. Surely, there could be a peace made that would satisfy all. And so, I brokered that peace. I did what a father should do for his son when he is threatened. I saved your life, Jantalus."

He paused, collecting himself. "I should not have. Had I known the true cost, I would not have. Addicus, Mordoc and I agreed that we would take a portion of your power. Each one of us would take a measure, reducing yours to make you something less of a threat. Split among the three of us, it would ensure that none of us had too much and posed the same danger that you did. It had risks of course, but we decided them worth the taking. Magic and life you see-."

"Are one," Jantalus finished for him. "I know. When you took my magic, you took a piece — three pieces — of my soul. Is that why I was lost for so long? Is that why my whole life was nothing but endless darkness with brief windows into the world?"

"Windows?" Joran shook his head. "There were no windows in the prison we created. What you saw were nothing more than bits of memory and imagination not too much unlike what you see now. Someday, we hoped, we would find a way to contain your magic and restore you. Until then, we did what we could for you. I fed you. Not food and water like most men need to survive. I fed you magic and with that magic, pieces of memory and thought that I could not help but share. What you think you saw, whatever images and sounds you might remember having experienced are just dreams stolen from me and mixed with whatever little your imagination could muster to add to them. I have no idea what you saw. I do not care. But whatever it was, it was a lie you told yourself to convince your mind that you were something close to alive."

"But I saw my mother die," he insisted. "I saw Mordoc kill her and you do battle with him."

"No. You did not. You saw something through my eyes, twisted to seem like your own. After we took your magic, I left Haven for a time to hide you and your mother in Drappel. I would return to Haven when I could, maintain my position and serve on the Council. Addicus and Mordoc stayed away as they promised. Addicus left Haven entirely and went back to Northshire. Mordoc stayed with me when I was in Haven but did not

ask where you were and did not try to find you. At least, not for a time."

"Your magic slowly twisted us all, Jantalus. Like a disease, it ravaged us, weakening us, breaking us down. Mordoc began asking where you were. We had not taken enough from you he said. He feared you were still dangerous. I did not understand it at first, but I came to realize that he was craving more of your power. I tried to refuse him, to make him see that he was being irrational, but he would not listen. He began working with the Sentinels, recruiting his own children to aid him. They sought out magic, finding anyone that used it outside of the approval of the Vicars and stealing it. He added more and more to himself, growing increasingly powerful. It was you he always wanted though and nothing else satisfied him. Finally, he found you. He used one of his daughters, Dianan, to gain my confidence and discover the truth. When I realized what I had done, I returned to Drappel and hid you away from him. When he arrived, you were gone."

"Mordoc was furious. He demanded you be brought to him, demanded that I submit to him as a representative of the council. I was a fool – I refused. He returned with his Sentinels and his children. Your mother and I fought back, but when she realized why we were fighting, realized what had been done to you, she abandoned me. She did not die Jantalus, she betrayed me. My own wife! She went alone for she did not know where I had hidden you."

He took a moment, seeming to compose himself. *"I drove them off and escaped. You and I ran for six years. Six years I took care of you like a mother cares for a helpless babe. We lived in caves and alleyways and stables. I ate the scraps from kitchens and wore the cast-off rags of beggars. All that time I kept you hidden. I ran so long I lost all strength and all will. I was broken, defeated. I did the only thing I thought left to me. I returned to Drappel and tried to find old friends to help me. Peridor Finn helped me, of course. He always did. He gave us a place to stay and kept us hidden. But people knew. They remembered. Sentinels had scoured the Censharn for years looking for us. The Alliance had bounties on our heads and eventually, we were betrayed. Mordoc came for us, leading an Alliance army with his Sentinels."*

"And so you called on Peridor Finn and all the rest to aid you," Jantalus broke in. *"That is how Drappel was destroyed. And Mordoc took me and brought me here, to Sentry."*

"Took you? No. You went of your own free will, boy. In the heat of battle, pressed on all sides and surely facing defeat, I made a rash decision. A decision I would take back if I could. I returned what piece of your magic I had taken. It revived you, gave you strength and life and the power to fight back. And what did you do? How did you respond to your father and allies under siege? You joined him. Him! The man who broke

our family, slaughtered your people and tried to take your very life for himself. You turned on me, accused me of trying to destroy you and stood by Mordoc's side as he decimated Drappel."

"I managed to get away with Mira and Khessa Rhenn's help. You fled with him, running here, an old, forgotten fortress that Mordoc hoped no other remembered. I chased after him, of course, after you both. I would end you if it was the last thing I did. Cirrin Ravensbourne and what men remained to him came with me, Peridor leading them. We chased you for weeks before we cornered you here. But as angry as I was, I let my need for vengeance blind me. You were cunning and you laid a perfect trap. You threw yourself on my mercy, begged forgiveness, accused Mordoc of manipulating you. And when I dared to be a father for an instant, I found myself trapped in your black fire."

"And Mordoc?" Jantalus asked, trying to decide if he believed it – any of it. He sensed no lie, only anger, but none of it sparked any memory in him. It was as if he were hearing a tale involving total strangers.

A wry smile creased the lined face. "Justice, I suppose, came next. The kind of justice that only a bitter man can appreciate, perhaps, but I did. As soon as you betrayed me, he betrayed you. He nearly had you, but you fought him off, drove him away. You were spent and dying, and so you trapped what was left of your magic here, with me, thinking someone would come to save you and you could take it back. Peridor did come, but he misunderstood it all and bore you away. The rest? You know what came next far better than I."

Jantalus turned, paced away and stood with his back to the image of his father for a long time, thinking it all over, trying to decide what to make of it. Was there truth to pluck from a sea of fiction? Was this the tale of a bitter, angry man who had betrayed him trying to justify himself by painting his son as something worse and deserving of what had been done? Was it all a lie and Joran Kathias and the strange being he spoke to now were not the same man at all? Was it all true to the best of this creature's ability to recall and interpret it but inaccurate nonetheless?

All possibilities, he conceded. Good possibilities, if not in their likelihood, at least in concept. All of them would provide a measure of cushion against the verbal bludgeoning he had just taken. A bit of justification or even absolution would go a long way to making it all a bit more palatable. He held on to those possibilities for a moment, tested the strength of them and then let them melt away like a snowflake on his skin.

Everything he had heard was the truth. Every word. That was who and what Jantalus Kathias had been. That was the reality he was going to have to face if he wanted to escape this world of imagination locked within the ring of fire. The version Mira Rhenn had told him, while similar was missing the details she had no knowledge of and *contained enough lies to convince him to trap himself in the ring of fire.*

He turned back to the thing that represented his father. "How do I escape the fire?"

He shrugged. "I would assume your power added to what is trapped here would be enough. Part of what you see around you was created by what you trapped here when you betrayed me. It was the part of that force of magic that pulled you free when you tried to escape before. It is apart from you now, but it still belongs to you."

"And you?" Jantalus asked. "If I take back my magic and escape, what becomes of you?"

"I will cease to exist. For all I did, as hard as I fought for you, you betrayed me and now, I will die that you might live."

"And my mother? Mordoc? What of them?"

Joran's face flushed with anger again. "They'll be together soon enough. Oh, not as you think. Not yet. That body lying on the floor out there in the tower is not mine. The shade lied. It is Mordoc's. Once you had trapped my soul, he assumed my form. So much easier, you see, to crawl back to dear old Jilien on the council and beg forgiveness as Joran Kathias. Mordoc, after all, led an army to kill you only to be seen running off with you as an ally. I can only imagine he will find Aralyn as well and convince her he is me and mend that rift as well."

"And he still holds a piece of me?"

Joran nodded. "He and Addicus Malshere both. I pray they always do."

Jantalus shook his head at the creature. "Odd, don't you think, that you see no fault of your own in this?" The thing tried to respond, but Jantalus spoke over his words. "Maybe I am something twisted. Maybe I should have been controlled and contained. But why? I was a child once. You shaped that child. You created the man he became. Was I a freak? An accident of birth? Maybe I was. But what did you do? Help me? Guide me? Show me some other way? No. You worried for yourself and when things fell apart, you blamed me. When the power I possessed became too much to control, you took it from me. When your wife saw what you did to her son, you blamed me for driving her away. When I turned on you, you blamed me for not supporting the man who did me wrong at every turn. Everything you have suffered is as much your doing as mine."

"That is not-."

"It is," Jantalus insisted, cutting him off. "It is true. That is the source of your hate. You do not hate me. You hate yourself for your weakness, for your anger and for your lack of any quality a father should possess."

Before he could respond, the world about them suddenly dimmed, fading to black for an instant before returning to how it had been. Jantalus looked about himself in wonder.

"What was that?"

A slow, wicked smile spread across the face before him. "Another comes. Addicus has come. My prayers are answered."

Jantalus surged forward and seized the smiling face, jerking the proxy that stood for his father's soul forward. "If any god was inclined to listen, you should have prayed for mercy."

With a wild, furious cry, Jantalus summoned all of his magic in a thunderous rush of power that broke over everything and drowned it in a sea of black.

Chapter Thirty-Seven

Sentry came into view just as the nearly full moon broke over the tips of the mountains. Streaming down from a nearly clear sky, it lit their way like a hundred lanterns and painted the huge tower of the town in silver against the backdrop of the starlit sky. Tyris and Stilthius paused, taking in the sight of it and what it meant for them. They were close now. Whatever could be done for Halonni and Jantalus would be done soon. That meant the walking dead, evil spirits and even Addicus Malshere.

Tyris Menion glanced up ahead at the trail where it bent to the right and climbed to the edge of the town. This was the end of it in every sense. He knew what lay ahead and what their chances were. They had no magic to fight the power of a Necromancer. Shantara was with them, but she was only waiting for a chance to betray them and had been from the first. If he had anywhere else to go or anything else worth fighting for, he would have turned and started back down the mountain in an instant.

Instead, he tapped his brother's arm and pointed to the brilliant moon. "If you have his ear, you might want to whisper something into it."

Stilthius raised his hammer into a stream of silver light. "He knows, Tyris. He put the desire in my heart. If it is his will, we will survive. If not? I can only ask that he look after our friends."

Shantara looked back from where she and her brothers had continued along the trail. "Changed your minds?"

Tyris smiled back at her with no warmth. "Just wondering when you'll be changing yours."

She laughed. "Surprises make life worth living, outlander." She turned away again, took two steps and stopped as if rooted to the ground.

"What is it?" Caleb asked beside her, casting a warning glance at the Menion brothers.

Shantara was shaking her head, her black eyes wide. "We are too late. Addicus is here."

As if she had heard, Halonni gasped, her head flinching up from Derek's shoulder. Her eyes snapped open, all gray with streaks of black as they settled on Tyris Menion. He hurried to her as her hand stretched out for him. He caught the hand, her icy fingers wrapping about his. He had to lean close enough for their cheeks to touch to hear her speak.

"Addicus. Get me close. I can take back what he stole if he is weak or distracted."

There was probably a better chance of Hunnaris coming down from the moon to fight for them, but he simply nodded. Her hand clutched his even tighter when he tried to pull away. "Jantalus. He's here too. His power...overwhelming everything. More than a match for Addicus. More..."

Her feeble whisper finally broke off and she slumped back against Derek, her terrible eyes still fixed on him, but her strength spent. He gave her hand a final squeeze and then released it.

Stilthius was beside him again as Tyris started back toward the Tassarens, waving the Avaruns after him. "You know Addicus will have Shaddix and the rest with him. If they fight for him, those Black River fucks will carve this lot up without trying."

"I know."

"That's on top of Addicus being more than Shantara can handle by her own admission."

"I know that too."

"Just making sure."

Tyris glanced over at him. "That's all? Just making sure I knew we were fucked? No advice? No help?"

Stilthius shrugged. "Help? If I had a few hundred Tulins waiting to rush into battle with us, I would have produced them by now. Like you said, we're fucked."

"You aren't making this better."

His brother caught his arm and dragged him to a halt. "Listen to me. You listen close. I've seen this before."

"I know that. We've been here a hundred times. Different names, maybe – different people around us. We always clawed our way out." Tyris shrugged. "We'll find a way this time."

"No," Stilthius told him. "I mean I've seen *this*. Right here. Right now. This is where I've been led. This is where Jantalus Kathias's road was supposed to take us."

"You don't know-."

"Yes, I do. This is it. The full moon is on us. The battle waits and our enemy is unconquerable. This is everything we have lived for, Tyris. Tonight, here, now, our kullars await."

The big man shook his head. "Or we're just in the wrong fucking place at the wrong fucking time-."

"Are you two coming?" Caleb called back to them. "Addicus will have Jantalus and be home by the time you're done."

"Fuck off!" Tyris called back. He turned back to his brother. "Luck. That's why we're here. Good luck, bad luck, whatever it was, we're here because that's how things happen. You can call it a god. You can see some destiny. I see a stable in a little shit of a city that we happened to share with a couple poor bastards that were being hunted by these shits." He gestured vaguely in the direction of the Tassarens. "If we hadn't spent the last year drunk, gambling and whoring, we wouldn't have assumed they were coming for us and picked a fight. That's how this started. You can think we were destined to fight those bastards, but now they're helping us and us them. Where is Hunnaris's plan in that? Why is it about Addicus and Sentry now? Why does it change every time you're proven wrong?"

Stilthius held up his hands. "I'm not perfect, Tyris. I read the signs as best I can."

"Signs? What signs? There are none. You dream this shit or whatever happens. But there is no sign. You say you believe, but he gives you nothing to believe in. Faith for the sake of it, Stilthius. That's all you have. Look around you. These people, you and me and Halonni included, are going to fucking die. You see that, don't you? And why? Devoc and his people because they believe in some fucking spirits that live in the mountain that so far have done nothing but freeze our balls and skin our knees. You for a god who doesn't give a shit about you or anyone else. Halonni because she's in love with that black-eyed bastard who butchered a whole town full of people before he forgot who he was. And me? I have no friends beyond that butcher and that poor, dying girl. After them, I have you – mad as shit and talking to the fucking moon. So we all die for what brought us here."

He heaved a deep breath. "But dead is dead Stilthius. And we're just dead men who haven't hit the ground yet."

To his surprise, Stilthius smiled. "Heathen bastard! We will make this night if only so I can live to hear you say you were wrong."

Tyris shook his head. "You're the maddest fuck I've ever met."

"Outlanders!" Shantara called back. "Addicus is moving, headed away from us. He may have found Jantalus. We move now or this is all for nothing."

Tyris nodded and drew a deep breath. "I hope Hunnaris is listening for once," he muttered to his brother.

Stilthius lifted his hammer between them. "He always listens. He just isn't much for answering."

"Left," Tyris shouted to Devoc. "Tell Chanok to move his men left. My brother, Lorum and I will stay right with Shantara and the others." He caught Derek's shoulder as everyone shifted into position. "You stay with me as much as you can. Not too close, but don't leave my sight. If I fall, you stay with my brother."

"And if you both fall?" Derek asked, his face flushed with fear and anticipation.

Tyris laid his huge hand on Halonni's head. "Run like hell and take her with you."

He left the boy without another word, hurrying to where Stilthius waited with Lorum and the Tassarens. Caleb was scowling at them, obviously not in agreement with the truce his sister had negotiated with them. Rossin stared up at the tower that loomed above with a blank expression that made Tyris wonder if he was seeing any better than Devoc.

"I am no match for Addicus," Shantara was saying. "The best I can hope for is to delay him, draw his attention to me."

"A few seconds is all I'll need to put a knife in his throat," Caleb said, producing the weapon and spinning it in a tight circle. "He's only a man." He gestured to Tyris and the others. "You fools just keep whatever men he has off me until it's done."

"And if you fight him as well as you fought me?" Stilthius asked.

Caleb bristled and took a step toward him, but Shantara put a hand against his chest and shoved him back. "Rossin's focus will be Addicus as well. Between the two of them, we have at least some chance."

"Some?" Lorum Ravensbourne asked, eyeing them all with undisguised doubt.

Shantara shrugged. "Would you prefer no chance?"

Lorum snorted, spat and turned away.

Shantara turned her black eyes back to Tyris. "Just keep whatever rabble Addicus sends to stop us away while we work."

"We'll do our part," Tyris told her. "And we'll be watching for what happens after the old man is dead."

She flashed him a wicked smile. "That does put our little alliance to rest, doesn't it? Maybe you should hope he kills me."

She was gone before he could reply, ordering everyone else after her with a sweep of her hand. The score of Avarun warriors, Chanok at their head with Devoc leaning on his strong arm, fanned out and approached the town from the left side of the path. The Merions and Ravensbournes stayed behind Shantara and her brothers, approaching from the right. Shantara moved without thought for an ambush or trickery, sensing, Tyris assumed, that there was none or simply not caring. He hoped for the former, but almost expected the latter.

Sentry was nothing but a scattered collection of ruined stone buildings, all gaping holes and collapsed roofs. The wind rushed through the town, funneled by the stone walls that remained, blowing snow and ice. The barren streets were still dusted with snow at their edges, though it was obvious that men had moved through recently. Their tracks led to the center of the ruins and stopped.

Gathered there, all mail, blades, and flapping cloaks were Shaddix and his Black River mercenaries. They had formed a knot of steel and muscle between a pair of buildings, blocking access to the street behind them that led to the base of the tower. They did not move as the force of Avaruns approached, waiting in their position, prepared to defend it.

The eyes that peered out from their ranks glimmered black in the silver moonlight.

"Turned," Tyris heard Shantara hiss. "Addicus has made them his own. They will fight without fear or pain. They will not break or surrender."

"There!" Stilthius called, pointing.

Tyris followed the line of his finger to a solitary figure moving down the street behind the mercenaries, tall and spare and wrapped in his familiar gray cloak.

Addicus.

The old man seemed to feel their eyes upon him. He stopped where he was and turned. His black eyes swept over them before fixing on Shantara. She was the threat to him and he knew it. His hands trust out toward them as if dismissing them. Immediately, Shaddix and his men started forward, weapons ready. Addicus Malshere watched them a moment and then turned away once more and headed for the tower.

"A line!" Stilthius called to Devoc. He dragged the top spike of his hammer across the hard earth, drawing a ragged cut. "Tell Chanok to form on this line!"

Devoc repeated the orders for his people and the Avarun warriors followed Chanok to the spot. Through Devoc, Stilthius ordered them to ready their spears and stay where they were. Shaddix and the men of Black River were marching straight for them, showing no reaction to the defensive position that had established. Half their number and walking in a simple line without any strategy for attacking, they were still the superior force. The Avaruns were clad in heavy cloaks and leathers while the Black River men wore full coats of mail and bore shields. Shantara had promised they would fight without fear or pain. Any one of them would be three of the Avaruns.

Tyris called Lorum to his side and ordered Derek to step away. Together with Stilthius, they anchored the right side of the Avarun line while Caleb and Rossin Tassaren took the left, Shantara a few steps behind them. They had not been told to do so, but seemed to understand what Stilthius was trying to accomplish. The Avarun warriors were only there to hold a static position. Their spears would keep the Black River men at bay for a few moments while Tyris and the others cut at their flanks. If Shaddix showed no other intention beyond walking straight into the Avarun line, it would be a simple enough matter to execute. The only question was how quickly Tyris and the rest could carve through the possessed men before they crushed the Avaruns with superior weapons and skill.

"What the hell is that?"

Tyris pulled his attention from the advancing mercenaries to where Lorum Ravensbourne pointed with the tip of his broad sword. Behind Shaddix and his possessed men, a horde of dark shapes began to emerge from the shadows of Sentry, plodding into the moonlit street from alleys and the cover of shattered buildings. The mob was a tattered mass of shredded clothing and burnished armor, all swords, axes and spears glazed with ice and snow. Hollow eyes stared out from ragged hoods and loose-fitting helmets. Their flesh was gray and sagging, preserved by the cold from rot, drained of all life. A score were visible on the street, crowding in behind Shaddix and his men, with more than Tyris could count filtering in behind them.

These were Devoc's walking dead, a wild tale of a crazed old man proven true. A murmur swept through the Avarun warriors and they began to shuffled backward, their line wavering. Chanok was shouting at them, his dark face twisted with rage, spittle flying from his mouth. Tyris caught Shantara's black gaze and the Necromancer shook her head, her broad face ceased with grim resolve. Too many, Tyris knew, even for her.

He bumped his brother's arm with his elbow. "Still think this is where Hunnaris wants us?"

Stilthius hefted his hammer and stared at the advancing enemy, shaking his head. "I do not doubt him - yet."

"Yet?"

"I'll give him a few more seconds."

The first thing he experienced was the memories he had lost.

Like a wave, they crashed over him, the sounds a roar, the images bright like the sun. Jantalus felt himself shaken, his very soul rocked as if struck. He clung to his father as the flood threatened to overwhelm him and carry him away, his magic bound tight to the other's, anchoring him and holding him fast. He fought to hold his very being together, pulled first one way and then the next, everything about him falling part and being rebuilt in an instant. He did not feel pain, only a sense of something bearing down on him and suffocating him with its sheer size and power.

He willed himself to stay in control, fight down the panic and drink it all in like dry earth absorbing the rain. The rush of sound and light eventually settled into an even flow. There was too much to process and interpret at once, so he simply accepted it and put it aside for the moment. Already he was beginning to understand the fractured nature of what he would be when it was finished. Mira had warned him that recovering himself would be like replacing the shattered glass in a mirror. Even if he found all of the shards, the cracks and chips in the glass would forever distort the image.

The image that was for him his father and the magic he had possessed stood in the false grove with the false cottage and trees before him still, eyes wide and staring, mouth frozen in a silent scream. They were still inside this ethereal world of his mind's creation, still acting on a purely mental level. Everything he saw and felt and smelled and tasted was simply a visual interpretation of his magic surrounding what was left of his father's and bending it to his will so that he could absorb it all.

His father's magic was strong, a raging fire that followed the flood of memories and burned through him as he took it all. It resisted him, a snarling, raging beast of a thing that refused to be moved. At first, Jantalus thought it was his father fighting him out of a sense of self-preservation. That would have been a senseless gesture. Joran Kathias was not going to be saved. He was nothing but a swirling bit of magic and memory preserved from total annihilation by the ring of black fire that burned at the top of the watchtower at Sentry. He had no chance for escape, no chance for another life. He had been doomed the moment he was trapped. He knew that and still wasted his time fighting against his inevitable destruction.

Jantalus came to understand as he fought to wrestle the magic away from his father that the resistance was one of rage and hate. It was a final, desperate attempt to delay him, to deny him what he had lost and keep Jantalus from taking back what part of him was trapped here. Addicus Malshere was close, Joran had claimed. He was hoping to slow Jantalus until the other arrived to ensure he would never be whole again.

The realization of it enraged him and he redoubled his efforts to break his father's defenses. He summoned all of his strength, all of his magic, and renewed his assault. In the proxy world his mind had created, his hands tightened against his father's face, fingers digging into flesh. Joran Kathias shuddered in response, his knees buckling, but Jantalus held him up, refusing to loosen his grip. He felt the walls his father had built began to crumble and the magic seeped through the cracks and into Jantalus.

The image of the man before him began to change, crumbling along with those defenses. He began to shrivel like an old husk, the flesh seeming to melt away from his bones. His skin peeled away; his eyes sank into their sockets. In seconds, what had been his father was now a wasted, almost skeletal thing. A faint moan escaped his thinning lips and the wild shuddering became a feeble twitch.

Jantalus stared down at the wasted thing with no sense of pity or remorse. This creature was nothing to him. Not a father. Not a friend. Not even a person. It was a tiny shard of a soul that trapped magic and no more. He continued to drink of that soul — of that magic — until it was gone.

The image of Joran Kathias faded until it was dust that slipped through his fingers. Everything his father had been was gone. The piece of his soul and the power it contained belonged to his son now. Jantalus sensed that what he had taken contained a fragment that had once belonged to him, a piece of the magic his father had stolen along with Addicus and Mordoc. Theirs and more, he realized. Some of what he had taken was what part of his father had survived his imprisonment in the ring of fire. It was something Jantalus had never before possessed, and, perhaps, had no right to.

Payment, he decided. Payment for a life stolen from your child.

He felt stronger now. It was not simply a renewal of the strength lost in his journey to Sentry or the battles fought along the way. He was more complete. Some of the holes in the very core of his being had been filled. Some, but not all. The ring of fire had trapped two souls and their magic, he had been told. The image of Joran Kathias had represented one. What, then, was the other?

Jantalus looked about himself once more. The grove. The trees. The cottage. The hounds on the front porch. The old stump and the axe. These were his creation. But how could they have been? His memories of home had been from the inside to out. He had seen the place in Drappel days ago, but it was shattered, burned, and broken. He might have imagined the details, but he thought not. Everything was exacting – perfect. It was a memory, but not his own. At least not a memory the man he was now possessed.

He knelt in the grass, his fingers passing through the blades. They were green and fresh and full of life. The soil was soft and damp. The wind was tinged with the smells of hickory. The sun was warm on his face.

This place was alive. Alive with magic.

His magic.

He pressed his palms down against the earth and closed his eyes. He could feel it. He could feel a drumming pulse to it. A heartbeat. He had but to take it.

In the space of time between thought and action, his body came alive with searing pain unlike any other. It dwarfed any magic he had ever wielded, any cut or blow he had sustained. It was all he could do in the world of imagination he had created to open his eyes and force his head around to the source of it.

Standing at his back, between him and the bit of memory and imagination that looked like home, was a tall, thin man in gray robes. One long arm stretched out toward him, bony fingers extended. Black fire streamed out from those fingers, knifing through the space between them and engulfed Jantalus Kathias. He was helpless under the assault, his breath stolen away by the pain, his strength sapped by other's magic. The man's head lifted, the thin smile and black eyes catching the sunlight that streamed down around them.

Addicus Malshere.

Chapter Thirty-Eight

Shaddix and the possessed men of Black River had halted their advance and were waiting for the walking dead to join their ranks. The dead were still fifty yards away while a dozen paces separated them from the waiting spears of the Avaruns. Not all sense, it seemed, had been taken from the mercenaries by their subversion at the hands of Addicus Malshere. They saw the risk of coming forward and understood the need to wait to be reinforced by the horde of shuffling corpses that continued to filter into the street. They were vulnerable now, but in a moment, they would be unstoppable.

"It might be our only chance," Stilthius muttered as they watched it all play out.

Tyris never failed to be amazed at his brother's ability to know exactly what he was thinking. It, more than most other things, was the reason they were still alive. Not that it was going to help them here. They were going to need more than a score of terrified men and a blind magician to stop what was coming. Thwarting Addicus, saving Halonni and finding Jantalus had all been worthy enough goals, but they were not going to make it off the street. This was their end if they chose to stand here.

What Stilthius knew he was thinking was that they could attack the Black River men, cut them down and then face only the horde of walking dead. It was a simple matter of prolonging the inevitable by Tyris's estimation.

He shrugged and gripped his double-bladed axe in his big hands. "Fuck it."

With a wild cry to the Tassarens at the other end of the line, he plunged forward, Stilthius to his right and Lorum Ravensbourne to his left. Caleb and Rossin hesitated only a moment and then seemed to understand what the Menion brothers were doing. Shantara stayed where she was, watching and waiting. Chanok and his men, spurred on by the reckless courage of the others, sounded their war cry and charged.

The mercenaries of Black River met the charge without flinching, shields locked and swords ready. They caught the Avarun spears and knocked them aside, countering with thrusts of their swords from the safety of their shield-wall. A stagnant line formed where the two forces had met and held for but a moment. Like a pair of black giants, Tyris and Stilthius crashed down on the left side of the Black River line. Axe and hammer forced a pair of shields aside and Lorum Ravensbourne thrust between them, his sword finding an exposed throat.

Tyris was in the gap created by the fallen man before it closed, his axe sweeping in wicked cuts. A back handed stroke took the top of a man's head off, spattering blood across the faces of the nearby men. He kicked another in the face, nearly flipping him over backward and sending him crashing away. Cuts and thrusts clipped his mail shirt, but he kept scything with his axe, beating men back.

Stilthius was beside him in an instant. One great stroke of his hammer crushed a man's jaw, turning his head so sharply his neck cracked. Tyris shifted to put his back to his brother's, a tower of steel in the center of the melee. The entire left side of the Black River line was scattered and broken. Four of the mercenaries lay at the Menion brothers' feet and Caleb and Rossin Tassaren had felled two more on the opposite flank. The Avarun spears held the others in the center, penning them in while staying clear of their swords. Robbed of their sense by Addicus's magic, the mercenaries stood their ground and slashed away at the score of spears that corralled them, their flanks crumbling.

Tyris hacked at the nearest man, batted his sword aside and split him at the base of his neck above the shoulder, nearly decapitating him in one stroke. He thrust him away, sending the flopping body crashing into another and risked a glance back at the advancing horde behind them all. The walking dead were nearly at their lines, empty eyes staring out, feet shuffling on the hard, snow covered street. They had not been fast enough.

The Avarun spearmen saw it too and began to retreat despite Chanok screaming at them. As they withdrew, the remaining Black River men slipped the trap and turned to fight. Rossin and Caleb were forced back. Tyris was caught between the possessed mercenaries and the advancing dead men. He crushed the skull of the nearest walking corpse, shattering it like rotted wood, but where one fell, three took its place. He nudged Stilthius, urging him to retreat. Turning in unison, their flanks covered as they withdrew, Tyris and Stilthius pulled back, rejoining the Avarun line as Chanok stopped their flight and reformed them a dozen yards back. Caleb and Rossin executed a similar retreat, Shantara waiting behind them.

Confused by the sudden breaking of the Avarun line and unaware of how close the walking dead had come, Lorum Ravensbourne fought on, locked sword to sword with Shaddix. Tyris shouted at him, calling for him to withdraw, but the rallying cry Chanok gave and the roaring response of his warriors drowned the outlander out. Before Tyris could reach him, one of the shambling corpses had him from behind, one hand seizing a handful of his cloak, sword lifting. Lorum turned to meet the new attack, his guard slipping. Shaddix's sword thrust upward caught him under the chin and slid through his head from jaw to crown.

Derek called out as his brother's sword tumbled from his limp hand and blood gushed down his mail to pool at his feet. Lorum was still on his feet when the dead man who had grabbed him brought its sword down and sheared off the back of his head, crimson blood and gray brain spattering everything around them. Lorum sagged to his knees as Shaddix withdrew his sword and then pitched forward into the snow, soaking it red.

Howling in fury, Derek Ravensbourne was rushing forward, Halonni still limp and defenseless in his arms, grief and rage blinding him to the stupidity of what he was doing. Stilthius reached for him as he raced by, but Derek shrugged off his cloak as Stilthius seized it. The boy was just beyond the reach of both Shaddix and the walking dead when the realization of what he was doing stopped him. The enemy closed in on him, swords and axes lifted, cutting him off from his companions. Derek dropped Halonni to the ground and fumbled for his sword.

Tyris and Stilthius never hesitated. Ignoring the gibberish Chanok shouted at them, the brothers charged the wall of walking corpses that formed around Derek. They hacked and cut, crushed skulls and severed limbs, faster, stronger and more ferocious than the plodding dead men. The undead seemed endless. They came on despite losses, forcing themselves between Derek and the outlanders. The boy fought to clear himself a path back to the Menions, hacking like a mad man, but the enemy pressed him on all sides and threatened to pull him down. Still too far away to reach him, Tyris watched as Shaddix closed on the boy, his sword gripped in both hands and ready to strike.

Derek threw his sword up to parry the blow, shrinking away from the attack.

The blow never fell.

Shaddix stood where he was, sword held high, black eyes staring at the boy. It was as if he was frozen in place and could not move. Tyris saw Shantara moving from her position on the far side of the Avarun line, but it was curiosity etched on her broad face, not the concentration he had seen others who used magic show. With Stilthius at his side, he cut through the dead men that blocked his way and pressed forward. They formed a tiny island at Derek's back, forcing the walking dead away.

With the undead cleared away for the moment, Tyris saw what was happening. Still lying on the snowy street beneath Derek, Halonni had struggled up on one elbow, her hand fastened on Shaddix's ankle. A black aura wreathed her hand, like a bit of living shadow that was crawling up the mercenary's leg. Shaddix began to shudder and convulse and then crumpled to his knees before her. She dragged herself up, hands seeking his face, the blackness still washing over him.

All around them, the walking dead still pressed in, reaching for Derek and the Menions, but they showed no interest in Halonni or Shaddix. Tyris slashed away, driving back the closest while Stilthius jerked Derek away and shoved him back toward the Avarun line. The boy stumbled and turned back to them, his sword still clutched in his hand, his youthful face all confusion.

"Run, you stupid bastard!" Stilthius called before turning to meet an undead warrior as it jabbed at him with a spear.

Tyris reached for Halonni and then stopped, hesitant to disturb her as she used magic. The walking dead still advanced around them and they were in danger of being surrounded. They needed to move, even if that meant risking some calamity by pulling Halonni away. He set his teeth and snatched her arm, pulling her up.

She released Shaddix and the mercenary flopped onto his back, staring up at the moonlit sky without moving. Halonni offered no resistance as Tyris dragged her back, her hands clutching his cloak for support. The dead pressed them still, slashing and stabbing, and Tyris shielded her with his own body, blade and spear pounding against his mail. Stilthius fought to keep the worst of it from them, his hammer raining thunderous blows as he shattered the half-rotted bodies.

In the chaos of the surging bodies, Stilthius tripped and went down, stumbling over the corpse of one of the Black River men as they backed away. The undead were on him at once, swords hacking and twisted hands reaching. Tyris called to the Tassarens for help as he rushed back to his brother, dragging Halonni as he went. The Necromancers stayed where they were, holding the line and making no move to risk themselves. Helpless to force them, Tyris began slashing with his axe, still supporting Halonni as he fought to save his brother. It was hopeless and he knew it. Too many of the undead pressed in.

Behind him, the walking dead had closed on Chanok and his warriors, the foremost spitting themselves on the Avarun spears as their fellows slipped between them to attack the terrified men. Caleb and Rossin were hacking away those who strayed close to their side of the line, still defending their sister who stood watching it all unfold as if it posed no danger. Through it all, Shantara had not helped their effort and did not look to be interested in doing so.

He hacked and shoved his way to his brother as the gray hands and gaping mouths snatched and snapped at him. Blows pounded against his mail, bruising deep but not breaking through. He kept Halonni close, always defending her first, using his body to shield her when he was not fast enough. The walking dead ignored her completely, every blow aimed at Tyris alone. It was not, he realized, that they were afraid of her or trying not to hurt her for another reason. As insane as it seemed to him in the moment, it was as if they did not even know she was there.

He crushed the skull of the dead man in front of him, finally clearing a path to Stilthius. He bent and caught him under the arm, heaving him up. Scratched by dirty nails and nicked by old, rusted blades, Stilthius was nonetheless alive, a broken nose and a jagged slash across his cheek the worst of it from what Tyris could see. He surged to his feet with his hammer still in his hands, driving the relentless crush of the enemy back as he stumbled after his brother.

"No." Halonni's hands clutched at him as he tried to lead them both back to the Avarun line.

Tyris shook his head and pushed on, moving her without effort, all but carrying her with one arm while he slashed with his axe with the other.

"Tyris. Stop."

He pushed her behind him and decapitated one of the walking dead as it reached for him. "We stop and we die."

Her hand lifted, finger pointing. "We'll die anyway."

He followed the invisible line she drew to the Tassarens. The three of them had left their position at the other side of the line and were moving around the flank of the massed dead of Sentry, skirting the buildings and slipping deeper into the town. Shantara caught his gaze for a moment and flashed him a wicked smile before disappearing around the edge of a stone building.

"What the fuck are-."

"Addicus has reached him," she answered as Stilthius stopped beside them, his hammer whirling as it kept the dead clear. Derek Ravensbourne had rushed forward from where he had retreated to and was fighting beside the big outlander.

"Jantalus you mean?" he asked.

She stared past him to the tower at the other end of the town, her eyes almost completely taken over by the black tendrils that snaked through them. "If he breaks Jantalus, we are all dead anyway. Shantara knows that. She is going to him. Going to steal the power for herself, though. She will not be content to stop Addicus."

Tyris pushed her back as the dead forced Stilthius and Derek to give ground. "She might be the only one who can!"

Halonni stepped in front of him, one hand still clutching his arm the other stretched toward their enemy. A tremor shook Sentry and the earth sudden split wide before her, dropping the walking corpses that milled about into a crevasse as deep as a grave. A great belch of dust and fine earth coughed forth as it swallowed them up. The disappearance of the foremost of the dead left only a handful near them. Tyris joined Derek and his brother and cut them down in a matter of moments while Halonni sank down on the ground at the edge of the great hole she had formed, too weak to stand.

Tyris was back for her at once, pulling her up by the arm and retreating several steps as more of the walking dead began to skirt the edge of the crevasse. She lifted her slate gray face and horrible eyes. "I am still weak, Tyris. Too weak to fight this battle. If I have any strength left, let me use it trying to stop Addicus. If we can free Jantalus-."

"Shantara may-," he began.

"Kill us after she kills Addicus," Halonni finished for him. "You know we can't trust her. We have to go, Tyris. I took the piece of Addicus's magic that possessed that man and used it to restore some of my own, but it is fading already. We have to hurry. We have to go while I am still of use to you."

Tyris gestured to the closing dead men. "Take their power, then."

She shook her head. "My connection is to Addicus. He commands these things, but his magic did not create them."

"Just fucking do it!" Stilthius called to him as he slammed his hammer into the face of one of the walking dead. "What the fuck are you standing here for? Do we have another choice?"

They didn't. They were going to die and how and why didn't mean shit now. Here, on the street ahead or at Addicus's hands at the tower – it was all the same Tyris figured. Halonni was probably wrong about having the strength to fight Addicus. He was probably wrong about Shantara fighting for them. Stilthius was probably wrong about them even bothering to try.

Fuck it.

He wrapped a huge arm about Halonni's waist and started toward the tower, cutting as he went. He screamed back for Devoc and Chanok, but never bothered to see if they heard or were even still alive to hear. Halonni's magic had given them a small opening to break for the street with only a handful of the walking dead to bar their way as the rest flailed about trying to navigate the huge hole.

With Stilthius at his left and Derek Ravensbourne at his right, Tyris Menion ran for the tower.

"Fighting is only going to make it hurt more, boy."

Addicus was close now, barely an arm's length away in the illusionary world of Jantalus's mind. The old man loomed over him as he sagged to his knees, the black fire still pouring from his gnarled fingers, the thin, weathered face split by a wicked smile beneath his gray cowl. The magic was draining him as it burned, draining out all of his magic and that he had taken from his father, stripping away parts of his very soul. Jantalus tried to resist through sheer force of will, but he could muster no defense against it.

An infuriating sense of ignorance filled him. Something in the back of his mind that he could not force himself to draw to the fore told him that he knew a way to defeat the magic Addicus was using. In fact, he was sure he had battled against it before. So much of what had been was still a murky, chaotic jumble to him that he could not seem to focus on what he needed. The ignorance fueled anger and frustration, but they were useless here. He could feel his mind and soul being torn down a bit at a time, pulled away and added to Addicus's own.

"Odd, don't you think?" the old man asked. "I fought so hard to defend you from them all. I even sacrificed my seat on the Vicar Council because I thought they were wrong about you. And after all this time and effort and killing, here I am. Here we are. Ironic."

"That you are no better than the Vicars? Than Mordoc and my father?" Jantalus tried to lunge at him, but only fell forward, catching himself with his hands and fighting without success to rise again. "I'd call it sad."

"That you won't be around for them to use as a killer? That another village won't suffer the way Drappel did because you couldn't control yourself? That someone like me — experienced, disciplined — will be the caretaker of this magic you treated like a whore?"

Jantalus raised his black eyes to the Necromancer, his teeth clenched and bared. "So this is about justice? About some selfless need to protect everyone from me? Spare me. You want what Mordoc wanted - to take what made me so far beyond your control and make it yours. Power. Nothing but power."

"Controlled power," the old man insisted. "Power applied where and when necessary. I was content to let your father make you into a man capable of making those choices. A pity he failed. To think of where we might all be today if things had gone as I hoped…"

Jantalus tried once more to rise and failed, his body trembling, his heart beating so hard and fast he thought it would fail him. He would not escape from Addicus's black fire. Even if he knew a way, his strength was insufficient for him to summon any magic. Everything he had endured, the struggle to reach Drappel and then Sentry, the pain and fatigue and anguish, had been for nothing. The moment of victory he had managed to achieve after believing himself trapped by the ring of fire had been torn away by the arrival of Addicus Malshere. The memories of who Jantalus Kathias had been would never really be his now. The chance to see the man he was and choose a future was gone.

He wanted to scream or cry or rage against it. Instead, he collapsed on his face in the illusion that was the grass beneath him. His mind was being overwhelmed, his magic and his will drained away by the second under the Necromancer's furious assault. He would resist with what little strength remained not because there was any hope in it, but only to delay Addicus Malshere's triumph another few moments.

Everything was fading, his mind falling into oblivion and slowly turning the world black around him when he felt another presence. A tremor shook the very ground beneath him. The black fire pouring from Addicus's hands eased for a moment. Too weak to take advantage of it, he managed only to raise his head and look up at the old man. Addicus was looking away from him, his hooded head turned to something behind him.

An explosion of power tore through the air and a new rush of black fire rolled up behind the Necromancer and engulfed him. Addicus cried out and staggered, nearly falling to his knees before Jantalus. His fists clenched tight and his body rigid, he refocused his own magic into a shell of black flames that surrounded him and formed a shield between him and the new magic that assailed him. It left Jantalus a moment to breathe, but he was spent and could not even force himself up to his elbows.

Still lying in the grass, his heart pounding in his chest, he heard Addicus hiss a single word through his clenched teeth.

"Shantara."

Jantalus took no comfort or hope from the rescue. One enemy traded for another was no improvement. It was only a matter of which one survived to kill him later.

Chapter Thirty-Nine

Tyris Menion slowed as soon as he came to the base of the tower from which Sentry took its name. They were in a small alley between two ruined buildings, separated from the tower by only a small, empty plaza. The door stood open, staring back at him like a great black eye. No bars. No gate. No obstacle barred his way. All that was left to do was walk up the three stone steps and enter the old fortress. Simple. Easy.

Too damn easy.

He saw no shadow move in the moonlight. He heard not footfall on the hard earth. He did not even feel a rush of air to prickle his skin or set the hairs of his neck on edge. Perhaps it was the years of constant battle or a life spent hunted. There would be a time, long afterward, when it had all faded to memory and he had occasion to think on it with some level of objectivity when he thought Hunnaris might have given him some warning in that moment. Whatever it was, he knew with no reason for knowing that the attack was coming.

He jerked Halonni close with his left arm, lifting her from her feet without effort and flung himself to his right, bowling Derek Ravensbourne over and knocking them all sprawling. The twin swords whistled past his head, the edge of one blade skipping off his mailed shoulder, the keen tip digging a jagged gash across the back of Halonni's hand where it gripped his cloak.

Tyris went down, his legs tangled with Derek's. He twisted his body, slamming down against the boy, but managing to keep Halonni from being crushed between them. Barely conscious, still dazed by the magic that devoured her from within, she cried out in pain, her injured left leg wrenched at an odd angle. Tyris had a handful of her cloak, dragging her to the side as he lifted his axe, desperate to regain his feet and defend them.

303

Everything moved too slowly. The world was a slow drumbeat of time, one moment after another. Caleb Tassaren had recovered from his wild swing and was squaring himself to finish them. Over his shoulder, Stilthius struggled against Rossin, his hammer deflecting sword and dagger. Derek was thrashing beneath him, kicking and flailing, his attempts to stand impairing Tyris's own. Caleb stepped forward, swords lifted, a perverse smile twisting his lips.

Tyris shoved Halonni off him, jerked free of Derek and raised his axe. All too slow. All too late. The twin swords caught a sliver of moonlight, flashing silver.

Before they could fall, Stilthius's hand snatched Caleb Tassaren's neck, engulfing it completely, yanking him back and bearing him to the ground. His hammer lifted, but he was exposed, his flank left open and Rossin plunged forward. Into the gap of his armor at the armpit, the madman's knife dug while the sword lifted to parry the hammer. Stilthius shuddered with the force of the blow, the hammer still descending. Caleb tried to parry the blow, but the steel head of the weapon crushed his arm at the elbow, snapping bone like deadwood. Caleb cried out, the sword tumbling from his hand. His second sword thrust out, skewering Stilthius through his thigh.

Tyris finally gained his feet, bellowing like a maddened animal. He charged Rossin Tassaren as the twisted man laughed like a maniac, sword and knife stabbing at Stilthius again. Up into the exposed armpit the knife slid again and again, too many times it seemed for how fast Tyris was closing on him. Through it all, Stilthius held Caleb Tassaren's neck in his huge hand, squeezing and jerking, tossing the Necromancer about like a doll in a child's grasp. His hammer hung from his limp arm as Rossin stabbed him repeatedly, blood flying in long, red lines across the snow-dusted street.

Rossin turned to Tyris in time to get one huge boot in the face as the outlander hammered into him. The madman fell away, his sword flying free of his grasp. He rolled across the street, regained his feet, and lifted the bloody knife. There was a dull, lifeless haze to the black eyes as they watched Tyris come for him. One wicked, merciless stroke of the great axe severed the hand holding the knife at the wrist. Rossin did not scream or even flinch. He simply stared at the blood that bubbled out of the mangled stump as if it belonged to someone else.

Tyris spun back around and sheared his head in half just below his nose. Blood, skin and bone erupted in an angry streak across the snow as they top of Rossin's head fell away. His body slumped to the ground where it was.

Tyris turned away at once, thinking only of his brother. There was no way, he told himself over and over. There was no way to survive this.

Stilthius bent over Caleb Tassaren, one hand still latched on his neck. The Necromancer had gone limp and Stilthius no longer shook him. Blood streamed down his brother's right flank and the sword protruded from his thigh still. He hunched over, his shoulders heaving, hammer still loose in his grip.

Tyris found no strength to move as he watched his brother. No hope.

Stilthius released Caleb Tassaren at last, his good hand reaching for his hammer. He gripped it tight and set the steel head against the earth. Slowly, shaking with the effort, he used it to force himself upright. Behind him, Derek had struggled to his feet, drawing Halonni up with him. She sagged against him, her left leg bent, the toe of her boot hovering off the ground. Her hands gripped his cloak, her gray and black eyes fixed on the dying outlander.

Stilthius did not look at them or even Tyris. He lifted his face to the stream of pale moonlight that shone down on them and sighed. "As you have asked, I have done."

Tyris took a step toward him. "Stilthius."

His brother did not respond, his eyes fixed still on the full moon above him. "As you have asked, Hunnaris. Always."

Nothing moved about them. The wind seemed to die completely for an instant. The constant, grating sound of the dragging feet of the walking dead that still approached all about them fell silent. Tyris could not even hear the sound of his own breathing.

Slowly, his arm shaking with the effort and blood pouring out of his side, Stilthius raised his hammer to the moon – to his god.

Kinthane.

Tyris flinched as if struck. He looked to Derek and Halonni but neither of them gave any indication that had heard anything. When he looked back at Stilthius, his brother was smiling.

"Kinthane," he said, holding his hammer up before his face, his eyes all reverence and awe. "A good name. A worthy name."

He coughed and fell to his knees.

Tyris finally hurried to him, catching him before he pitched forward and holding him up. Derek brought Halonni and joined them, sinking down beside them in the blood stained snow. Stilthius lowered the hammer to the street and then reached out to take Halonni's face with his good hand.

"You find him, girl. You help him. Hunnaris led me here. He gave me my kullar – Kinthane. But his will goes beyond me. My life is a tool, a means to safeguard you so that you can finish this. Finish this, Halonni!"

She tried to speak, her hand coming up to cover his, but she choked on her words and shook her head. Stilthius nodded and let his hand drop. He fumbled for his hammer and lifted it once more. He thrust it toward Tyris. "Take it. Take Kinthane."

Tyris shook his head. "No. It is your kullar. Take it with you when you go to Hunnaris."

Stilthius shoved it at him again. "I go to an eternity of peace at his side, feasting, celebrating. I do not need it. Take it and go. Help Jantalus. Your kullar waits. I believe it. I know it, Tyris."

Tyris was shaking his head, but no words came.

"Take it!" Stilthius struck his mailed chest with it. "Find a man worthy of it and tell him my tale."

Footfalls pounded against the street as Tyris closed his hand about the steel haft and he raised his eyes to a knot of shadows that flickered in the moonlight along the alley. Derek was on his feet in an instant, sword gripped in both hands. Tyris was half risen himself when a familiar, dusky face poked through the shadows.

Chanok. He was limping from a long gash along one thick calf and he was still dragging the blind old magician along with him. Devoc seemed unharmed, his milky eyes flickering about them as he tapped his walking stick along their path. Behind them, a handful of the Avarun warriors remained, all torn and bloodied, eyes wide with fear as they cast hasty glances over their shoulders. Tyris followed those looks to a growing mass of muddled shapes, noticing once more the scraping sound of shuffling feet.

Chanok slowed his approach, his dark eyes fixed on Stilthius as he jabbered something in the Avarun tongue and Devoc nodded. "We have little time," the old man told them. "If we bind-."

"We have no time," Stilthius announced cutting him off. His bloody hands gripped Tyris's arm. "You cannot take me with you. I would slow you and that would be the end of you. You will leave me and do what must be done. If Hunnaris wills it, you can return for me. Spread my ashes here – here where Hunnaris blessed me with my kullar." He lifted his face to stare up at the mountains in the distance, all white snow gleaming in the pale moonlight. "It is not so very different from home, this place. It will be good enough for a warrior's rest."

Tyris gripped his brother in turn. "I'll not leave you here to be torn limb from limb by those rotting pieces of shit."

Stilthius drew a ragged breath and coughed again, doubling over in pain. He sucked air through his clenched teeth and then looked up again. "It will take time for my lungs to fill and drown me." He snatched his brother's hand and guided it to the hilt of the sword that was still skewering his leg. "When this is free, I will bleed out before they reach me."

Tyris had an argument prepared, but swallowed the words. Something in the look his brother gave him, something, he realized in that moment, that had been there for a long time, reached out to him. It was not grief, nor was it regret for how it had all come to this end. Stilthius was resolved to this.

"This is what you want?"

Stilthius took his brother's head in his bloody hand and bent it forward so that their foreheads touched. "It is what I have prayed for. What I have spent my whole life waiting for. Do not mourn. Do not grieve for me. I go where I have always wished to be. You heard. I know you did. I have my kullar. There is no pain. No sorrow. This moment is perfect, Tyris. Remember that when you remember me."

"The dead-." Derek was saying, but Tyris was not listening.

He felt Stilthius's hand close over his own on the hilt of the sword. His brother's eyes never wavered. He did not blink. A slow smile spread across his broad face. The look of joy remained even as his body jerked wildly. Tyris felt the warm rush over his hands, but he held his brother's eyes and did not look away. The sword clattered to the ground. A calm came over Stilthius and the tension in his face relaxed. The smile slowly slipped away and his eyes grew heavy. He slumped forward, his head against Tyris broad shoulder.

Derek was screaming at him and Chanok and his men were jabbering in their nonsense language. Tyris ignored them. He clasped his brother to him, turned him to one side and gently laid him against the snow-covered street. He wiped blood from Stilthius's face with the edge of his cloak and then rose.

Behind him, the shambling undead of Sentry were pressing close, driving the remaining Avaruns ahead of them, filling the narrow street and spilling out into those adjacent. Tyris lifted Kinthane in one hand and his axe in the other. For a moment, his gaze fixed on the advancing horde, his thoughts wild with the promise of a warrior's stand, a charge into certain death and an end to it all. The moment passed, his brother's last words ringing in his ears. There would be no remembrance if he threw away his life now.

He turned and caught Halonni up about the waist, ignoring the stricken look etched on her slate-gray face and the sorrow in her eyes. All but dragging her, he started for the tower, drawing the others after him with a jerk of his head. Chanok came at once, carrying Devoc as much as helping him, his warriors a step behind. Derek backpedalled after them, watching the advancing undead with his sword held before him like a shield.

They crossed the little plaza and were on the steps of the tower when the boy called out.

Tyris Menion turned, following the pointing sword Derek held to the alleyway they had just left. Emerging from the shadow in advance of the horde of walking dead, two bloody swords gripped in his hands, Caleb Tassaren fixed them all with his black eyes. He took two steps toward them, stopped and bent his neck so that his ear touched his shoulder. It made an audible clicking sound and he straightened again before stalking toward them once more.

"That's impossible," Derek muttered as he staggered back toward Tyris and the others.

"Magic," Halonni hissed through clenched teeth. She straightened slightly, one hand still fastened on Tyris's arm. "He'll kill you if I don't stop him."

Tyris tightened his arm around her. "No. Jantalus needs your magic. I will hold him here. You go."

"I'll-." Derek began.

"Stay here with me," Tyris finished for him. "I need all the swords we have for when the dead reach us." Derek tried to object, but Tyris ignored him and turned to the Avaruns. "Devoc!"

The old man released Chanok and tapped forward with his staff.

Tyris carefully eased Halonni toward him. The girl caught the old man's arm and he clung to her in turn. "She will be your eyes, old man. You will be her strength."

Halonni caught his hand when he tried to turn away. "You can't Tyris. He's too much for you."

The outlander shook his head. He had no time to argue this. Caleb Tassaren was coming slowly, carefully, but he was coming and an army of walking corpses was coming with him. He bent and kissed the top of her head. "Then you hurry back. You bring that black-eyed son-of-a-bitch with you and tear this lot to fucking pieces."

She wanted to say something in response, to argue perhaps or even say good-bye, but he swept Halonni and Devoc both up in the circle of his big arm and all but shoved them up the steps to the door of the tower and through into the dark chamber beyond. He gave them no chance to even look back before he pulled the doors closed behind them and turned back to his enemy.

Derek, Chanok and the Avarun warriors formed a half circle with him at the base of the steps, Tyris centered.

He lifted his axe and Kinthane toward Caleb Tassaren in challenge.

Chapter Forty

Every staggering inch of progress made through the dark chamber of the tower was agony for Halonni Vilcris. Even with Devoc bearing most of her weight, she jarred her aching body with every hopping step, sent hot knives of pain lancing up and down her left leg. Once she caught the toe of her boot, stumbled in the debris, and nearly fell on her face. Instinct overruled sense and she put her injured leg down to steady herself. Her resulting cry echoed though the empty chamber as both legs crumbled beneath her. Devoc was there at once, his gnarled old hands pulling her back up, wrapping about her and dragging her on. She sagged against him, her teeth grinding against the pain, her face all cold sweat.

At the end of the chamber was a spiraling staircase that led into the heights of the tower. The twenty feet from where she stood to the first step might have been a thousand times that for all the strength she had to cross it.

"The spirits here rage against the dark magic," Devoc muttered as he dragged her along. "They will grant you their strength to battle it."

Halonni shook her head. The old man was mad. Beyond mad, in fact. His spirits were nothing here. His ability to speak with them and sense them might have been some latent talent for magic he had never been trained to use, but it was not what he thought it was. No sentient being here resisted the intrusion of Addicus or the Tassarens or defended Jantalus. The power that hung in the air about her was that of the spirit world and the strange, inexplicable magic Jantalus wielded. Devoc could believe what he wished, but she knew better.

She could sense the Necromancers here, Addicus and Shantara both. Their magic challenged Jantalus's, but it raged against each other's as well. She had feared they were working in concert against him, but it seemed the

Necromancers were battling each other as well. Divided, Halonni could not imagine they stood a chance against the level of power she had sensed when she had first approached Sentry, but Jantalus was failing. His magic ebbed and with it, his very life. How he had gone from so much intensity to barely being perceptible among the swirling magic was something she could not explain. She knew, however, that she was not mistaken. He was not only losing the fight – Jantalus was dying.

They reached the steps and paused, Halonni grasping the rail for support, her body alive with pain and Devoc tapping the metal steps with his staff trying to get a sense for how he was going to navigate them. They were narrow, too narrow for them to walk abreast. That would mean one of them leading the other. Devoc's blindness and her inability to stand on her own seemed to rule them both out. He could not climb the steps without her nor she without him.

He reached out, clutching at her until he found her arm and pressed his staff into her hands. "Go," he told her. "I'll trip you or myself and be the death of us both. Go without me. I will stay here and summon the spirits to aid you."

She shook her head, not thinking that he could not see her. "Devoc, the spirits don't-."

His hands gripped her shoulders and turned her toward the steps. "Go, girl. The spirits don't need you to believe in them. They are what they are."

He was mad and foolish and wasting his time and breath, but she had neither of her own to spare fighting with him. His staff gripped tight in one hand and the other clutching the handrail, she dragged herself up the stairs, groaning and hissing air between her teeth with every step. She was going to fall and break her other leg or roll head over heels down the steps and break her neck, she was sure of it. Every impossible step that she managed to conquer did not reassure her. She kept pushing off with the staff and pulling against the hand-rail, dragging her useless left leg behind her, so exhausted, sick and hurt that everything was starting to go numb.

Jantalus was up there and he was dying. She told herself that repeatedly, first in her mind and aloud by the time she reached the open trapdoor at the top of the stairs. Too weak to force herself up with the staff, she crawled with two hands and her one good knee, dragging her other leg behind her. She noticed the bloody gash on the back of her right hand for the first time as she pulled herself up, wondered where it came from and then put it out of her mind.

At the center of the room, a ring of black fire burned, raging high toward the domed ceiling with no visible source of fuel. A small section of it was incomplete, like a door left open through which she could see people. Jantalus was standing rigid at the very center, his head thrown back and his mouth open in a silent scream. A strange, faceless figure more shadow than man lay crumpled at his feet. Behind him, his long, thin fingers locked on Jantalus's head and face, stood Addicus Malshere. He too stood like a statue, locked in place with his face twisted in pain and surprise. Shantara was the last of them, her thick hands on Addicus in turn, and a cruel, satisfied smile twisting her lips. None of them noticed Halonni's arrival.

The power of their minds linked them all, Halonni realized. Addicus had attacked Jantalus and Shantara had attacked him in turn. The urge to lash out, to use her magic to get them away from Jantalus and crush them rose up in her, but she fought it down. Simply using her magic to kill them while they were unaware of her might kill Jantalus as well. Time was slipping away, but killing Jantalus by being foolish was not the answer.

"He needs to be separated from Addicus and given time to escape the ring of fire."

Halonni started at the voice and risked a quick glance behind her, thinking it was Devoc who spoke. The voice had been a woman's, and she was not surprised when she did not see the old man. She looked back at where the three struggled amid the black flames and saw a translucent figure gliding toward her. It was a woman, all white and silver lines, the echo of a spirit passed from the mortal world.

Halonni forced herself up on her good knee, bracing herself with Devoc's staff. "Who are you?"

The ghostly woman shook her head. "It doesn't matter now. I thought to destroy Jantalus when he came here, to end all of this and be done. I failed. Addicus or Shantara will claim his power. Better that he have it than them. As mad as that sounds to my ears, it is true. I sense the magic that you possess. You must stop them. I would beg you kill them all, but I think you have come to save Jantalus. Better him than the other two, if a choice must be made."

"But-."

One translucent hand lifted. "Jantalus fails and the Necromancers will have what is his. You must break Addicus's hold on him and he must escape the black fire. Once he is free, he may be able to fight back if he survives being torn away from Addicus while their minds are one. The circle of fire draws his strength - suppresses his magic while it feeds theirs. Do what you can, girl. Do it. Now."

Halonni had more questions than she could make sense of in the moment. Who and what was this ghost and what had she done? What did she know of Addicus and Shantara and how did she come by her judgment of them or Jantalus? What was the ring of fire? What was Jantalus doing in it? All of those questions and more flooded her mind and were shoved aside an instant after they occurred. It did not matter. Perhaps there would be time later. Perhaps not. What mattered was now.

She was already summoning her magic when it occurred to her that the apparition had lied. In an instant of panic, Halonni feared she had been duped into helping the enemy destroy Jantalus. If so, it was too late to stop herself. Instinct would have to rule over thought. Her sense of things would have to be enough.

The moment her magic began to burn in her blood, Halonni became keenly aware of just how weak she was. Everything she had taken from the possessed Shaddix had evaporated in an instant, leaving her only the feeble, fractured Halonni Vilcris beneath. Her power began to falter even before it had begun, sputtering and dying, evaporating into the cold mountain wind that rushed through the open windows of the tower. She trembled and sighed, her strength gone and her resolve crumbling. She had nothing left to call on, no reserve or hidden will to tap into. Everything she had was spent and she had come this far, suffered so much, only to fail.

She dropped to the floor again, her feverish face pressed against the icy stone. Unable even to lift her head, she stretched out her hands, dug her fingers into the seams between the stone blocks of the floor and pulled. How she managed to drag herself even the single pace she did amazed her. Again, she reached out and caught the edges of the stone and pulled, dragging herself across the floor like a slug. Her fingers were torn and bleeding, old wounds and new. Her knee bumped along behind her, catching every crack and crease. But she was beyond pain now.

Jantalus would be dead before she got there, she thought, cursing every inch she managed to crawl as a pathetic thing to have accomplished. She willed him to fight on, to live until she could make her way to him. She was shouting at him as she reached the ring of fire, her voice gone hoarse with sickness, fatigue, and the strain of everything that had befallen her. What began inside her as a command for him to be strong and resist came out as a desperate, garbled cough. If he understood – if he were even capable of it – she never knew, but something kept him alive for the eternity it took her to reach them.

She dragged herself past Shantara, the Necromancer's cloak brushing her face as she crawled by. Her hand stretched out, her fingers, all gray and streaked black beneath the skin sliding up Addicus's pant leg. Her warm, sticky flesh dug into his thin calf and she gripped him with what little strength she could muster. His magic was flaring and surging, battling against Shantara and he was too overwhelmed to resist this new attack.

What was hers was still there, inside of him. Everything he had taken, all of those bits and pieces that were missing from her, called back to her.

She summoned her magic again and, again, it sputtered and threatened to die like a candle beside an open window. But what was left of her clashed against what he had taken with just enough force to create the spark of magic and flare to life.

Addicus screamed, his whole body convulsing violently. Halonni felt her power growing, his magic feeding hers through the connection between them. Her magic swelled within her, gaining strength. Battered and weakened, her body shook with the strain of it, her mind and will stressed to breaking. The world before her eyes was going black and she felt everything begin to spin. She had all she could control. It would have to be enough.

She released Addicus and slammed her open palm down on the floor before her. Earth magic rose up from the stone, building power and then exploding outward. The floor tore apart from itself, shards of stone blasting forth from the gaping hole that formed. The force of the explosion tore Addicus away from Jantalus and sent him crashing into Shantara. The Necromancers tumbled away, arms and legs flailing.

Halonni's magic died an instant later, the invisible barrier she had formed to block the force of her magic from herself and Jantalus crumbling. She collapsed to the floor again, this time without even the strength to raise her head.

A chance, she told herself. At least I have given him a chance.

The magic felt limitless.

Shantara and Addicus had vanished from his mind, their relentless assault abruptly ending and leaving him alone in the illusionary landscape of his own mind with nothing but the images of his own creation – those formed by the magic that had once been his. He ran his fingers through the grass that was not really there and felt the power anew.

It flowed into him once more, rushing like water pouring into a gaping hole suddenly formed beneath it. He felt his strength returning, his magic renewed. All that he had lost in his battle with Shantara and Addicus was being replaced. He was not himself, he sensed, but he could not remember ever having been whole from the moment he had come awake in Durn's home weeks ago.

The magic that he absorbed now was not something apart from who he was, but a piece of what had been missing. It was rebuilding him from within, restoring Jantalus Kathias to the man he was supposed to be, not adding to who he had been of late. A moment of fear came with the realization, a return to the question of just who and what he had been and whether or not he would want to be so again. The fear disappeared into the tide of the magic, drowned in the invigorating power that merged with him. He saw no point in further questions, no reason for doubt. This was happening and could not be stopped.

What he would become remained to be seen. But it could no longer be changed.

He felt a moment of quiet peace as the last of the magic flowed into him. For the space of a heartbeat, he stood in a void of pure blackness, all pretenses gone, and the magic that had formed the image of his old home no longer a separate thing. Everything was his. Right or wrong, better or worse, he was – while still a fractured man – more complete than he had been. He was battered and worn still, the physical and mental struggles he had endured weighing on him. His magic, however, was stronger within him than he had ever felt. His memories were not yet whole, but in his mind, he felt less chaos, less empty spaces between the images of the past. Some of what he had seen for so long in senseless fragments had been forged into something not yet perfect, but far more clear.

He had taken a first step to being whole.

He allowed himself only that instant to feel the sense of comfort it lent before the struggle outside of his mind, back in the physical world of the tower of Sentry, called to him. He felt new magic from beyond the phantom world he experienced. It was not Addicus and Shantara, though he could still feel them. It was a third power. He concentrated a moment, reaching. It was...

Halonni!

Like a man breaking the surface of the murky water that had pulled him down and nearly drowned him, Jantalus Kathias tore the very fabric of the void that surrounded him and reached for the light of the physical world.

Chapter Forty-One

Caleb Tassaren lunged with both swords leading, sweeping up for Tyris Menion's face, looking to slip beneath his guard and finish him in one pass. The outlander slapped the blades aside with his axe, knocking the smaller man sideways and jabbed at him with the spike atop Kinthane. Caleb ducked beneath the blow and spun away, whirling in a circle to cut at him again. Tyris recovered in time to deflect the twin blades, pressing forward, trying to back the Necromancer against the wall of the nearest building. Caleb was too smart and quick to be cornered, disengaging and dancing out of reach.

He was fast, too fast for Tyris to simply overwhelm with a flurry and hammer through his defenses. For all of his love of ambush, Caleb Tassaren was a skilled swordsman and patient enough not to overcommit to an attack and leave himself vulnerable. He knew his swords were at disadvantage against the longer reach of the axe and hammer Tyris wielded and he was waiting for openings to slip beneath them to make his cuts. The men circled each other for a time, neither foolish enough to give the other an opening. Tyris allowed the stalemate for a few moments, but he knew what the bastard's game was.

Chanok and Derek could not possibly hope to defeat the horde of walking dead that pressed in around them. They were already retreating, stabbing and slashing to keep the undead at bay, the two of them and the handful of Avarun warriors who remained a tiny island in the sea of walking dead. Too many to stop, he knew. A man would fall at some point, opening a hole in their pathetic little half circle around the base of the tower and the rest would be overrun. Caleb Tassaren would wait and simply crush them all through force of numbers.

He pressed the attack once more, trying to force Caleb Tassaren to stand and fight where he could overwhelm him with size and strength. Again and again the smaller man darted out of his reach, agile, fluid and too aware to be backed into a corner. Tyris possessed speed far greater than a man of his size should have, easily deflecting any counter the Necromancer could throw at him, but in terms of agility and pure foot speed, he could not keep pace with him. Every retreat and sidestep carried Caleb Tassaren away from the cut of the axe and the fall of Kinthane, always a hand's breadth from danger, always just a second ahead.

Conscious of the time he wasted, desperate for an opening, Tyris lunged, stopped just short of a full attack and braced himself for the Necromancer's counter. Caleb took the opening, slashing backhand with one sword, aiming to cut him across the face. Tyris turned his axe to catch the blow, hooking the sword under the crescent tip of the blade and jerked Caleb forward. He rammed the spike atop Kinthane's broad head into the smaller man's gut, burying it deep and twisting. Caleb Tassaren screamed and thrashed, shoved himself back from the outlander and backpedalled away. Tyris gave chase at once, his axe slashing down. Caleb deflected the attack wide and was running again.

The Necromancer clutched at his belly a moment, one sword pointed out toward Tyris as he circled. "Not so easy, big man." His face split in a wicked grin. He drew a breath and straightened, lifting his tunic as he did. The skin beneath was streaked with blood, but even as Tyris watched, the wound from the hammer sealed itself, vanishing completely.

Tyris glanced to his left, a moment of doubt seizing him. He needed help here, someone to corral the bastard and let him cut until no magic was strong enough to repair it all. No aid would come, though. Chanok was down, groping for his fallen weapon, his eyes glazed over in a daze and blood dribbling from his nose and mouth. Derek Ravensbourne stood over him, his sword whirling in a wide arc, trying to force the undead back while the Avarun recovered. The men around them were wavering at the sight of their leader on his knees, bleeding. They needed Tyris more than he needed them.

Tyris needed to finish this. Now.

He straightened and let his weapons dip slightly, staring into the black eyes that watched him. "Fuck it, then. I'll play no more games with the spineless shits of this land. A pair of tits and you'd make a complete woman. You fight none of your own battles, show no courage when you do and make sport of everything. You are weak, worthless and beneath me. You play at some delay, I thought, hoping for those mindless corpses to come and then to overwhelm and kill me. Strategy, you might tell yourself. Clever are you?"

Caleb Tassaren did not lower his weapons, but the mocking smile returned. "It seems to be working."

"Yes," Tyris conceded. "Not because it's a smart plan, though. It's working because you've nothing hanging below your cock. It's working because you're not enough of a man to face me. You ambushed my brother because he would have torn your worthless head off in a fight. You avoid me now because you are too weak to face me alone."

The smile vanished, Caleb's chiseled face growing dark. "You'll not goad me into stupidity, outlander."

Tyris sucked a mouthful of phlegm and spat it across the space between them, wetting Caleb's tunic. "Good words – for a sad little girl huddled in a corner shitting herself. Do what you will." He pivoted to one side and pointed to the tower door. "I am going to kill your sister or whatever that black-eyed bitch is."

He turned his back on the Necromancer and started for the tower, hammer and axe hanging loose at his sides.

He would have to be quick when it came, quick and perfect in his timing. Caleb Tassaren was no fool, he would anticipate a trick. He would be ready for some trap. Tyris could give nothing away. He was taking a chance with not only his life but Chanok and Derek's lives as well. If Caleb sensed what he was doing, he would leave him and go to finish them, leaving Tyris facing not only the Necromancer, but the undead as well. He had to be convincing in his indifference or they were all dead.

He quickened his pace, adding to the sense that he had abandoned his companions and focused on the battle in the tower. He risked no glance backward, paused for not a moment, his eyes fixed on the open doors, his weapons steady at his side.

He blocked out the hammering of his pulse in his ears, ignored the scraping, dragging feet of the undead on the cold ground and the grunts of pain and exertion from Derek and the Avaruns. His whole world was the footfalls that began behind him and approached, starting slow and hesitant and then gaining speed and force as anger and desperation finally took hold of Caleb Tassaren. Tyris's words had set the bait. His abandoning the battle to aid Halonni was the hook that drew the Necromancer on. He might be able to deny his personal need to battle the outlander, but he could not allow Shantara to be thwarted. Why else, Tyris reasoned, was he not in the tower with his sister to begin with?

He waited until he could almost feel the warmth of Caleb's breath against the back of his neck and then struck. The trap was expected, the attack a foregone conclusion. Caleb knew it and Tyris knew that he did. The real trick, of course, was disguising the attack. More obvious than anything about these Tassarens, more than their skill and magic and determination, was their pride. They were an arrogant lot from what Tyris had seen, sure of their magic and their superiority. Mostly, though, of their intelligence. They were smarter than their prey. It was a natural belief among those who hunted others.

Tyris Menion was no man's prey. As much as the black-eyed bastards, he was a hunter, a killer, a predator. These Tassarens were the kind of hunters who lay in wait and struck when they had their prey's back. Tyris was the kind that met his enemy face to face and put strength against strength. Caleb Tassaren was too smart to allow for that. He knew he was not strong enough to stand and fight. Tyris had to play the Necromancer's game if he was to have him.

He whirled about just in time to meet Caleb Tassaren at arm's length, Kinthane cutting a hard, swift arc toward the smaller man's head, a great steel promise of instant death. It was a perfectly timed blow, flawlessly aimed and impossible to parry for all of its speed and force. It was exactly what Caleb Tassaren had expected and he avoided it exactly as Tyris anticipated he would. The Necromancer dropped to a crouch and drove one sword straight up under the arc of the hammer, seeking to gut him. Tyris knew from the moment the attack began that he would miss with Kinthane. He continued to rotate, spinning completely about, stepping forward with his trailing leg. Caleb Tassaren's sword slid up the edge of his thigh, tearing a bloody gash and deflecting wide. As his sword arm thrust high, Tyris's axe completed the spin, chopping down at the exposed leg below the thrusting sword arm.

The blade bit deep through leather, flesh and bone, sheering the leg at the knee in a red geyser. Caleb Tassaren let loose a terrible wail and tottered to the side, collapsing on the hard ground, one sword skidding away. Blood spurted from his severed leg as he thrashed, one hand clutching, his scream a long, endless shriek. Tyris Menion came forward to stomp on the wrist of his sword arm, pinning it to the earth. Caleb Tassaren stared up at him with his black eyes, his face twisted with pain and rage, his white teeth clenched tight. Already the fountain of blood was slowing, the stump of his leg healing over.

Tyris brought his axe down again, severing the arm he stood on at the elbow. The wailing began anew, body thrashing and blood spurting. Another hacking blow tore off the second arm. The second leg took two. When he was done, Caleb Tassaren simply stared up at the sky, blood oozing from the torn flesh where his limbs had been, his magic sealing the edges, but not replacing what had been lost. His mouth froze in a scream and he could not summon enough breath to continue. His chest heaved and what was left of his body bucked and reared, convulsing in agony.

Tyris spat in his face. "Heal from that, pig-fucker."

He took no time to celebrate his victory. There was no time to even catch his breath. He turned from the twitching, blood spattered Necromancer and rushed for the knot of men and the sea of shambling, twisted corpses that pressed in on them. Hammer and axe scything, he cut a path to them, crushing skulls and hacking off arms. He drove the nearest of the undead back, clearing a path so that Derek could seize a handful of Chanok's cloak and pull him away. Blood poured from the man's side where a broken spear still protruded. He was clutching his sword, desperately trying to gather his legs beneath him and failing.

Derek dropped him on the steps behind them and returned to Tyris, putting his back to the outlander's. Three of the Avarun warriors were gone, pulled down and swallowed up by the crush of attackers. The four who remained formed a defensive screen before Chanok. The undead filled the entire plaza before them so that none of the street was visible.

"Too many," Derek muttered over his shoulder. "It is over."

Tyris kicked at the nearest of the walking corpses, shoving it back into those behind. "Not yet. I think Chanok is waiting for something."

Chapter Forty-Two

Pain.

His head. His ruined left hand. His aching shoulders and knees. The moonlight was bright enough to burn his black eyes. Everything was pain.

I'm alive.

The ring of black fire still burned around him, but part of it was missing, a corridor of sorts now broke the circle of flames. Halonni lay there, the stone floor torn apart beside her as if dug by some huge hand that had reached down, scooped a handful of the rock, and ripped it free. She was gray like slate and shot through with streaks of black, her little body shaking with every feeble breath she gasped. Her eyes were closed and her face was pressed against the cold stone. He bent, reaching for her, and then stopped.

They were still near.

Shantara and Addicus. He could feel them. They were alive. The ring of fire blocked his view of the room, but they were there. He glanced behind him to the space that had been his prison. It was empty. He found no sign of the formless creature that had been the sum of Joran Kathias and the fragments Jantalus had left with him at Sentry. Everything that was had become part of him. Addicus - and, through him, Shantara - had taken some of that in turn.

Jantalus would take it back.

He had just stepped over Halonni, clearing the ring of fire, when Shantara attacked him. She was standing off to one side, using the barrier of the flames to disguise her position, waiting in ambush as the Tassarens always did. Black fire erupted from her outstretched hands, a whirling cone of cold flame that rushed across the space between them. Jantalus raised his bandaged left hand, bloody and swollen, fingers stiff and useless. A shimmering barrier rose up and stopped the black fire just beyond his outstretched palm. Shantara's magic surged against his, battering his defenses, hungry and desperate, but he held.

His black eyes met hers through the wild flicker of the fire and he saw her blocky face go slack, her strong jaw dropping. She understood, she saw what he had become. He started for her, his hand still held out before him, her magic deflecting off his as he closed the distance between them. She hammered at him again and again, her magic a relentless, frantic assault that was doomed to failure. His free hand balled into a fist as he closed on her, his power building. Shantara held her ground for a moment and then began backpedalling, her magic faltering and sputtering

He bore down, rising up like a dark specter over her. Her fire scattered, unfocused and impotent. She shrank back from him, her eyes riveted on his as her body curled against the tower wall. She tried to shield herself with a shell of black flames, warding him away. His right fist came up, crackling with white lightning, turning the air between them acrid and bathing their faces with pale light. His hand drove down, the lightning shattering her feeble shield like glass. His hand opened as it reached her face, his fingers digging into her flesh. She screamed, high-pitched and terrible, tears flooding her eyes and spilling down her cheeks.

His thumb hooked her nostril, his middle and forefingers dug into her eyes as he jerked her face close. Blood ran as she shrieked and thrashed, begging and pleading words lost in her screams.

Mine, bitch. Give me back what is mine.

White light exploded between them, crackling lightning pouring from his hand and into her. The screams choked off and her body went rigid. Jantalus felt her breaking apart from within. Everything that made her what she was - the magic, the power of her will, the discipline - crumbled before the power of the white lightning. The magic she had stolen from him through Addicus came rushing back first, and then a measure of her own. He added it to his, bent it to his will and made it a part of himself.

When he had all he desired, he released her. The lightning faded away as she slumped to the floor, blood dripping from her nose. She looked up at him, one eye ruined, the other filled with blood. Her hands reached out for him, shaking and weak as they grasped at the edge of his cloak.

"Spare me," she mumbled, her voice quivering, the words tumbling from her lips. "Spare me and I'll tell you anything – everything."

He reached down with his good hand and jerked her to her feet by her tunic. His face leaned close, his black eyes boring into hers. "I'd rather watch you die."

She pawed at him, shaking her head and pleading. He thrust her away and summoned his magic, a ripple of force exploding from his hands. It slammed into her, lifted her up and thrust her away. Through one of the huge, empty windows that lined the room she sailed, her head dashed against the stone frame, splitting open in a crimson rush. She did not scream as she tumbled through and fell away.

Jantalus was staring out after her when he felt the old man. "Addicus."

He turned to find the Necromancer bent over Halonni, one thin, gnarled hand entwined in her long, midnight hair. He looked up at Jantalus with a crooked smile that was both fear and mocking.

Jantalus took a step toward him. "You have something of mine, old man."

Addicus lifted Halonni's head by her hair. "Two things, boy. I'll trade one for my life."

The sorcerer's hand came up. "I'll kill you and take both."

The old man cocked his head to the side. "Will you? Are you sure you can? Oh, you're strong, you twisted fuck. But you're ignorant. You have the power, but not the knowledge you need to use it. I have a piece of her, boy – an important piece. She's dying and what I have of her is the only way to save her. If you take it from me, can you return it to her unchanged? Is it worth the risk that you'll not be able to restore what I have taken?"

Jantalus stayed where he was and watched the old man, measuring him. As much as he thought he should know better, he believed Addicus. More importantly, he doubted his ability to do what was needed. The old man was right, he was ignorant in this. He did not know what had been done to Halonni or what needed to be done to help her. If he killed Addicus, he was killing her as well.

"What will it be, boy? Time slips away. She has none to spare."

"How will I know what you have done will save her life? How do I know she will not die after you leave?"

The old man shrugged. "How do I know you'll not try to kill me the moment I turn to leave? We both are taking risks here. Believe me, if I was not so weak from Shantara's ambush, I'd be tearing you apart now, not bargaining this little bitch's life for my own."

Jantalus's hand knotted into a fist, the white lightning wreathing it once more. Addicus had another piece of him, a part of his magic and his soul. For all the gaps in him now filled, the old man had the pieces to fill so many more. His chance to reclaim who and what Jantalus Kathias was could slip away from him if he chose poorly. Everything had led him here, to his precious answers and the completion of the man who had been shattered. He had so much. With Addicus, he would have everything that was lost except for the pieces Mordoc Tassaren had taken.

Finish it here and I have but one man to hunt. I can kill Addicus and return to what I was.

He lowered his hand, his magic fading away.

No. Better to be who I am. Halonni believed in a choice between what was and what would be. I will choose who Jantalus Kathias will be, not be forced into what he was.

"Help her."

Addicus Malshere stared at him, obviously stunned by his choice. "I will take her from here and when I am safe I will-."

"Now," Jantalus said, cutting him short. "You will help her and you will put the dead who walk this place to rest. Do both, or I'll kill you and take my chances."

"And how can I trust your word?" the old man snapped.

"How can I trust yours?"

A wicked grin split the weathered old face. "Fair enough, boy." He released Halonni, dropping her back to the floor. She was limp and made no sound or movement. Addicus pressed his hand against her stricken face, his magic rising. "Thought you'd choose to kill me," he muttered.

"Another day," Jantalus responded.

Addicus's black eyes flicked back to him. "Damn fool."

The old man bent his head in concentration and Jantalus felt the power of magic on the air. Halonni's body went rigid, a gasp exploding from her lips. Her back arched off the tower floor and her hands curled into fists. Addicus gripped her throughout, his eyes closed and his face tight with concentration.

An instant later, it was done. Addicus's hand lifted away and Halonni slumped to the floor once more. Gathering his cloak about him, the Necromancer rose. He squared himself before Jantalus, his eyes riveted. "It is done."

Jantalus closed on him, watching him as he came, prepared for any trick or sudden attack. Addicus backed away as he approached, the men circling like dueling swordsmen. Jantalus dropped to one knee beside Halonni, his hand pressed against her throat. Her skin was pale once more, the black streaks beneath it had vanished. Her heartbeat was strong and regular, her breathing shallow but even.

"And the walking dead?" he asked, still watching Addicus. The power that he had sensed outside the tower seemed changed.

The old man shrugged. "Dismissed." He held up his hands defensively. "Before you break your vow and kill me, know this – I have given her a memory, a piece of information eradicated from your own mind that you did not regain from your father or the magic left here. It lives inside of her as long as I live. When she wakes, you will have it. If I die, it will be lost to her."

Jantalus rose. "Just a memory?"

The old man nodded quickly. "A memory, I swear it. Nothing more. Leverage to keep myself alive."

Jantalus gestured to the trapdoor behind the old man. "Go. Now. Before I change my mind."

Addicus Malshere dipped his head slightly. "Gladly." He backed away, felt behind himself carefully with the toe of his boot and began descending the stairs below backward, watching the sorcerer as he went. "Jantalus."

He looked up from Halonni.

"Do not come looking for me. Your father, despite what you may think, was my friend. Your mother as well. I never wished them ill. I would not bury their son if I do not have to. If this is about Jantalus Kathias remaking himself, then leave what was in the past. All of it."

"Will you? Will Mordoc and his children? Can I just forget it all and not worry that one of you will not be coming for me when my back is turned?"

Addicus shook his head. "I will go, Jantalus. You'll not see me again. Mordoc? He has dozens of children, blood and otherwise. They may never stop. They are trying to piece him back together as you have tried to complete yourself. You and I and Mordoc are so entwined in each other that none of us will be our own again - not completely. A whole Mordoc and a whole Jantalus cannot exist. Do you understand? If he is to be Mordoc as he wishes to be, you must die."

"And you will not seek to be more?" Jantalus asked. "You're so sure, after all of this, that you'll never come for me again?"

The old man shrugged. "I had a chance, a moment of advantage. I lost it. I didn't get old by pushing my luck, boy." He pointed to Halonni. "When she tells you what I have left with her, act on it, Jantalus. Act on it before it is too late. Perhaps I have failed the Kathias family. Perhaps I could have done better along the way. What I have given to you through her is a small gesture of penance, then. Use it."

He was gone before Jantalus could ask anything else, ducking below the surface of the floor and down the spiraling stairs that led to the base of the tower and beyond. Jantalus could feel the magic that permeated Sentry retreating. Addicus had kept his word twice over. Halonni, weak, injured and too ill to move, was nonetheless restored. He had also recalled the magic he had used to twist the spirits of the mountain into giving new life to the dead.

Jantalus dropped to his knees next to Halonni, exhaustion washing over him like a wave, his battered body and worn spirit aching from the ordeal. His power was still strong within him, his magic a burning, raging thing, but his strength had faded. He pulled Halonni up against him, cradling her head in his lap and bent so that his forehead touched hers. He had very nearly battled Addicus, his anger pushing him. Now, he wondered if he would have been as terrible an opponent as the old man had feared.

He closed his eyes and sighed.

Better that I chose as I did. Better for everyone.

Chapter Forty-Three

"Jantalus."

He opened his eyes to see Halonni staring up at him. She managed a weak smile and then lifted her hand to look at it, turning it over before her eyes. "I am-."

"Back to yourself," he told her.

The hand reached up to his face. "You saved my life."

Jantalus shook his head. "You saved mine, Halonni. More than coming here and stopping Addicus and Shantara - you saved mine."

She looked about them. "Addicus?"

"Gone. Shantara is dead. We are safe."

Her gray eyes found his again. "I have to tell you-."

Voices from the chamber below drowned out hers and heavy footfalls hammered on the iron stairs. Tyris Menion thrust into the room in a thunderous charge, all blood and sweat and steel, hammer and axe held ready. A boy followed him, youthful face smeared with blood, a sword gripped tight. The outlander looked about them, panting like a raging beast, eyes wild. After a moment, he lowered his weapons and turned to Jantalus and Halonni.

"The old man got past us," he muttered.

Jantalus nodded. "I let him go. We had a bargain."

Tyris looked less than pleased with the revelation but simply nodded. "The dead collapsed where they were. Sentry is empty."

Jantalus looked to the trapdoor in the floor, waiting and listening. No one else came. "Stilthius?"

Tyris Menion shook his head. "Walking Hunnaris's heathered fields. He waits for his stubborn little brother, I think."

"I am sorry, Tyris."

The big man shook his head again. "Don't be. Stilthius came here looking for something. He earned his kullar. He found what he always wanted. There is no sorrow in that." He gestured to the boy. "Derek Ravensbourne. He searches for his father."

"Cirrin?" Jantalus asked, remembering. "Gone. Gone with Mordoc."

The boy started. "Mordoc? But-."

Tyris raised a hand to silence him. "There will be time later, boy." He knelt next to Halonni. "You're tougher than you look, girl. Still too short, too skinny and pale as snow, but the equal of any Tulin warrior I ever met."

Halonni took his big hand in both of hers and sighed. "Just the four of us, then?"

The outlander shook his head. "Devoc and a pair of men. Chanok too. He's hurt, hurt bad, but he's no weakling." He turned to Derek. "Gather what you can – food, blankets – anything you can find." He looked back at Jantalus as Derek disappeared down the stairs. "I need some time. I promised Stilthius I would spread his ashes on the mountain."

Jantalus nodded. "I can help-."

"No." Tyris laid a big hand on his shoulder. "I promised him. I will do it."

Jantalus knew better than to argue with him.

They spent the remainder of the night and all of the next day in the tower. Jantalus moved Halonni down to the first floor, away from the open windows and the frigid wind that never ceased. He bundled her in the spare cloaks Derek found and let her rest. They had no food, but they melted snow for water and waited while Tyris worked. Derek watched the outlander for a time, reporting that he was building a pyre out of what scraps of old wood remained amid the shattered, crumbling buildings of Sentry. Then, the boy disappeared for the balance of the day. He returned haggard with grief and exhaustion and said nothing when asked beyond that his own brother was resting now.

Jantalus spent the time wandering the tower, speaking only to Derek when he had something to report or asking Devoc about the injured Chanok. The little man was as strong as Tyris claimed, resting and waiting with the rest of them, his wound bound with strips of cloaks salvaged from the dead. He made no complaint, looking as though he understood and accepted the explanation Devoc had translated for him about why they waited.

Jantalus went once to the upper floor of the tower to see what had become of his temporary prison. The ring of black fire died away slowly, consuming the fragments of magic that remained around it and then disappearing all together. The shade of Mira Rhenn went with it, Jantalus assumed. He never saw her again, though Halonni mentioned once that the shade had spoken to her. The sorcerer could not sense her presence any longer, or the presence of any magic but his own and Halonni's left in Sentry. The spirits, Devoc volunteered, were at rest at last.

He found Caleb Tassaren outside the steps of the tower, dismembered but still alive. Jantalus left him screaming and thrashing for hours before having a pair of Avarun warriors take him to the northern edge of the town and heave what was left of him into the gorge there. Jantalus assumed his magic was sufficient to kill the Necromancer, but the idea of Caleb living a long, tortured life at the bottom of a hole somewhere appealed to him. Perhaps, he mused, it appealed to him a bit more than it should have.

He spent much of his time assimilating old memories, making sense, finally, of pictures that had once been too broken to see clearly. As promised by Mira Rhenn when she had confronted him, the mirror he held up to himself had been mostly restored, but the cracks remained and the image was blurred. It was something more than what he had, but not everything he had hoped for.

He learned things about himself and others he had longed to know. He learned things he never wished he knew and would have forgotten again if he were able. The lie he had lived, the half-existence of darkness interspersed with moments of light were exactly as his father's shade had promised. It had all been illusion. The bittersweet memories of his days spent in his parent's home, rescued from his endless isolation by his mother's gentle touch and sweet smile were nothing but imagination. His father was a twisted, spiteful creature who had broken him, used him, and tried to make him something of a slave. His mother was an unwitting accomplice for a time, but had finally fled when she learned the truth. She thought him dead now, he imagined. She was with Mordoc Tassaren, not knowing he wore her husband's face.

What was he to think of her? She had returned to the man she thought was her husband knowing what he had done. Should Jantalus consider that approval? Resignation? He considered the question for hours, arriving at more possibilities and answers than he could keep count of and then decided on none of them. She was alive. Mordoc was alive. He would find them, confront them, and have it resolved.

Now, he had more to consider than them.

During the brief time Halonni was awake that day, they sat together in the corner of the room at the base of the tower, huddled in their cloaks speaking in whispers. They shared the tale of their separate journeys after he had left her at the Avarun camp. He told her what he had experienced in the ring of fire and who and what he had been. He explained his choice when confronted by Addicus and why he had made it. She listened throughout and did not stop him, only nodding when she felt he was hesitating, encouraging him to go on when he was unsure.

He resolved that he would find his mother and Mordoc. He would confront them with what they had done and have answers for the questions that remained. The question of Halonni's father remained as well. It had been weeks since they had left Durn in Marcester under the guard of Sentinels. Addicus had warned that the Tassarens were many and might never stop. Their need to have Jantalus and help their father would drive them to anything. Durn was neither beyond their reach nor beneath their attention.

He had a plan of sorts formed for dealing with it, but it did not last long.

When he had finished relating all that had happened to him, Halonni spoke to him of what Addicus had given her. The memory he left with her was Jantalus's once, stolen away when so much else had been taken from him. What it told him was no small thing. It was a bit of information, a few seconds worth of conversation, but it changed everything. It stunned him, rendered him speechless and sent his mind spinning with possibilities. He was still considering what the revelation meant for him and what lay ahead when Halonni drifted off to sleep, leaving him alone to contemplate it.

Night had fallen again when Tyris Menion returned to them and announced he was finished. He had roamed the area all about Sentry gathering what he could find for a proper pyre and was ready to move on. He would light it as they left, he told them, let it burn and allow the wind to scatter his brother across the mountains beneath the light of the moon. They gathered what little they had come with, Jantalus carrying the sleeping Halonni, and followed him out.

Sentry was a cold, desolate thing, the broken, twisted corpses that had roamed it only a few hours before collapsed into heaps, scattered about like leaves thrown by the wind. With Addicus's magic gone, they had fallen where they stood. A few had been moved to make way for walking and Tyris had cleared a place for his brother's final journey.

The pyre was a mixture of scraps found in the ruined town and deadwood scavenged from a day's worth of searching along Kiranon. Tyris had worked for hours to shave small bits into proper kindling to ensure it would catch and burn. The dried old logs and broken timbers formed a strong support for Stilthius. Still clad in his mail, he lay atop the platform with his hands folded across his great chest, the moonlight falling on his dark face.

Tyris stood with Jantalus a moment, a small tin bowl he had found and filled with tinder smoldering in his hands. He looked up at the moon, at the pale light that streamed down on them from the cloudless sky, and sighed. "I send him to Hunnaris with nothing. His last wish was that I take Kinthane. I feel like he goes alone now."

"Your brother believed in Hunnaris," Jantalus told him. "He believed his god goes with him. That is why he had you keep the hammer. Because he feared leaving you alone."

Tyris thought on it a moment and then nodded. He drew a breath and then walked across the small plaza before the tower to where his brother lay. He brushed a bit of debris from the bloody mail and wiped at his brother's cold face. His hand lingered there a moment, his head bent, and then he thrust the battered tin bowl and the fire that flickered inside of it into a gap in the base of the pyre. The dry wood caught at once, billowing smoke and erupting with flame. Tyris turned away from it as it flared and surrounded his brother, burning high into the moonlit sky. He paused only a moment, looked up at the shining ivory disc above, and then walked back to where the others waited.

He put one arm around Jantalus's shoulders, one around Derek's, and walked them away from the pyre, away from Sentry and away from Kiranon.

None of them looked back.

Chapter Forty-Four

They made the descent to the valley under the light of the nearly full moon. Even wounded, Chanok led them, picking his way through the trails and bluffs with Devoc at his side. Jantalus carried Halonni as they went, refusing all offers of help from Derek and Tyris. The path they were taking, the outlander advised, was not exactly the one they had come by. With time being less important now, Chanok chose an easier way, making good progress while avoiding the most treacherous places. The ever-present wind made for numb hands and faces, but the light of the Avarun camp below drew them on with a sense of hope and purpose.

It was not yet dawn when they reached the valley floor, the horrors of Kiranon and Sentry behind them. They returned missing so many and having gained something yet to be judged for its worth. For a time Jantalus thought that no matter what came of his recovered past and the magic that came with it, he might never be deserving of what was lost. Stilthius Menion might have found a fulfillment in what he had done, but that was his own judgment. Jantalus judged the life lost and the damage done to the one he carried down the slope of Kiranon as prices not so easily justified.

Derek Ravensbourne spoke to him for a time as they walked, concerned for the fate of his father and desperate for any information Jantalus might have. Derek maintained a cautious respect, an understanding that something beyond his comprehension had been done and it weighed more on Jantalus than any concern for Cirrin Ravensbourne. Jantalus knew little beyond the fact that the boy's father had left Sentry alive and in the company of Mordoc Tassaren. Whether Cirrin believed him to be Joran Kathias because of his appearance or if he knew the truth, Jantalus did not know. Their destination was a mystery as well, though, if his father had been right, Mordoc might try to return to the Vicars. That meant Haven or another Alliance city, he decided.

Derek accepted the information with a measure of disappointment in the lack of detail, but his appreciation for what little Jantalus provided seemed genuine enough. He said no more about it, in any case.

Gyun greeted them at the edge of the camp. The news of so many fallen left the old woman stricken, but she welcomed Devoc and Chanok with no small relief. She opened her home and that of her brother to them all at once and she sent for her attendants and healers. After washing and dressing their wounds, the Avaruns provided clean clothes, fresh water and food. The fires were piled high and warm blankets provided. The few who returned from Sentry were soon asleep in the warmth and safety of the Wydant camp.

The sun had nearly risen to the highest point in the sky when Jantalus woke and went to peer out the flap of the tent. The camp was bustling with activity, returned to the constant moving of men and beasts as the Avaruns went about their daily routines. He spied Chanok among them, limping along and wincing, his hand clutching his bandaged side, but keeping pace and working with the rest. The Avarun raised a hand when he spotted him and Jantalus returned the gesture before ducking back inside.

Tyris was asleep still, stretched out along one side of the fire, so tall that he nearly took up the width of the tent. A good washing had cleared away all of the blood and the mostly whole brown skin beneath said that much of it had not been his. Skinned knuckles, a shallow gash to his thigh, scrapes and bruises were the worst of it. Tyris Menion had battled Necromancers, the walking dead and an entire mountain set against them without a single significant wound to his body. Jantalus considered the hole inside of him, the void left by his brother and thought perhaps the Tulin way was such that Tyris would soon find a peace with that, too. He would grieve, but not in a way most men thought of it. Tyris might not have had Stilthius's strength of faith in Hunnaris, but he had enough faith in his brother to believe he had died a happy man.

Jantalus stepped over the outlander and skirted the fire to where Halonni lay wrapped in blankets, nearly lost in the pile of bedding. Her eyes slipped open as he settled down beside her, still glazed with sleep, her mouth twisting in a faint half-smile.

"Restless?"

He cradled his injured hand and tried wiggling his fingers. They complied, but not with any enthusiasm. "Uncomfortable."

She sighed and rested her head against his arm. "You should try more of that tea they gave me. I could sleep for a month."

"You need to."

Her hand came up to his face, turning it toward her. "Did you find what you wanted in Sentry?"

He looked away from her a moment, thinking. "What I wanted? No." He shrugged and looked back at her. "But what I needed. Enough, I suppose, to make a choice."

"What choice?" she asked, blinking to stay awake.

"The one you always insisted I could. The choice between then and now. Between who I was and who I could be."

A playful smirk teased at the corner of her mouth. "Is that your way of saying I was right?"

Jantalus shook his head. "You could be, someday," he told her after a long pause.

He turned to look at her, but she was asleep again. Had she heard him? Perhaps not. It did not matter – not now.

He eased her back against her pillows, pulled the blankets up around her slender shoulders and kissed her midnight hair.

Good-bye, Halonni. I hope you understand. I hope you can forgive me.

He rose and searched for his boots, finding them on the other side of Tyris and slipping them on. He gathered his cloak and a spare, an old canvas bag and one of Tyris's knives. Devoc would be able to provide food and water, he supposed. If not, he would manage without both for a time. He cast one long, last glance at the sleeping girl, pulled his cowl about his head, and ducked out into the light.

"Jantalus."

He had five steps behind him when Tyris's voice stopped him where he was. He turned to find the giant emerging from the tent, a blanket draped about his massive shoulders. Barefoot, he walked to where Jantalus waited, an eyebrow cocked as he looked down at him.

"Too much rest for you here?" he asked. "Somewhere better to be?"

Jantalus looked off to the east where the sun lay across the snow-glazed peaks of the Tijian. "A place called Halbor. I have to hurry."

Tyris nodded. He knew. Jantalus had told him everything Halonni had shared with him about the memory Addicus had left with her. "Now?"

"I don't dare wait. I might be too late already."

The outlander drew a deep breath and let it out slowly. "Didn't tell her you were going, did you?"

Jantalus shook his head.

"That girl loves you, you know."

"No. She is in love with an idea – a possibility. I'm not sure if it's real. Not yet, anyway."

Tyris nodded, but he did not look convinced. "You aren't going to let me come with you, are you? She'd be safe. These people would protect her."

Jantalus shook his head again. "No. Not like you will. I trust no man in this world but you, Tyris Menion. I can't imagine why you did what you did, why you risked so much, but I can never repay that debt. Even so, I'm going to ask you for more. I'm going to ask you to watch over her. I promised her I would return to Marcester and do what I could for her father. I am breaking that promise because Devoc's people say Halbor is near, just beyond the edge of the mountains to the east. If Addicus was right, the Tassarens know what I know. They'll do what they can to get to me."

Tyris reached out and clamped a huge hand on Jantalus's shoulder. "I will watch over her. When she is stronger, we will ride to Marcester and look for her father. You meet us there."

"It might be better that I don't," Jantalus insisted. "You all might be better off if I stayed away until this is all through."

Tyris's hand tightened on him. "No brother of mine faces an enemy alone." His big face leaned close. "No brother of mine. We will wait in Marcester. You will come or I will tear apart this land to find you and beat your scrawny ass."

Jantalus seized the big hand and clasped it firmly. "That, I do not doubt."

Tyris helped him gather food and water, which Devoc and Gyun supplied without hesitation. In a matter of an hour, he had his pack filled and a simple map scrawled on an old animal hide tucked into his belt. Derek Ravensbourne would be cared for along with Tyris and Halonni. The boy was recovering from his own injuries, but had made it clear repeatedly that he was eager to be off and looking for his father. Gyun had wisely ordered her healers to give him a heavy dose of the medicine they used to put everyone to sleep.

Jantalus thanked the Wydant for all they had done and walked with Tyris to the edge of camp. His journey would take him south into Zantizan, retracing the route Tyris and the others had traveled with Addicus to reach the valley. From there, he would make his way back through Greylock Pass and, beyond it, Agron Pass once more. Another cut, one they had passed by many days before on their journey to Zantizan, would lead him through the eastern edge of the mountains and back into the Censkarn Valley near the town of Halbor. A few days they told him, hard and cold, and best left until the weather was better. But he was going and would not change his mind.

He paused at the edge of the camp and turned to Tyris again. "You will tell her why?"

Tyris laughed and shook his head. "I'll try, but she's got a temper I'm not sure I'll be able to handle." The smile slipped away and he drew a breath. "I will tell her. She won't like it, but I'll tell her."

Jantalus took the big hand in his own once more, feeling the other man's strength, his resolve. "Thank you."

Tyris gripped his hand, squeezing tight. "Marcester. Do not forget."

The sorcerer nodded and released him. "Marcester."

With nothing more to say, he hitched up his pack and started south, headed for the massive gray bulk of Mount Greylock. He looked back several times to find Tyris Menion watching him, standing fast and refusing to look away.

Tougher than old leather and as dependable as the sunrise I called him once. Look after her, my friend.

Halonni was awake when Tyris Menion returned to the tent that night. She was sitting up on her bedding, her eyes riveted to the tent flap. A spasm of pain flashed across her face when he ducked inside. She knew, he realized. She knew the moment it was he who had returned and not Jantalus.

"He's gone." She was not asking.

Tyris nodded slowly. "He has to do this, Halonni. He has to be sure he is who you wish him to be."

"I'm sure!" she insisted.

The outlander came to sit beside her, lowering himself to the pile of bedding Jantalus had used the night before. "My brother believed something, Halonni, that I never did. He could tell me over and over it was true, but he could not make me see it the way he did. I am not sure I believe it now. But I did learn something from him."

She shook her head, her face tight with anger, and her eyes hard. She was listening, but she did not yet understand. "What was that?"

"That what I believed for him meant nothing. It was Stilthius's faith – his beliefs – that brought him here. Not mine. He was never seeking my approval of his faith, Halonni. He was just trying to make me see why it drove him."

The tension drained from her face and she nodded. They sat together in silence a long time, staring out through the gap of the tent flap together and into the night beyond.

"You're smarter than you look, Menion," she told him finally.

He snorted. "I hope so." He laid a hand on her shoulder. "We will see him again, Halonni."

She covered his hand with hers, still peering out into the darkness.

"I hope so."

Chapter Forty-Five

Jantalus Kathias walked the streets of Halbor alone. Only a few stray dogs snapped and barked at him before scrambling away again. The slivers of lamp-light that filtered through the cracks in the shutters over the windows of the alehouses and gambling halls were all that lit his way. Raucous laughter and profane oaths mixed with the lively music and rhythmic thumping of cups on tables as the people within celebrated. There had been a wedding, he had heard a pair of men say as he passed them by several streets back. Two important families in the town were now one and the whole of Halbor was joining in the festivities.

He passed by it all without interest, his attention focused on a timber house that lay on a small hillock above the sparkling waters of Kynn Lake below. The moonlight danced on the surface, flashing like jewels. The steady rhythm of the water against the shore soon replaced the musicians he left behind as he made his way past the clapboard buildings of the town proper. He climbed the gentle earthen path to the low stone wall that surrounded the cottage, noting the light of the oil lamps and the flicker of a hearth in the window glass. Behind the house, a large barn stood dark and silent.

He gained the front porch, tapped gently on the oak door, and waited.

He heard the sound of a chair scraping across the floor and light footfalls approached. The latch clicked and the door swung in to reveal a woman. She was tall and lean, all trim muscle and fluid grace. Honey blond hair shimmered in the orange firelight as her sea-green eyes looked him over, hard and measuring. A pair of scars marred her otherwise pleasing features, one dark angry line starting behind her left ear and crawling down her neck to disappear into her tunic. The second, a thin white line, ran from the outer corner of her left eye to her jaw.

"Martiyana?" he asked.

He had been told that name by an old man he had stopped on the other side of town. Martiyana and Cormac. Horse traders who lived on the hill near Kynn Lake.

She peered into his cowl, confident, challenging and unafraid. "Who are you? What do you want?"

He reached up slowly, careful not to appear threatening. He slipped the cowl back from his face. Her eyes went wide at the sight of him, and a gasp escaped her.

"You know me?"

She nodded quickly. "They told him you were dead."

"They made me forget he ever existed."

She had his arm in an instant, dragging him inside, hurrying through the cottage to the open back door. He caught sight of bits of detail as she pulled him through, small touches of a craftsman's hand on the woodwork and masonry that made the house a home. The back door led to a small yard between the house and barn. It was still and lit only by what light spilled out from the opened doorway.

Just as they reached it, a man stepped into the light, his wiry arms full of firewood. He looked up at Jantalus with a flash of emerald eyes and rusty hair.

So much like mother. Exactly like her.

The firewood clattered to the ground. The man took a step toward him and then stopped again, shock and confusion twisting his youthful face.

Addicus did not lie. It is he. It has to be.

Jantalus stretched out a hand toward him, calm, reassuring. The hesitation eased as the other came forward again, his strong, calloused hand clasping firm. Relief flooded through Jantalus at the touch, an affirmation that made it all real.

No illusions or hallucinations or lies. Flesh and blood.

The man, Cormac, looked to his equally stunned wife and back. "Jantalus?"

He nodded in return.

"Hello, brother."

***

Thank you for reading Thinner Than Blood. If you enjoyed the book, please consider leaving a review at your retailer of choice. The sequel With Their Bones is available now.

ABOUT THE AUTHOR

Ed is a lifelong resident of upstate New York. He writes in the spaces around life as a husband and father.

Sign up for his mailing list to receive updates and a free story at www.edwardkryan.com.

Thinner Than Blood is the first book in the Mark of the Dead series. The sequel, With Their Bones, is available as of July 2020.

For more information or to contact him, visit Slate Run Publishing at www.slaterunpub.com.